JOYAMA™

VOLUME 1

CREATED, WRITTEN, AND ILLUSTRATED BY

DANIEL ISLES

DARK HORSE BOOKS

1

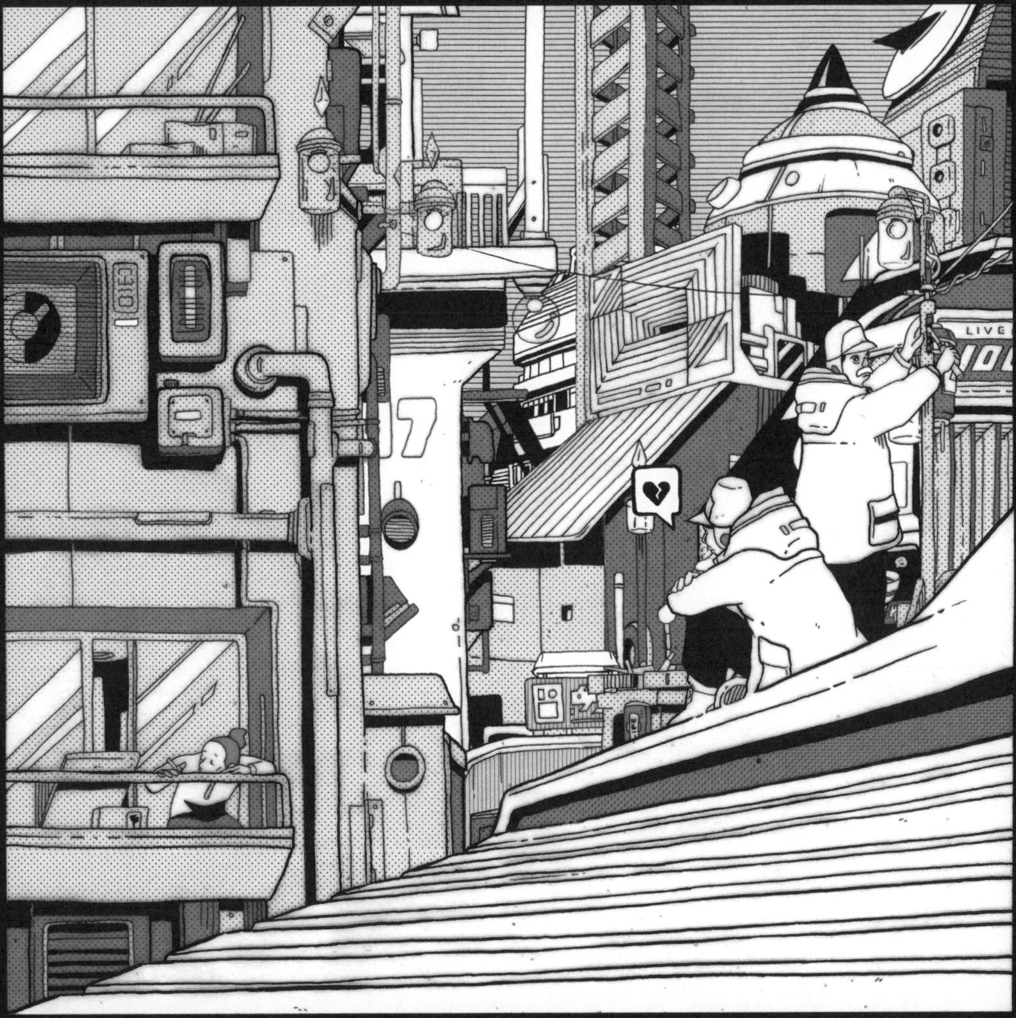
LIVE

"Bluecoats HQ,
this is transport
convoy Patrol 7."

"Good evening, Patrol 7,
how may we be of
assistance?"

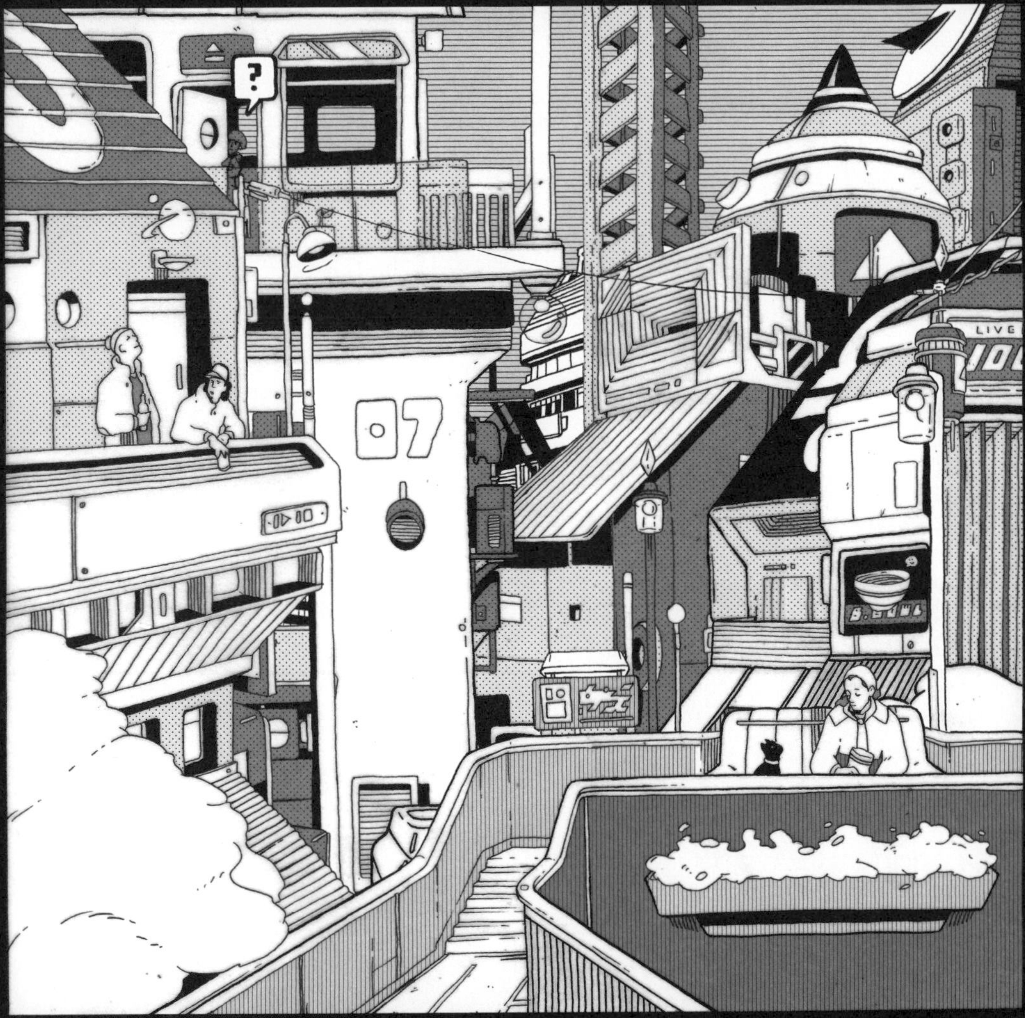
?
07
LIVE

"We have a high-profile Viper in transit.
Requesting clearance for the next checkpoint."

"Affirmative, Patrol 7."

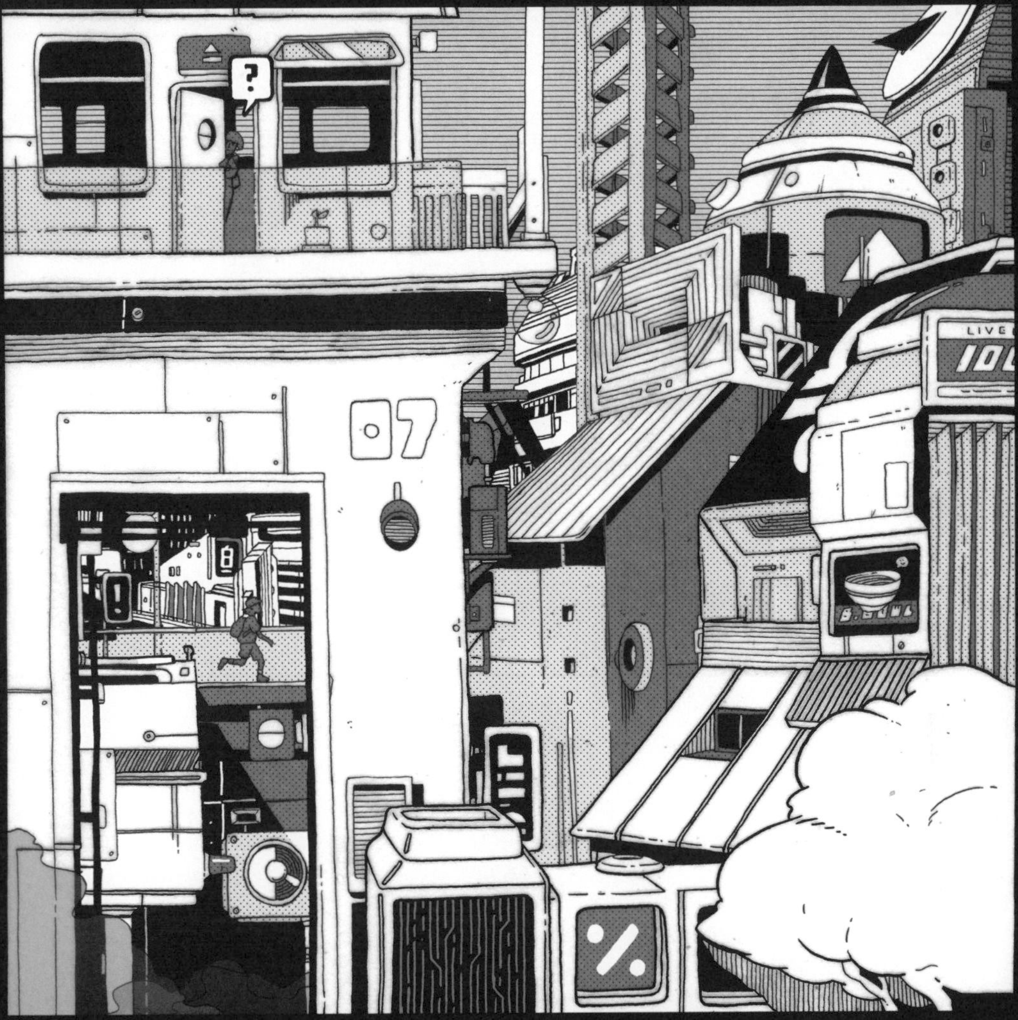
?
07
LIVE

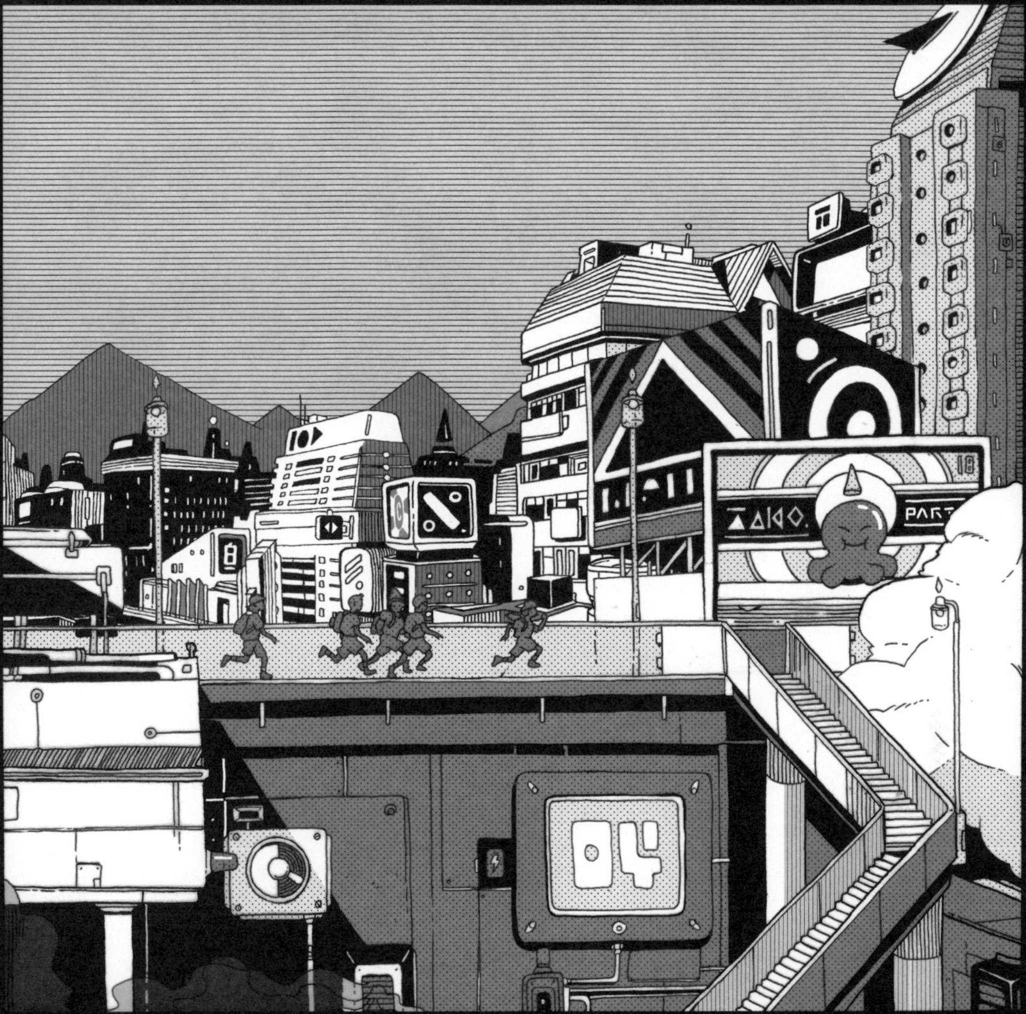
PART
04

"All lanes now cleared for your exit from..."

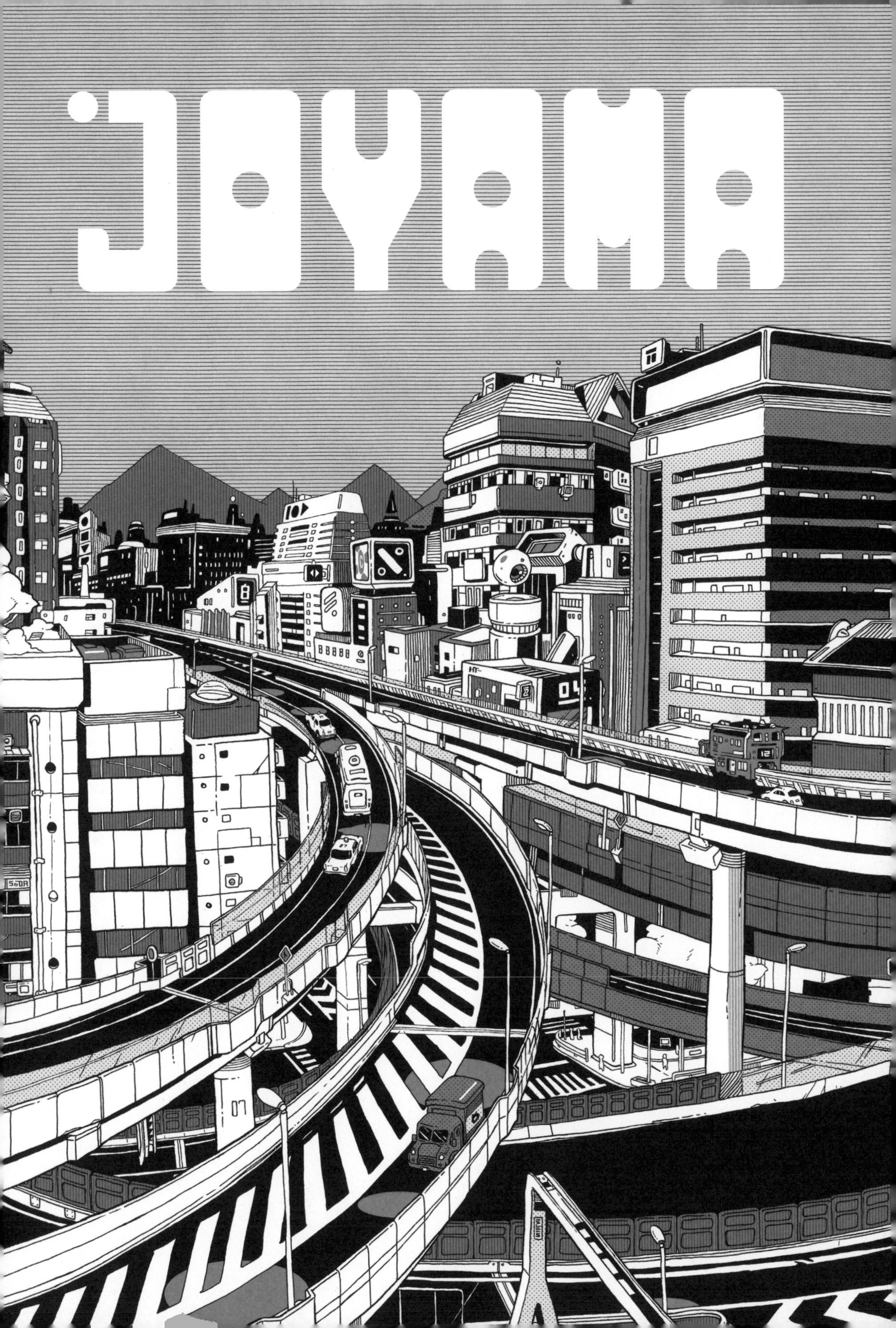
JOYAMA

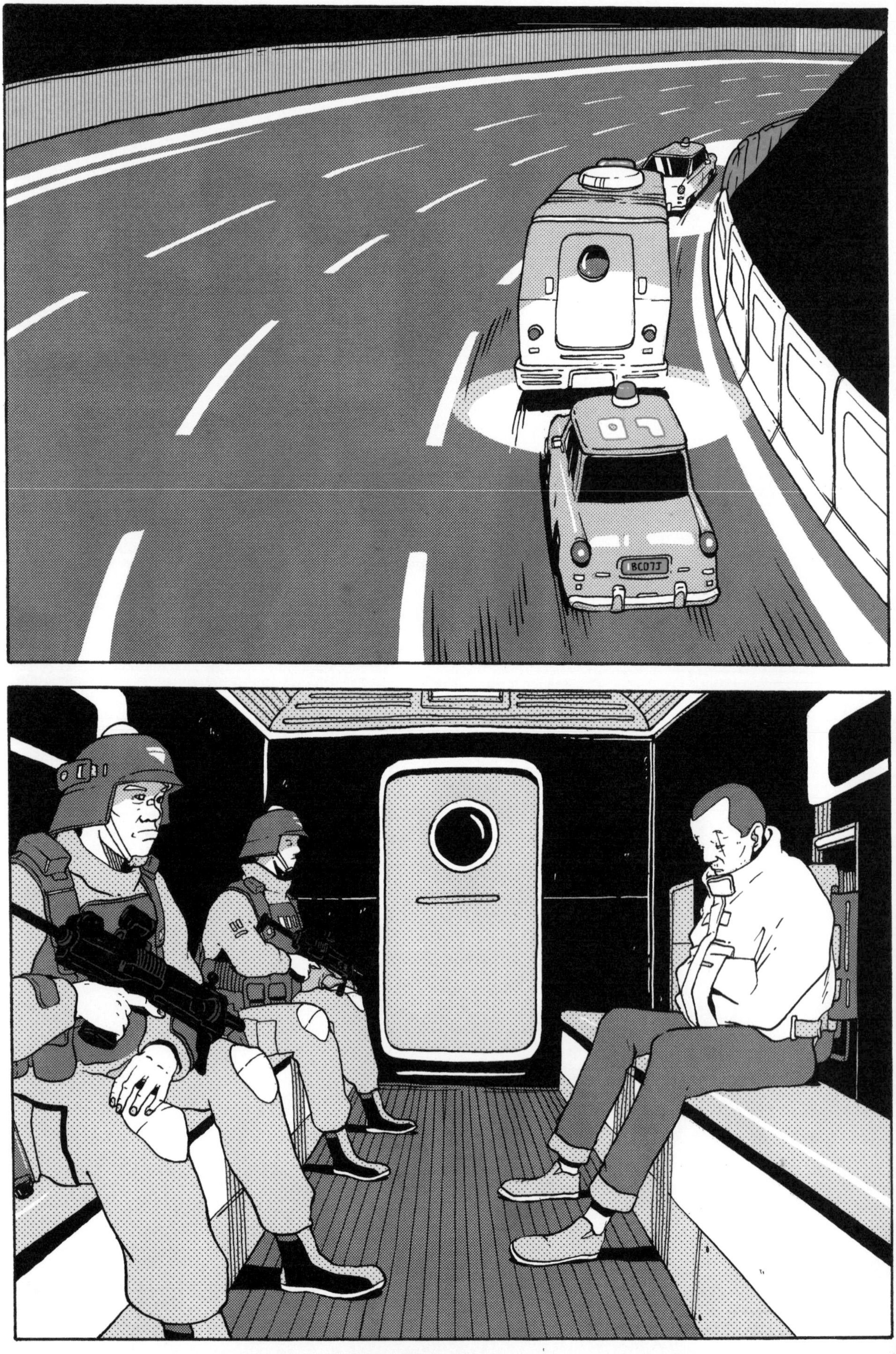
BC07J

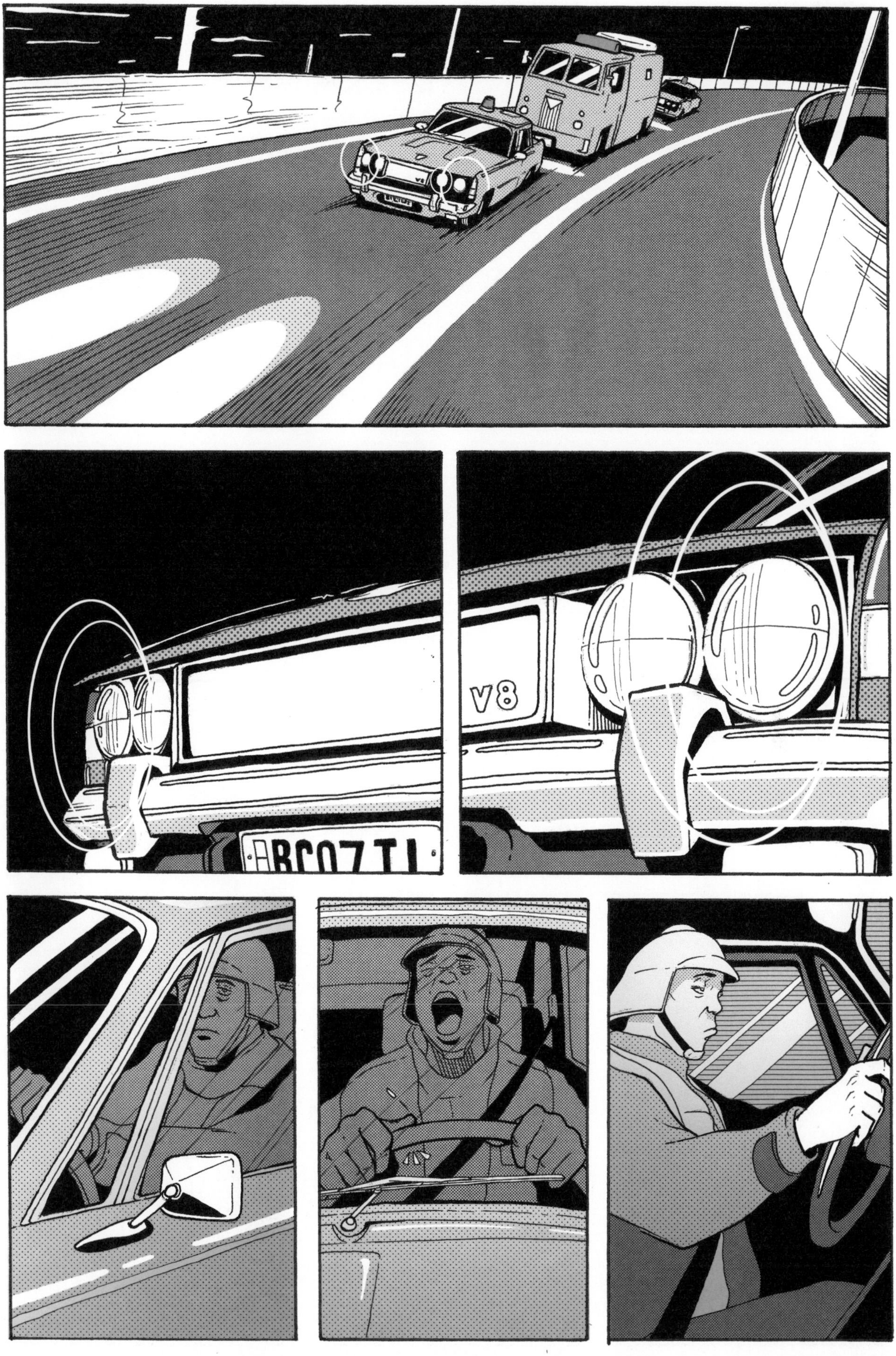
V8

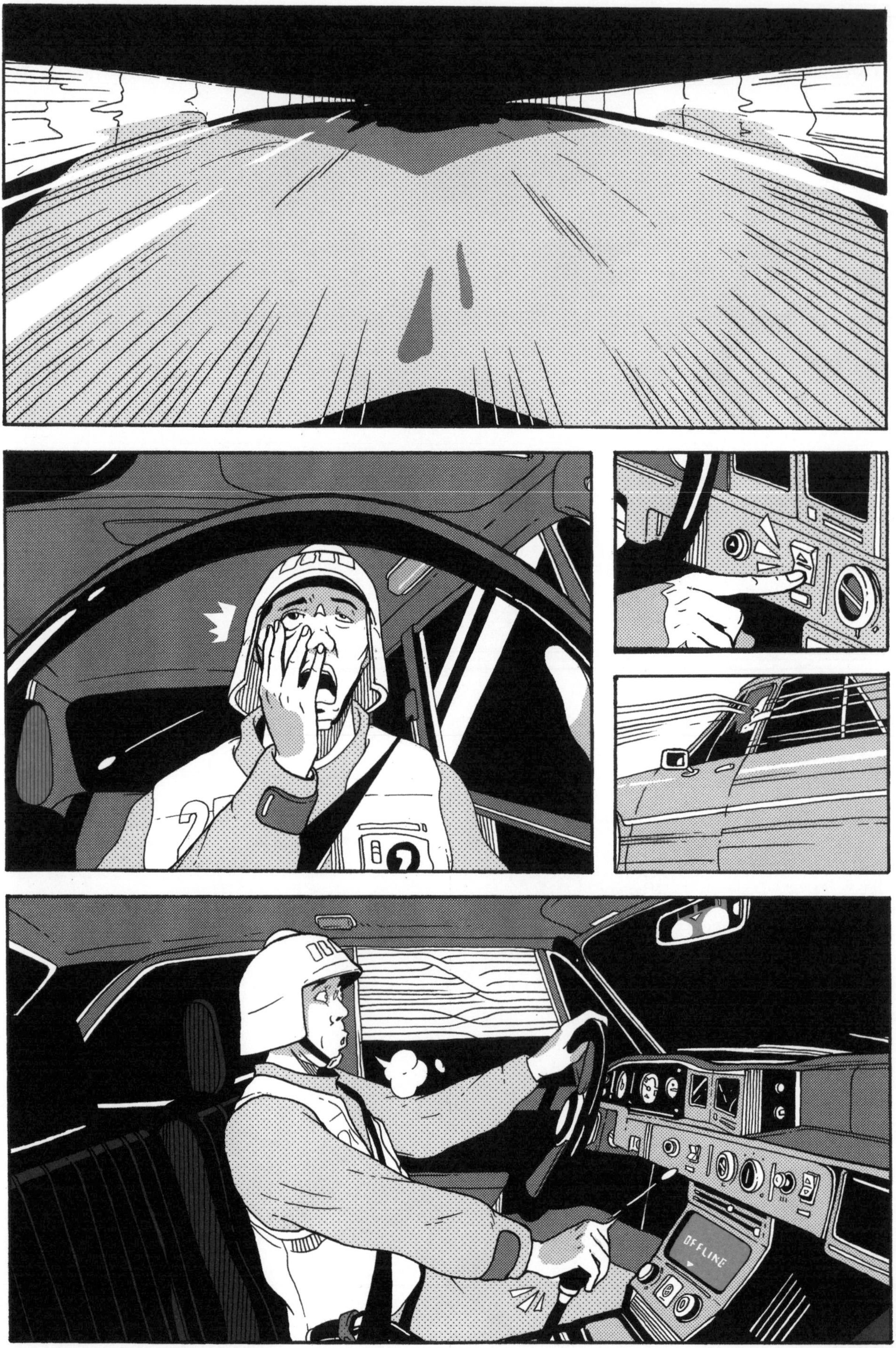
OFFLINE

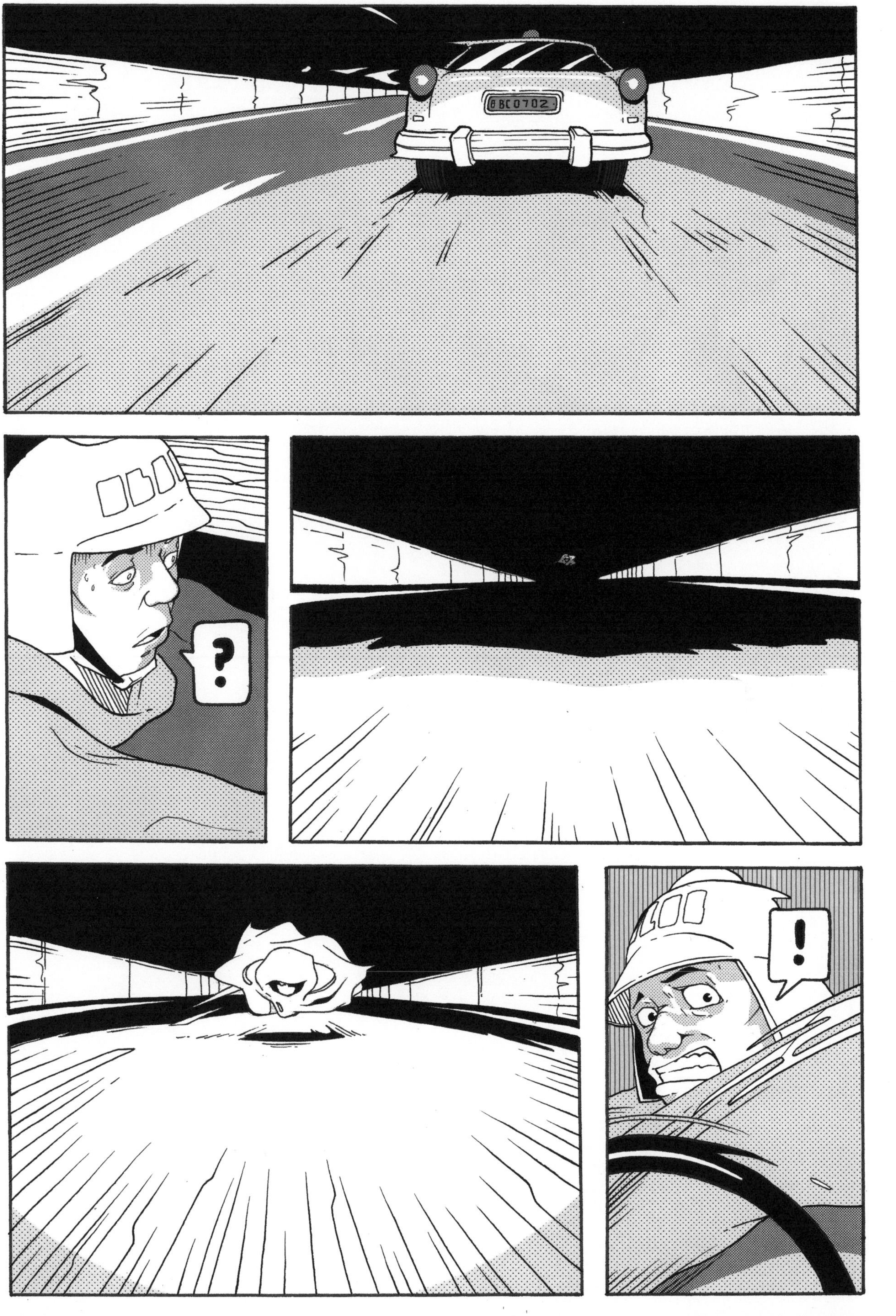
?
!

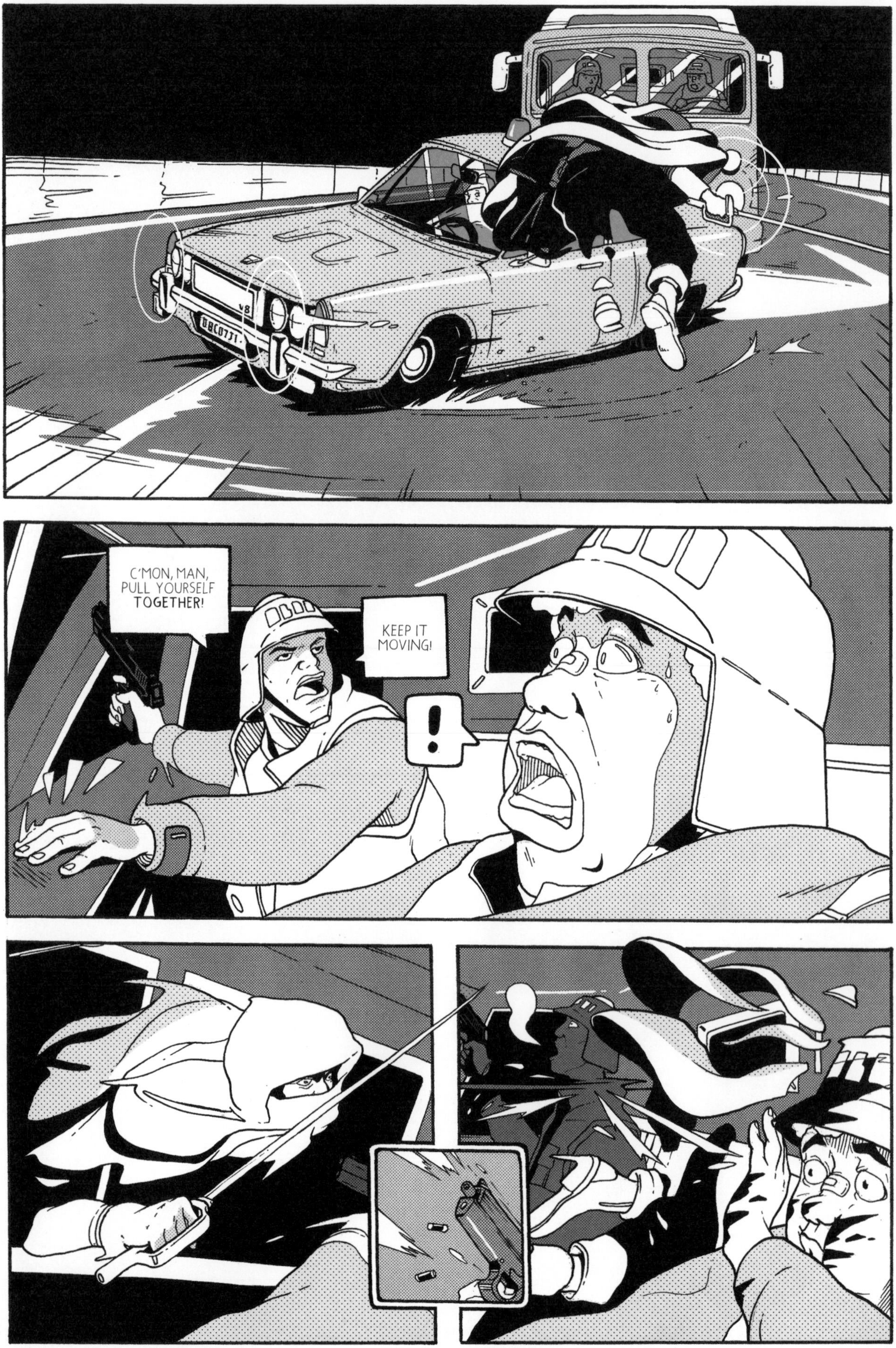
C'MON, MAN, PULL YOURSELF TOGETHER!
KEEP IT MOVING!
!

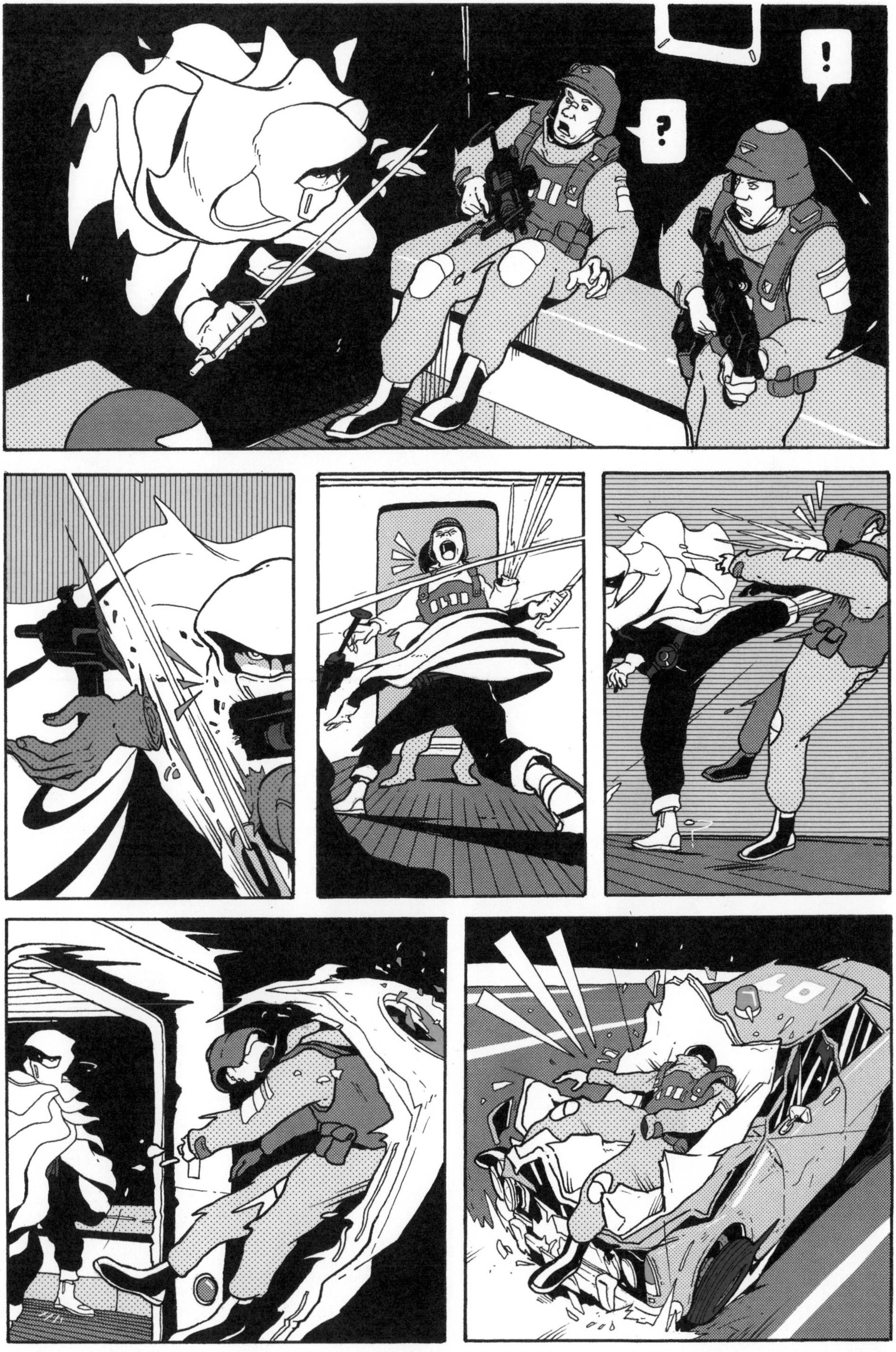
?
!

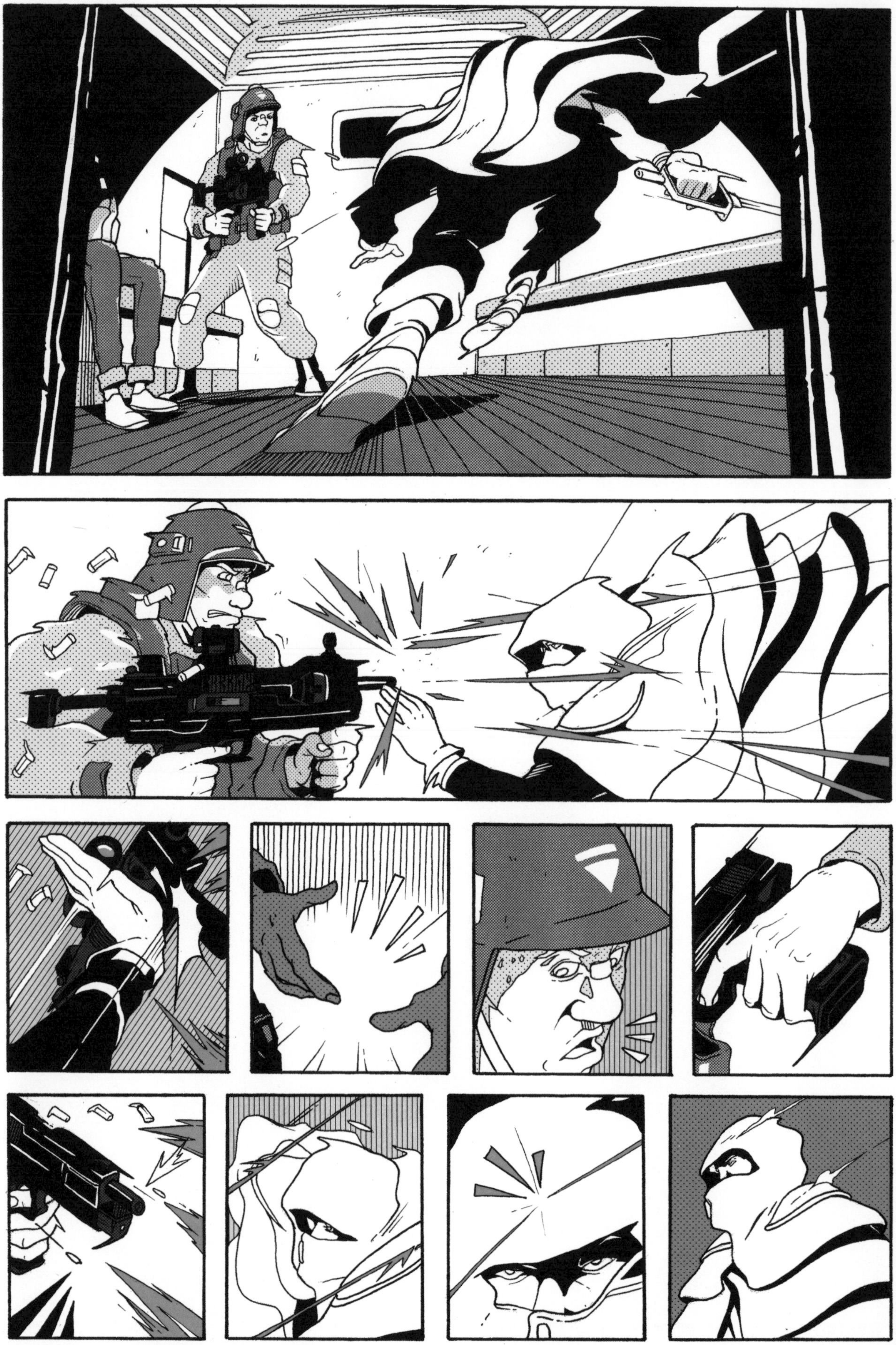

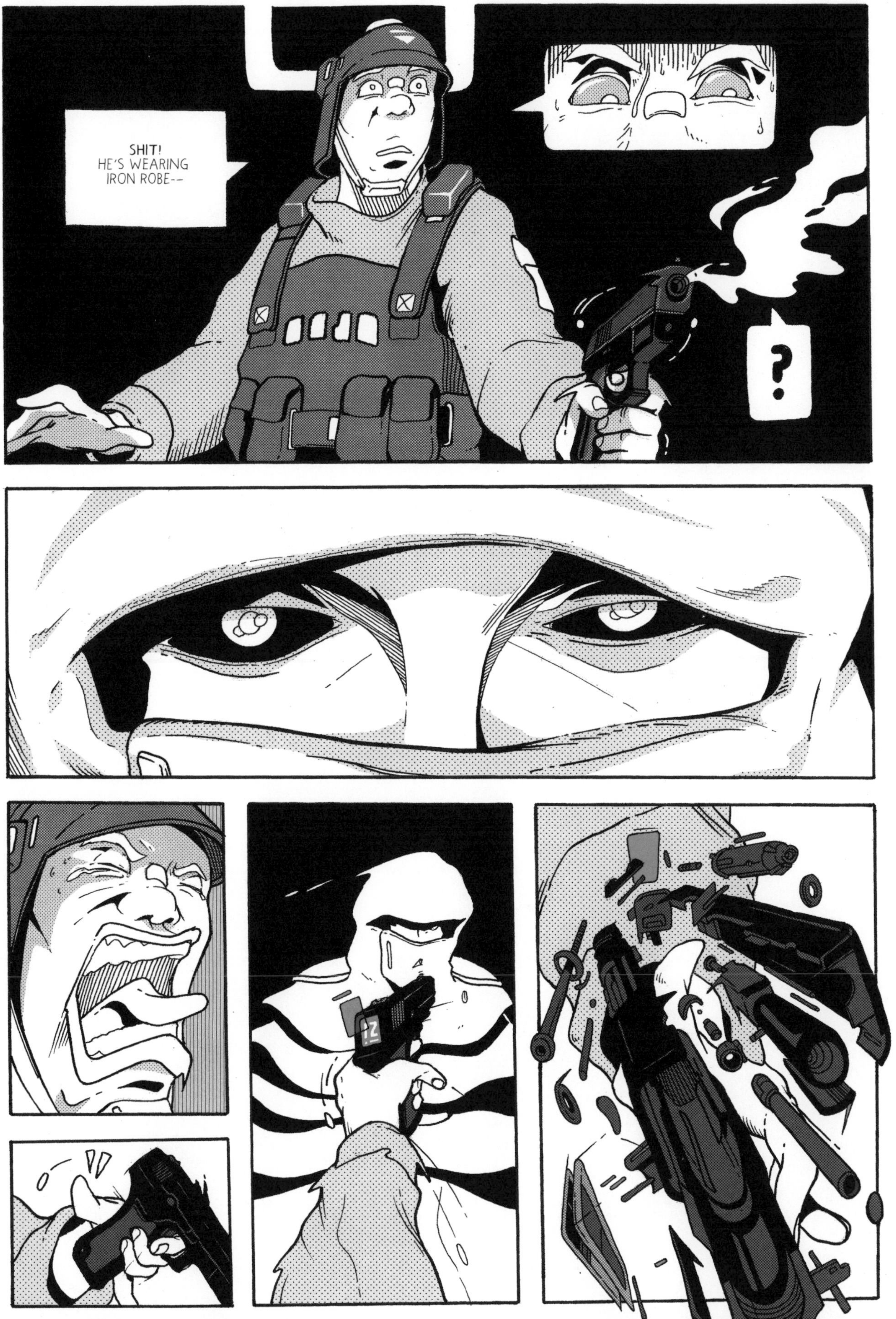
SHIT!
HE'S WEARING
IRON ROBE--
?

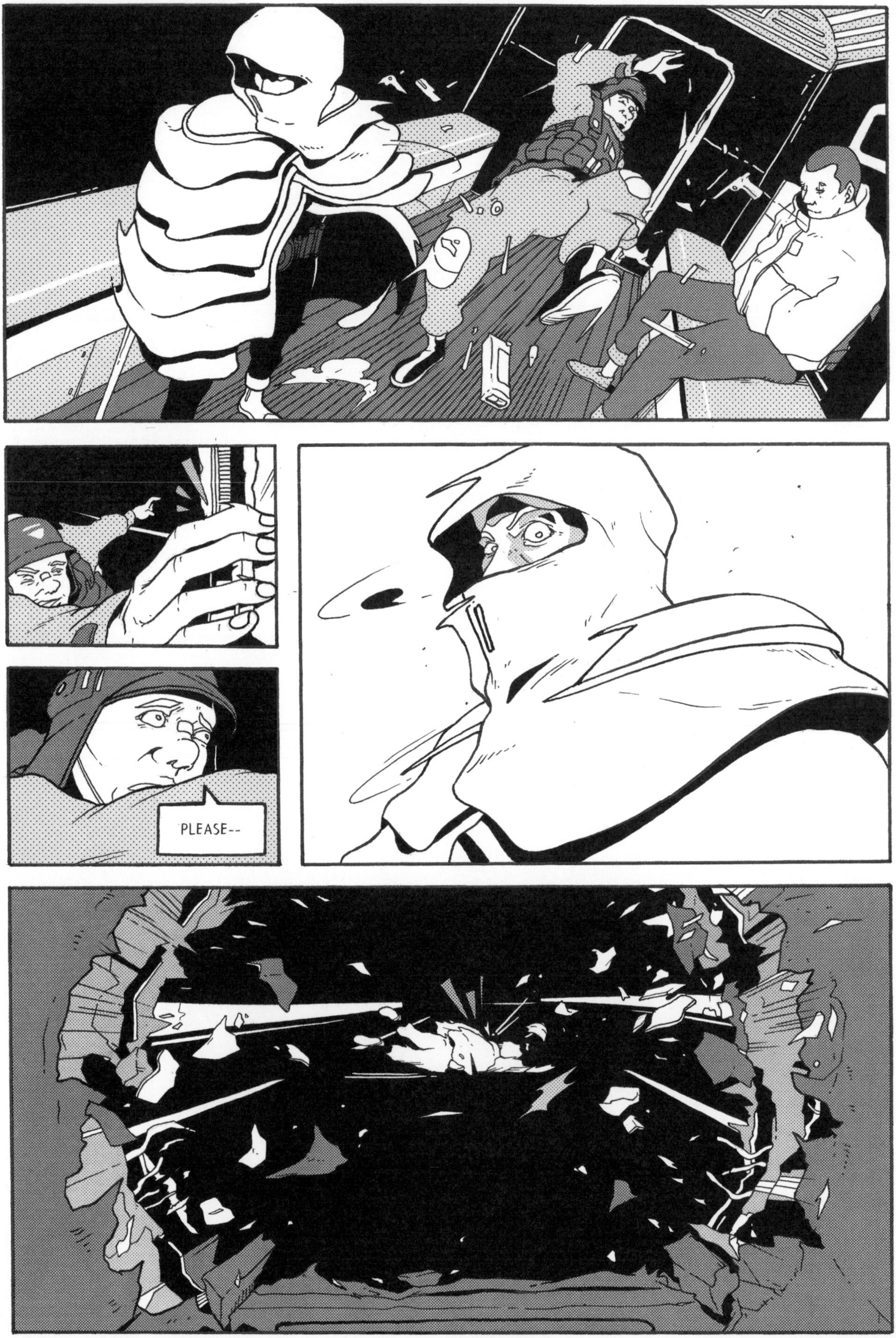

PLEASE--

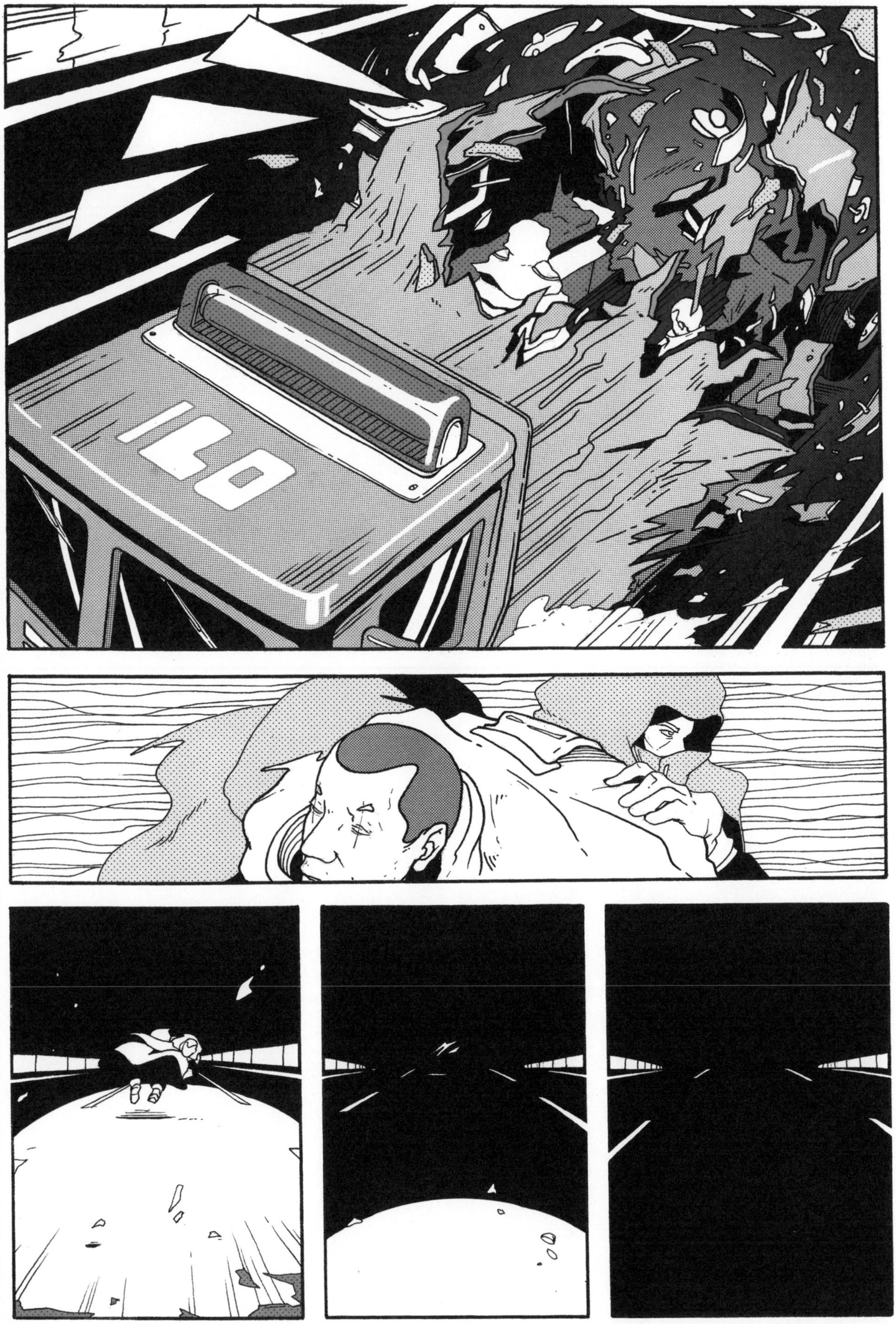

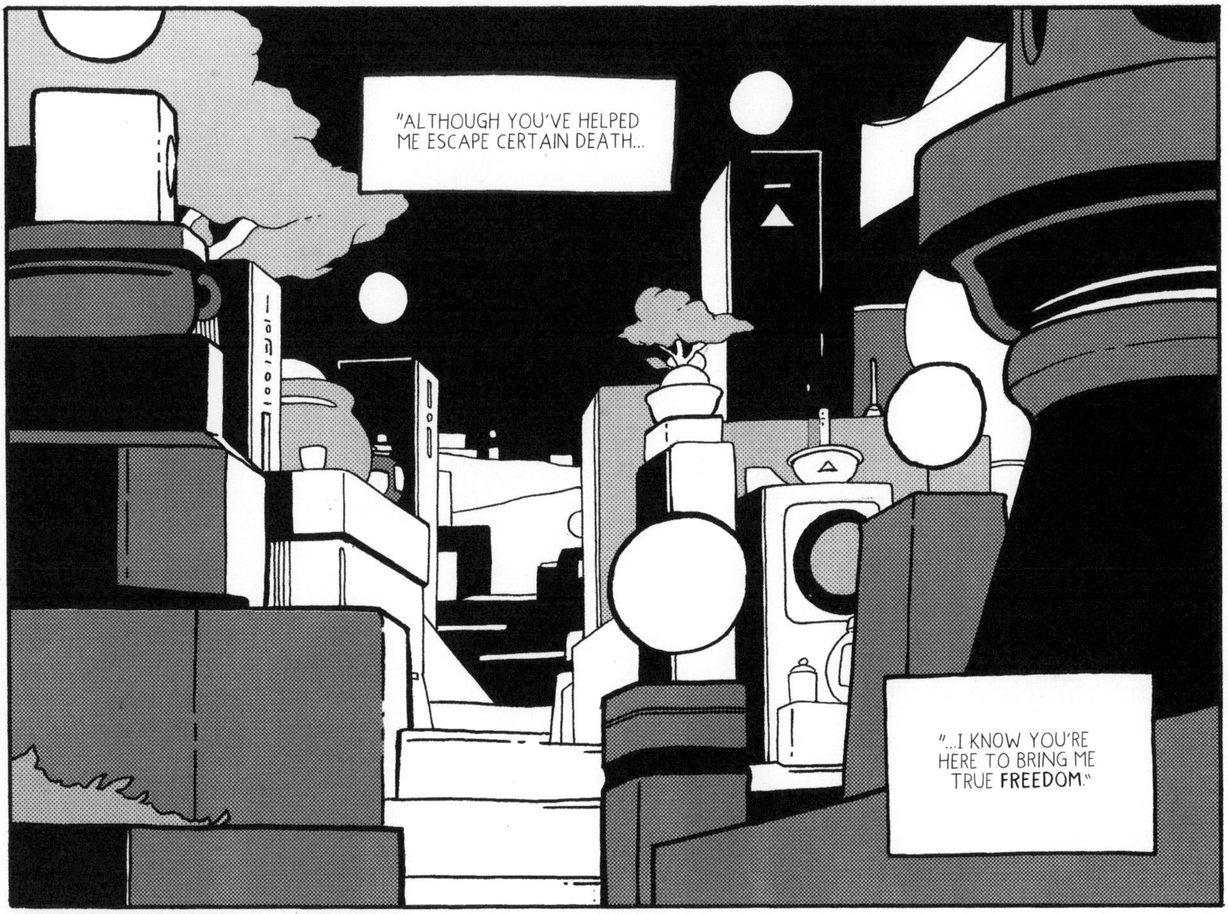
"ALTHOUGH YOU'VE HELPED ME ESCAPE CERTAIN DEATH...
"...I KNOW YOU'RE HERE TO BRING ME TRUE **FREEDOM**."

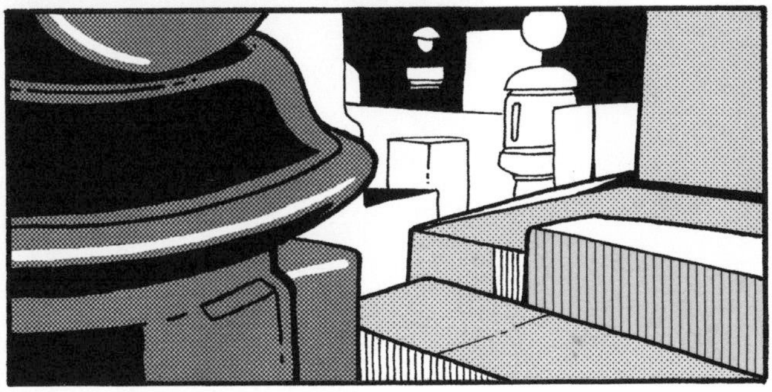

2

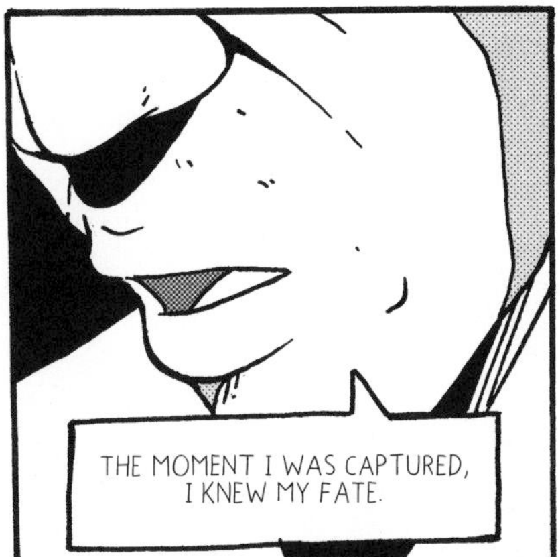
THE MOMENT I WAS CAPTURED, I KNEW MY FATE.

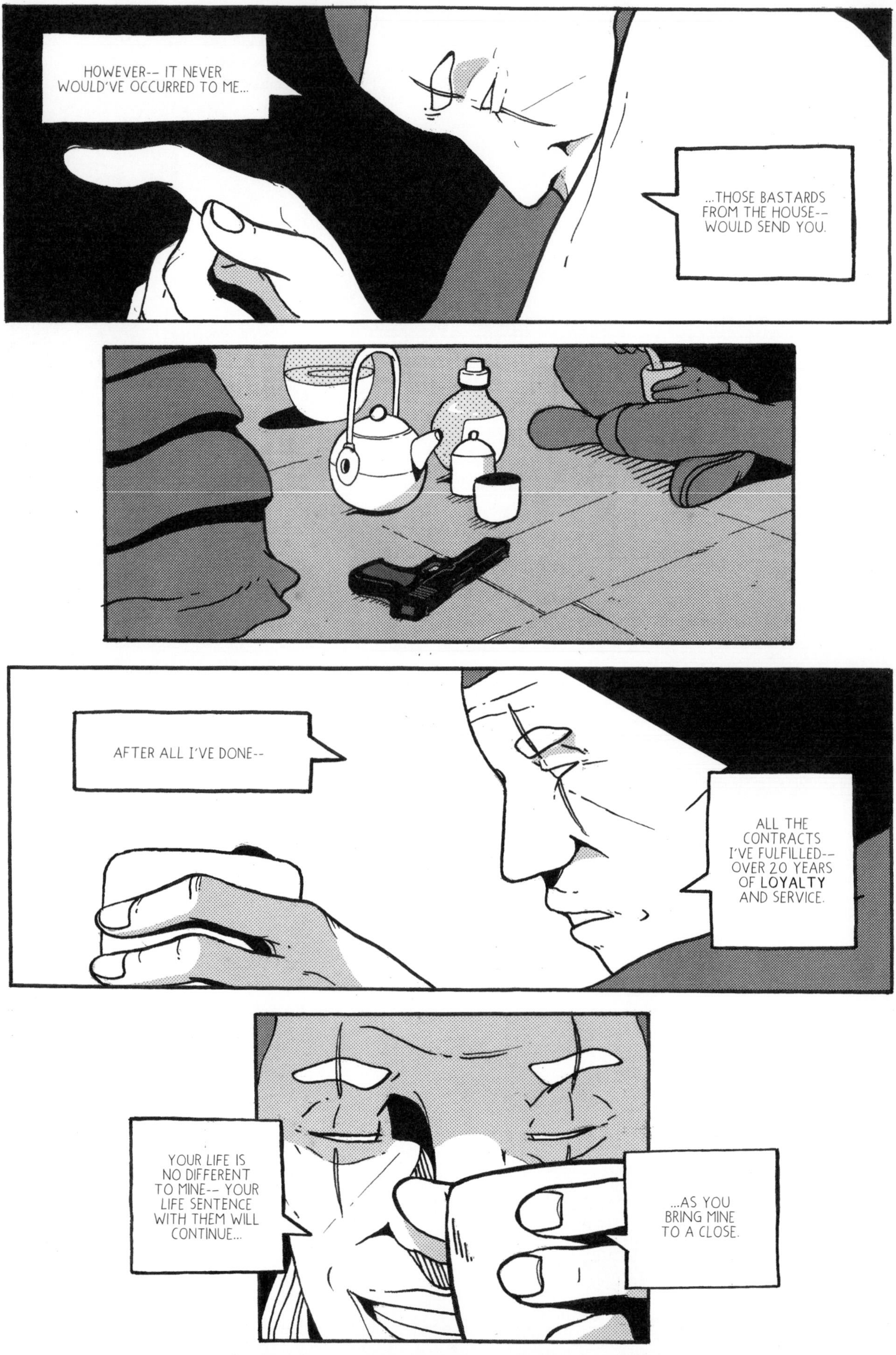
HOWEVER-- IT NEVER WOULD'VE OCCURRED TO ME...
...THOSE BASTARDS FROM THE HOUSE-- WOULD SEND YOU.
AFTER ALL I'VE DONE--
ALL THE CONTRACTS I'VE FULFILLED-- OVER 20 YEARS OF **LOYALTY** AND SERVICE.
YOUR LIFE IS NO DIFFERENT TO MINE-- YOUR LIFE SENTENCE WITH THEM WILL CONTINUE...
...AS YOU BRING MINE TO A CLOSE.

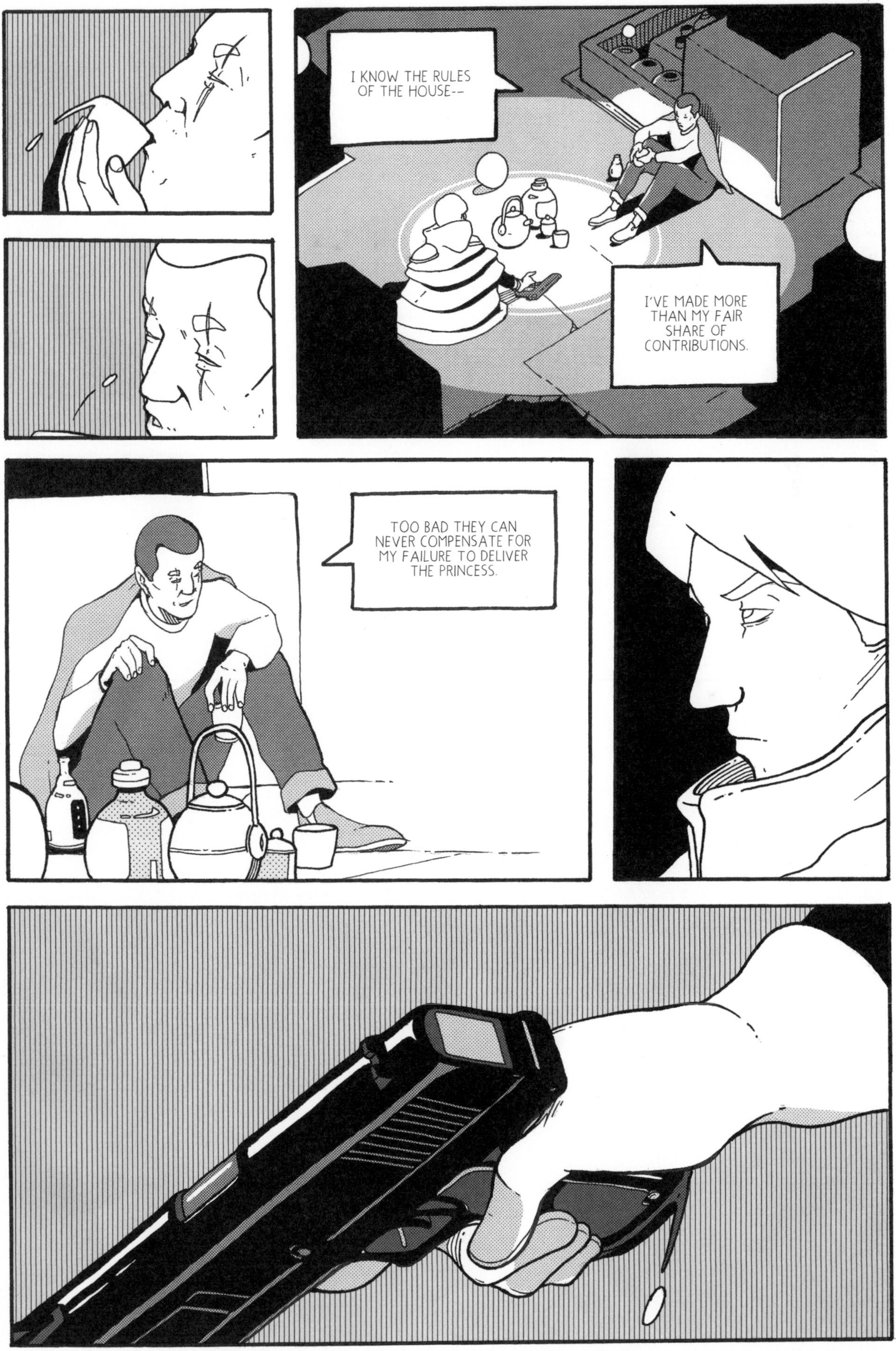
I KNOW THE RULES OF THE HOUSE--
I'VE MADE MORE THAN MY FAIR SHARE OF CONTRIBUTIONS.
TOO BAD THEY CAN NEVER COMPENSATE FOR MY FAILURE TO DELIVER THE PRINCESS.

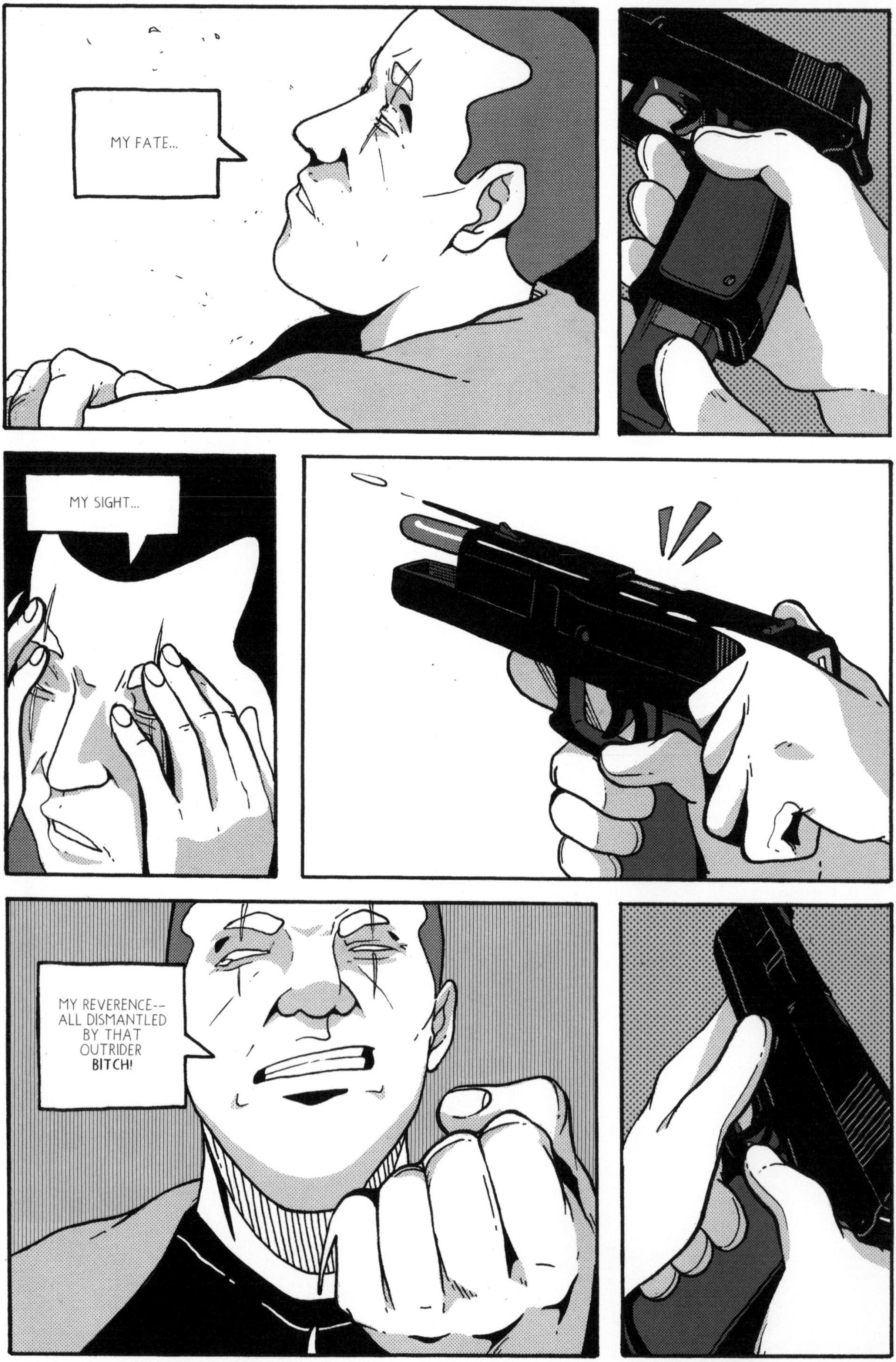
MY FATE...
MY SIGHT...
MY REVERENCE--ALL DISMANTLED BY THAT OUTRIDER **BITCH!**

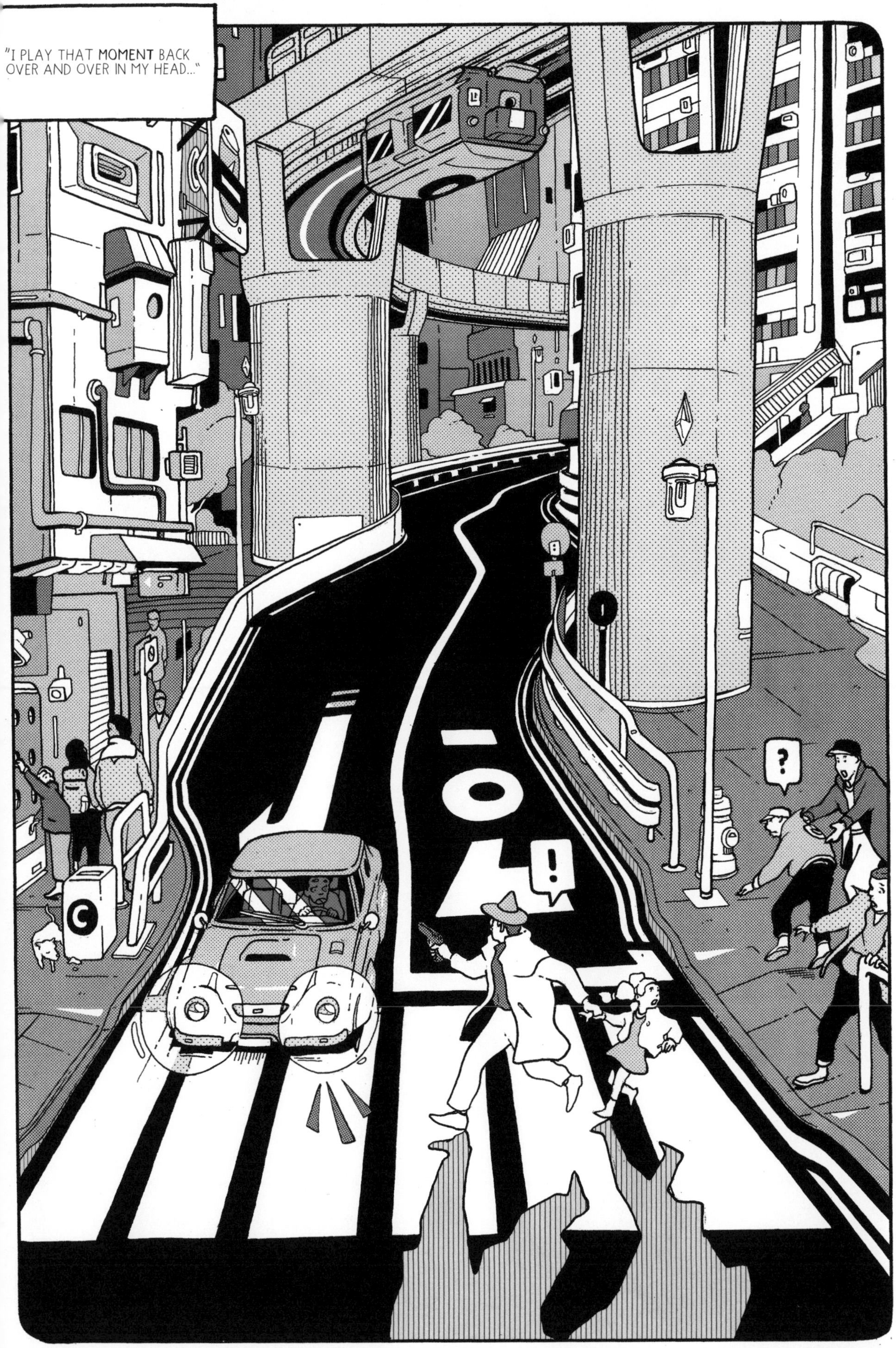
"I PLAY THAT **MOMENT** BACK OVER AND OVER IN MY HEAD..."
?
!

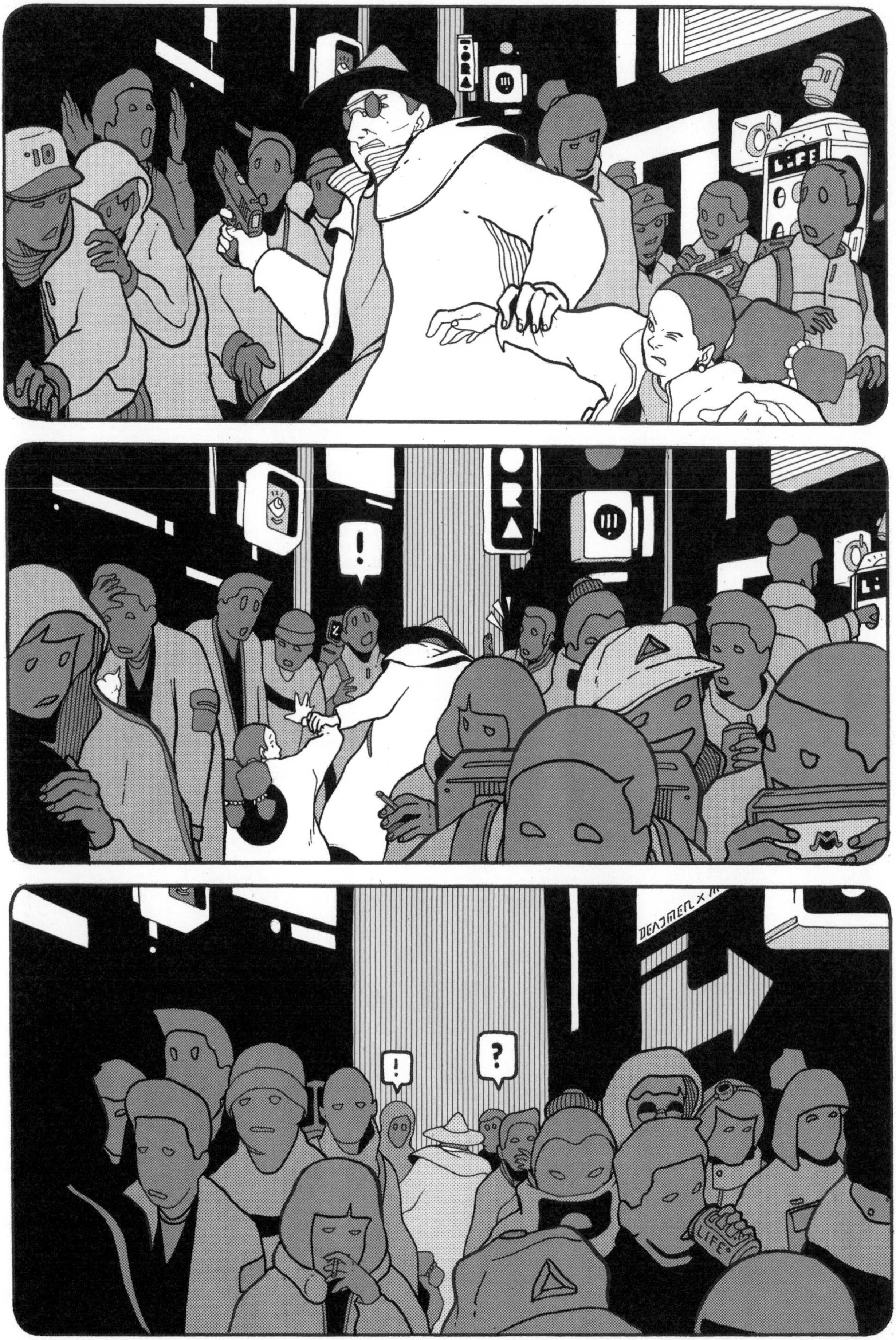
ORA
LIFE
!
ORA
!
?

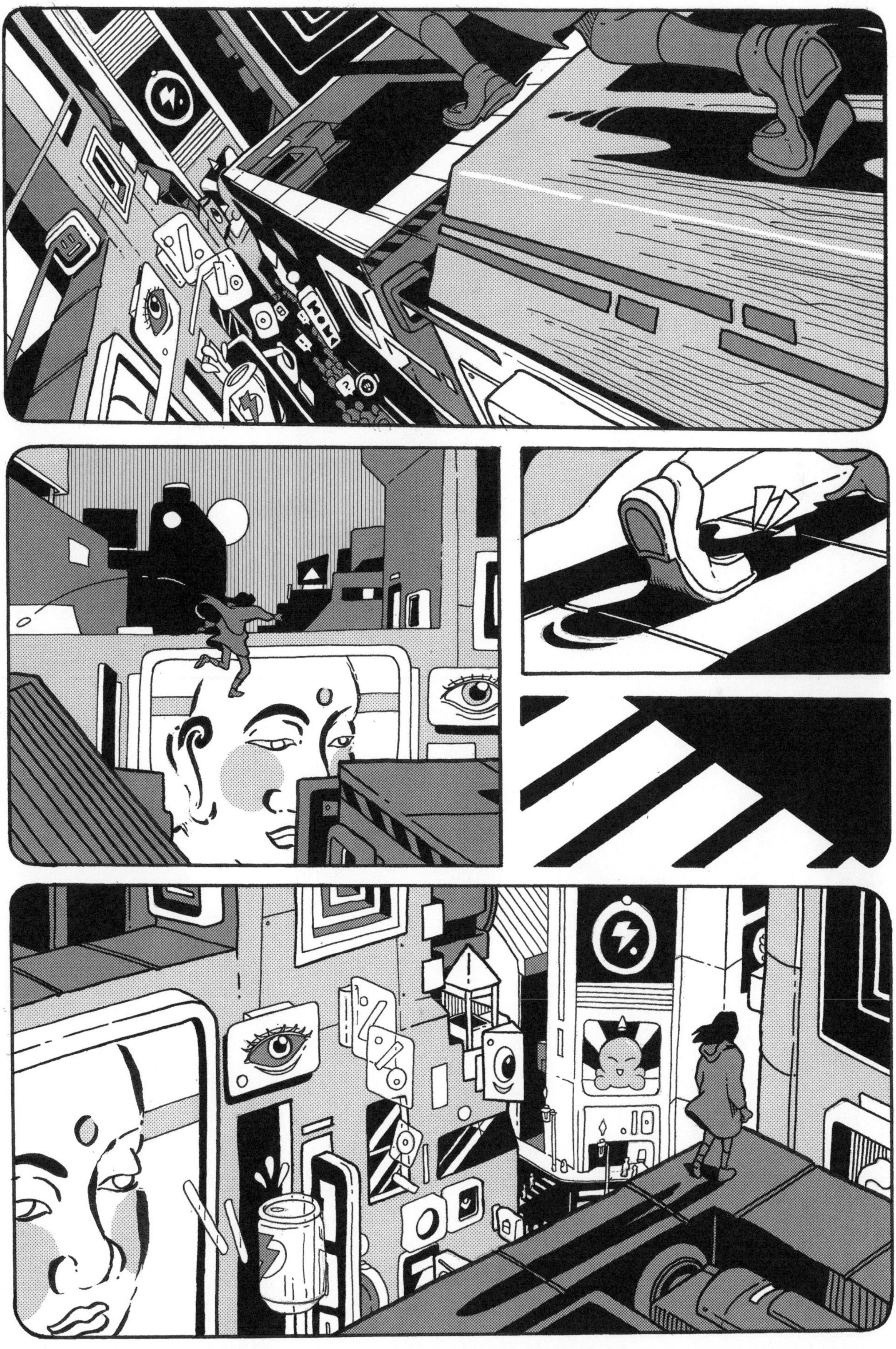

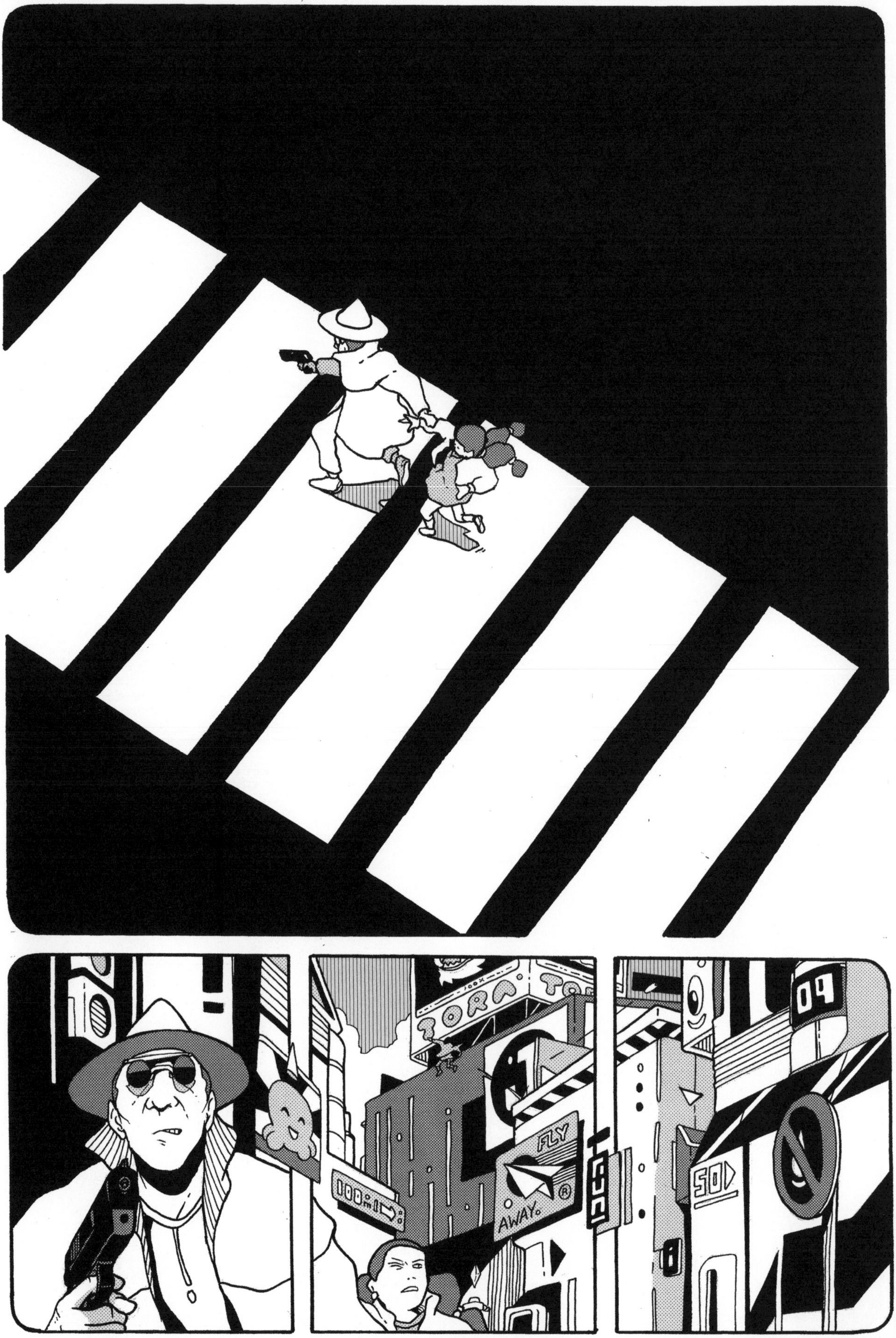
FLY
AWAY.
100m
50
09

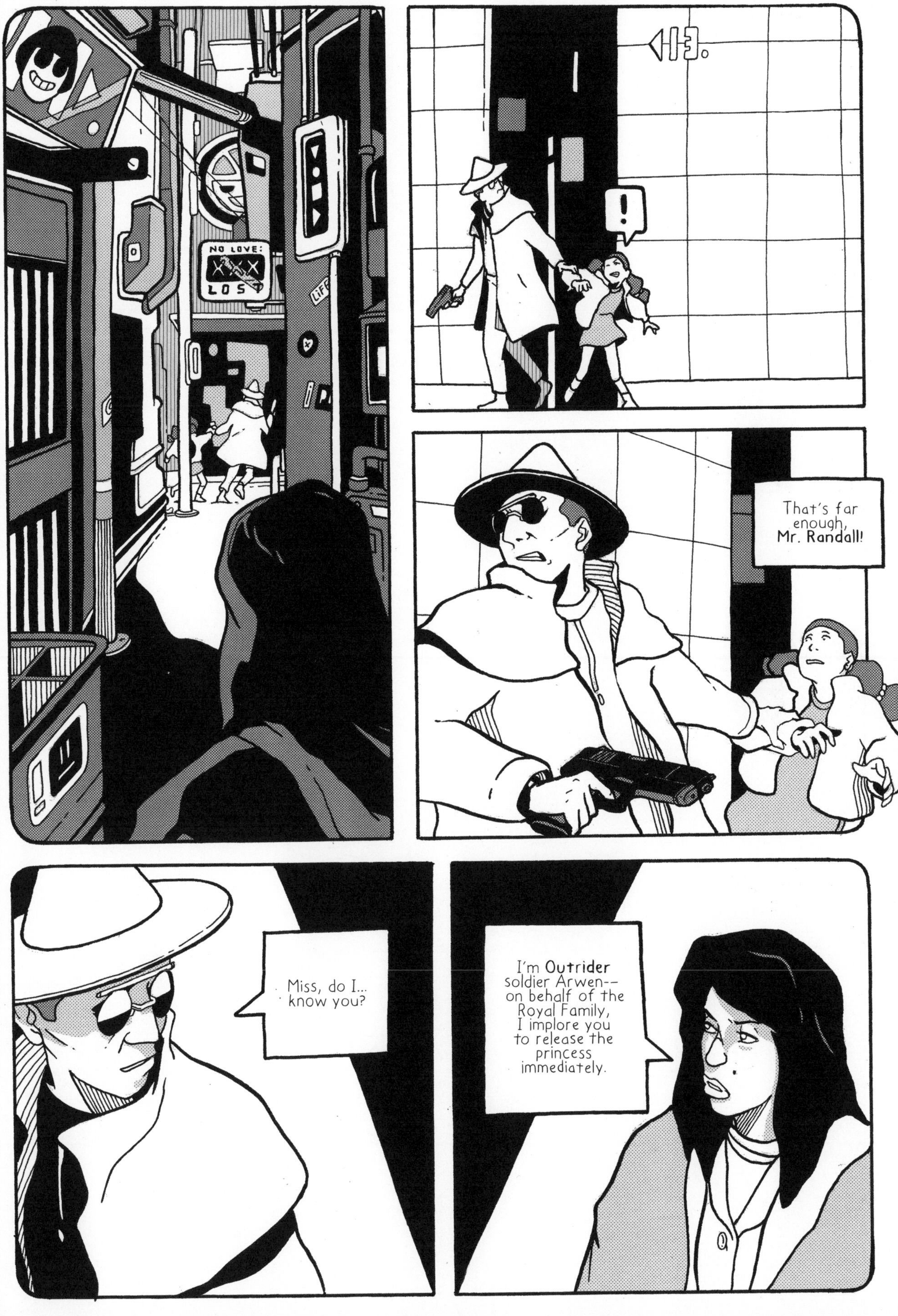
NO LOVE:
LOST
!
That's far enough, Mr. Randall!
Miss, do I... know you?
I'm Outrider soldier Arwen-- on behalf of the Royal Family, I implore you to release the princess immediately.

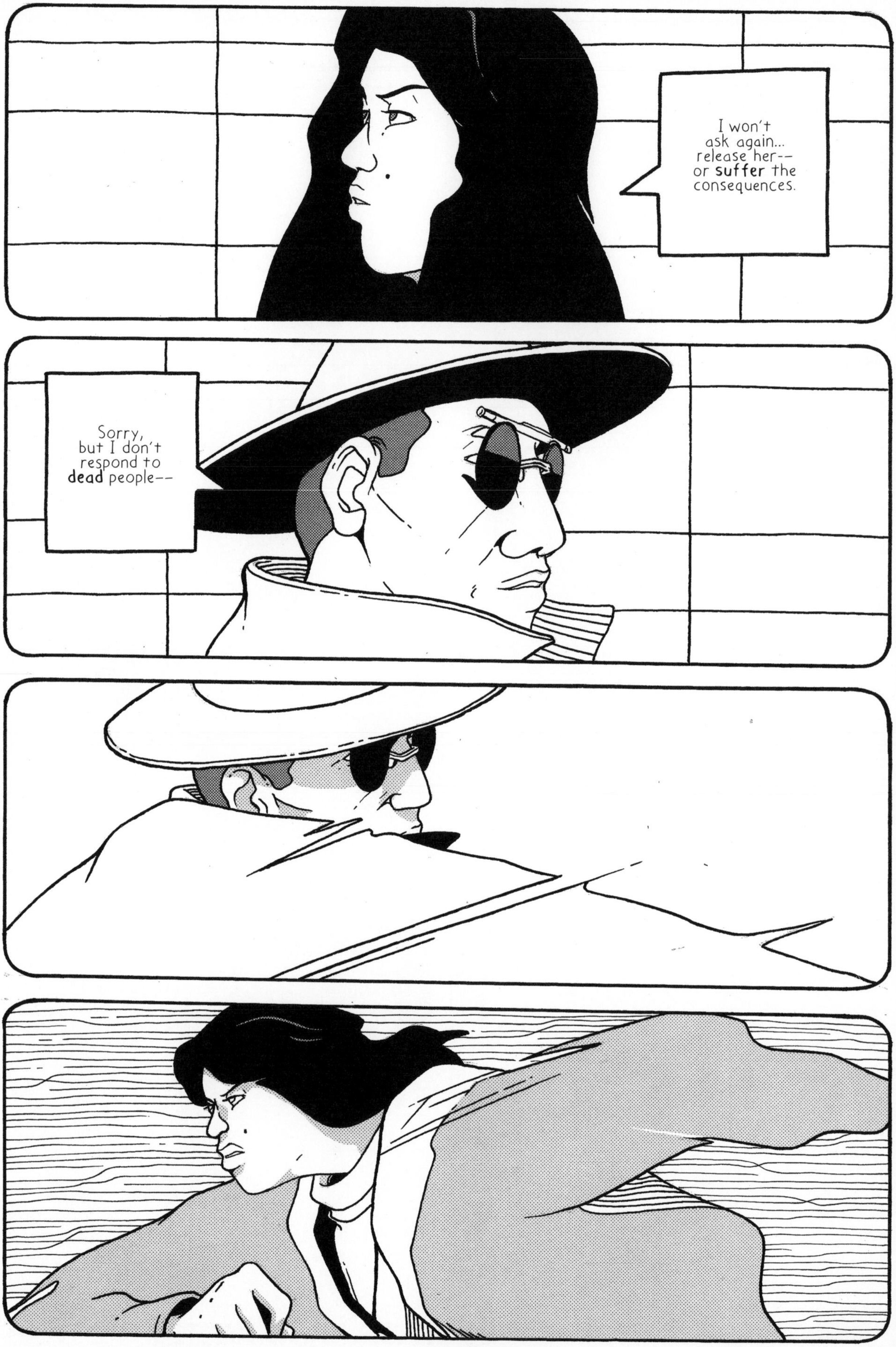
I won't ask again... release her-- or **suffer** the consequences.
Sorry, but I don't respond to **dead** people--

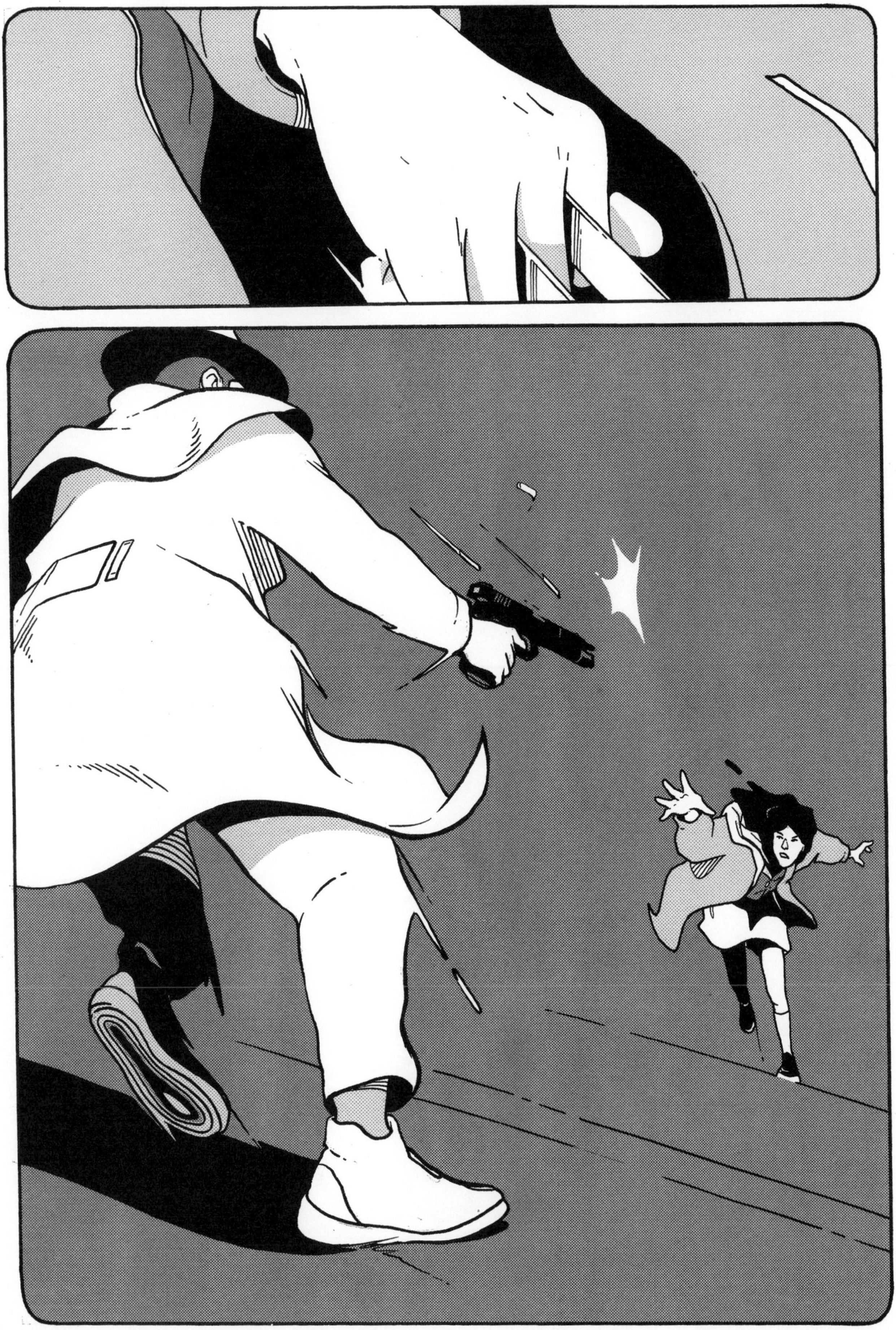

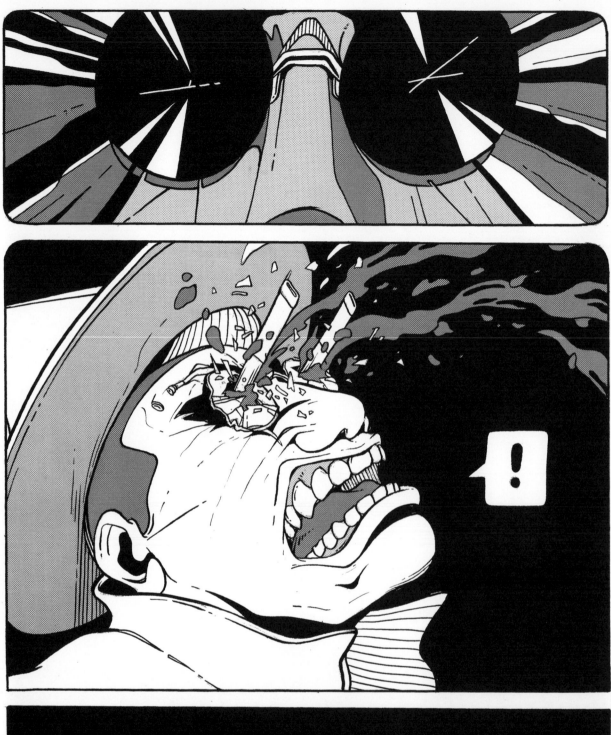

"...AND THAT'S HOW SHE BESTED ME."

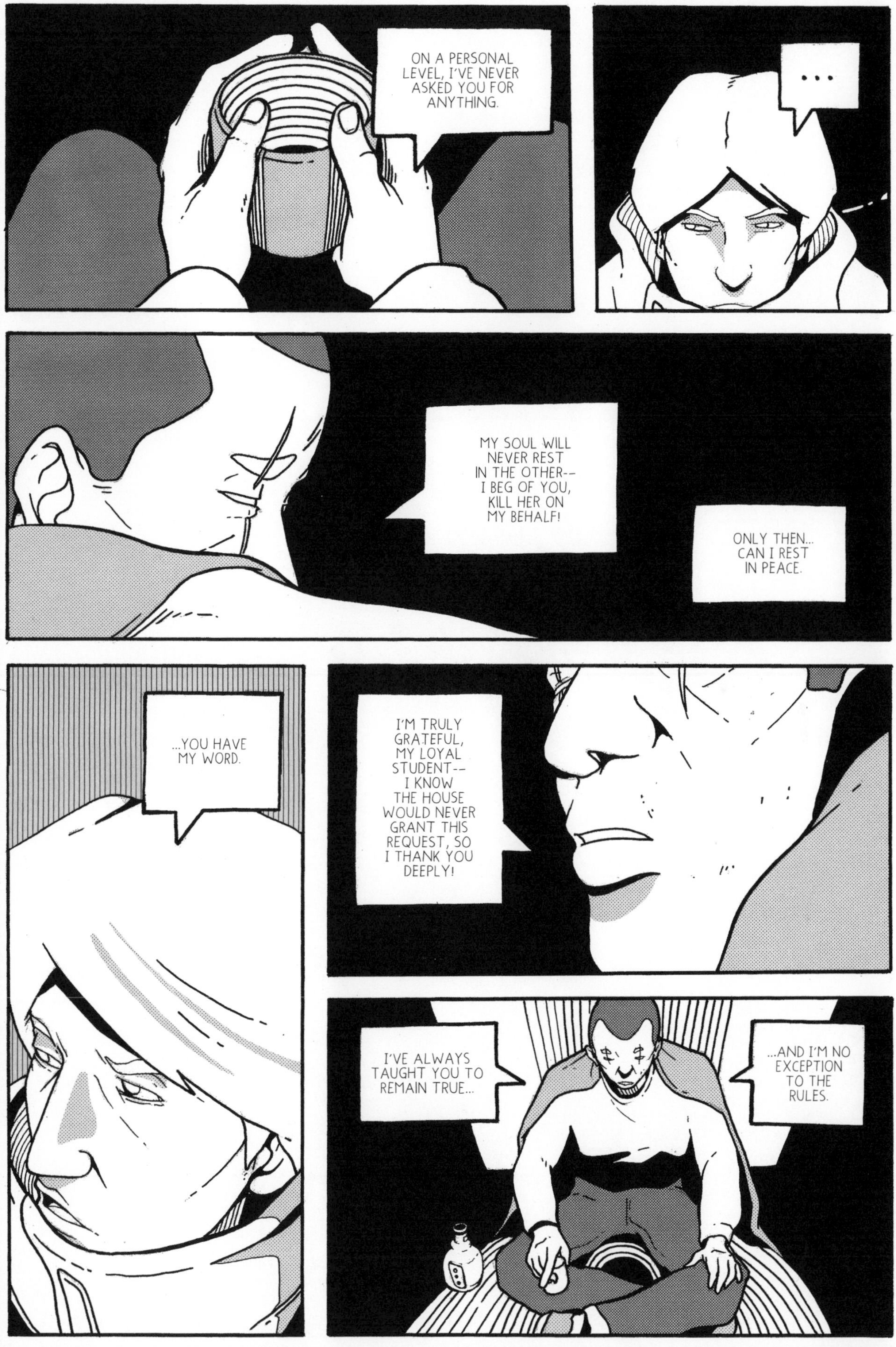
ON A PERSONAL LEVEL, I'VE NEVER ASKED YOU FOR ANYTHING.
...
MY SOUL WILL NEVER REST IN THE OTHER-- I BEG OF YOU, KILL HER ON MY BEHALF!
ONLY THEN... CAN I REST IN PEACE.
...YOU HAVE MY WORD.
I'M TRULY GRATEFUL, MY LOYAL STUDENT-- I KNOW THE HOUSE WOULD NEVER GRANT THIS REQUEST, SO I THANK YOU DEEPLY!
I'VE ALWAYS TAUGHT YOU TO REMAIN TRUE...
...AND I'M NO EXCEPTION TO THE RULES.

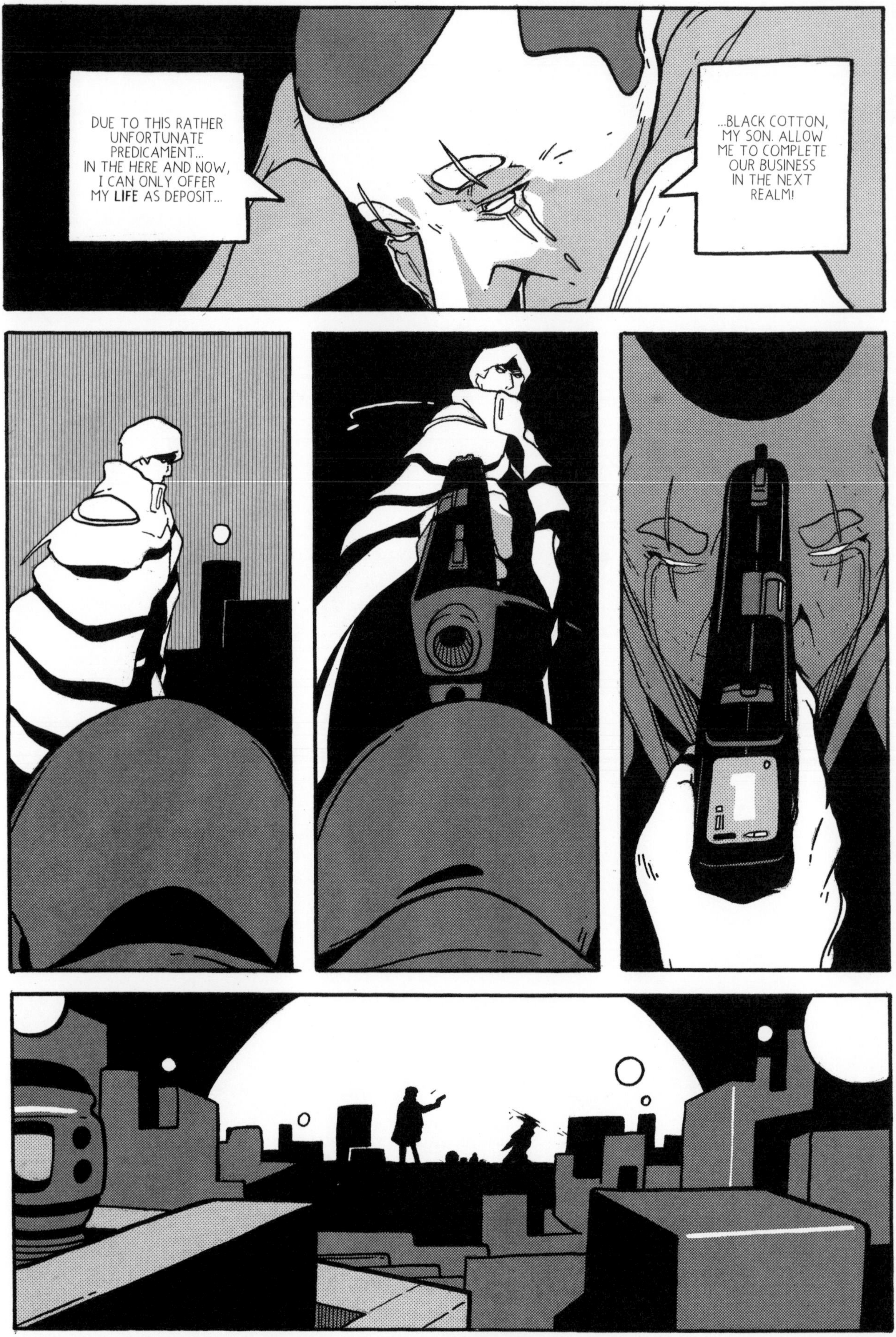

DUE TO THIS RATHER UNFORTUNATE PREDICAMENT... IN THE HERE AND NOW, I CAN ONLY OFFER MY **LIFE** AS DEPOSIT...
...BLACK COTTON, MY SON. ALLOW ME TO COMPLETE OUR BUSINESS IN THE NEXT REALM!

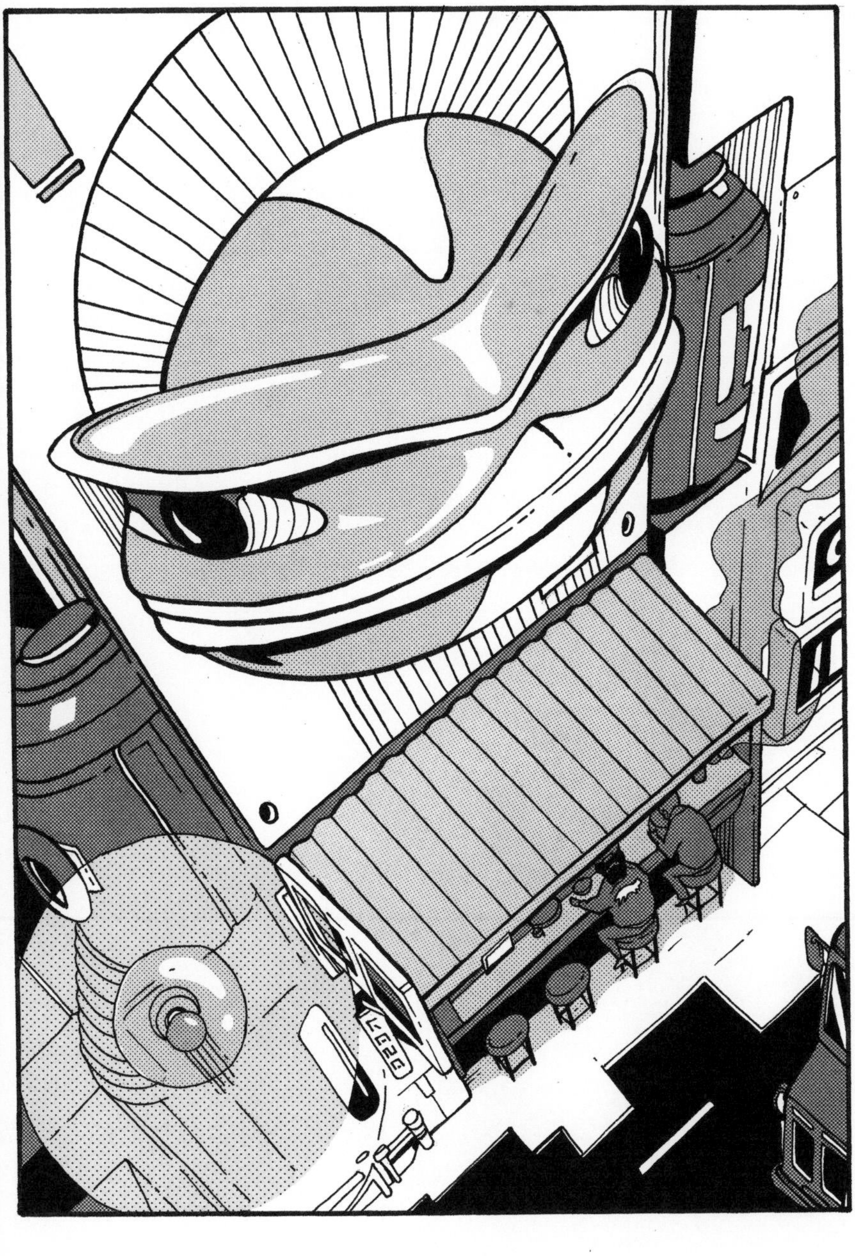

3

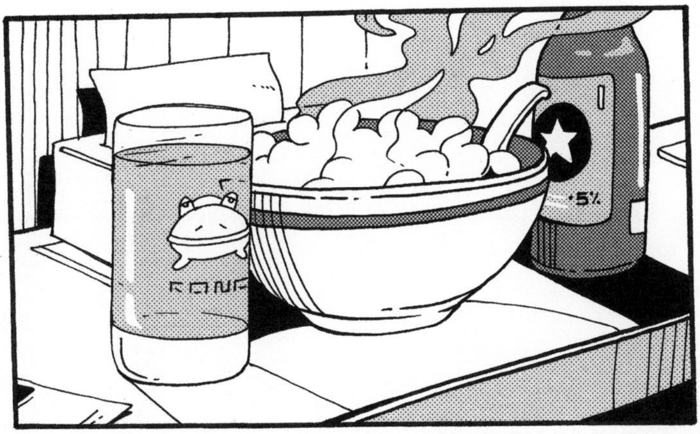

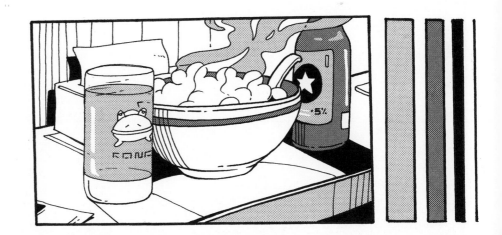

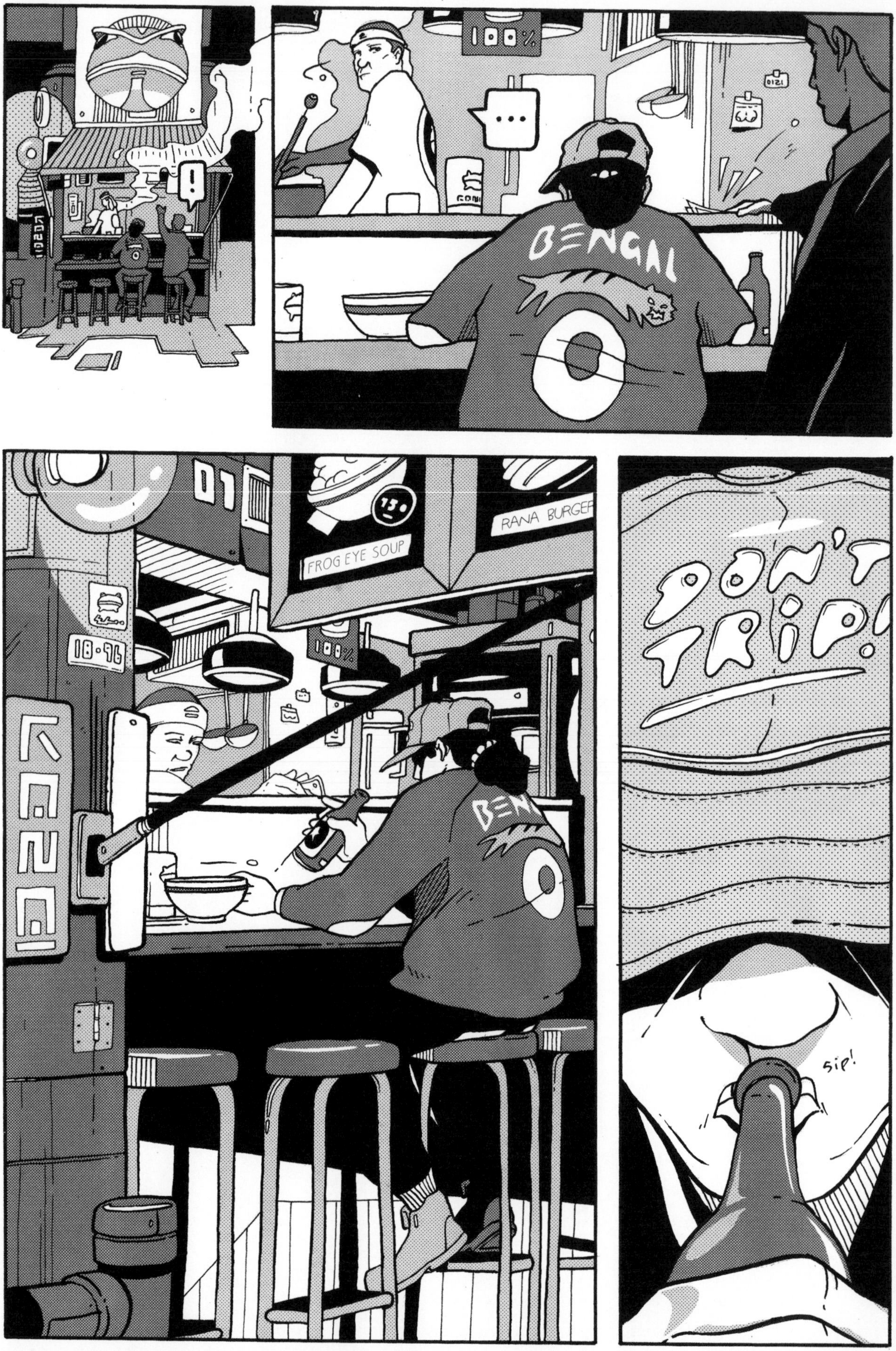

!
...
100%
BENGAL
FROG EYE SOUP
RANA BURGER
DON'T TRIP!
sip!

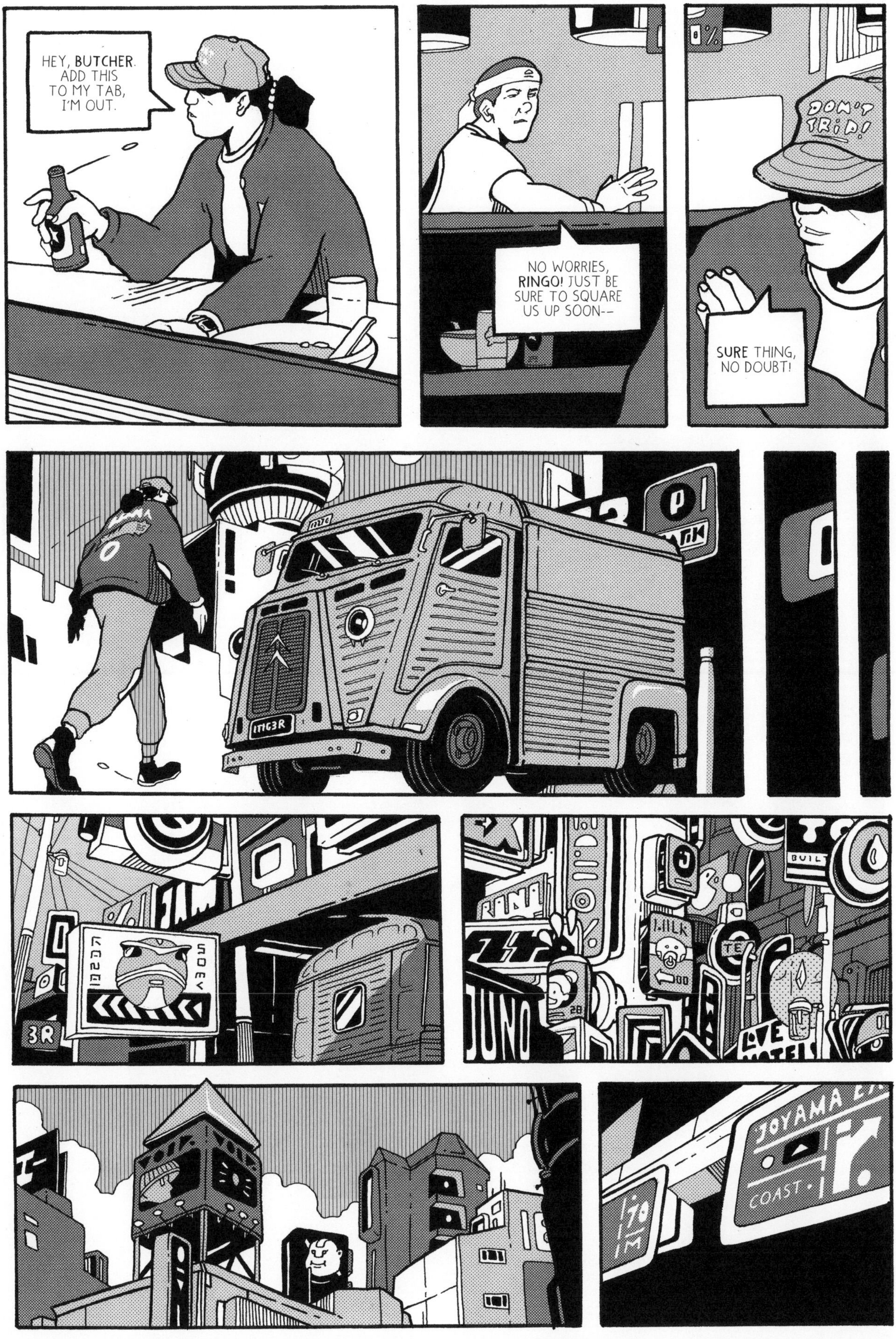
HEY, BUTCHER. ADD THIS TO MY TAB, I'M OUT.
NO WORRIES, RINGO! JUST BE SURE TO SQUARE US UP SOON--
DON'T TRIP!
SURE THING, NO DOUBT!
ITTG3R
BUILT
MILK
DUNO
LOVE HOTELS
JOYAMA
COAST
70

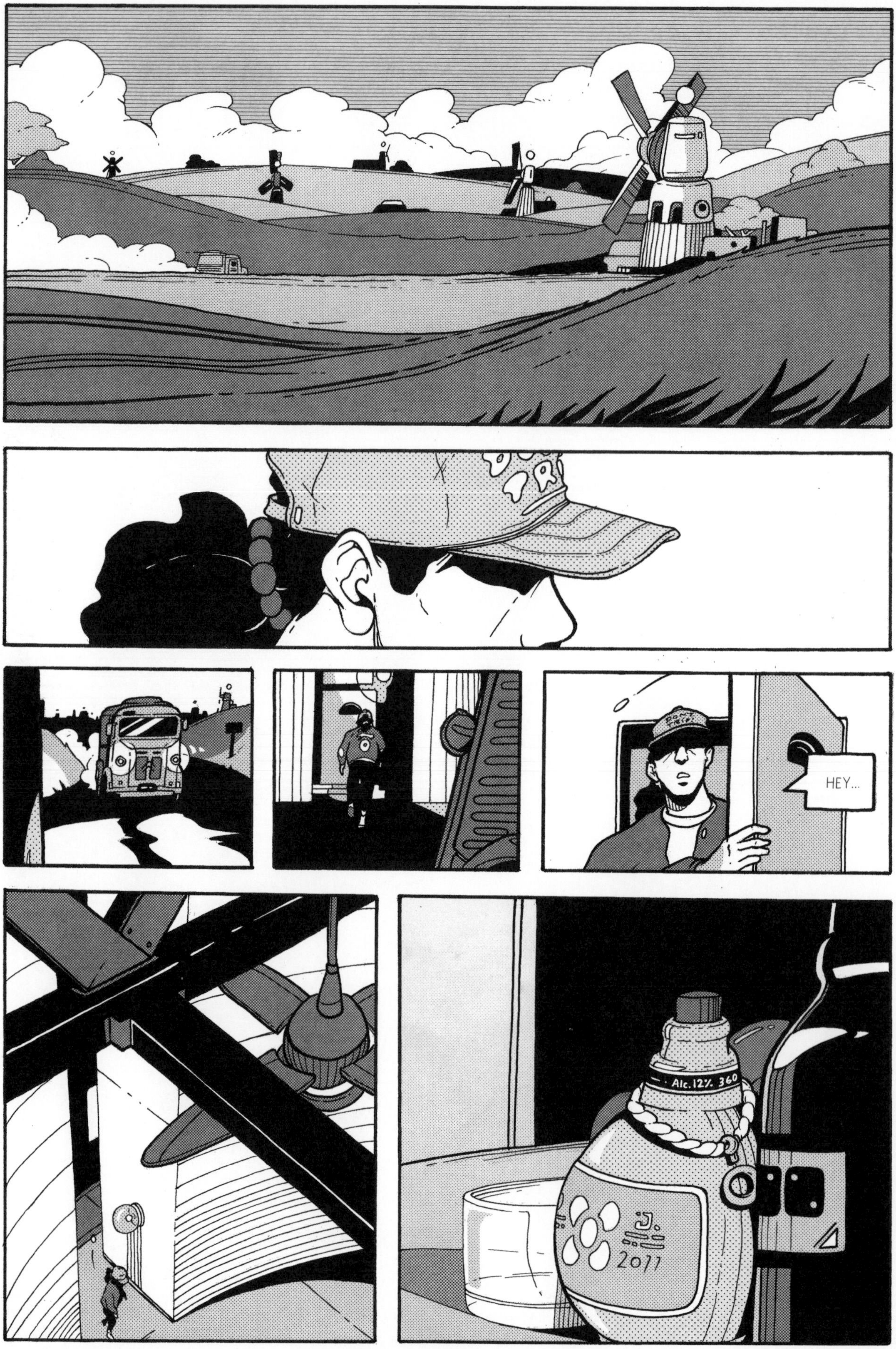
HEY...
Alc. 12% 360
J.
2011

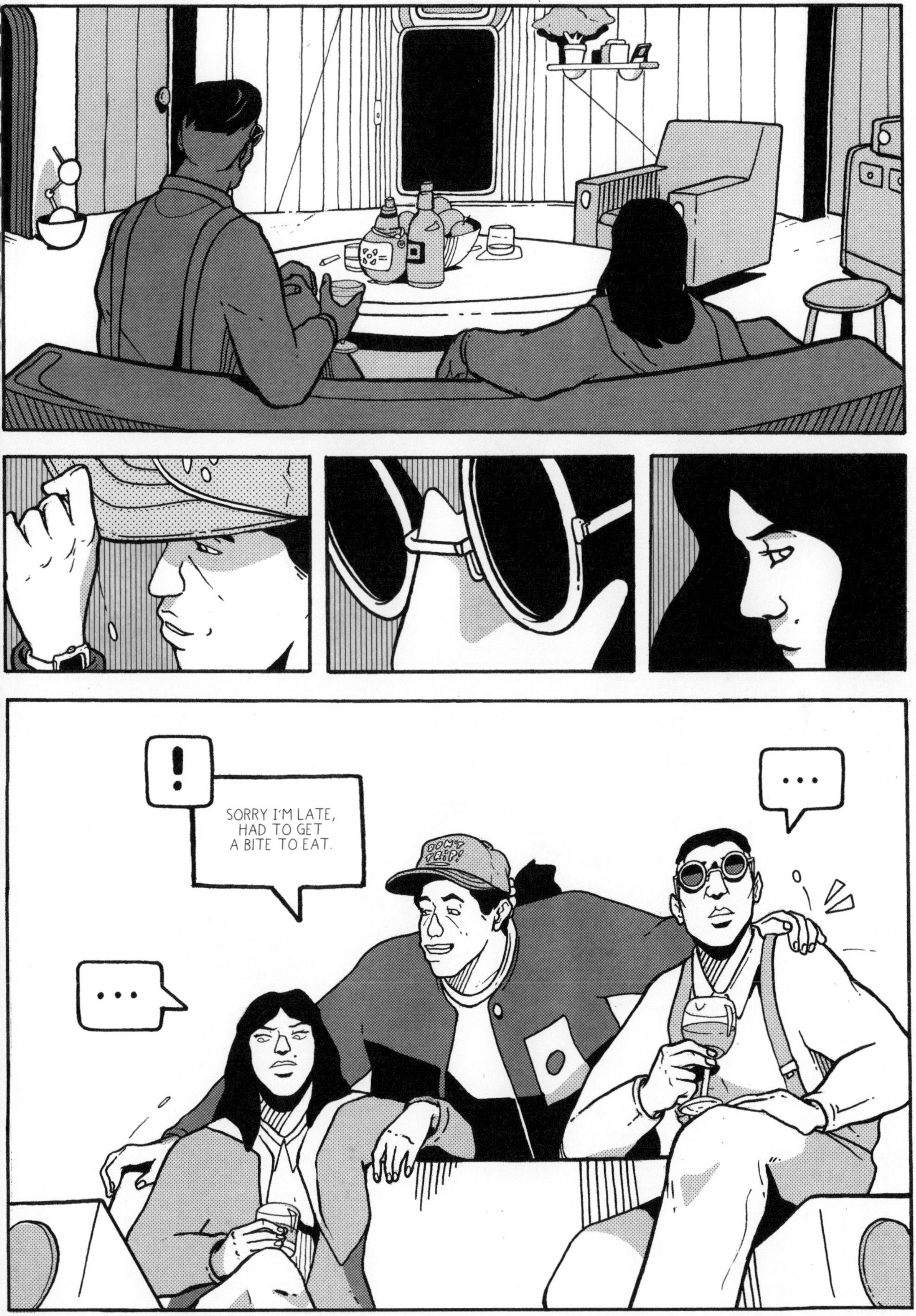
!
SORRY I'M LATE, HAD TO GET A BITE TO EAT.
...
DON'T TRIP!
...

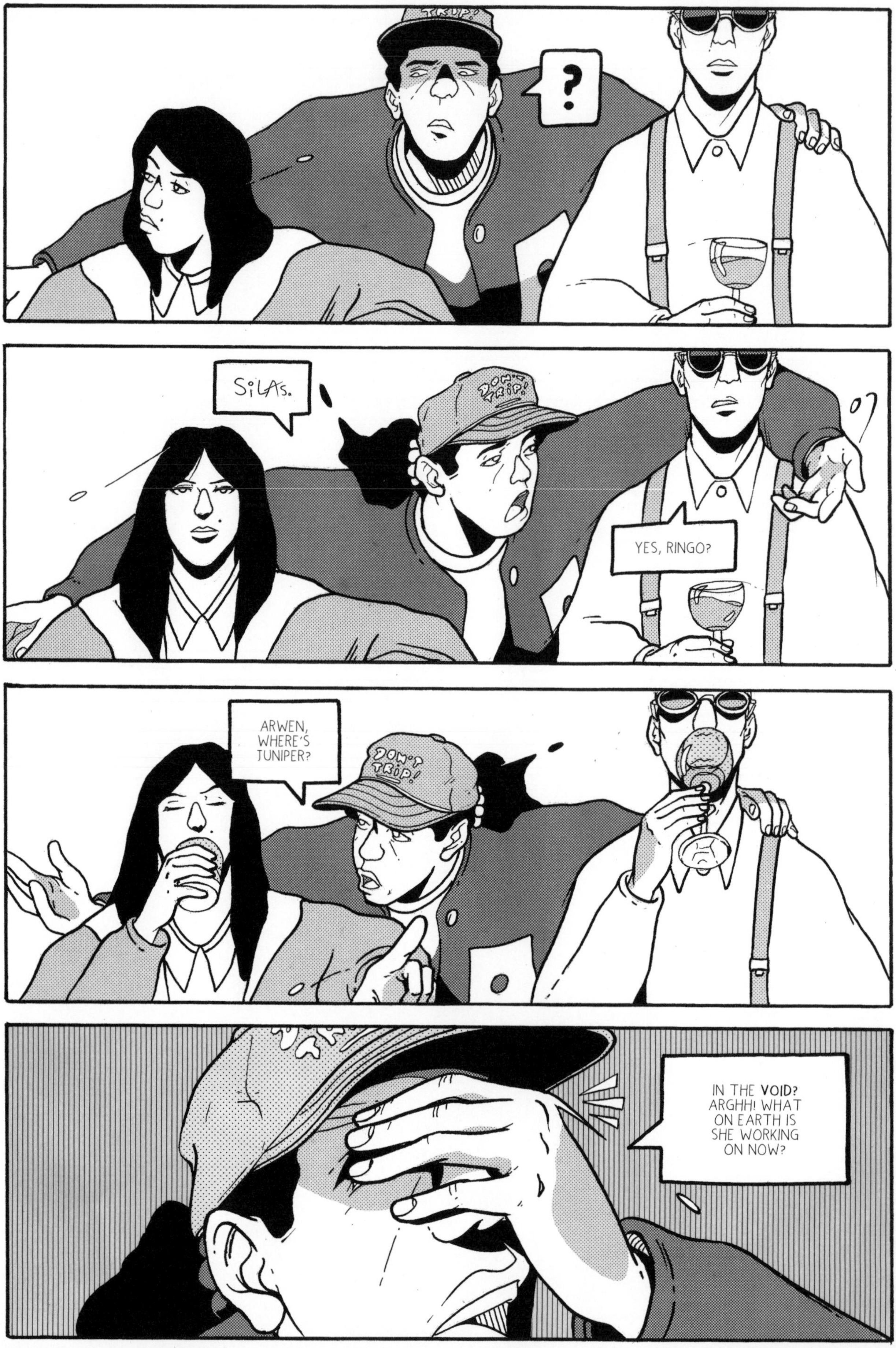
?
SILAS.
YES, RINGO?
ARWEN, WHERE'S JUNIPER?
IN THE **VOID?** ARGHH! WHAT ON EARTH IS SHE WORKING ON NOW?

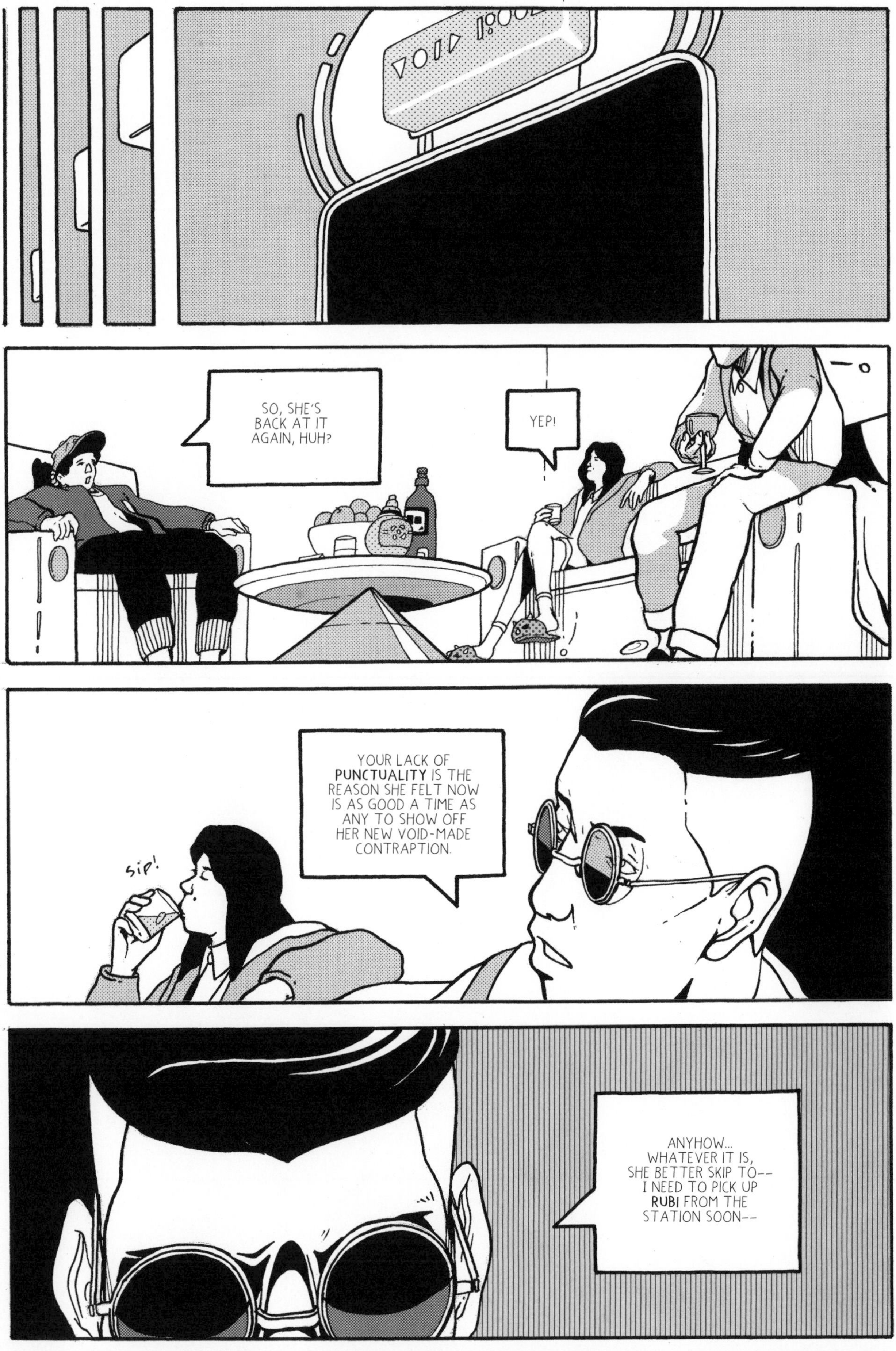
VOID !00
SO, SHE'S BACK AT IT AGAIN, HUH?
YEP!
YOUR LACK OF **PUNCTUALITY** IS THE REASON SHE FELT NOW IS AS GOOD A TIME AS ANY TO SHOW OFF HER NEW VOID-MADE CONTRAPTION.
SIP!
ANYHOW... WHATEVER IT IS, SHE BETTER SKIP TO-- I NEED TO PICK UP **RUBI** FROM THE STATION SOON--

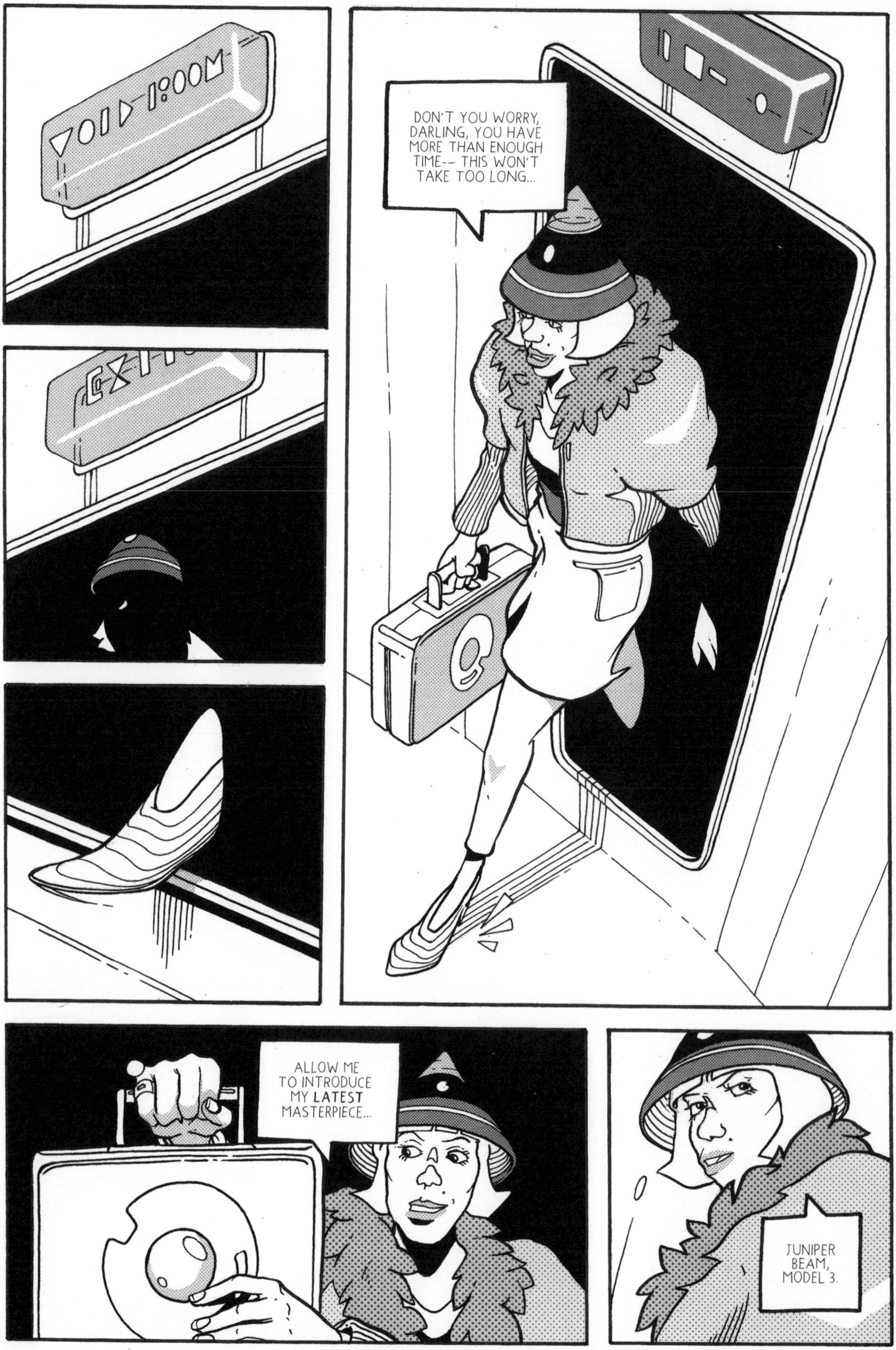

DON'T YOU WORRY, DARLING, YOU HAVE MORE THAN ENOUGH TIME-- THIS WON'T TAKE TOO LONG...
ALLOW ME TO INTRODUCE MY **LATEST** MASTERPIECE...
JUNIPER BEAM, MODEL 3.

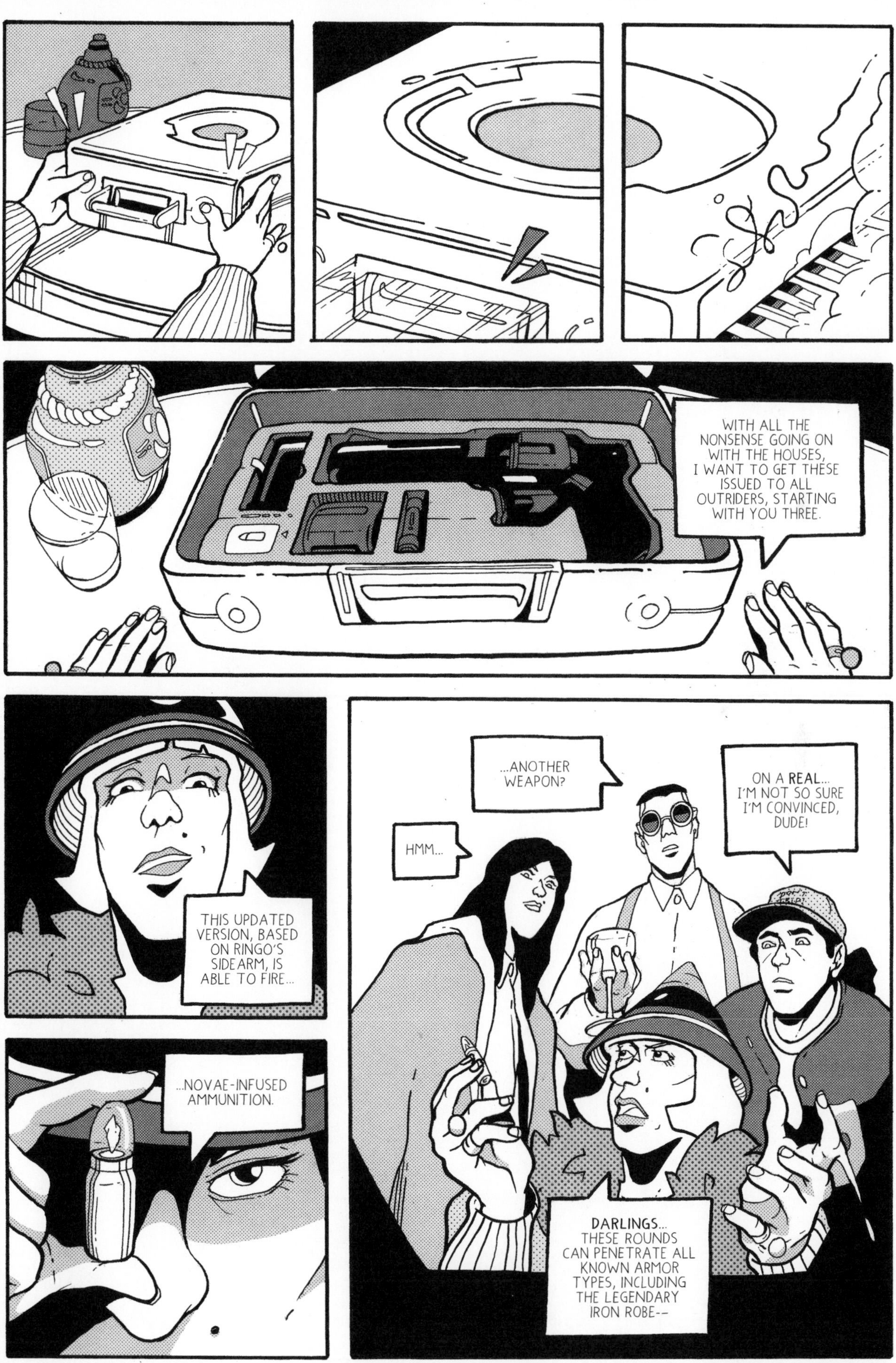
WITH ALL THE NONSENSE GOING ON WITH THE HOUSES, I WANT TO GET THESE ISSUED TO ALL OUTRIDERS, STARTING WITH YOU THREE.
THIS UPDATED VERSION, BASED ON RINGO'S SIDEARM, IS ABLE TO FIRE...
...NOVAE-INFUSED AMMUNITION.
HMM...
...ANOTHER WEAPON?
ON A REAL... I'M NOT SO SURE I'M CONVINCED, DUDE!
DARLINGS... THESE ROUNDS CAN PENETRATE ALL KNOWN ARMOR TYPES, INCLUDING THE LEGENDARY IRON ROBE--

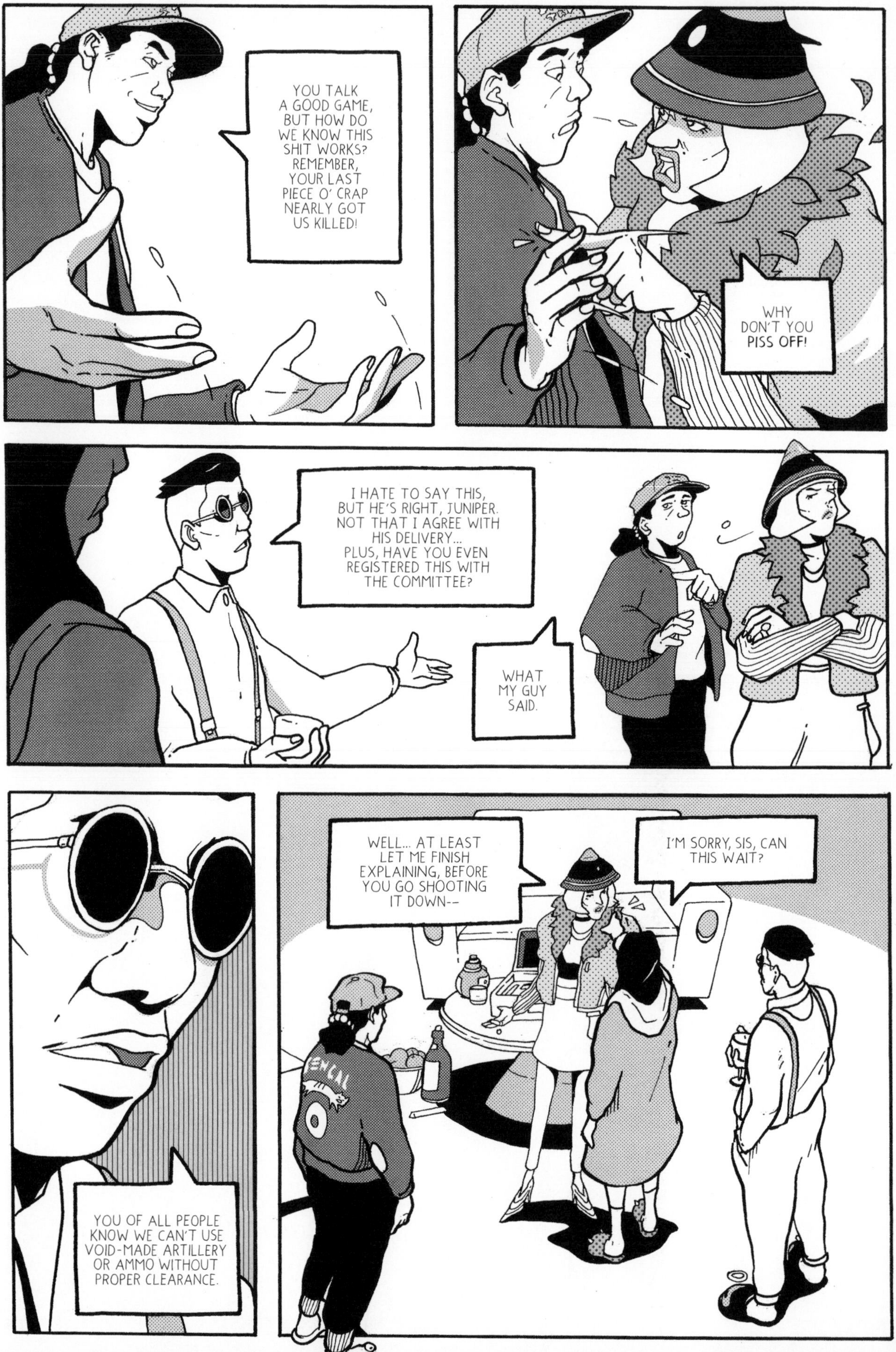
YOU TALK A GOOD GAME, BUT HOW DO WE KNOW THIS SHIT WORKS? REMEMBER, YOUR LAST PIECE O' CRAP NEARLY GOT US KILLED!
WHY DON'T YOU **PISS OFF!**
I HATE TO SAY THIS, BUT HE'S RIGHT, JUNIPER. NOT THAT I AGREE WITH HIS DELIVERY... PLUS, HAVE YOU EVEN REGISTERED THIS WITH THE COMMITTEE?
WHAT MY GUY SAID.
YOU OF ALL PEOPLE KNOW WE CAN'T USE VOID-MADE ARTILLERY OR AMMO WITHOUT PROPER CLEARANCE.
WELL... AT LEAST LET ME FINISH EXPLAINING, BEFORE YOU GO SHOOTING IT DOWN--
I'M SORRY, SIS, CAN THIS WAIT?

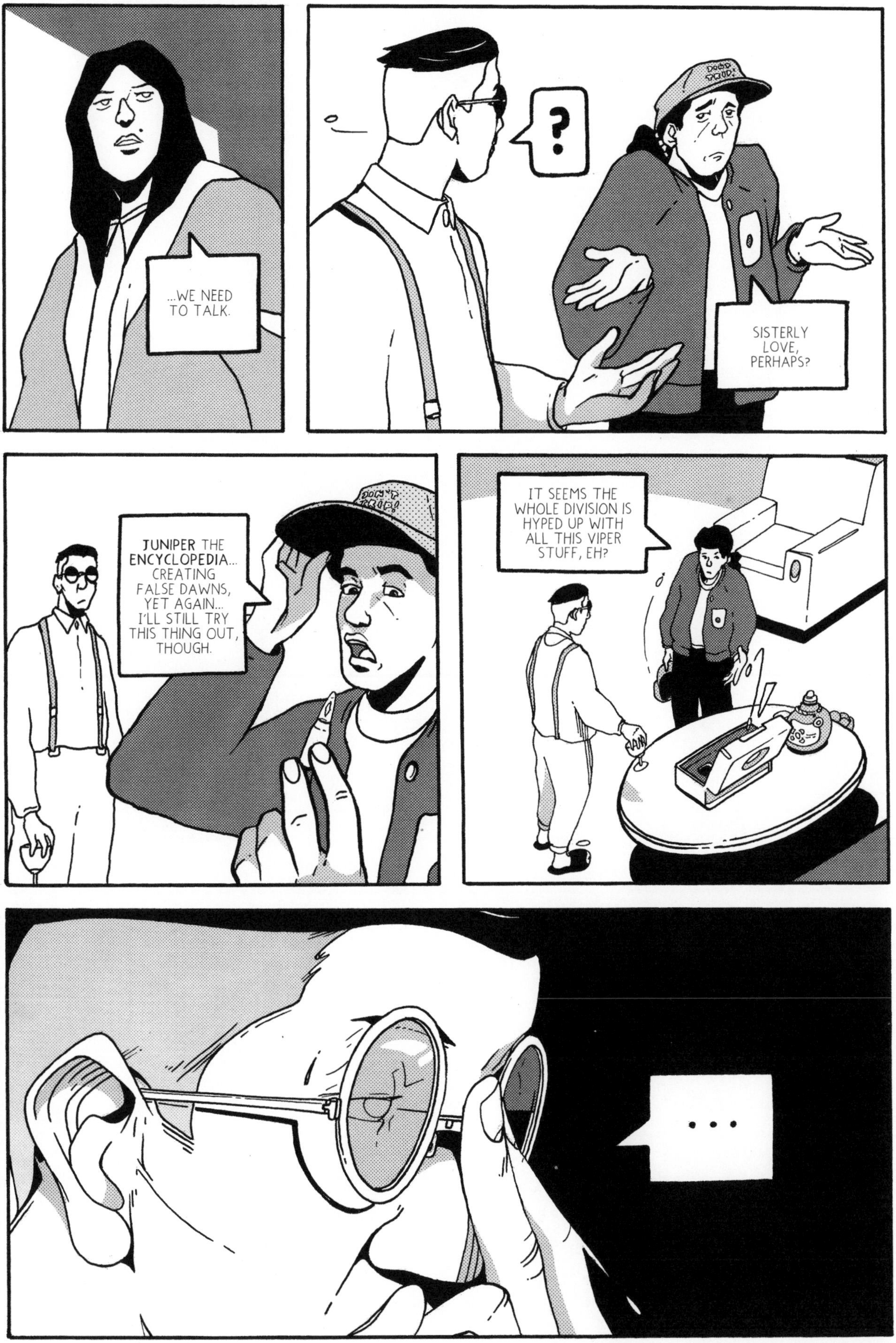
...WE NEED TO TALK.
?
SISTERLY LOVE, PERHAPS?
JUNIPER THE ENCYCLOPEDIA... CREATING FALSE DAWNS, YET AGAIN... I'LL STILL TRY THIS THING OUT, THOUGH.
IT SEEMS THE WHOLE DIVISION IS HYPED UP WITH ALL THIS VIPER STUFF, EH?
...

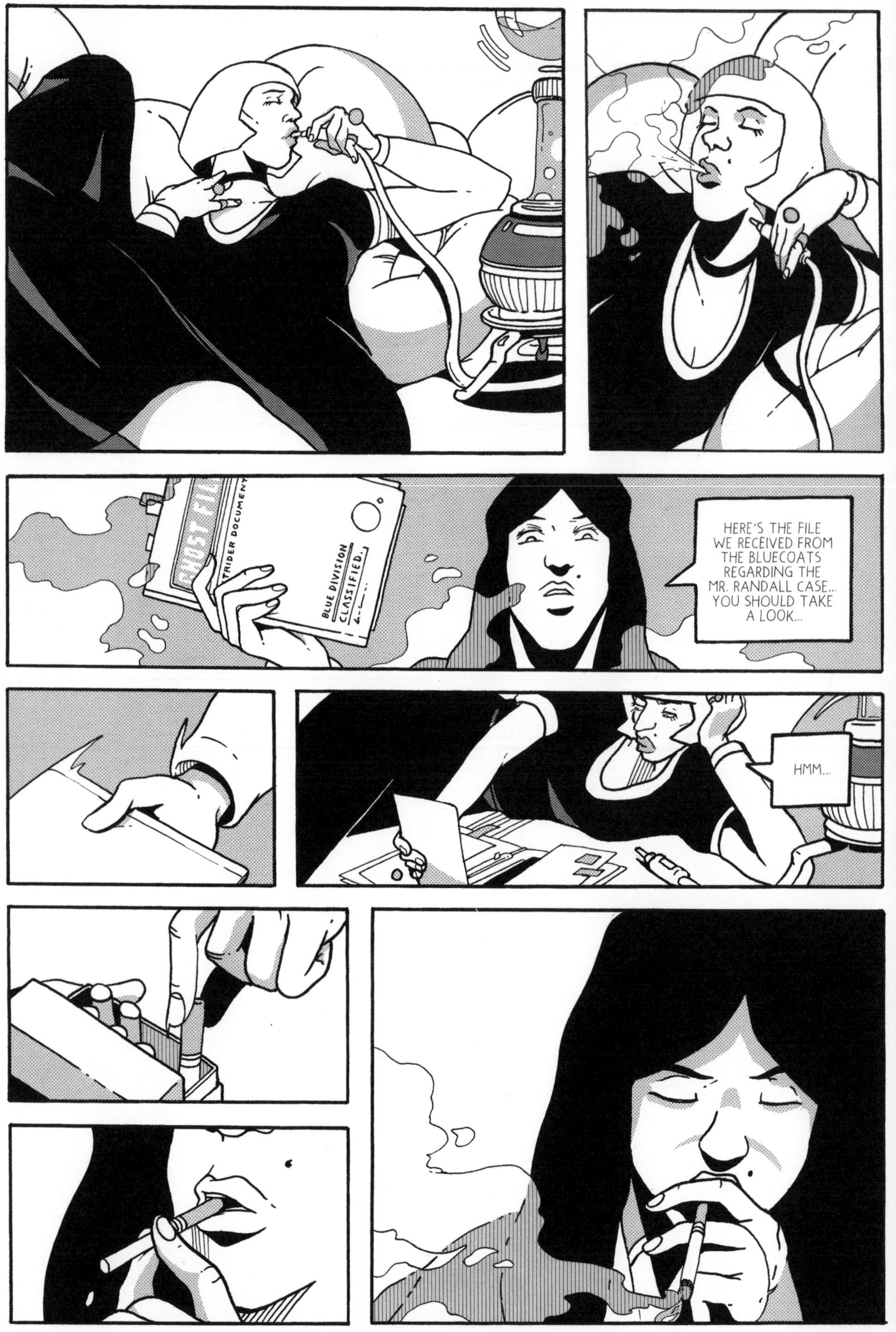
BLUE DIVISION
CLASSIFIED.
HERE'S THE FILE WE RECEIVED FROM THE BLUECOATS REGARDING THE MR. RANDALL CASE... YOU SHOULD TAKE A LOOK...
HMM...

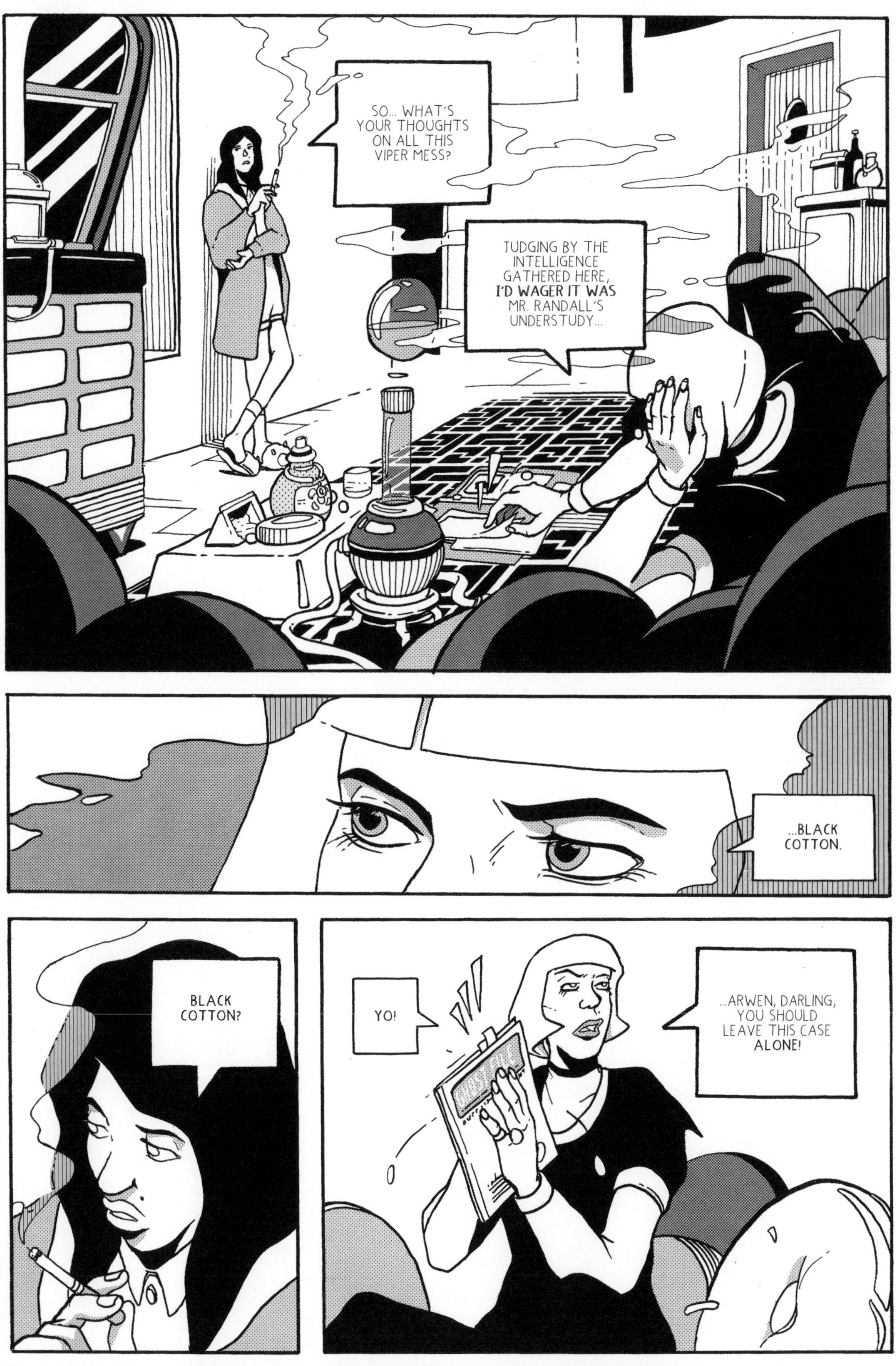
SO... WHAT'S YOUR THOUGHTS ON ALL THIS VIPER MESS?
JUDGING BY THE INTELLIGENCE GATHERED HERE, I'D WAGER IT WAS MR. RANDALL'S UNDERSTUDY...
...BLACK COTTON.
BLACK COTTON?
YO!
...ARWEN, DARLING, YOU SHOULD LEAVE THIS CASE ALONE!

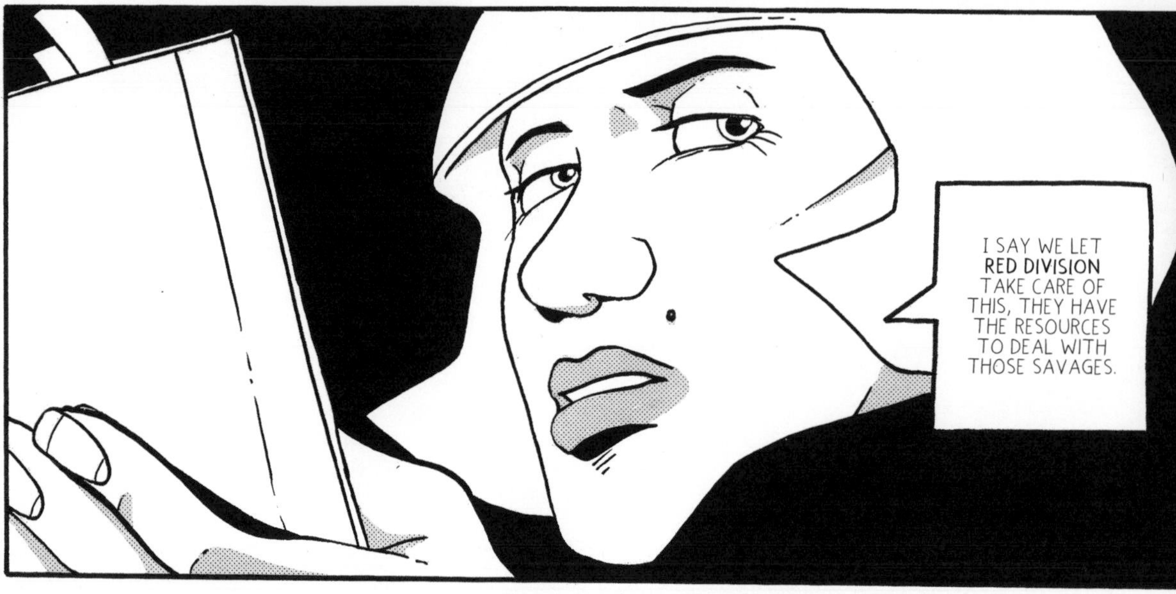
I SAY WE LET **RED DIVISION** TAKE CARE OF THIS, THEY HAVE THE RESOURCES TO DEAL WITH THOSE SAVAGES.

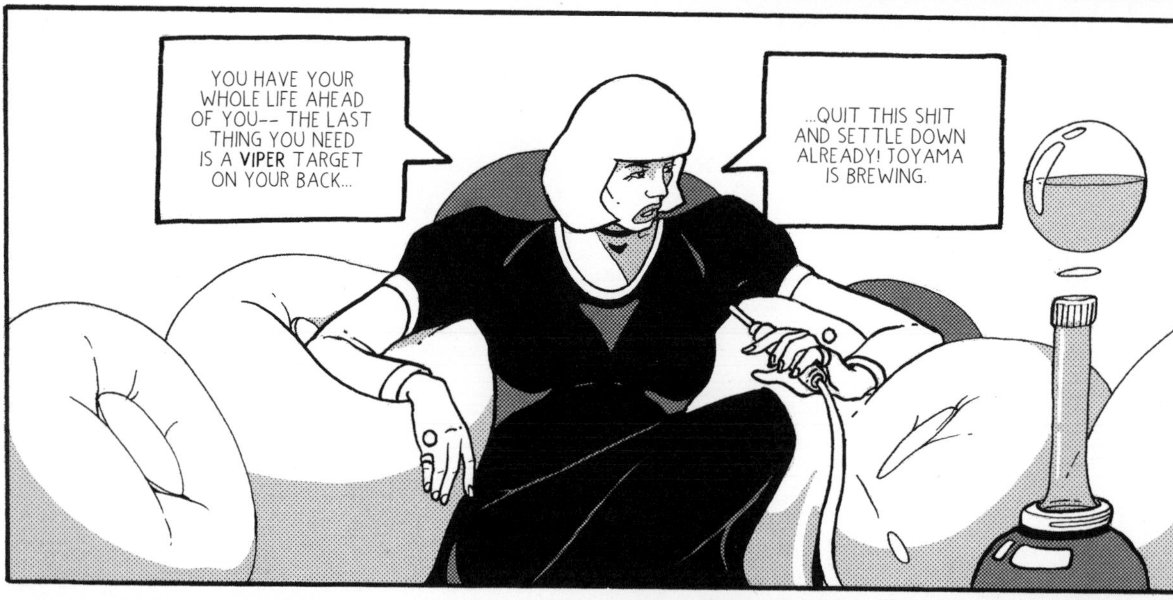
YOU HAVE YOUR WHOLE LIFE AHEAD OF YOU-- THE LAST THING YOU NEED IS A **VIPER** TARGET ON YOUR BACK...
...QUIT THIS SHIT AND SETTLE DOWN ALREADY! TOYAMA IS BREWING.

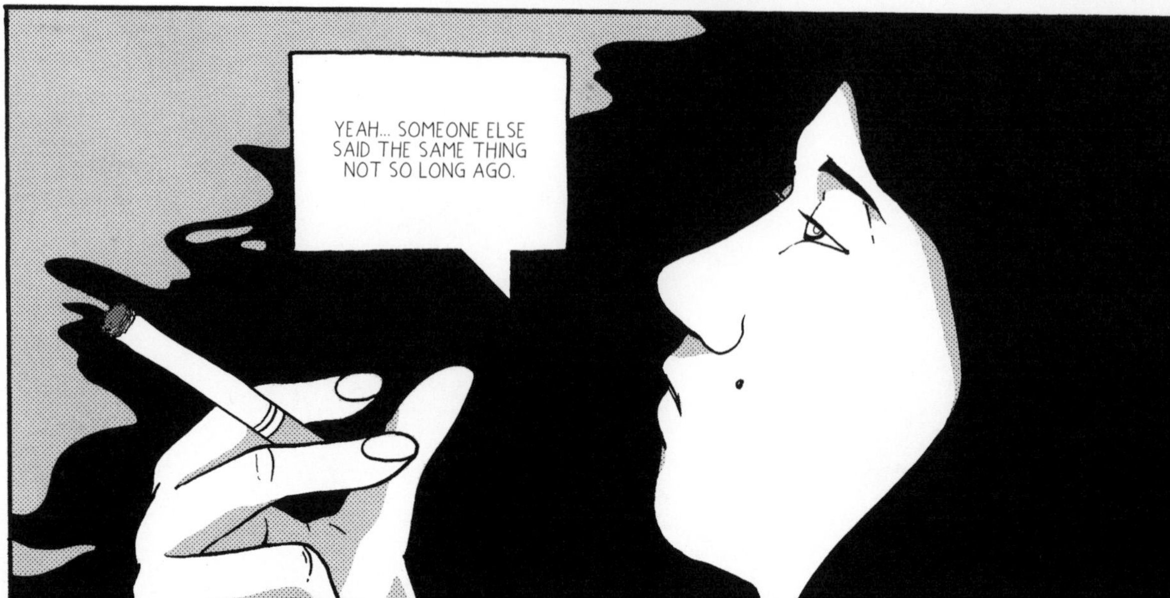
YEAH... SOMEONE ELSE SAID THE SAME THING NOT SO LONG AGO.

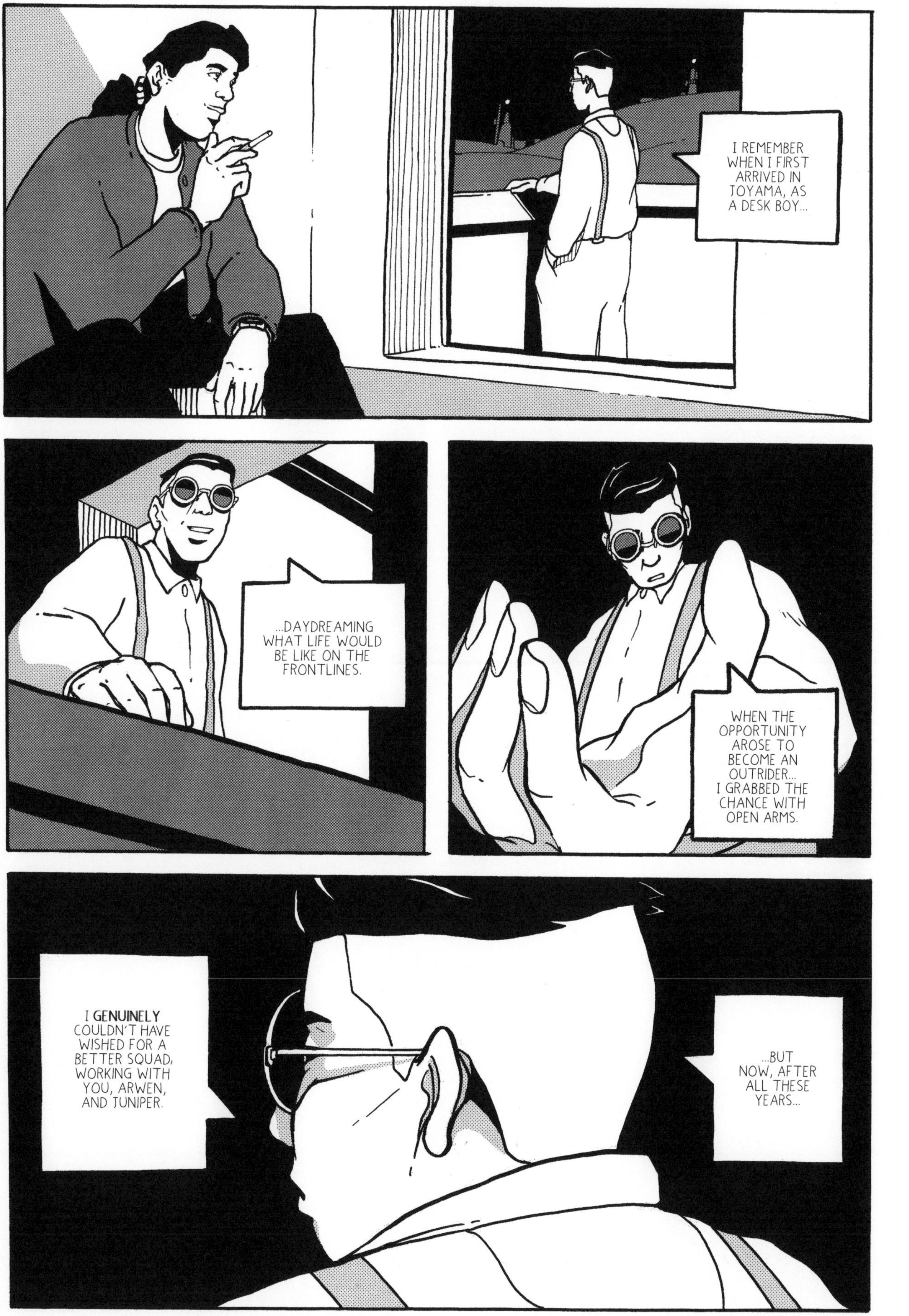
I REMEMBER WHEN I FIRST ARRIVED IN JOYAMA, AS A DESK BOY...
...DAYDREAMING WHAT LIFE WOULD BE LIKE ON THE FRONTLINES.
WHEN THE OPPORTUNITY AROSE TO BECOME AN OUTRIDER... I GRABBED THE CHANCE WITH OPEN ARMS.
I **GENUINELY** COULDN'T HAVE WISHED FOR A BETTER SQUAD, WORKING WITH YOU, ARWEN, AND JUNIPER.
...BUT NOW, AFTER ALL THESE YEARS...

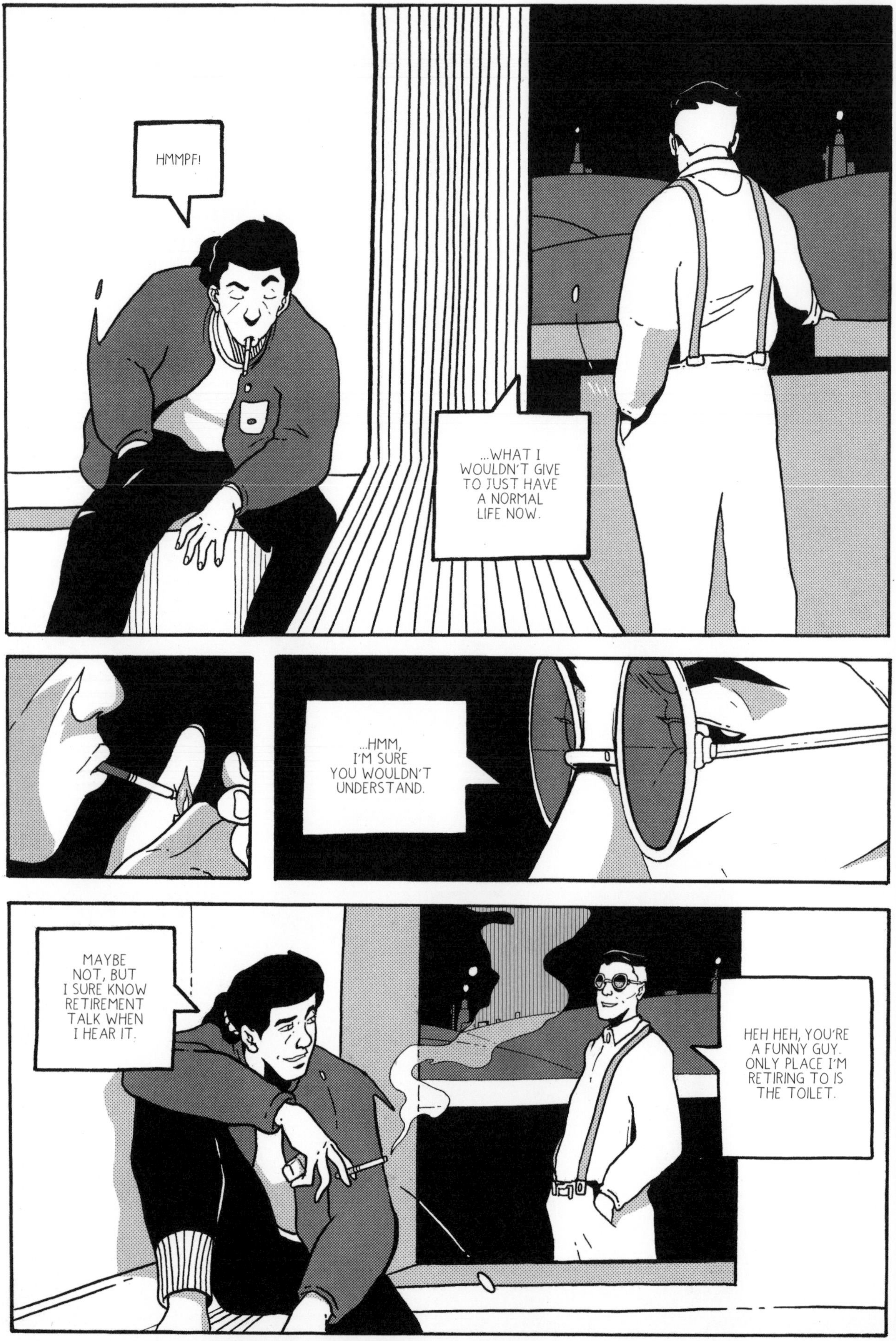
HMMPF!
...WHAT I WOULDN'T GIVE TO JUST HAVE A NORMAL LIFE NOW.
...HMM, I'M SURE YOU WOULDN'T UNDERSTAND.
MAYBE NOT, BUT I SURE KNOW RETIREMENT TALK WHEN I HEAR IT.
HEH HEH, YOU'RE A FUNNY GUY. ONLY PLACE I'M RETIRING TO IS THE TOILET.

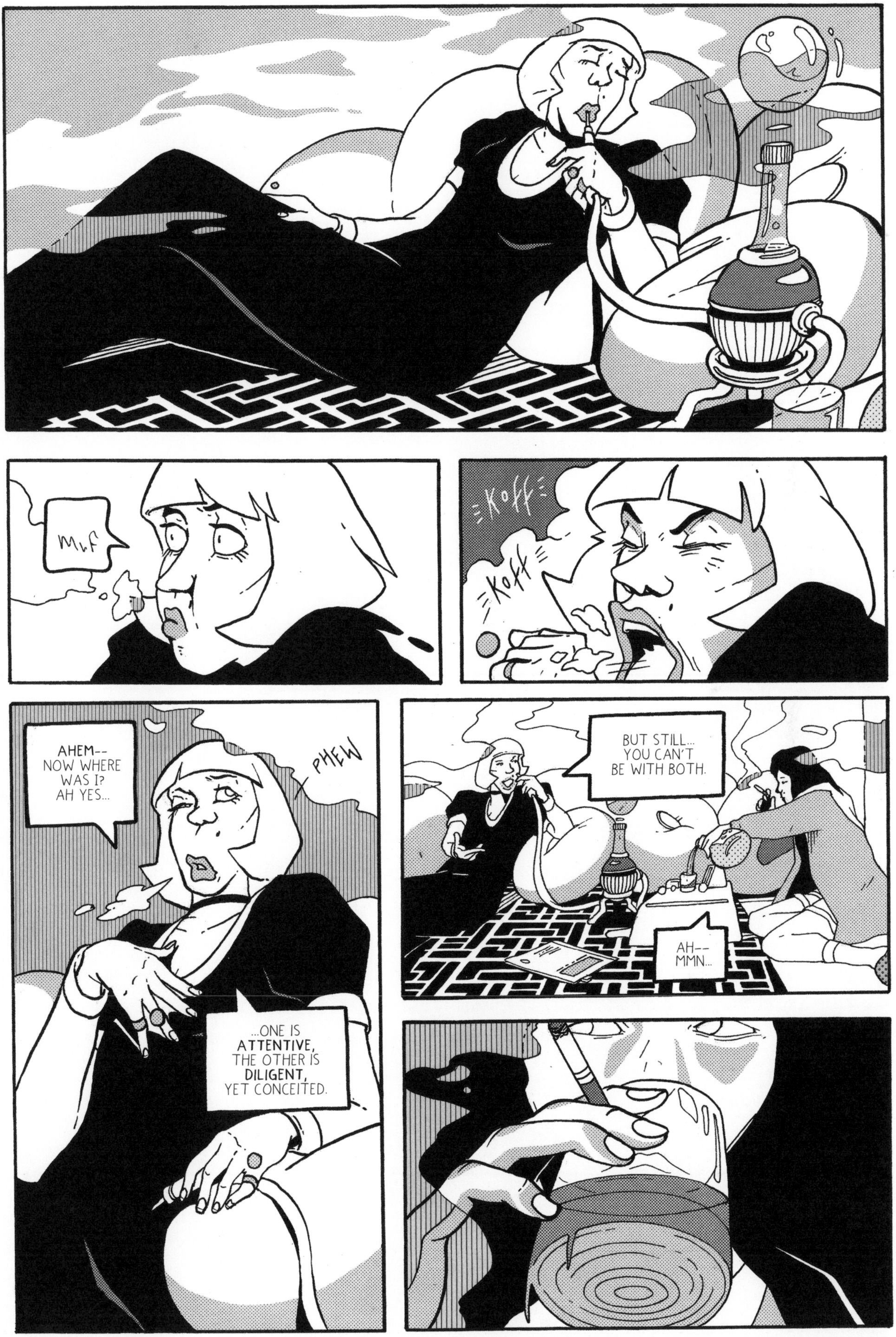

Mrf
KOFF
KOFF
AHEM-- NOW WHERE WAS I? AH YES...
PHEW
...ONE IS **ATTENTIVE,** THE OTHER IS **DILIGENT,** YET CONCEITED.
BUT STILL... YOU CAN'T BE WITH BOTH.
AH-- MMN...

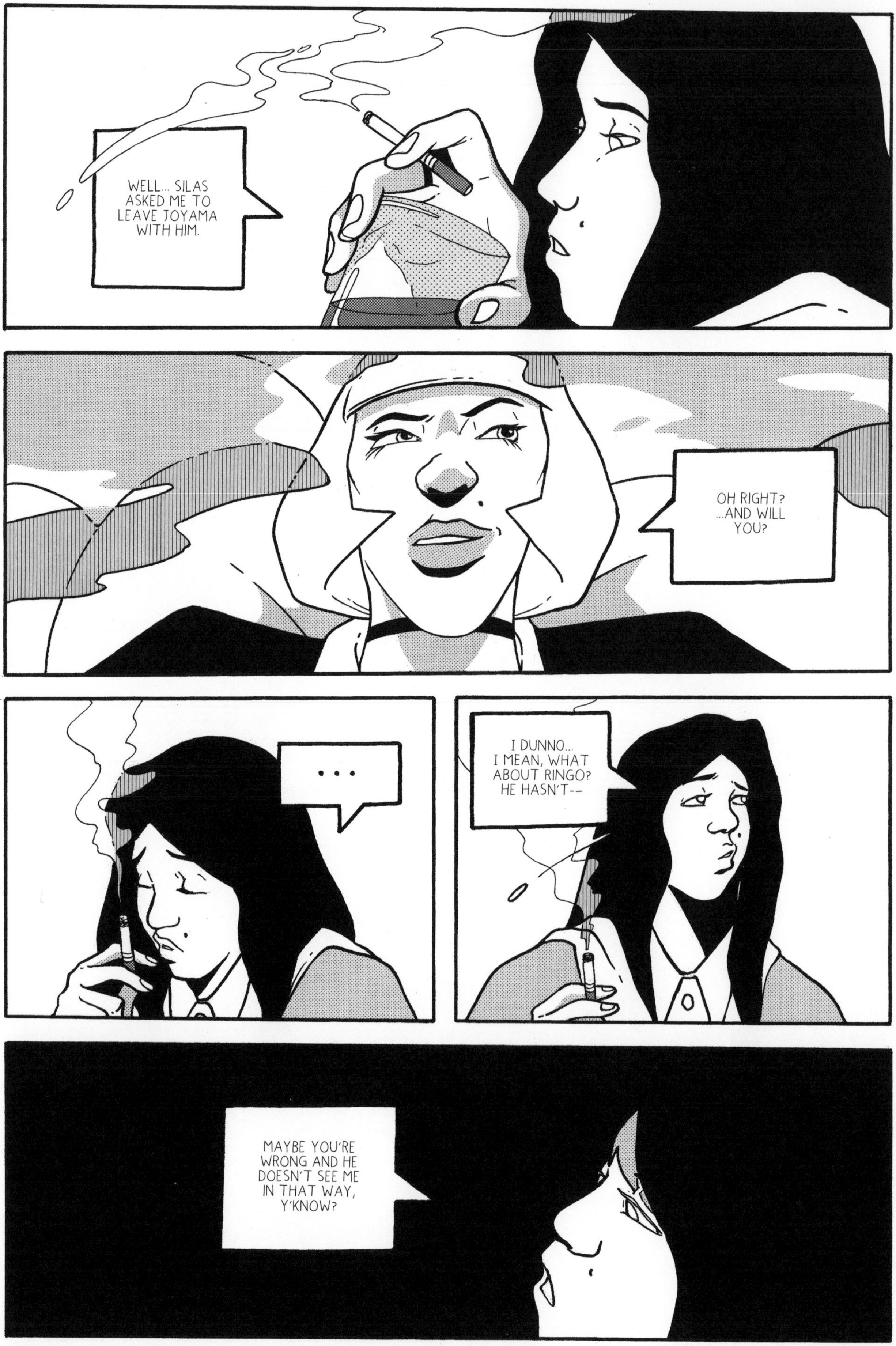

WELL... SILAS ASKED ME TO LEAVE TOYAMA WITH HIM.
OH RIGHT? ...AND WILL YOU?
. . .
I DUNNO... I MEAN, WHAT ABOUT RINGO? HE HASN'T--
MAYBE YOU'RE WRONG AND HE DOESN'T SEE ME IN THAT WAY, Y'KNOW?

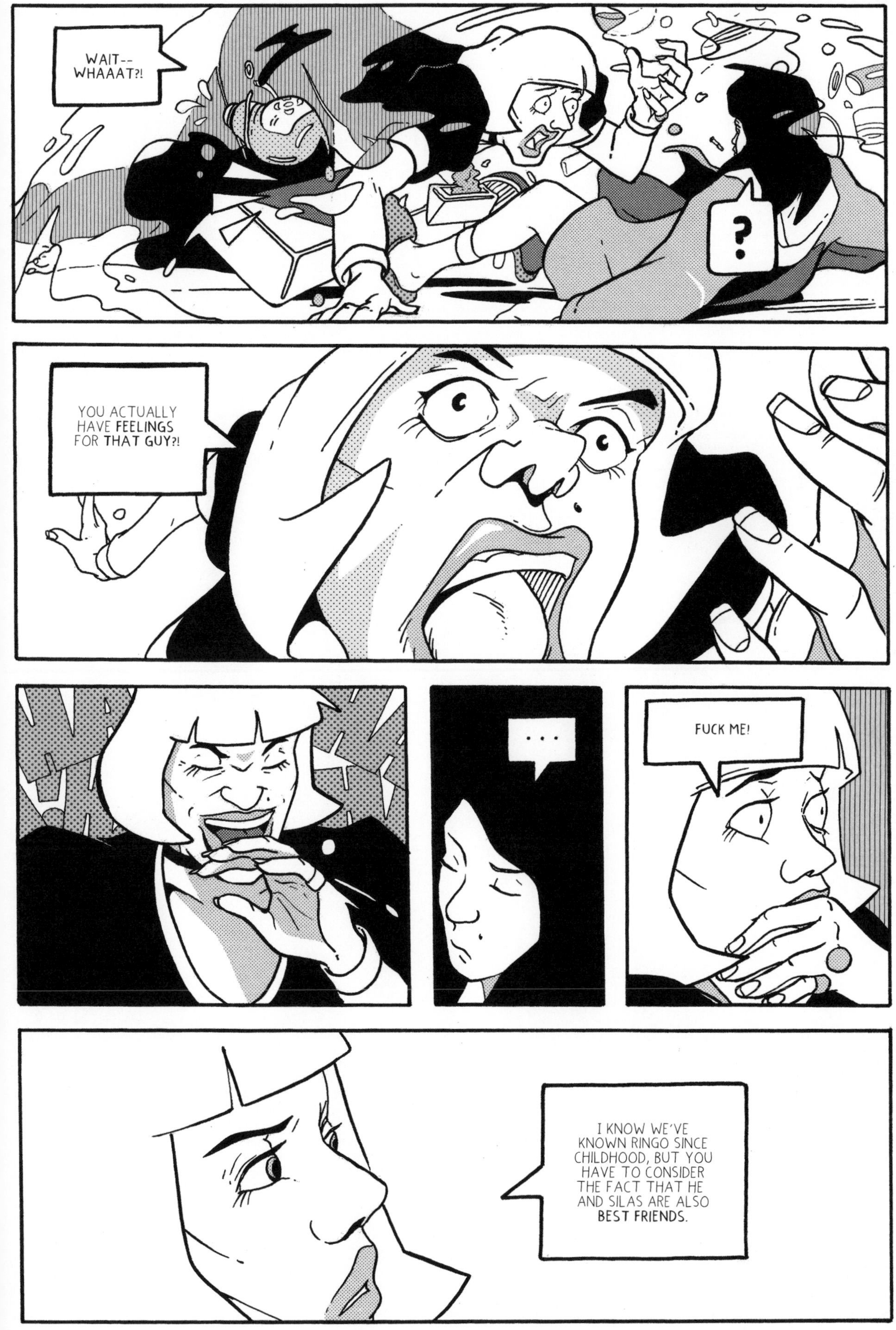
WAIT--
WHAAAT?!
?
YOU ACTUALLY HAVE **FEELINGS** FOR **THAT GUY**?!
...
FUCK ME!
I KNOW WE'VE KNOWN RINGO SINCE CHILDHOOD, BUT YOU HAVE TO CONSIDER THE FACT THAT HE AND SILAS ARE ALSO **BEST FRIENDS**.

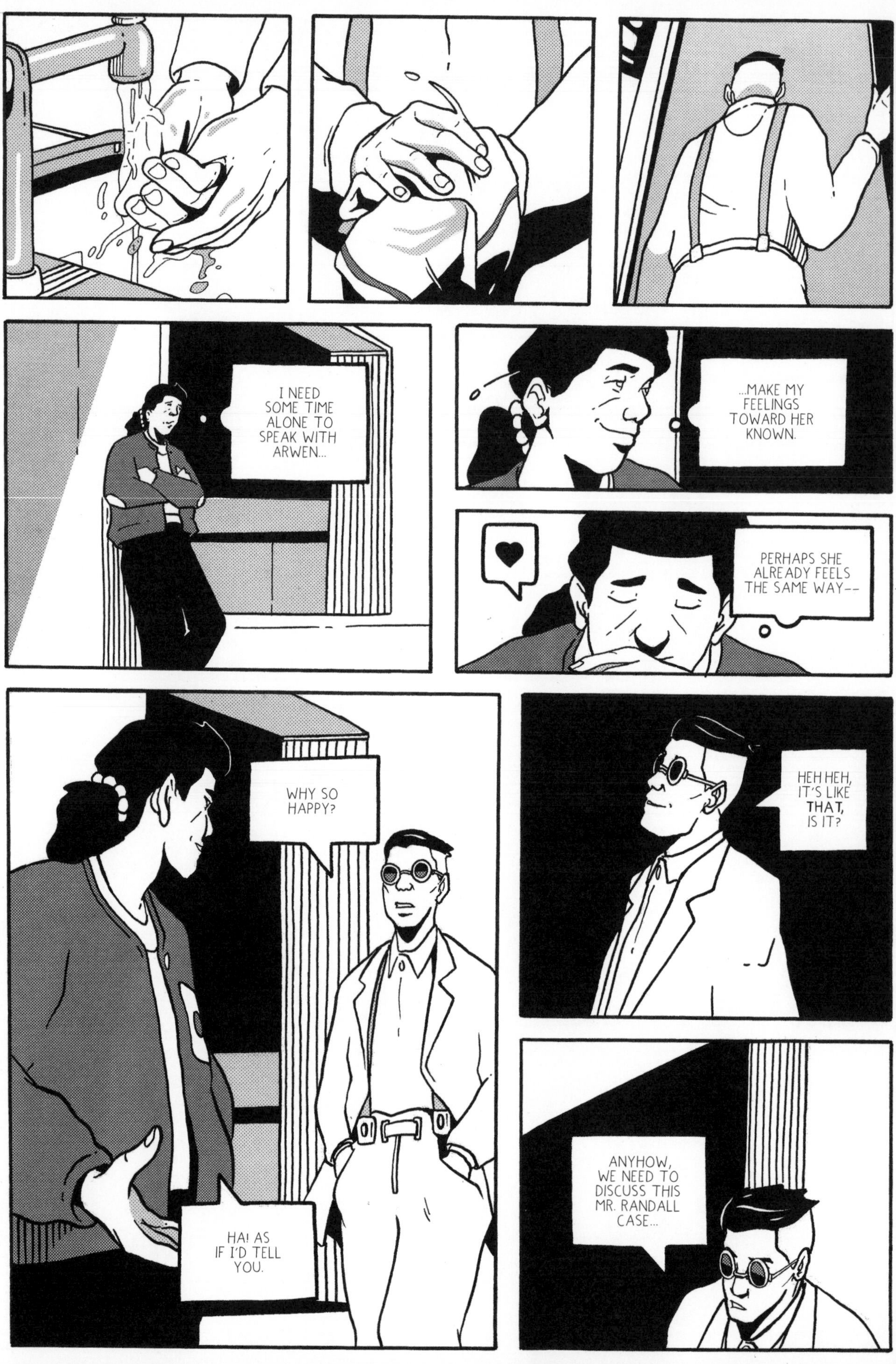
I NEED SOME TIME ALONE TO SPEAK WITH ARWEN...
...MAKE MY FEELINGS TOWARD HER KNOWN.
PERHAPS SHE ALREADY FEELS THE SAME WAY--
WHY SO HAPPY?
HA! AS IF I'D TELL YOU.
HEH HEH, IT'S LIKE THAT, IS IT?
ANYHOW, WE NEED TO DISCUSS THIS MR. RANDALL CASE...

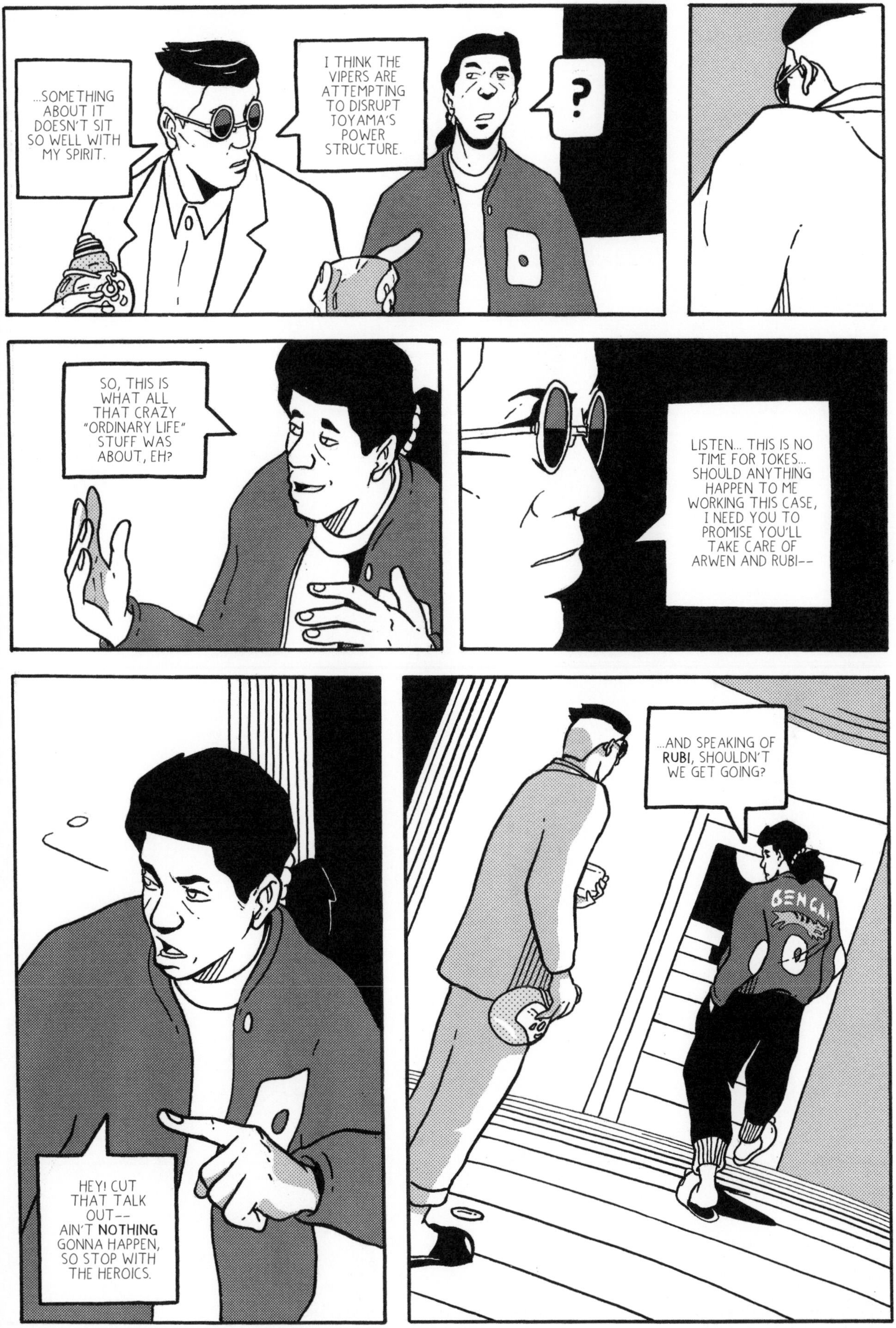
...SOMETHING ABOUT IT DOESN'T SIT SO WELL WITH MY SPIRIT.
I THINK THE VIPERS ARE ATTEMPTING TO DISRUPT JOYAMA'S POWER STRUCTURE.
?
SO, THIS IS WHAT ALL THAT CRAZY "ORDINARY LIFE" STUFF WAS ABOUT, EH?
LISTEN... THIS IS NO TIME FOR JOKES... SHOULD ANYTHING HAPPEN TO ME WORKING THIS CASE, I NEED YOU TO PROMISE YOU'LL TAKE CARE OF ARWEN AND RUBI--
HEY! CUT THAT TALK OUT-- AIN'T **NOTHING** GONNA HAPPEN, SO STOP WITH THE HEROICS.
...AND SPEAKING OF **RUBI**, SHOULDN'T WE GET GOING?
BENGAL

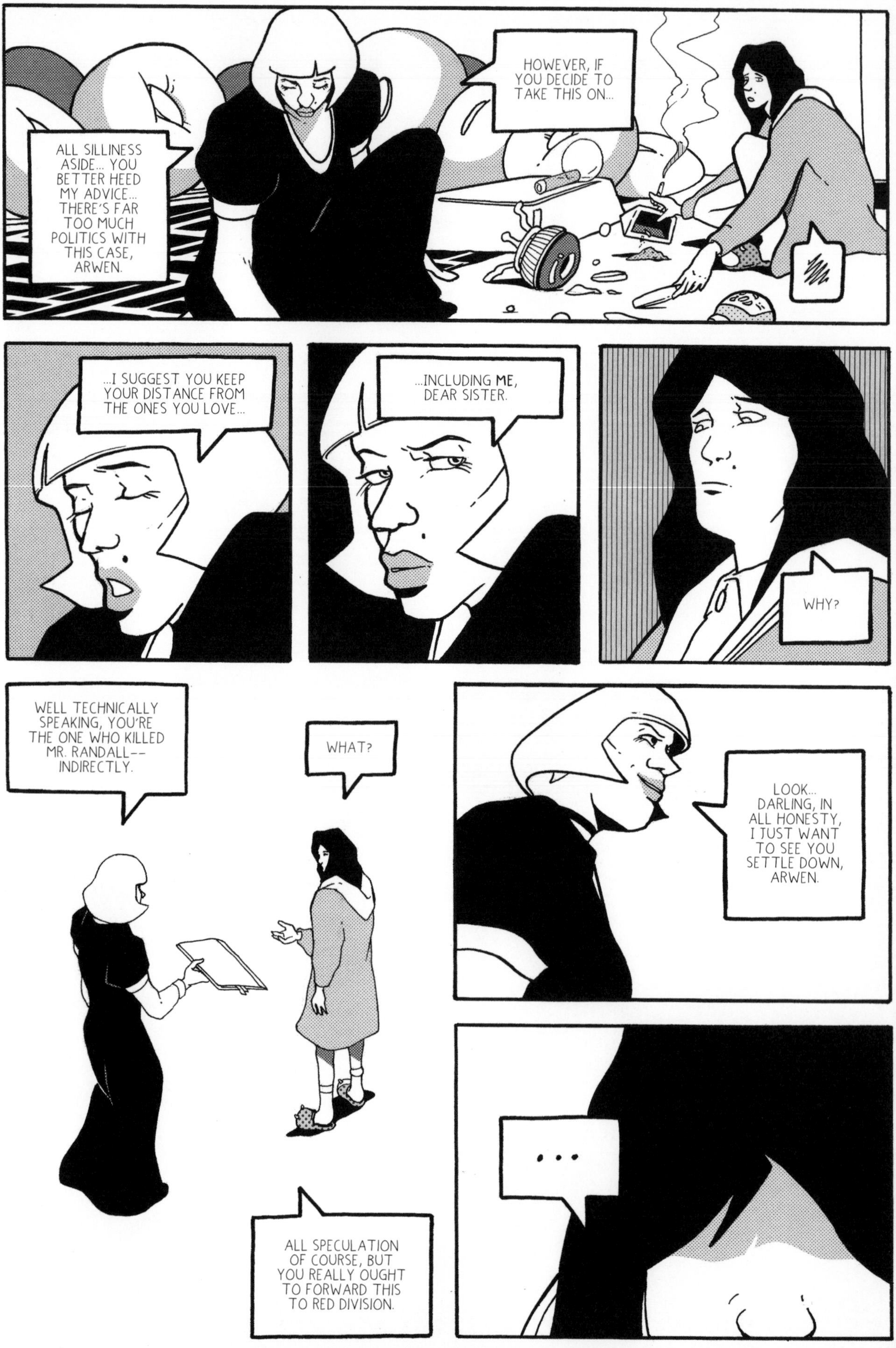
ALL SILLINESS ASIDE... YOU BETTER HEED MY ADVICE... THERE'S FAR TOO MUCH POLITICS WITH THIS CASE, ARWEN.
HOWEVER, IF YOU DECIDE TO TAKE THIS ON...
...I SUGGEST YOU KEEP YOUR DISTANCE FROM THE ONES YOU LOVE...
...INCLUDING ME, DEAR SISTER.
WHY?
WELL TECHNICALLY SPEAKING, YOU'RE THE ONE WHO KILLED MR. RANDALL-- INDIRECTLY.
WHAT?
ALL SPECULATION OF COURSE, BUT YOU REALLY OUGHT TO FORWARD THIS TO RED DIVISION.
LOOK... DARLING, IN ALL HONESTY, I JUST WANT TO SEE YOU SETTLE DOWN, ARWEN.
...

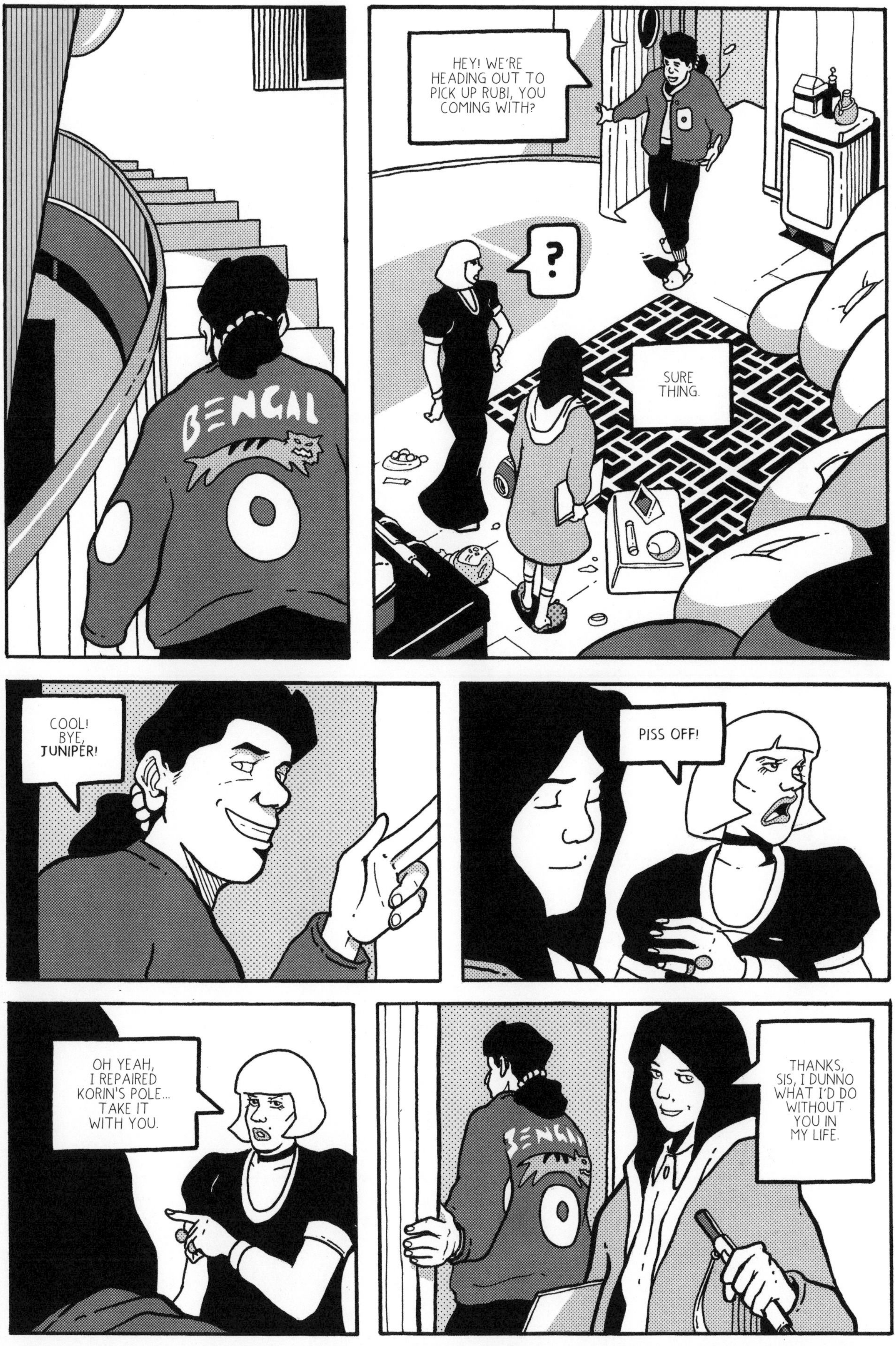
BENGAL
HEY! WE'RE HEADING OUT TO PICK UP RUBI, YOU COMING WITH?
?
SURE THING.
COOL! BYE, JUNIPER!
PISS OFF!
OH YEAH, I REPAIRED KORIN'S POLE... TAKE IT WITH YOU.
BENGAL
THANKS, SIS, I DUNNO WHAT I'D DO WITHOUT YOU IN MY LIFE.

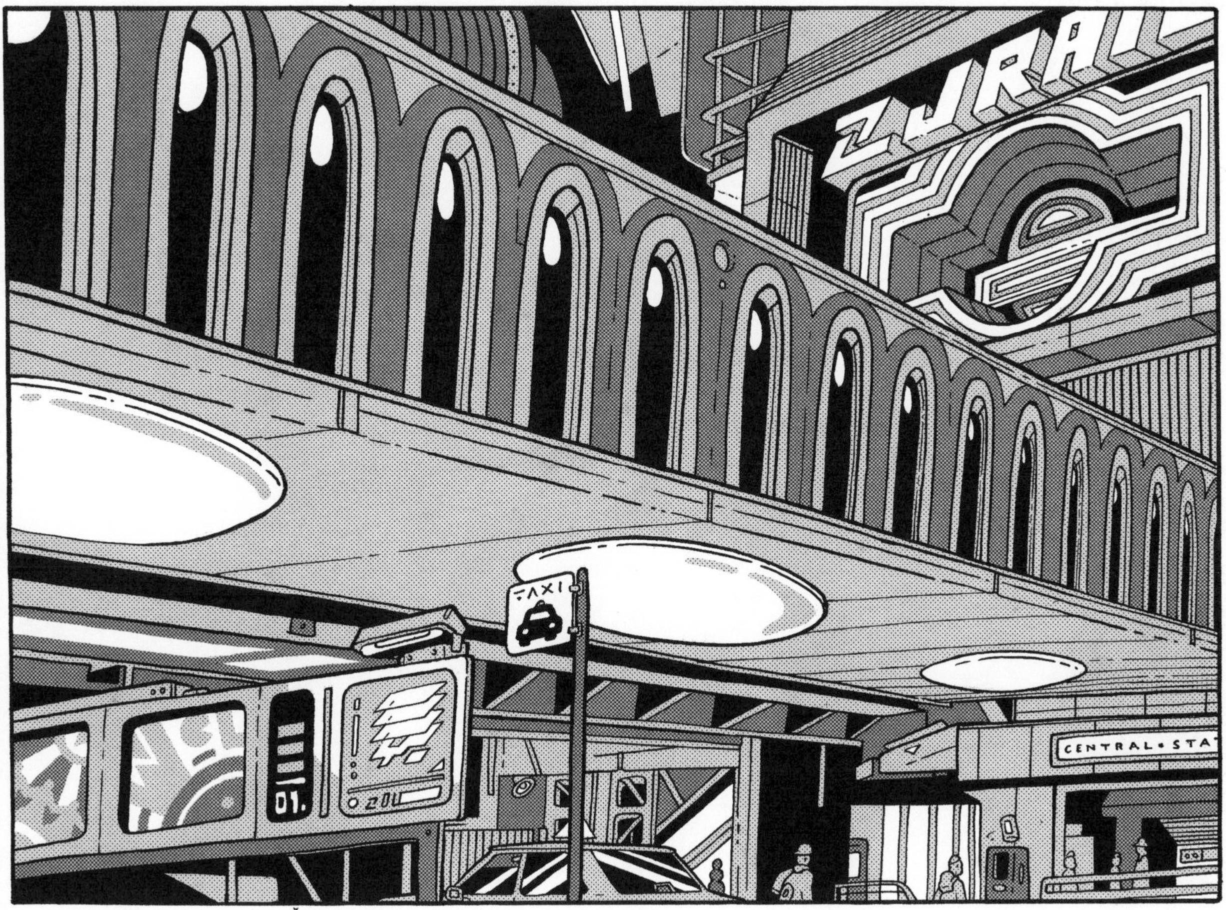
ZURAIL
TAXI
01.
CENTRAL • STAT

4

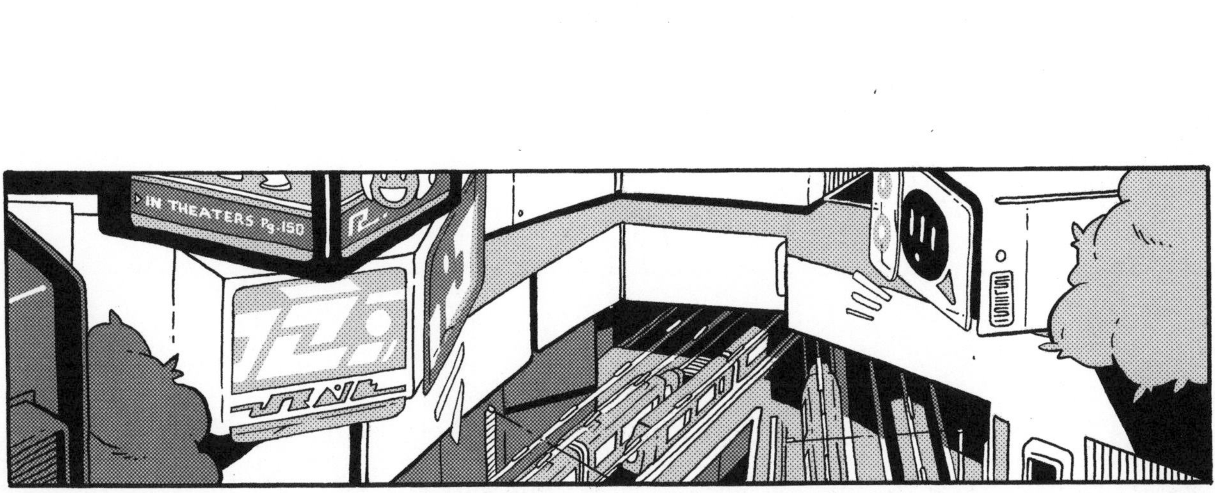
IN THEATERS Pg-150

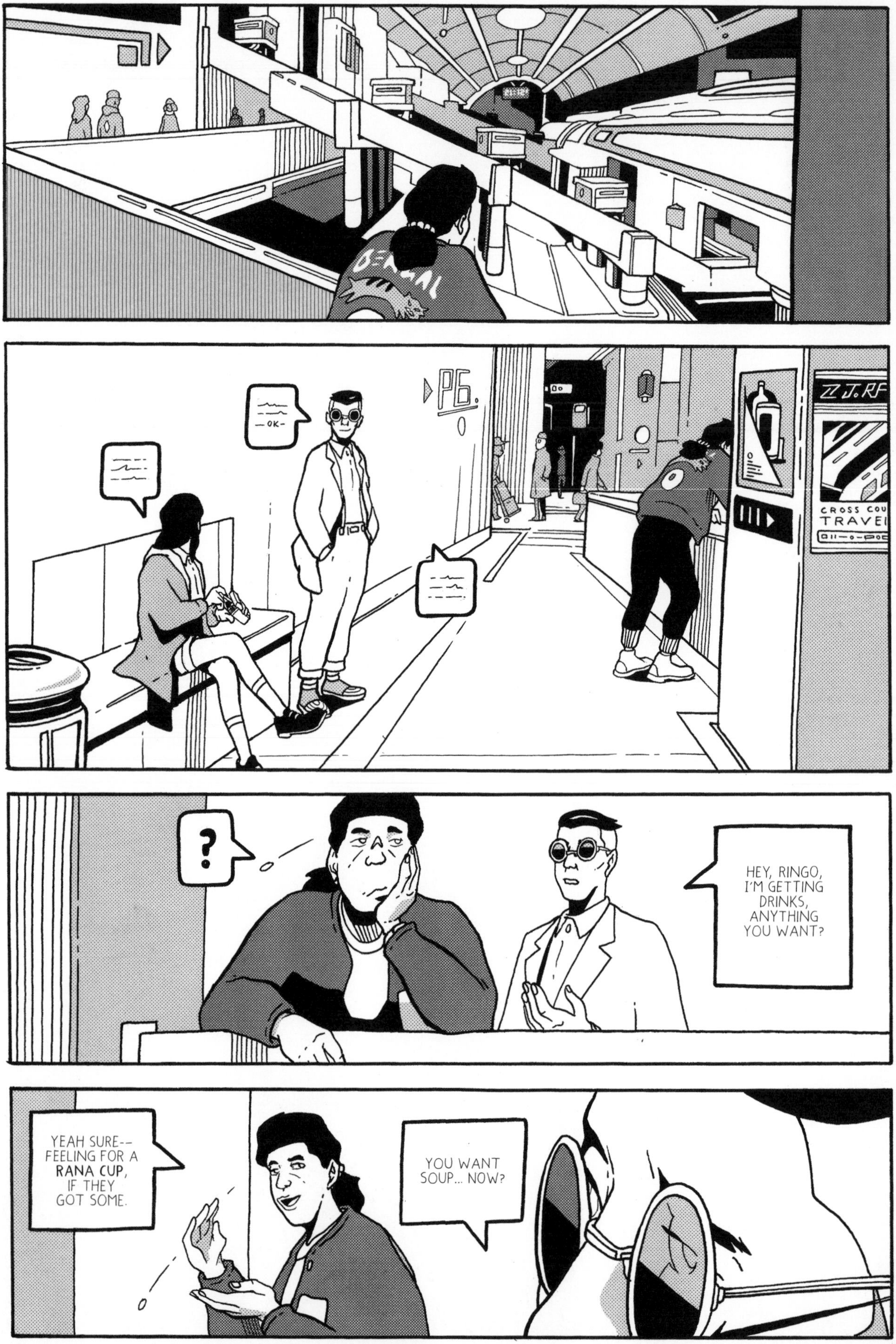
P6.
OK
CROSS COU
TRAVEL
?
HEY, RINGO, I'M GETTING DRINKS, ANYTHING YOU WANT?
YEAH SURE-- FEELING FOR A **RANA CUP**, IF THEY GOT SOME.
YOU WANT SOUP... NOW?

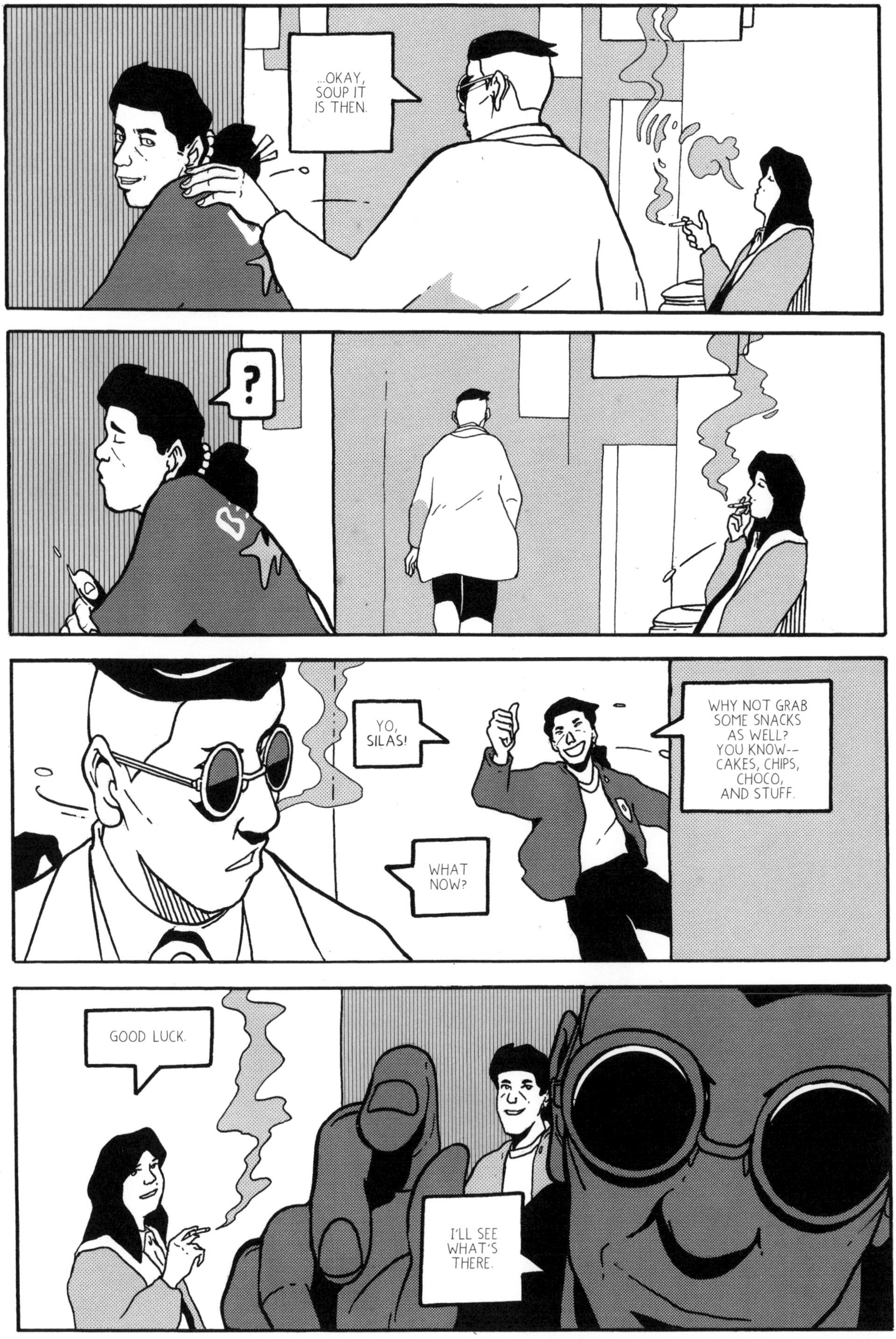
...OKAY, SOUP IT IS THEN.
?
YO, SILAS!
WHAT NOW?
WHY NOT GRAB SOME SNACKS AS WELL? YOU KNOW-- CAKES, CHIPS, CHOCO, AND STUFF.
GOOD LUCK.
I'LL SEE WHAT'S THERE.

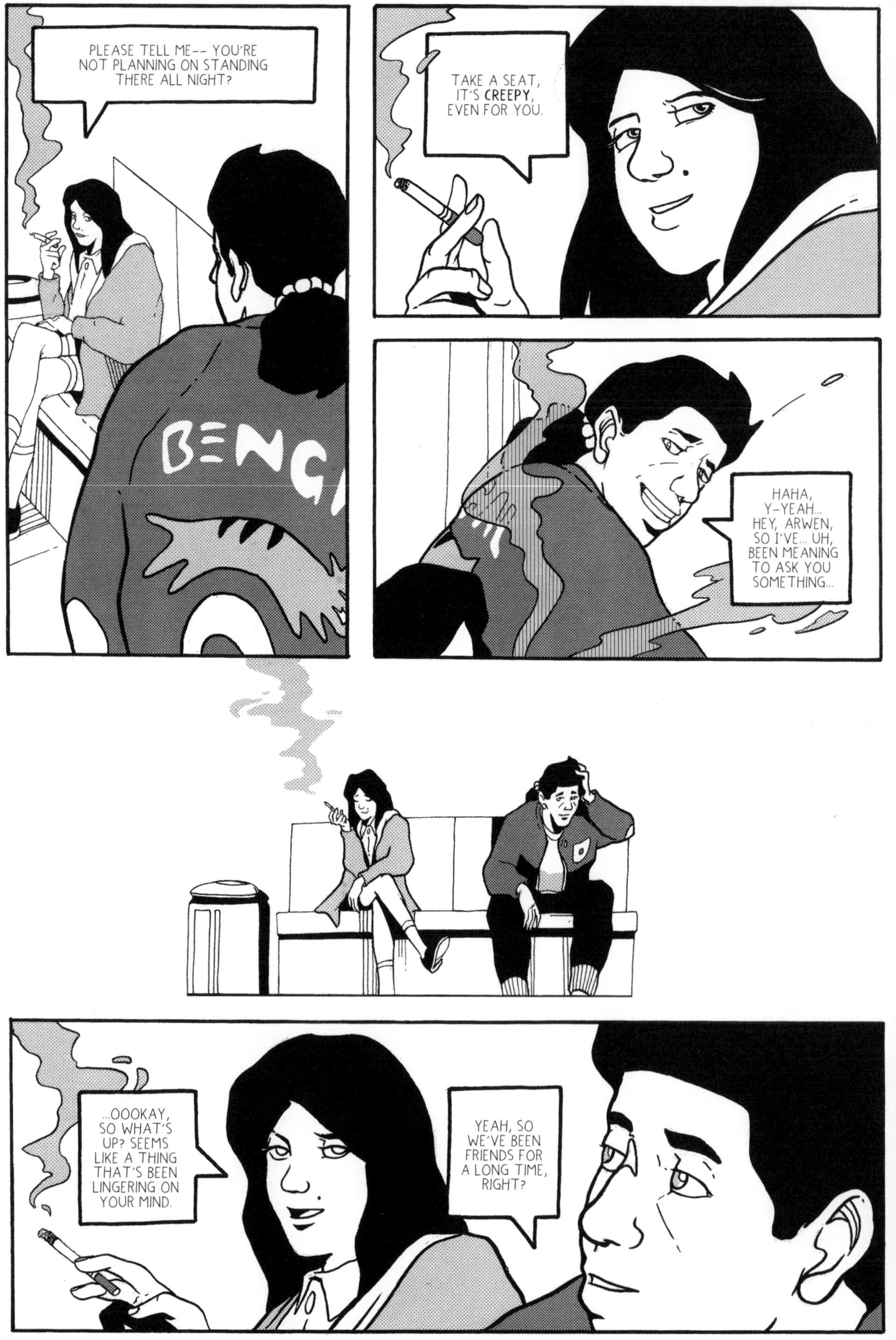
PLEASE TELL ME-- YOU'RE NOT PLANNING ON STANDING THERE ALL NIGHT?
TAKE A SEAT, IT'S **CREEPY**, EVEN FOR YOU.
HAHA, Y-YEAH... HEY, ARWEN, SO I'VE... UH, BEEN MEANING TO ASK YOU SOMETHING...
...OOOKAY, SO WHAT'S UP? SEEMS LIKE A THING THAT'S BEEN LINGERING ON YOUR MIND.
YEAH, SO WE'VE BEEN FRIENDS FOR A LONG TIME, RIGHT?

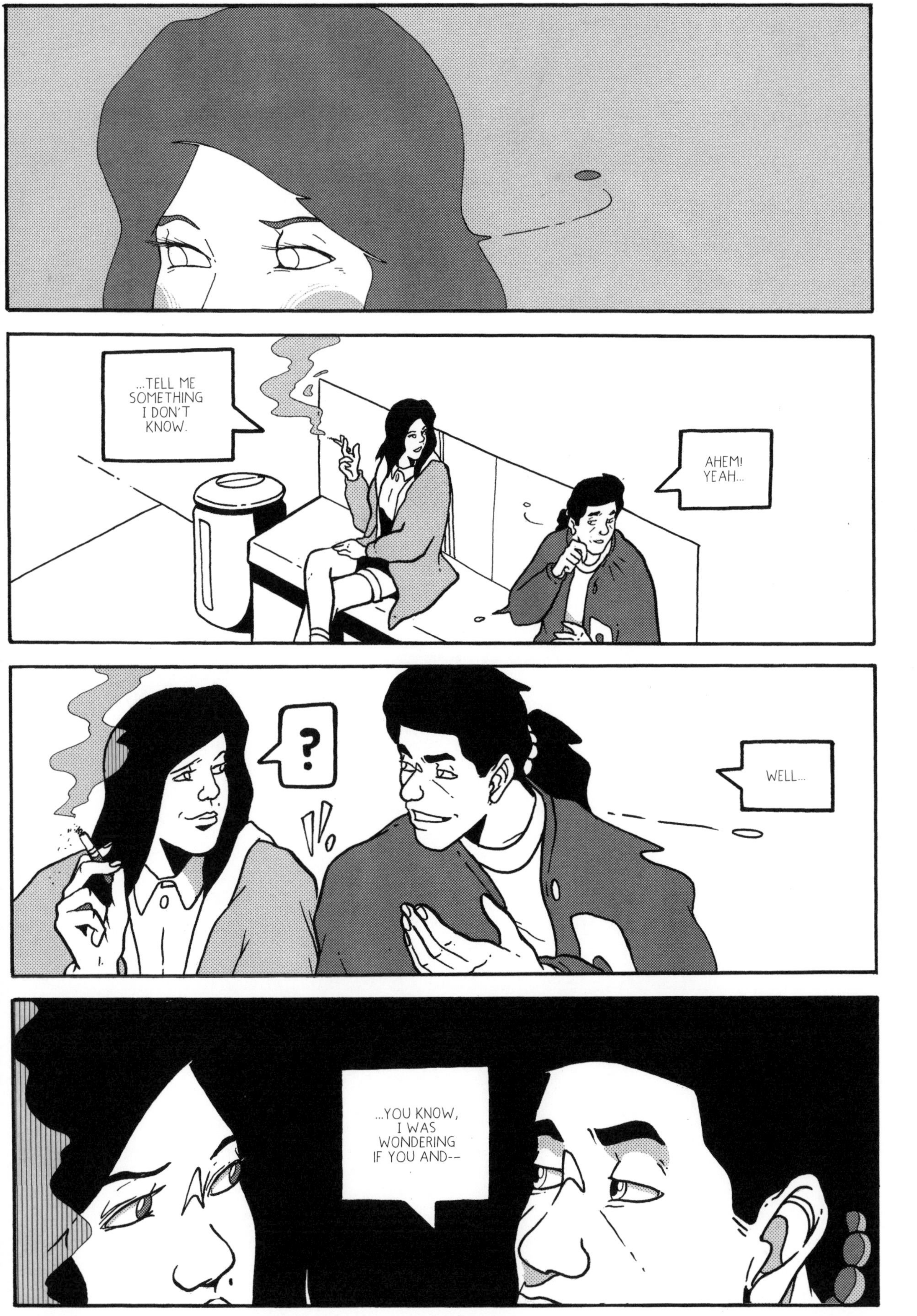
...TELL ME SOMETHING I DON'T KNOW.
AHEM! YEAH...
?
WELL...
...YOU KNOW, I WAS WONDERING IF YOU AND--

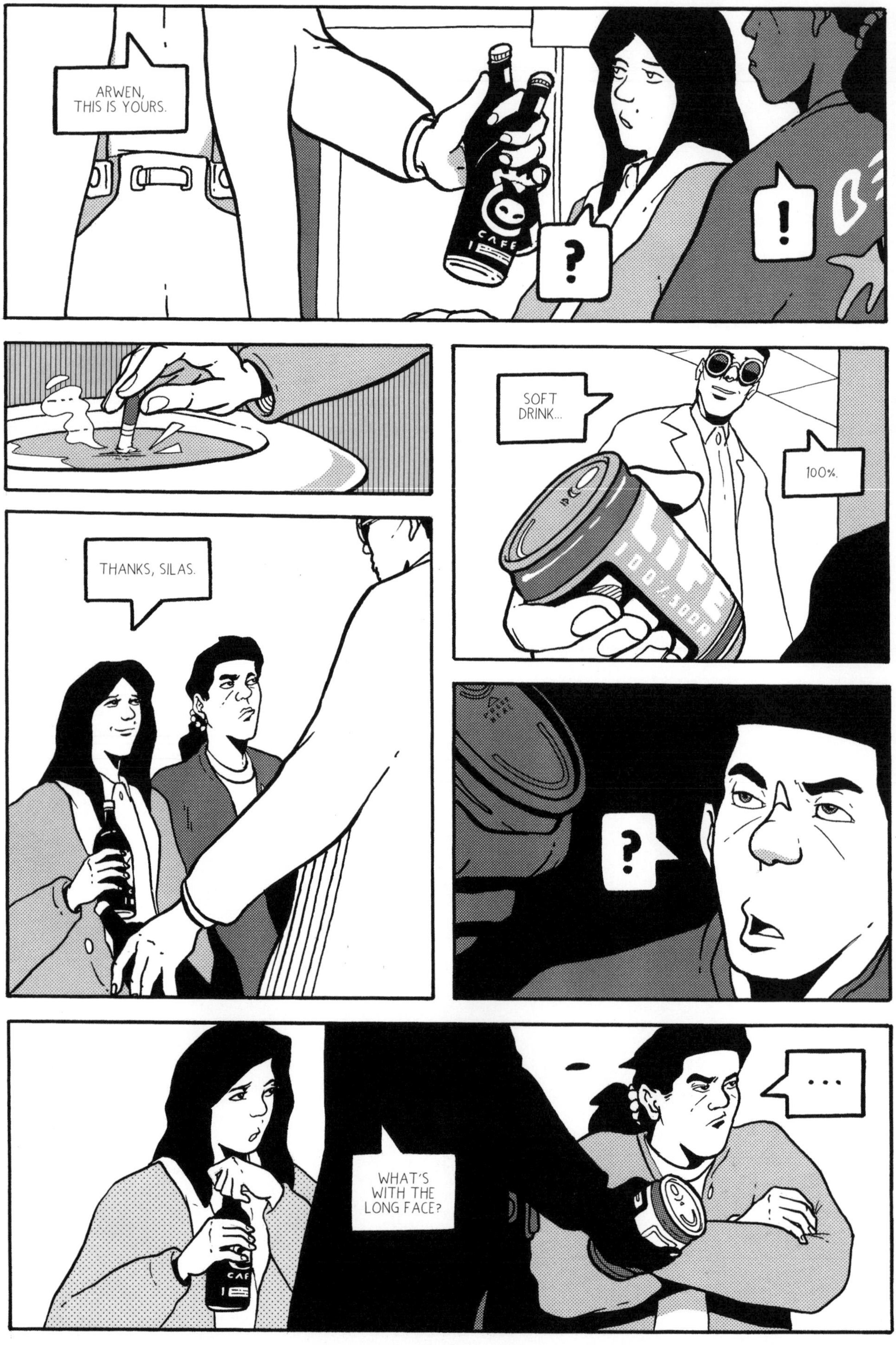
ARWEN,
THIS IS YOURS.
?
!
SOFT DRINK...
100%.
THANKS, SILAS.
?
WHAT'S WITH THE LONG FACE?
...

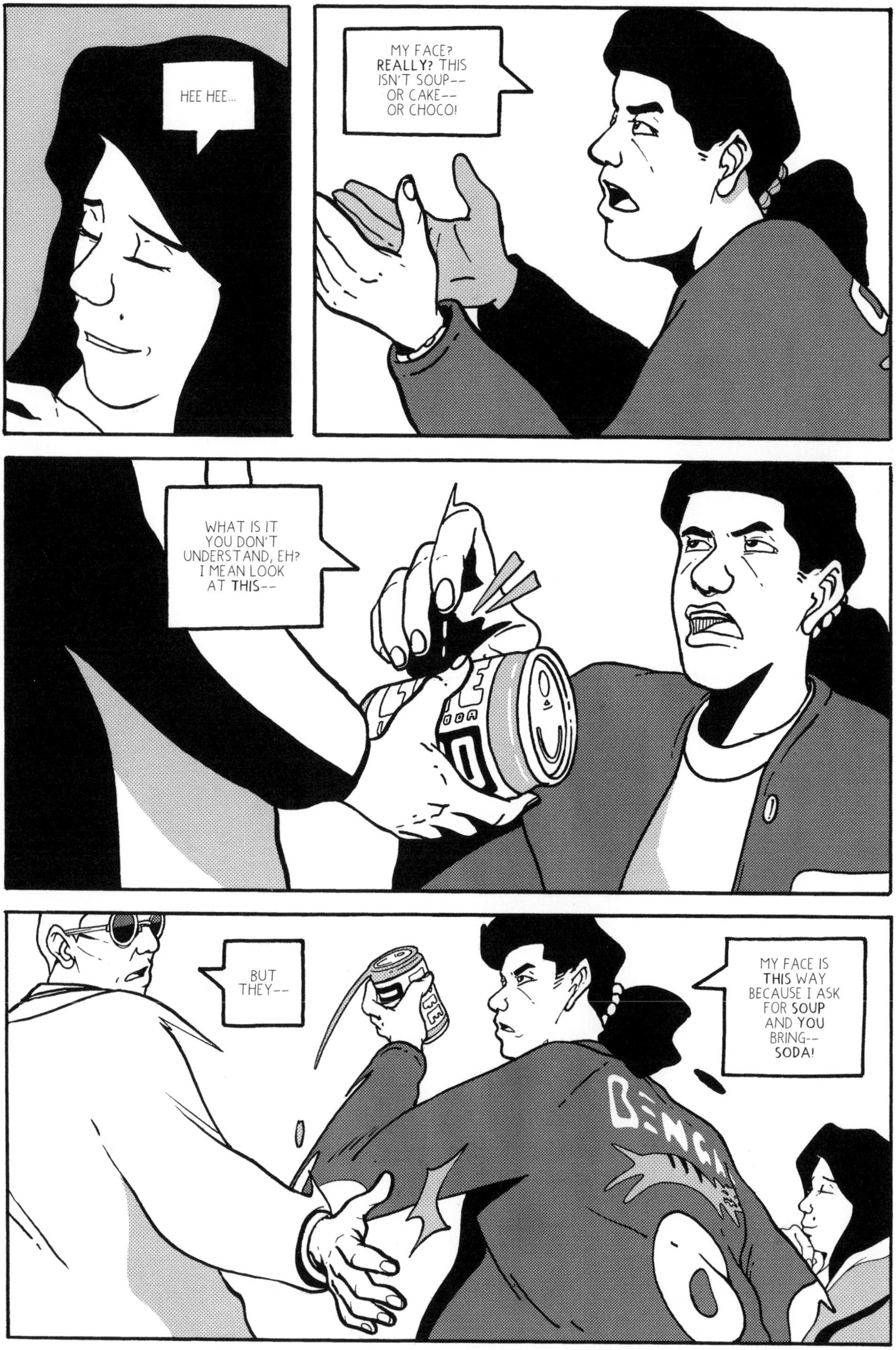
HEE HEE...
MY FACE? REALLY? THIS ISN'T SOUP-- OR CAKE-- OR CHOCO!
WHAT IS IT YOU DON'T UNDERSTAND, EH? I MEAN LOOK AT THIS--
BUT THEY--
MY FACE IS THIS WAY BECAUSE I ASK FOR SOUP AND YOU BRING-- SODA!

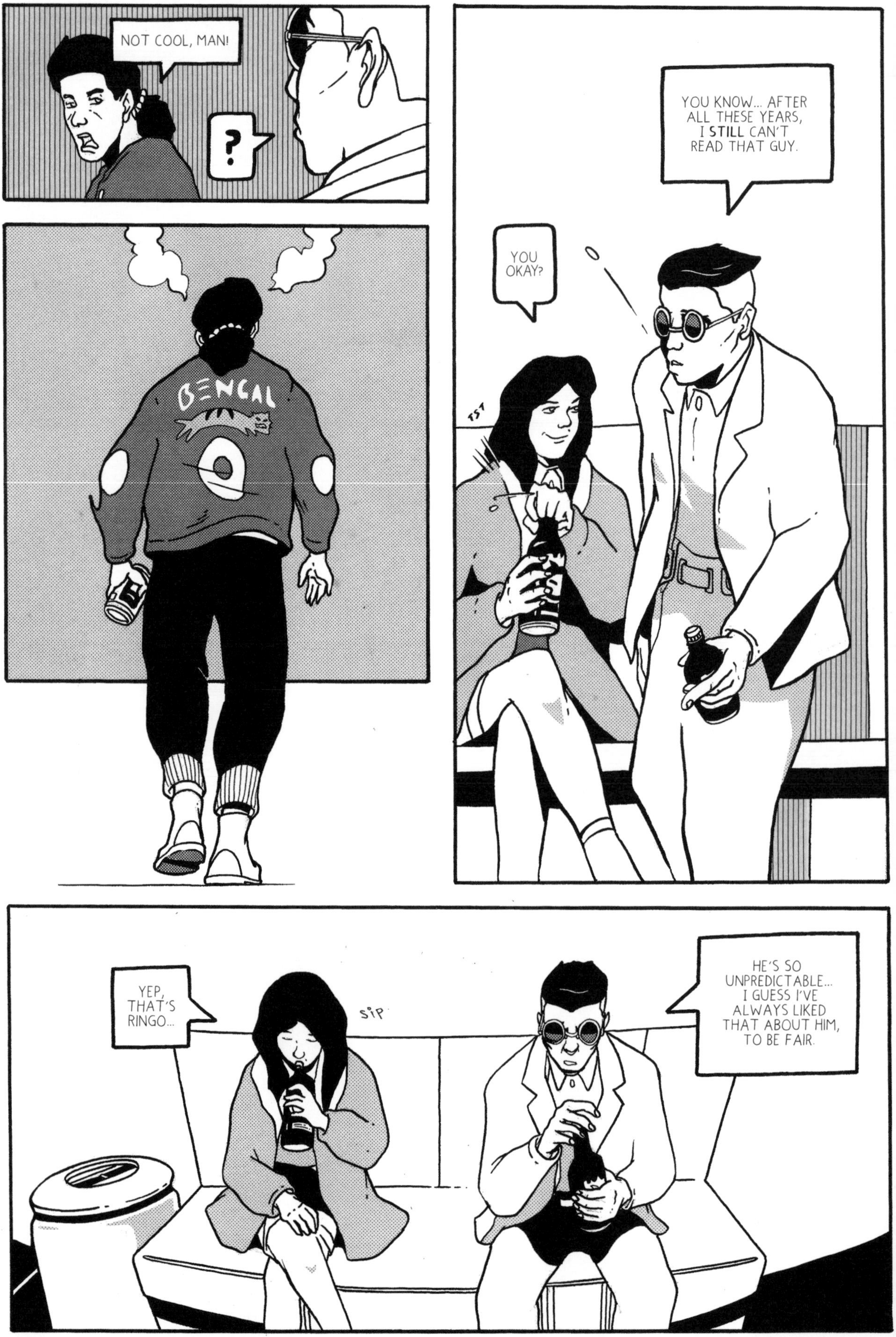

NOT COOL, MAN!
?
YOU KNOW... AFTER ALL THESE YEARS, I STILL CAN'T READ THAT GUY.
YOU OKAY?
TST
YEP, THAT'S RINGO...
SIP
HE'S SO UNPREDICTABLE... I GUESS I'VE ALWAYS LIKED THAT ABOUT HIM, TO BE FAIR.

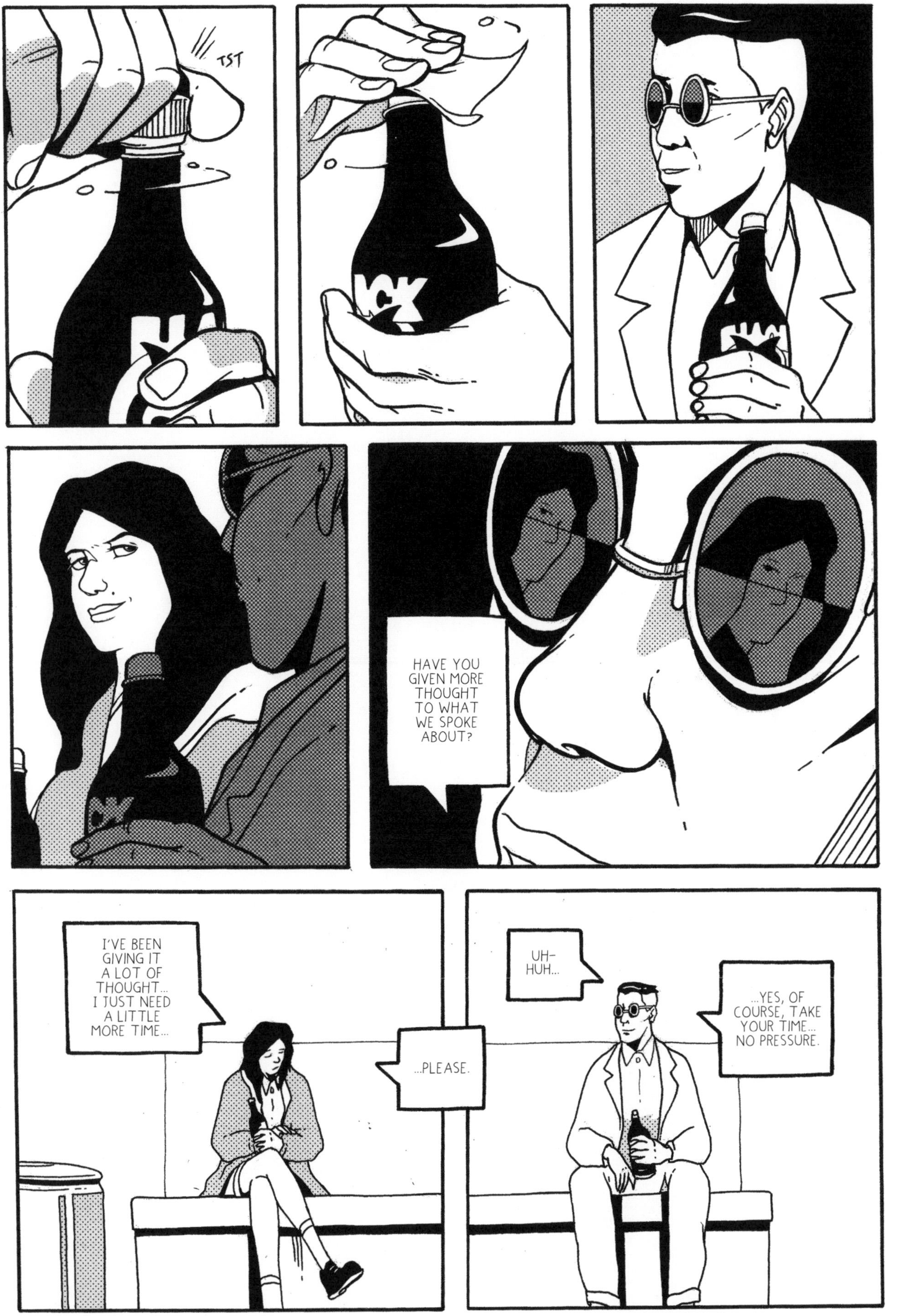
TST
HAVE YOU GIVEN MORE THOUGHT TO WHAT WE SPOKE ABOUT?
I'VE BEEN GIVING IT A LOT OF THOUGHT... I JUST NEED A LITTLE MORE TIME...
...PLEASE.
UH-HUH...
...YES, OF COURSE, TAKE YOUR TIME... NO PRESSURE.

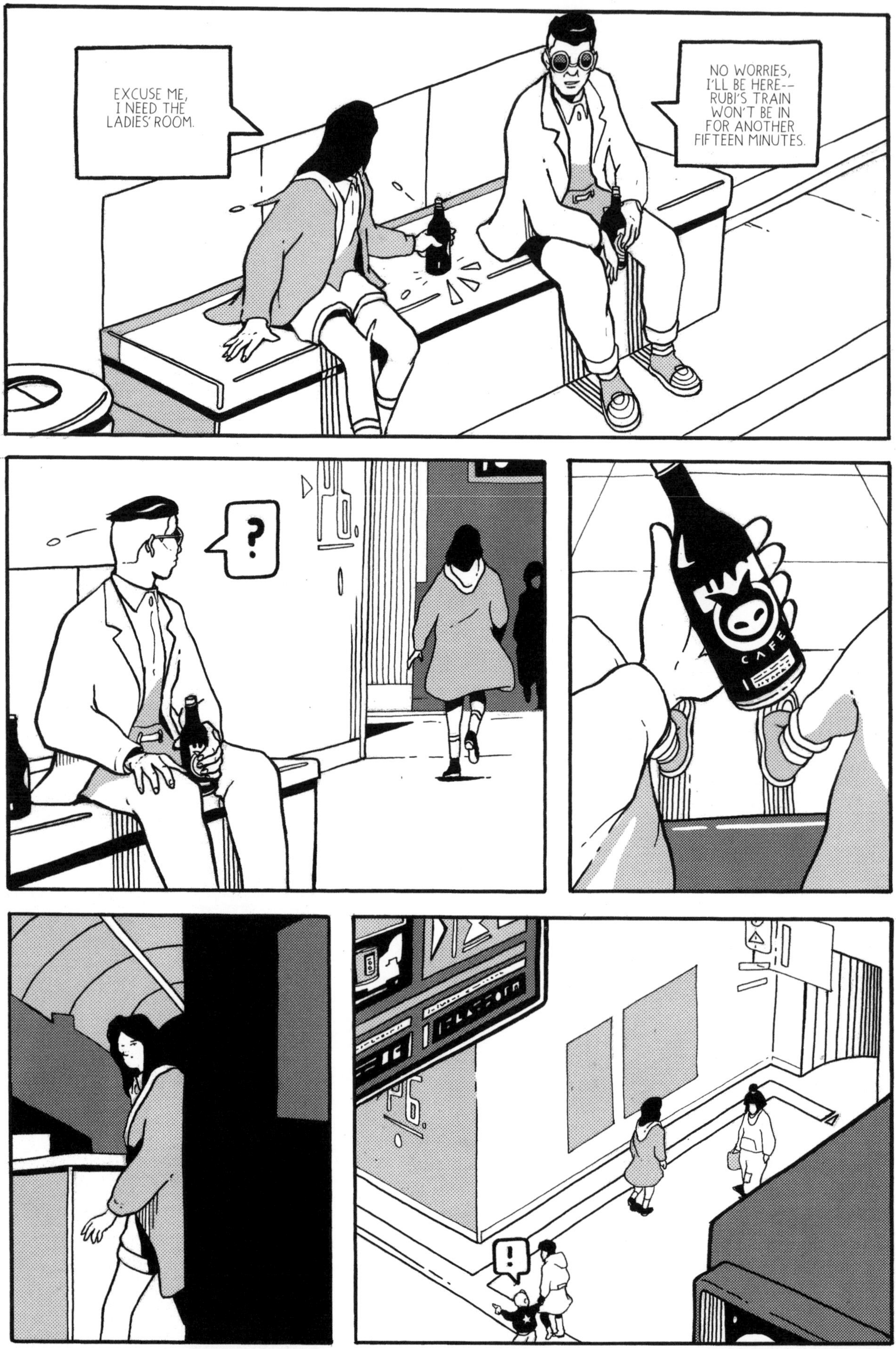
EXCUSE ME, I NEED THE LADIES' ROOM.
NO WORRIES, I'LL BE HERE-- RUBI'S TRAIN WON'T BE IN FOR ANOTHER FIFTEEN MINUTES.
?
CAFE
!

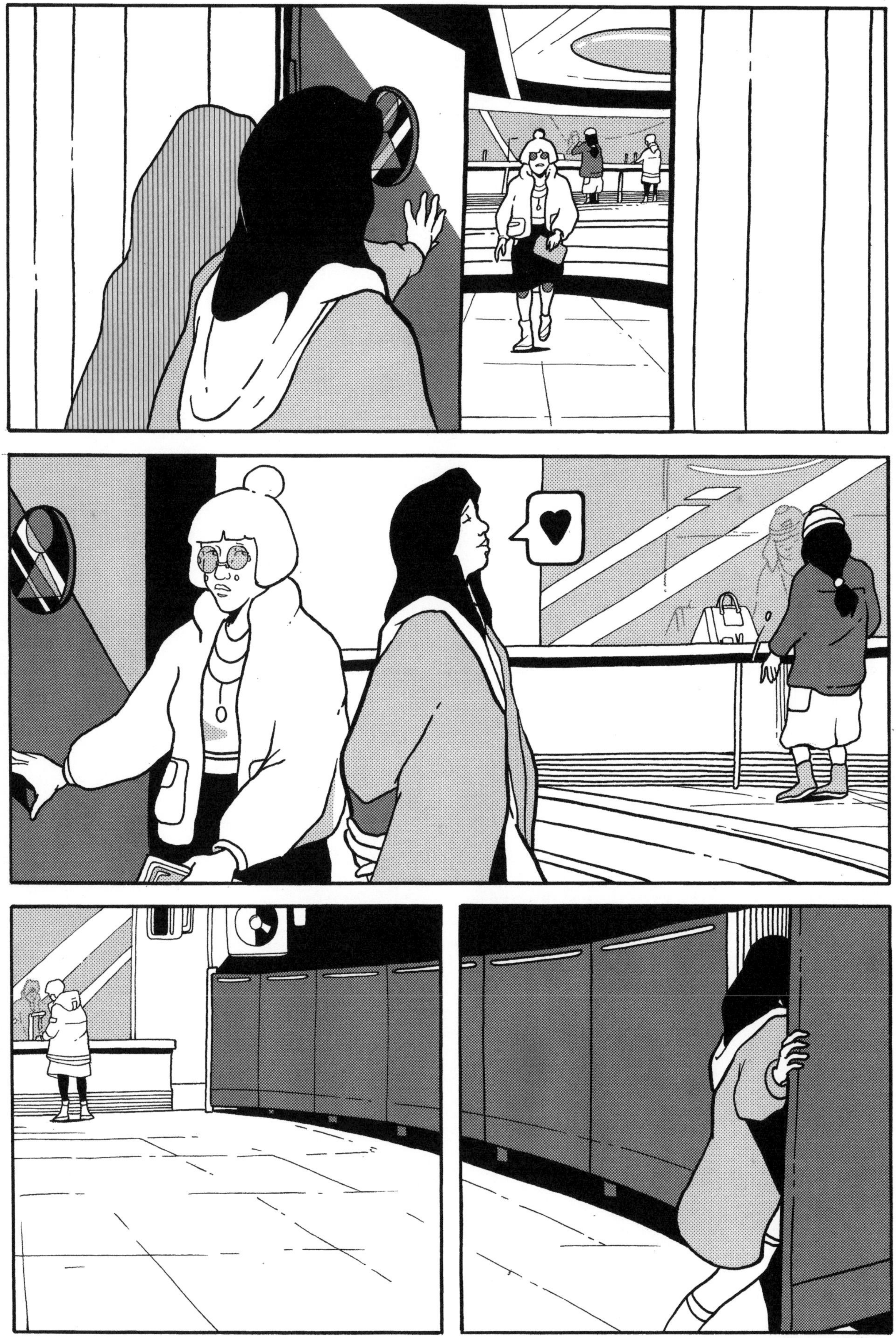

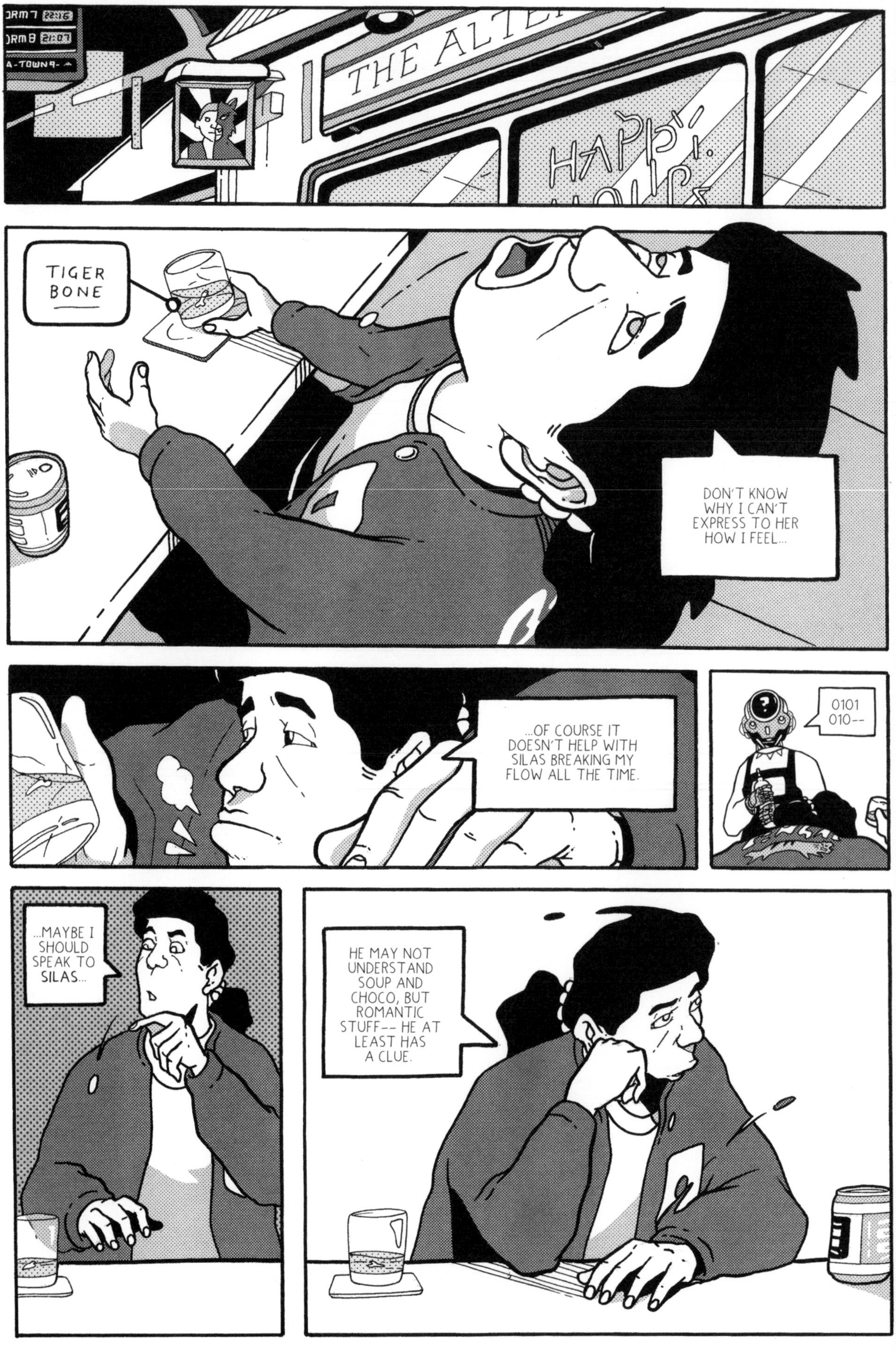
THE ALTE
TIGER BONE
DON'T KNOW WHY I CAN'T EXPRESS TO HER HOW I FEEL...
...OF COURSE IT DOESN'T HELP WITH SILAS BREAKING MY FLOW ALL THE TIME.
0101 010--
...MAYBE I SHOULD SPEAK TO SILAS...
HE MAY NOT UNDERSTAND SOUP AND CHOCO, BUT ROMANTIC STUFF-- HE AT LEAST HAS A CLUE.

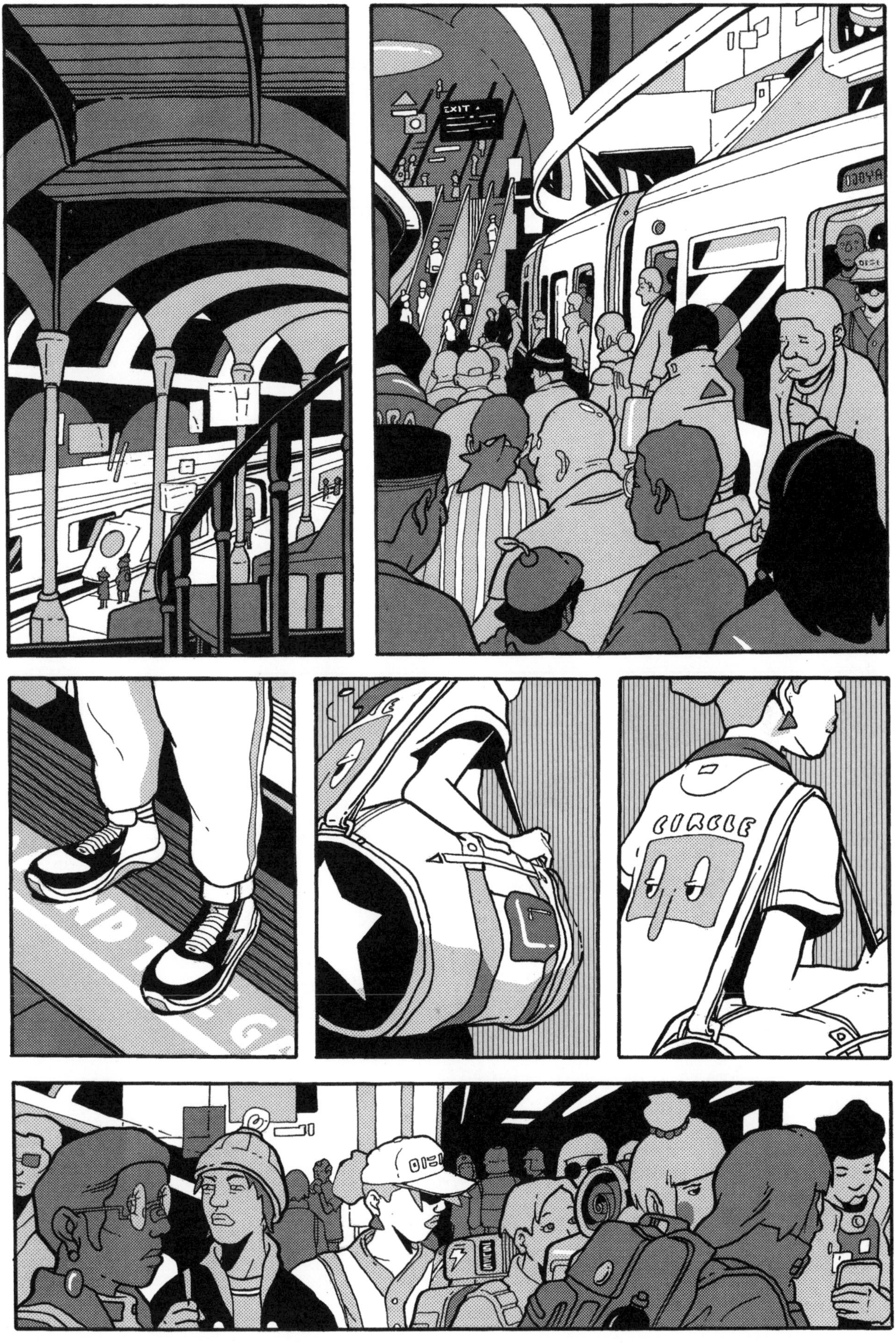
EXIT
CIRCLE

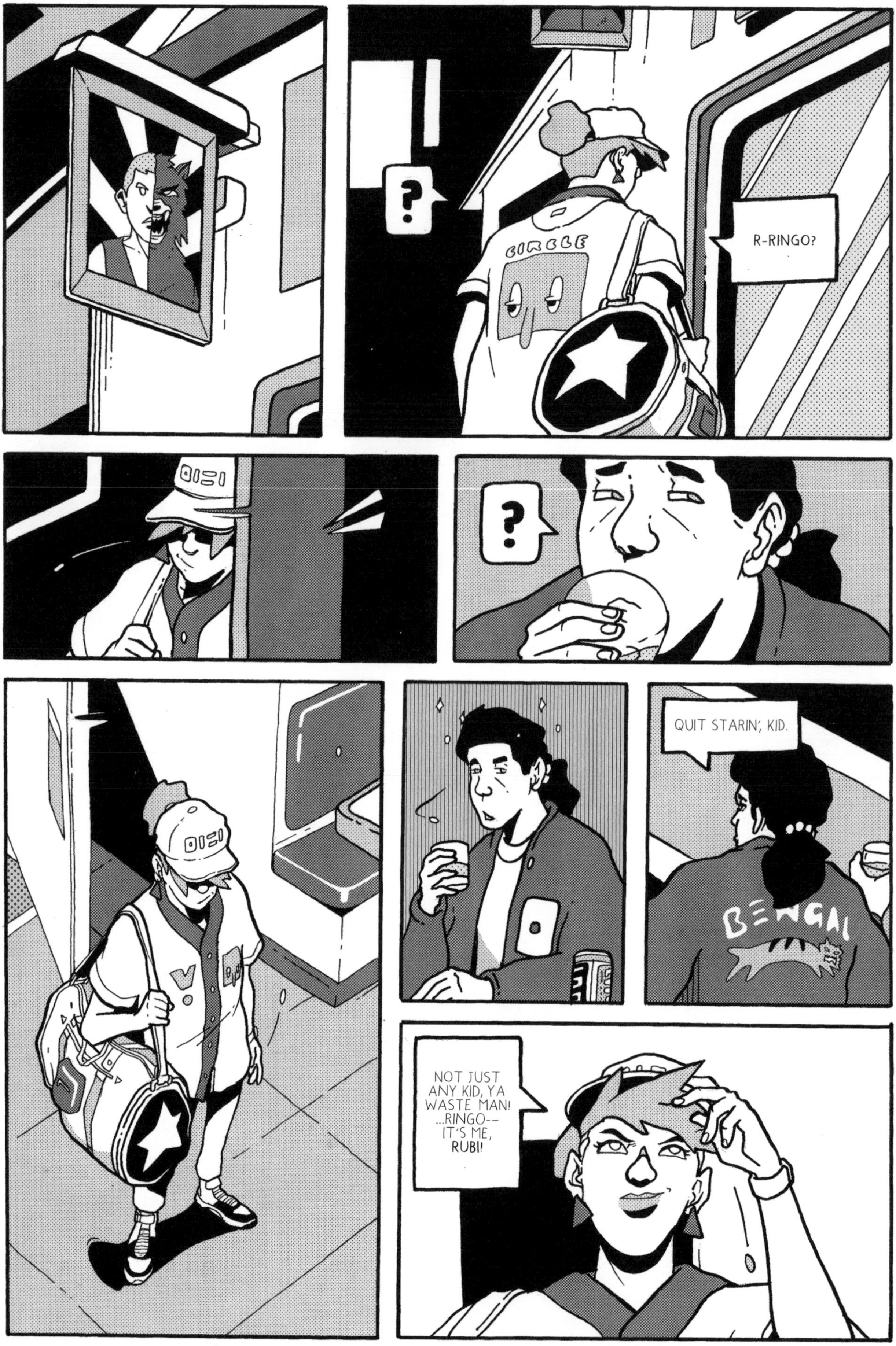
?
R-RINGO?
?
QUIT STARIN', KID.
NOT JUST ANY KID, YA WASTE MAN! ...RINGO-- IT'S ME, RUBI!

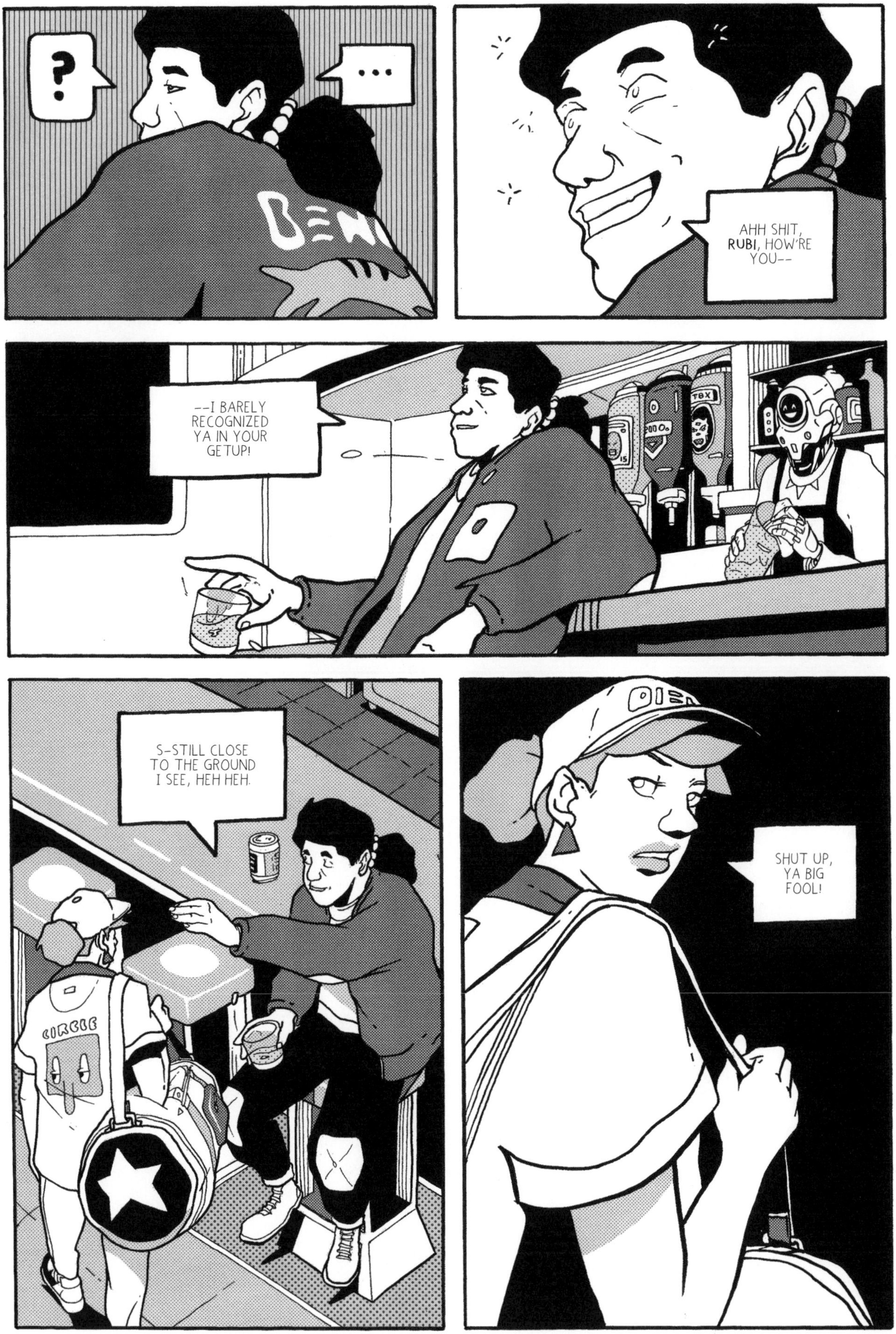
?
...
AHH SHIT, RUBI, HOW'RE YOU--
--I BARELY RECOGNIZED YA IN YOUR GETUP!
S-STILL CLOSE TO THE GROUND I SEE, HEH HEH.
SHUT UP, YA BIG FOOL!

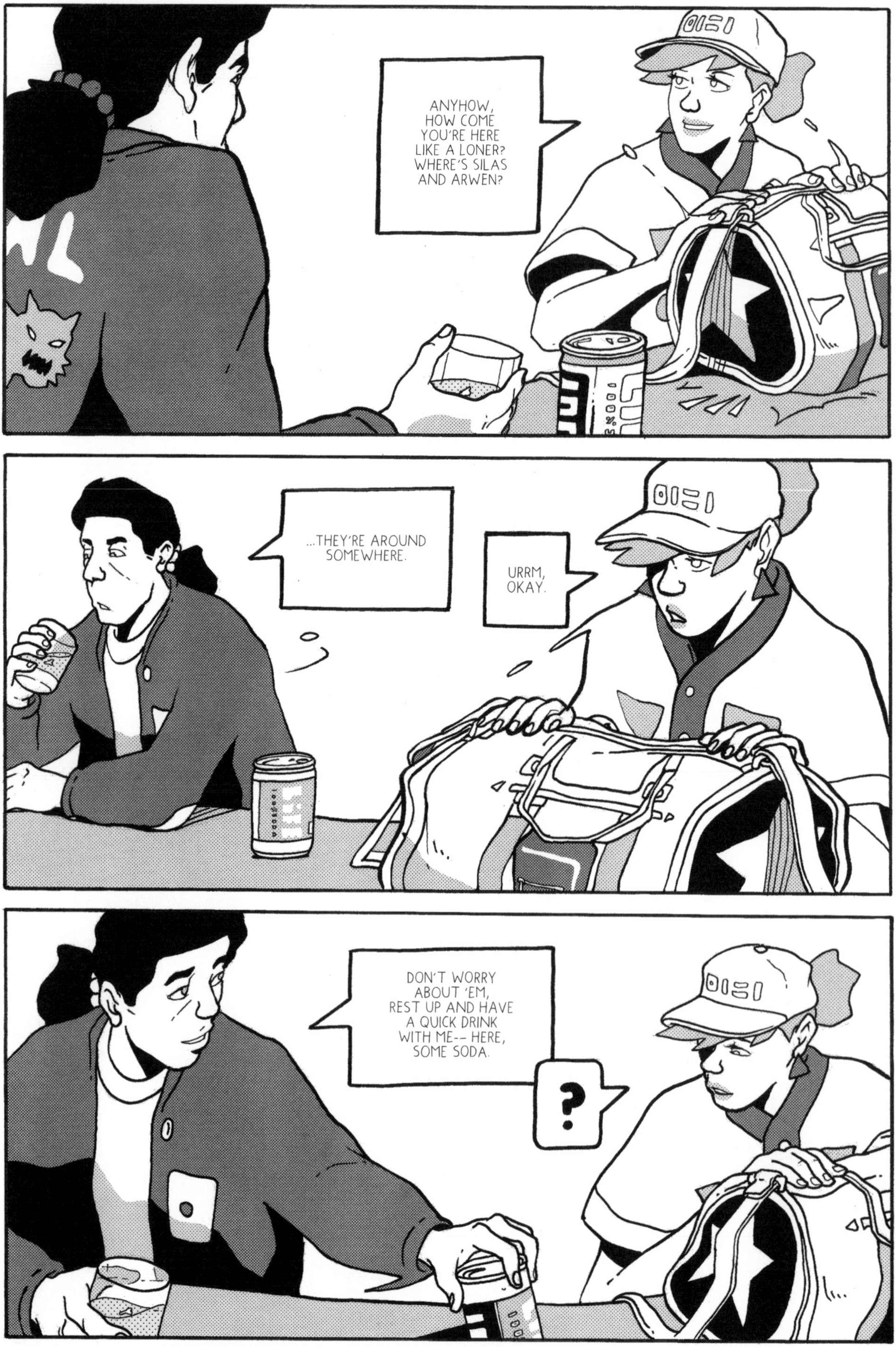
ANYHOW, HOW COME YOU'RE HERE LIKE A LONER? WHERE'S SILAS AND ARWEN?
...THEY'RE AROUND SOMEWHERE.
URRM, OKAY.
DON'T WORRY ABOUT 'EM, REST UP AND HAVE A QUICK DRINK WITH ME-- HERE, SOME SODA.
?

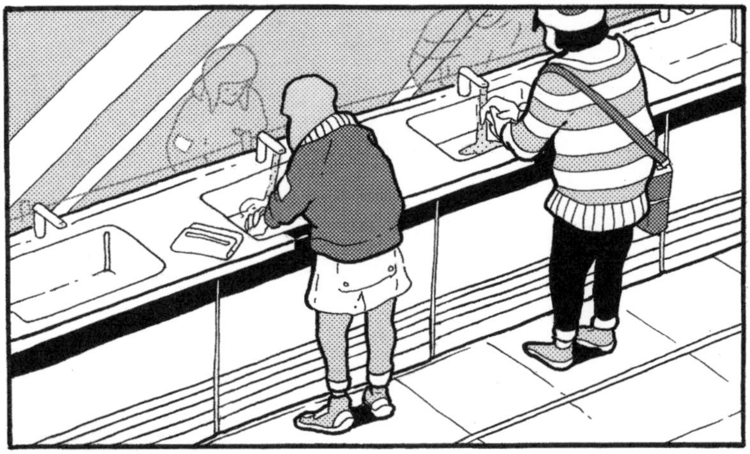

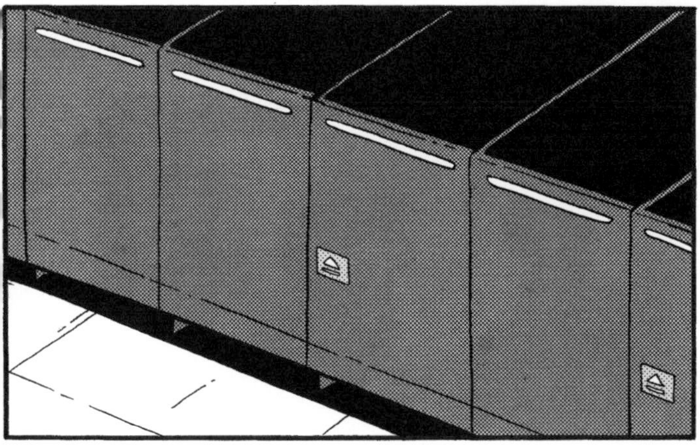

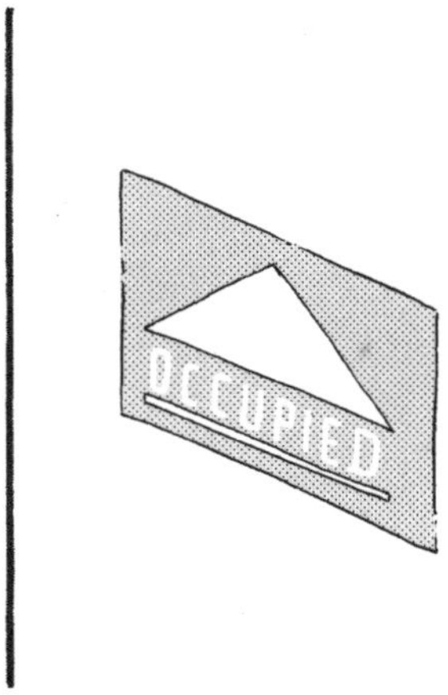
OCCUPIED

5

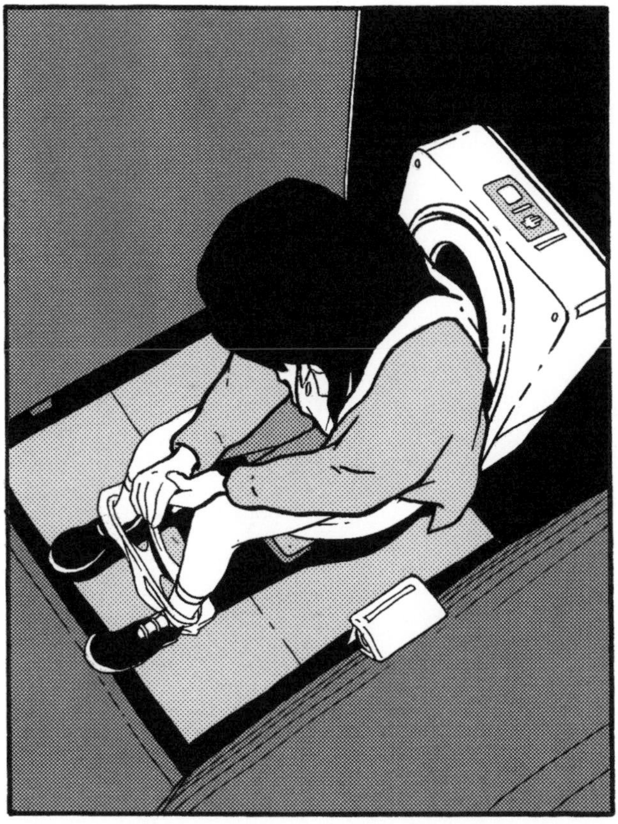

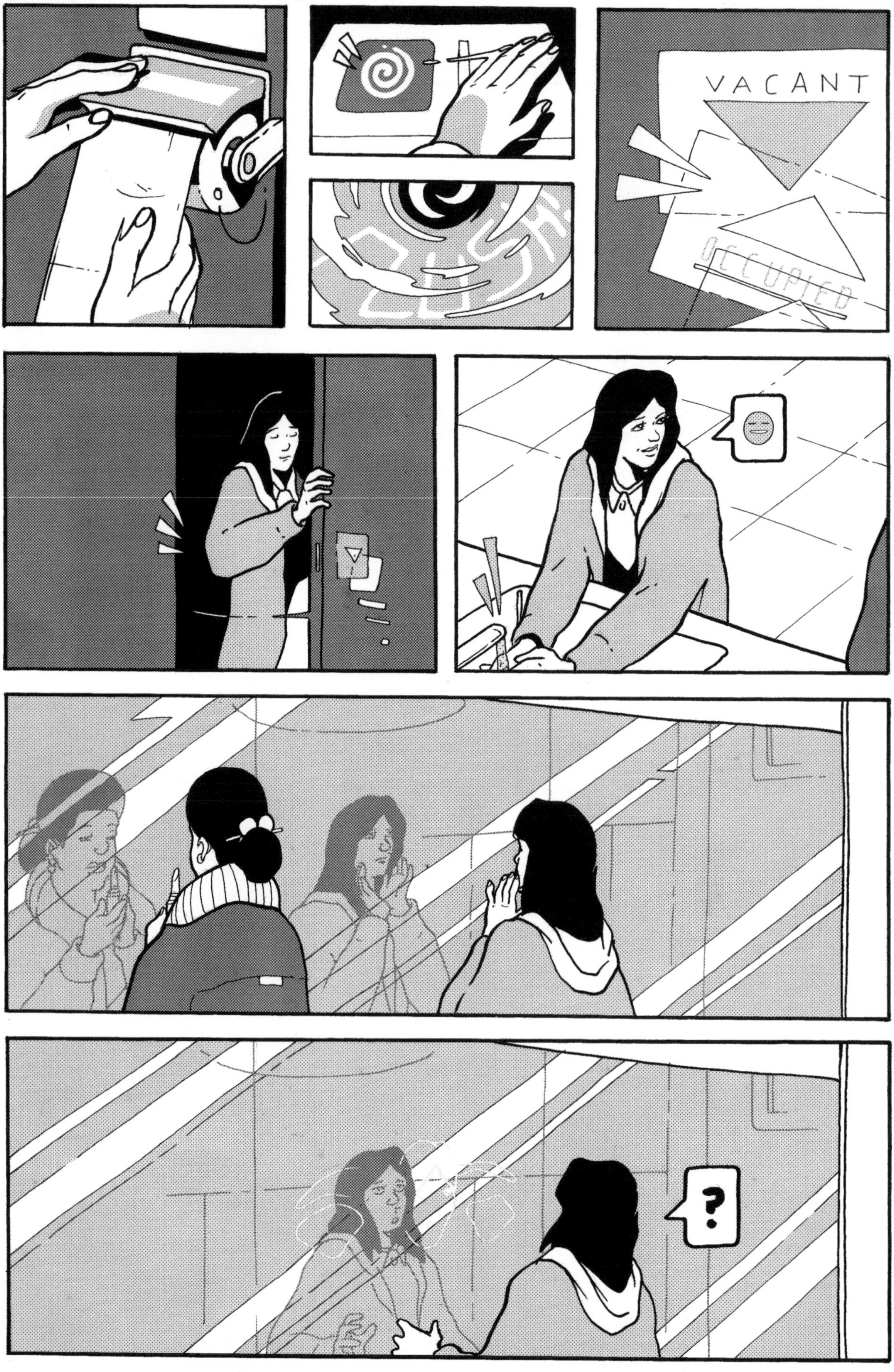
FLUSH
VACANT
OCCUPIED
?

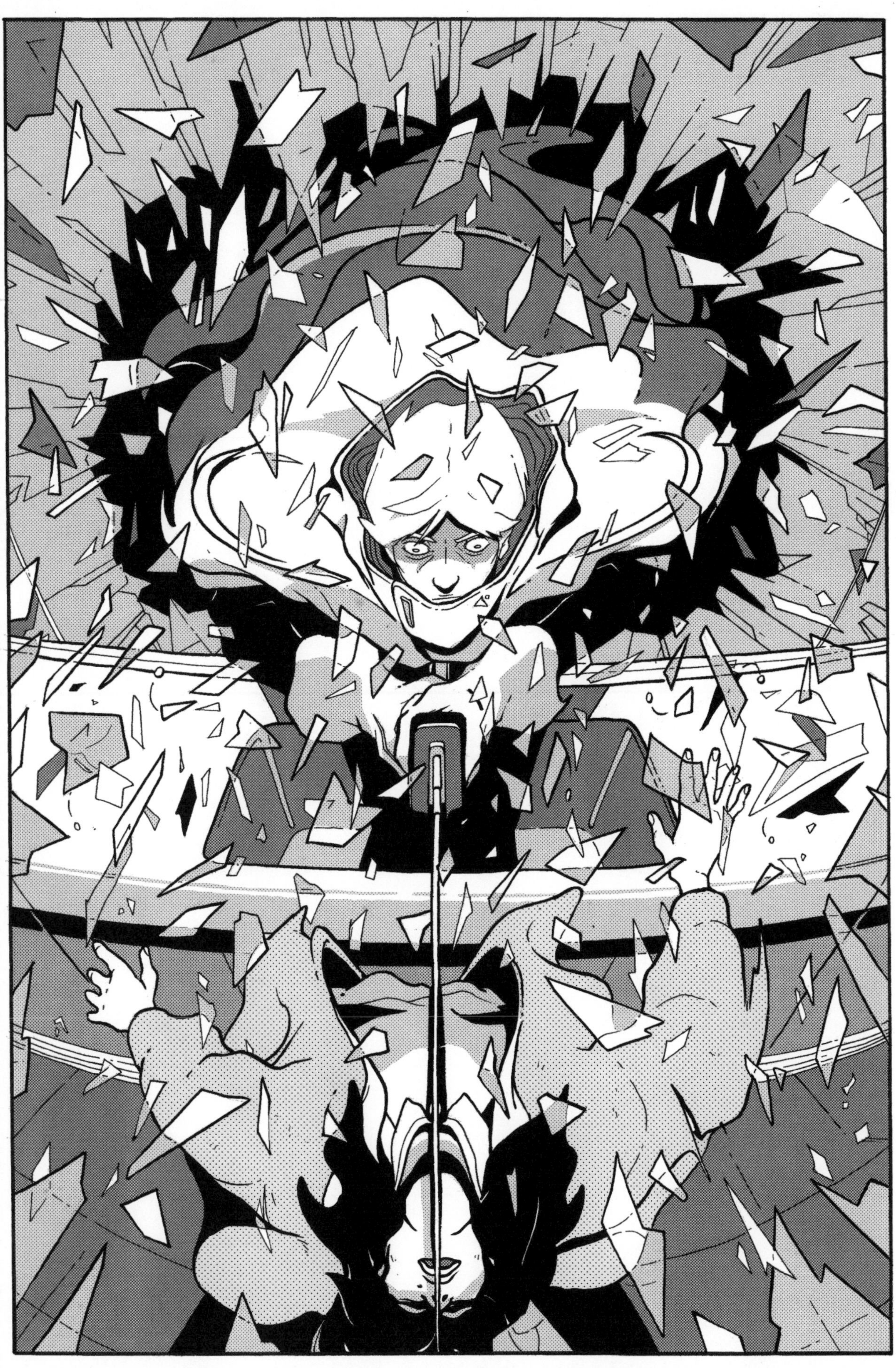

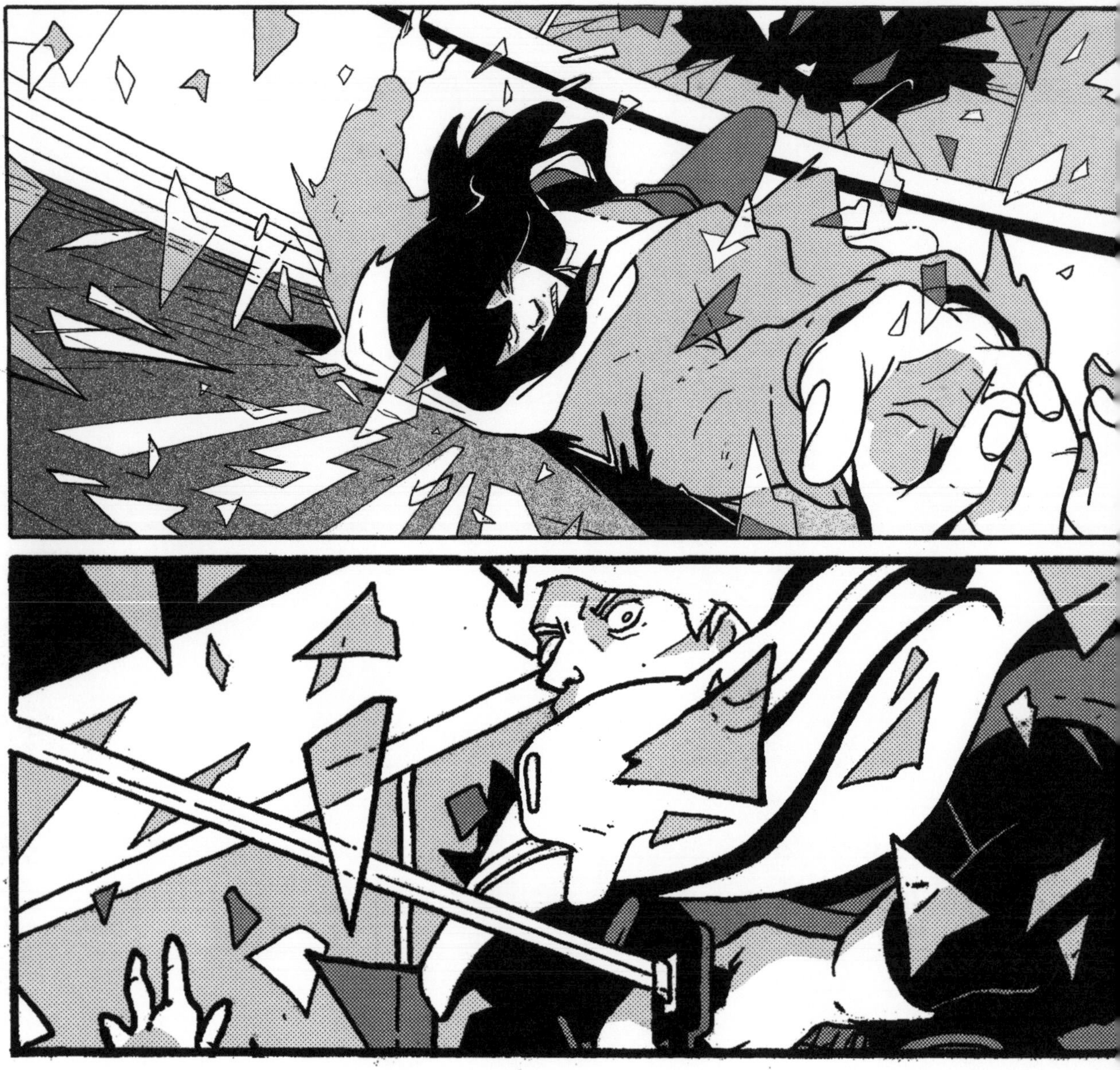

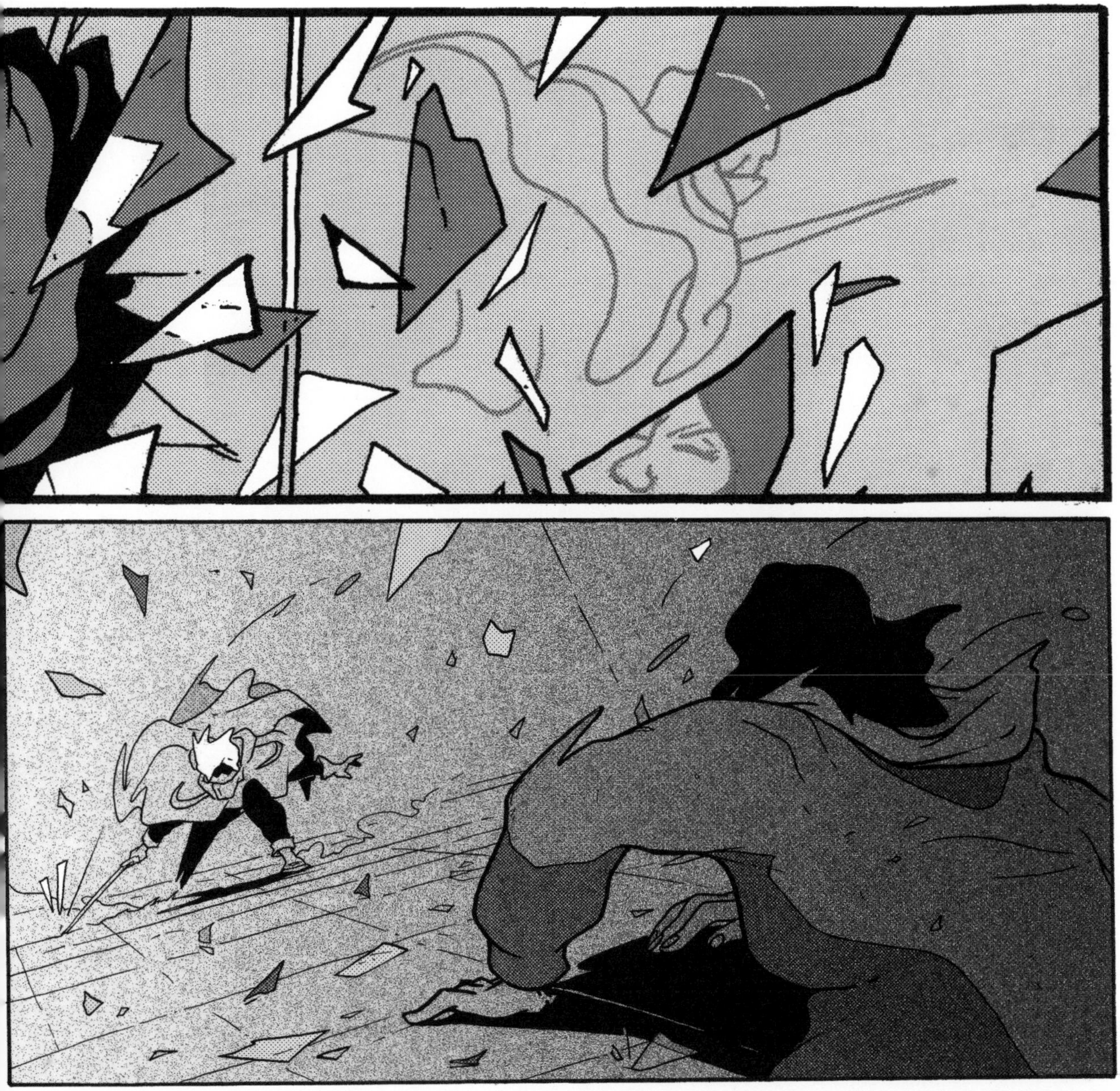

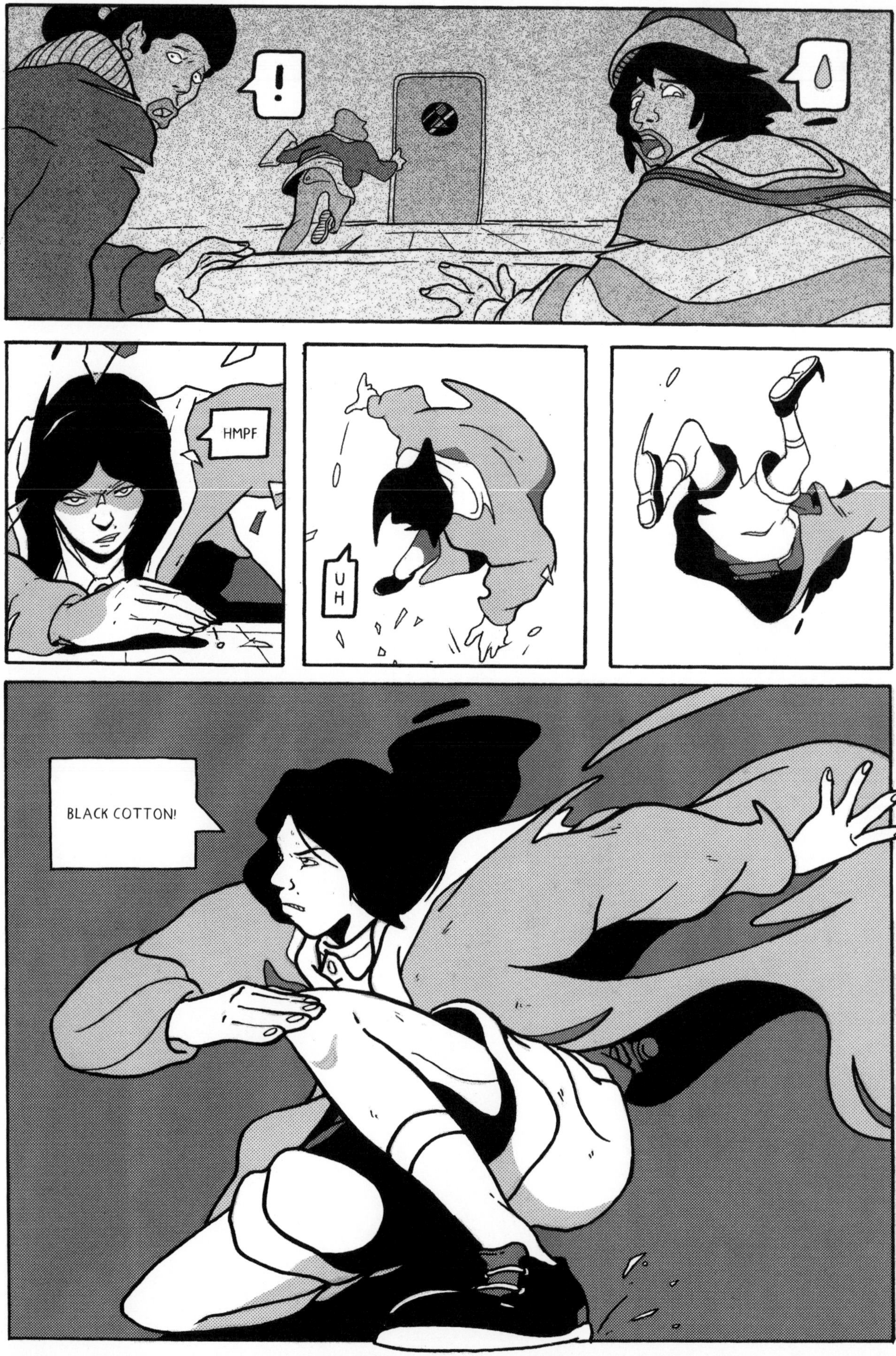
!
HMPF
UH
BLACK COTTON!

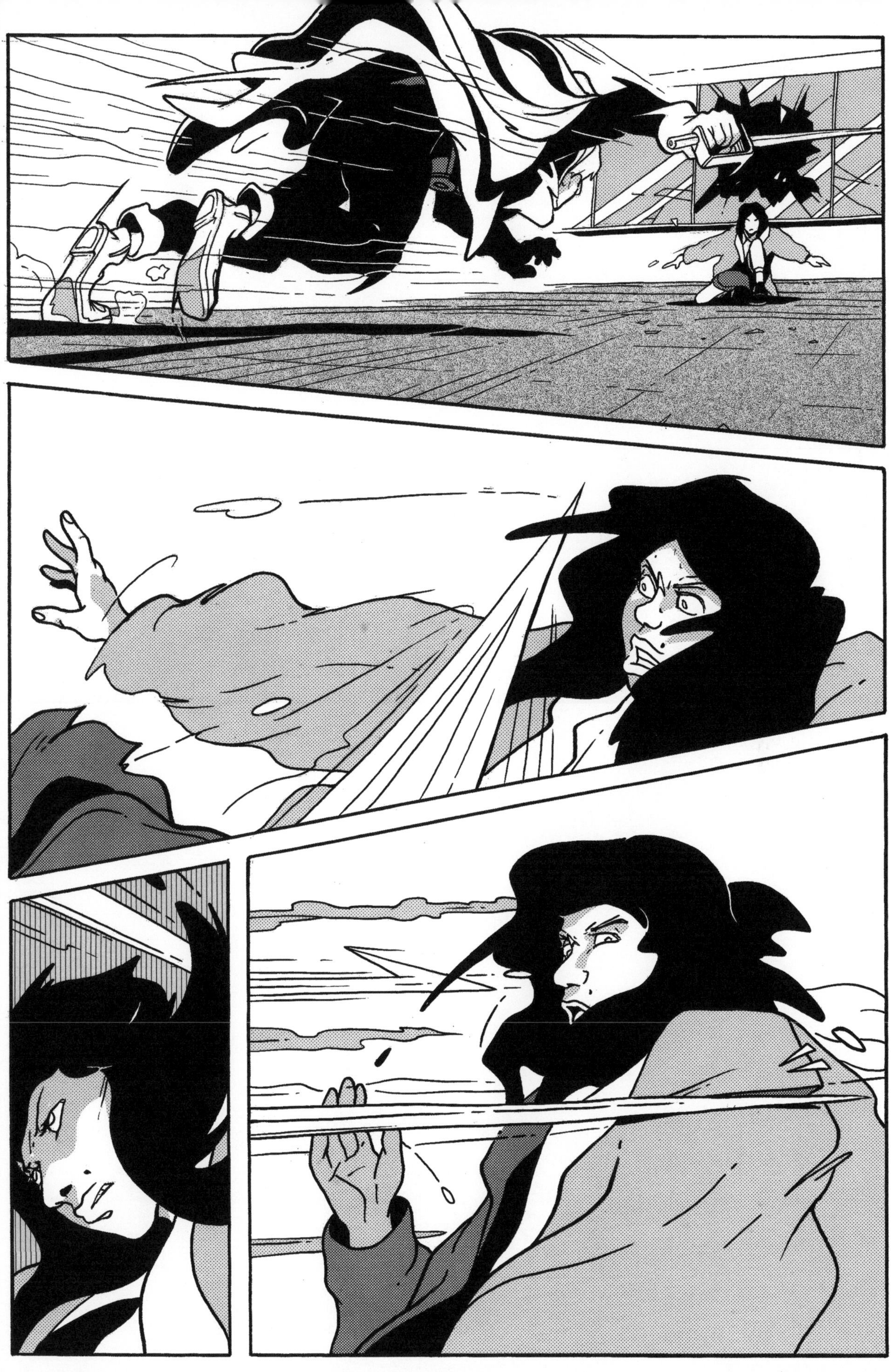

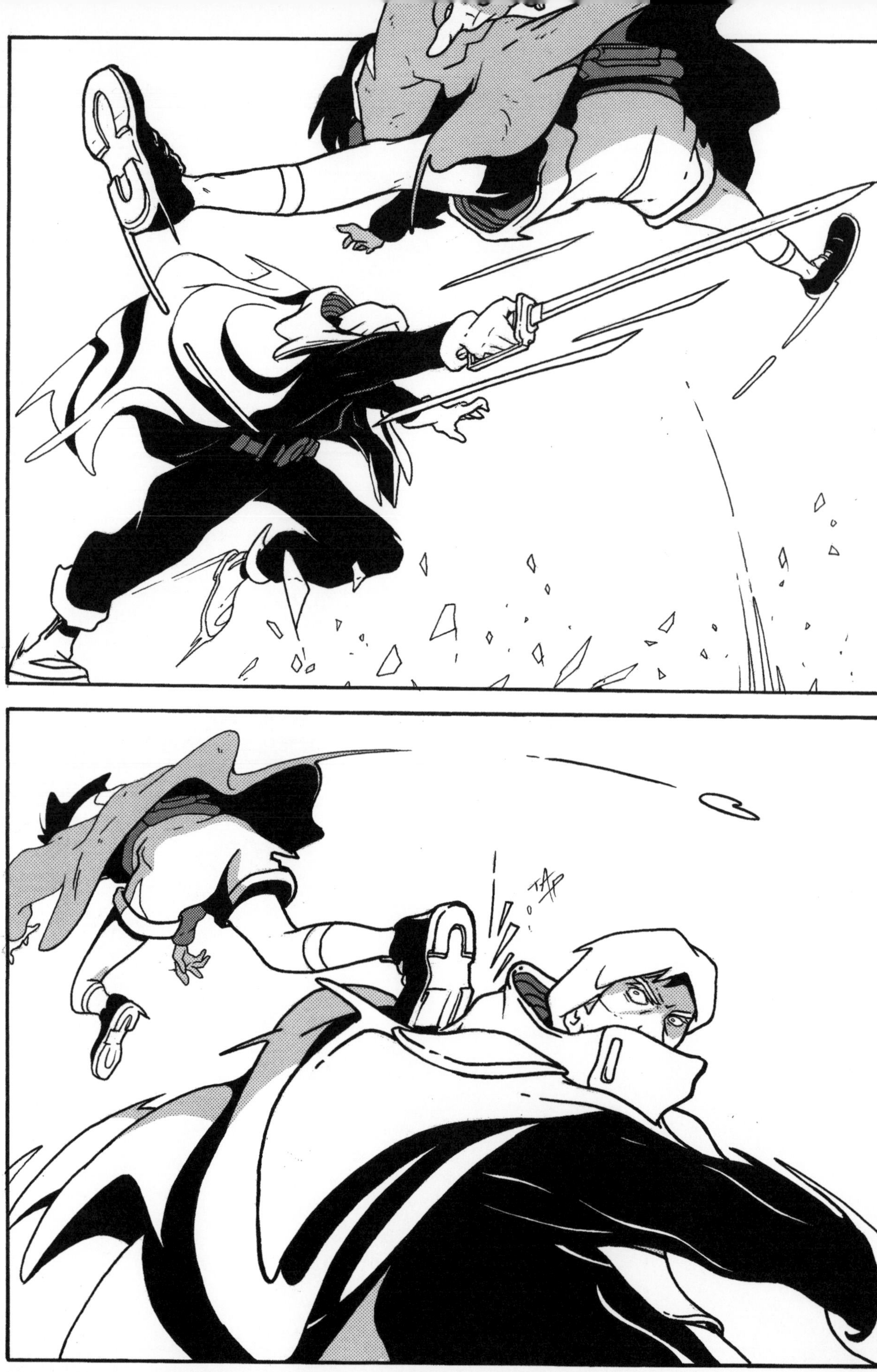
TAP

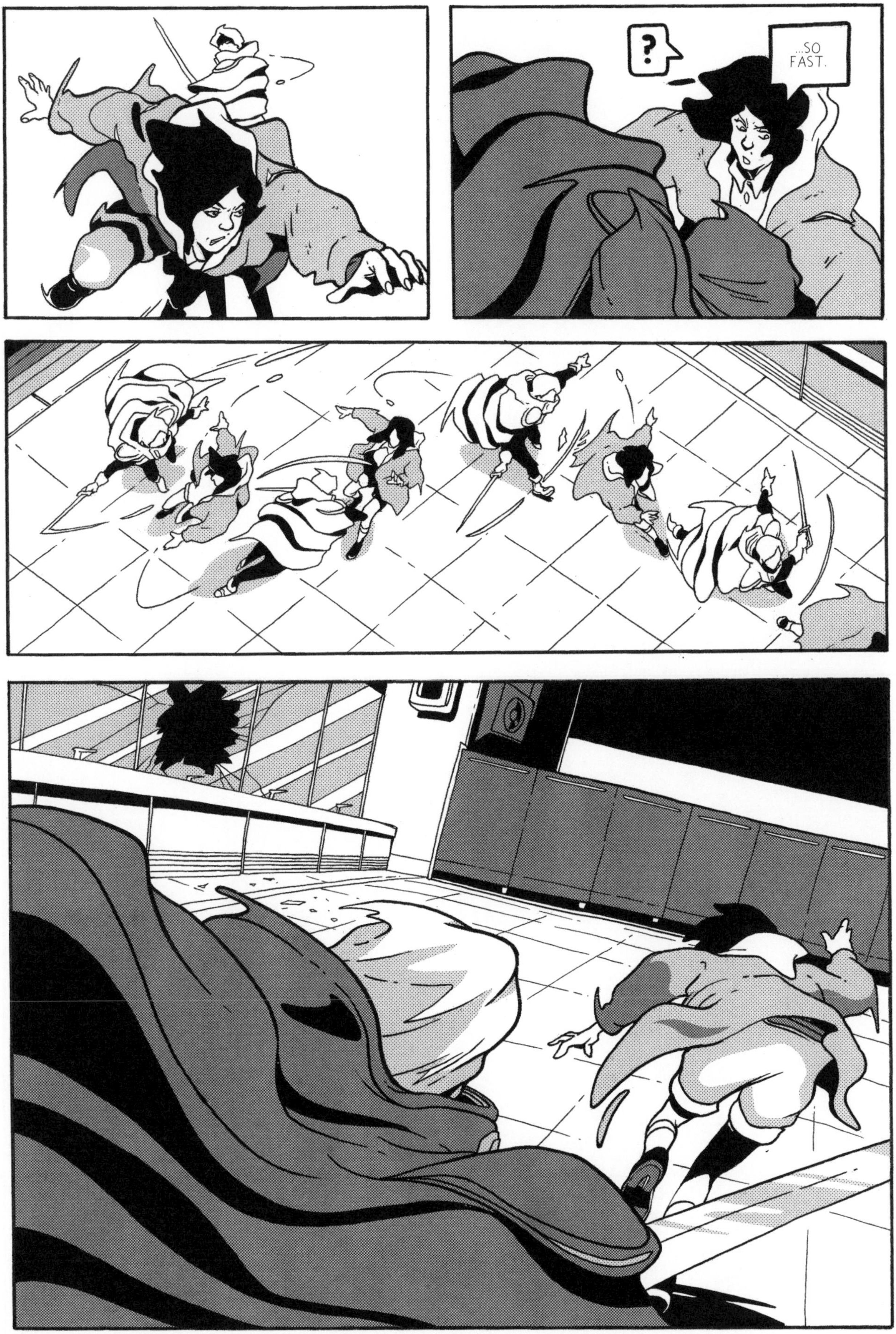
?
...SO FAST.

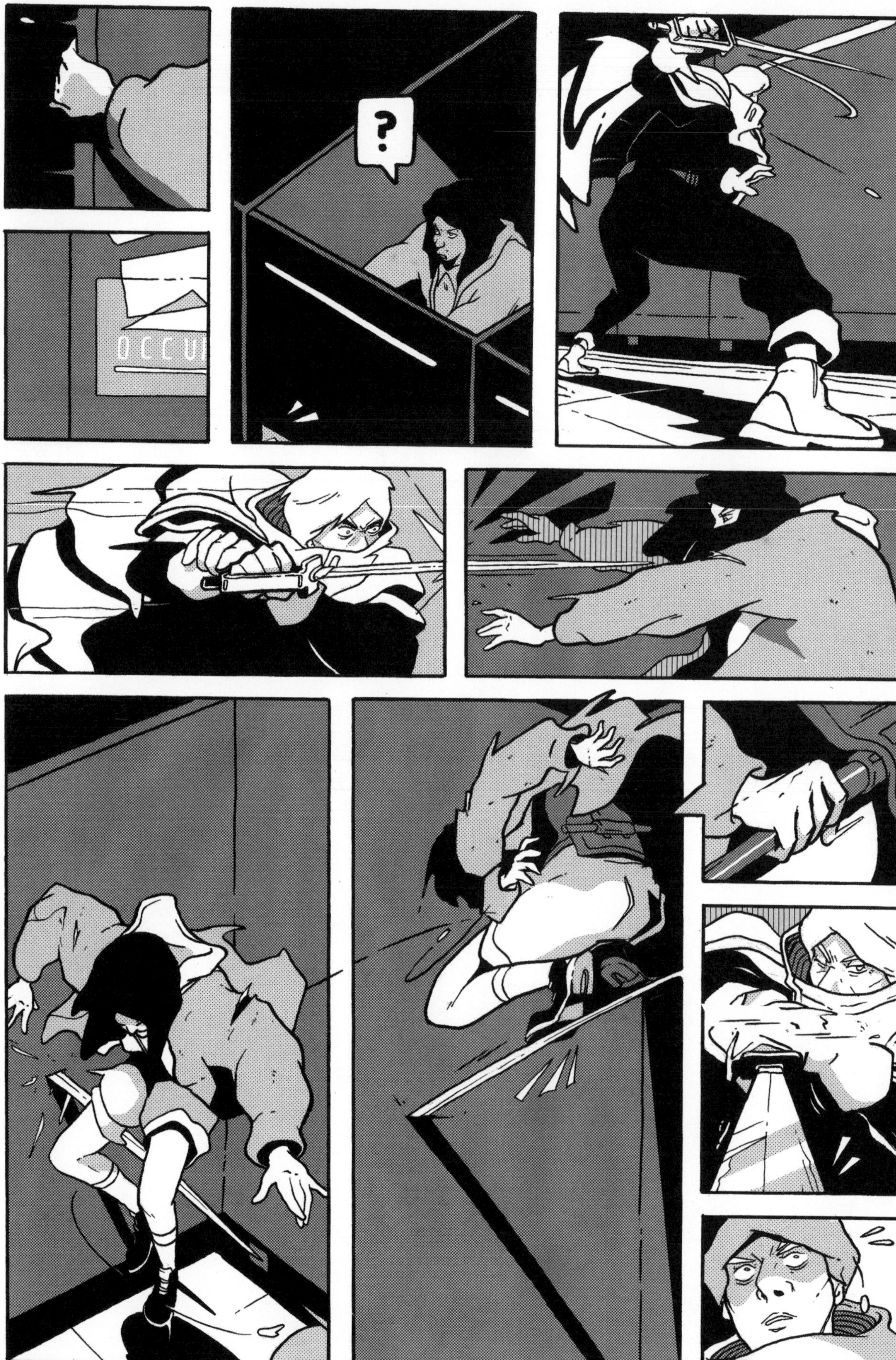
?
OCCU

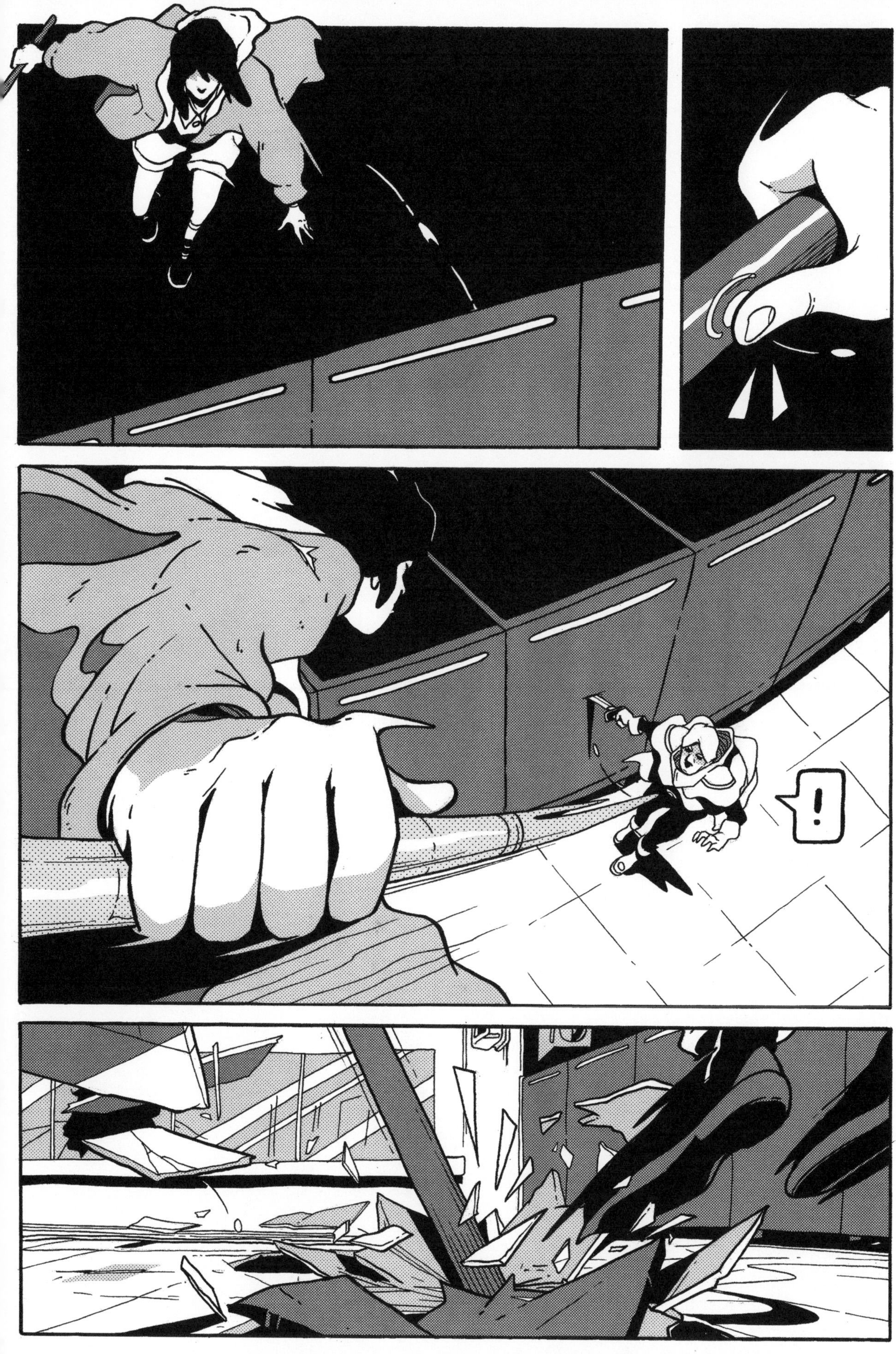
!

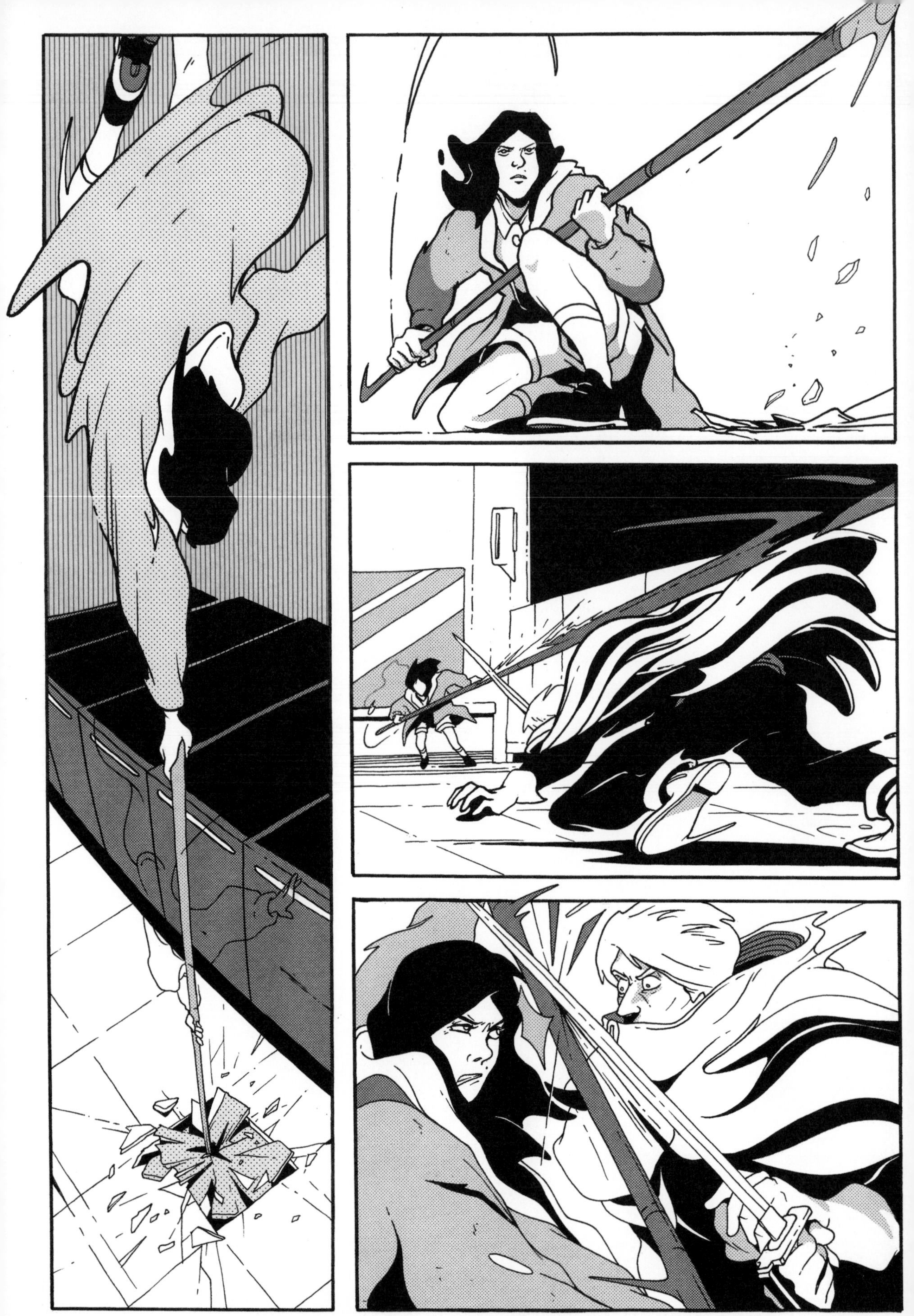

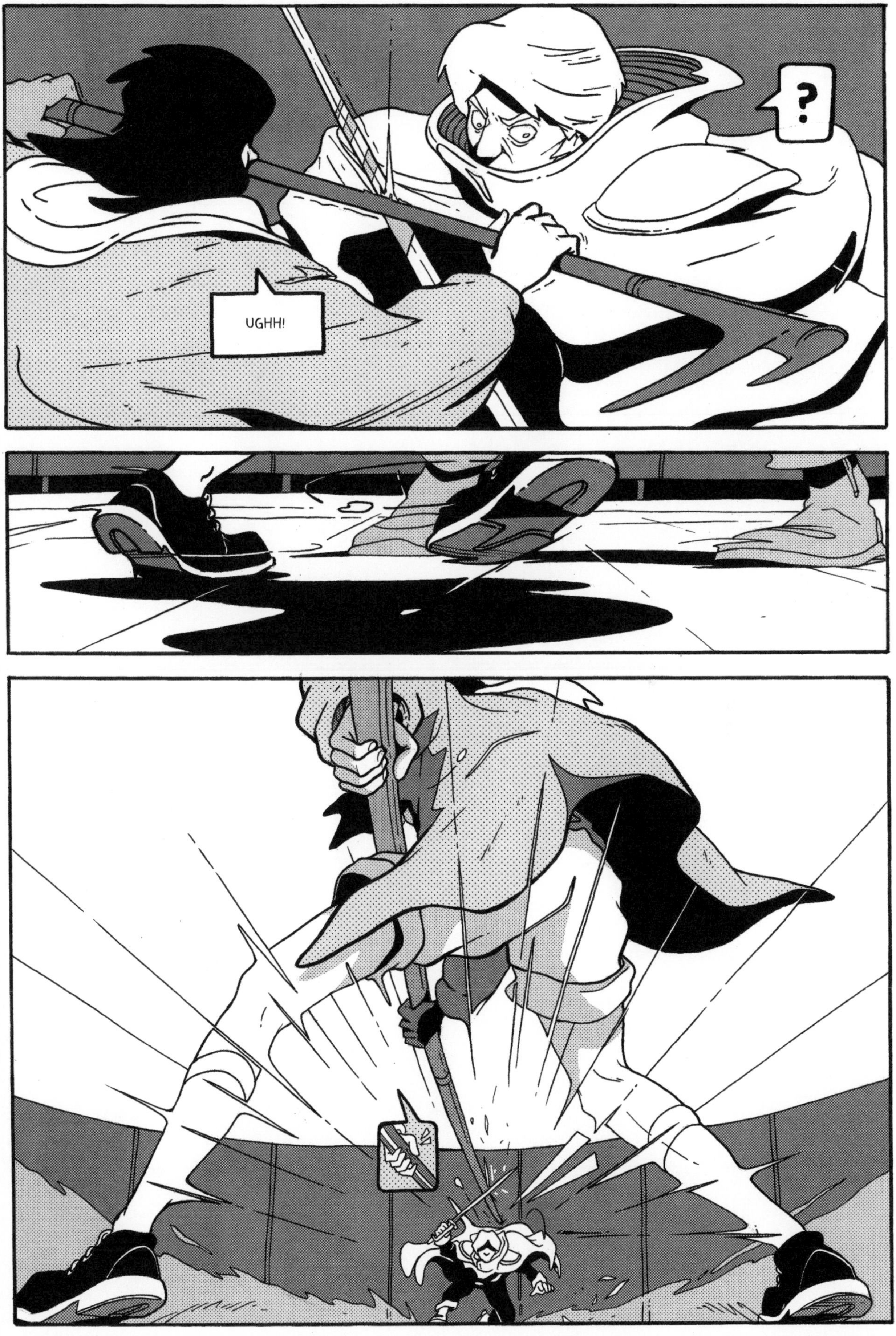

?
UGHH!

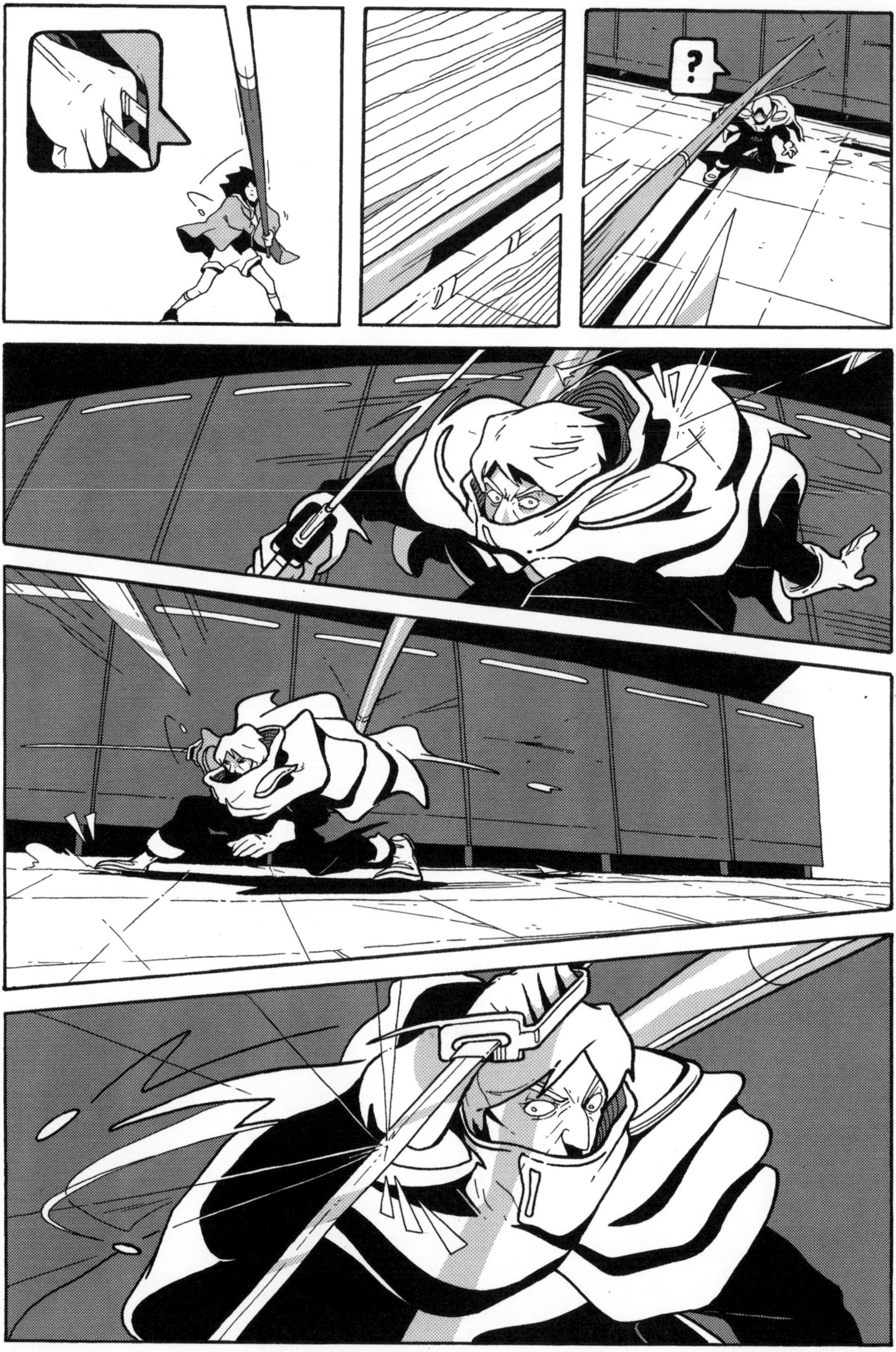
?

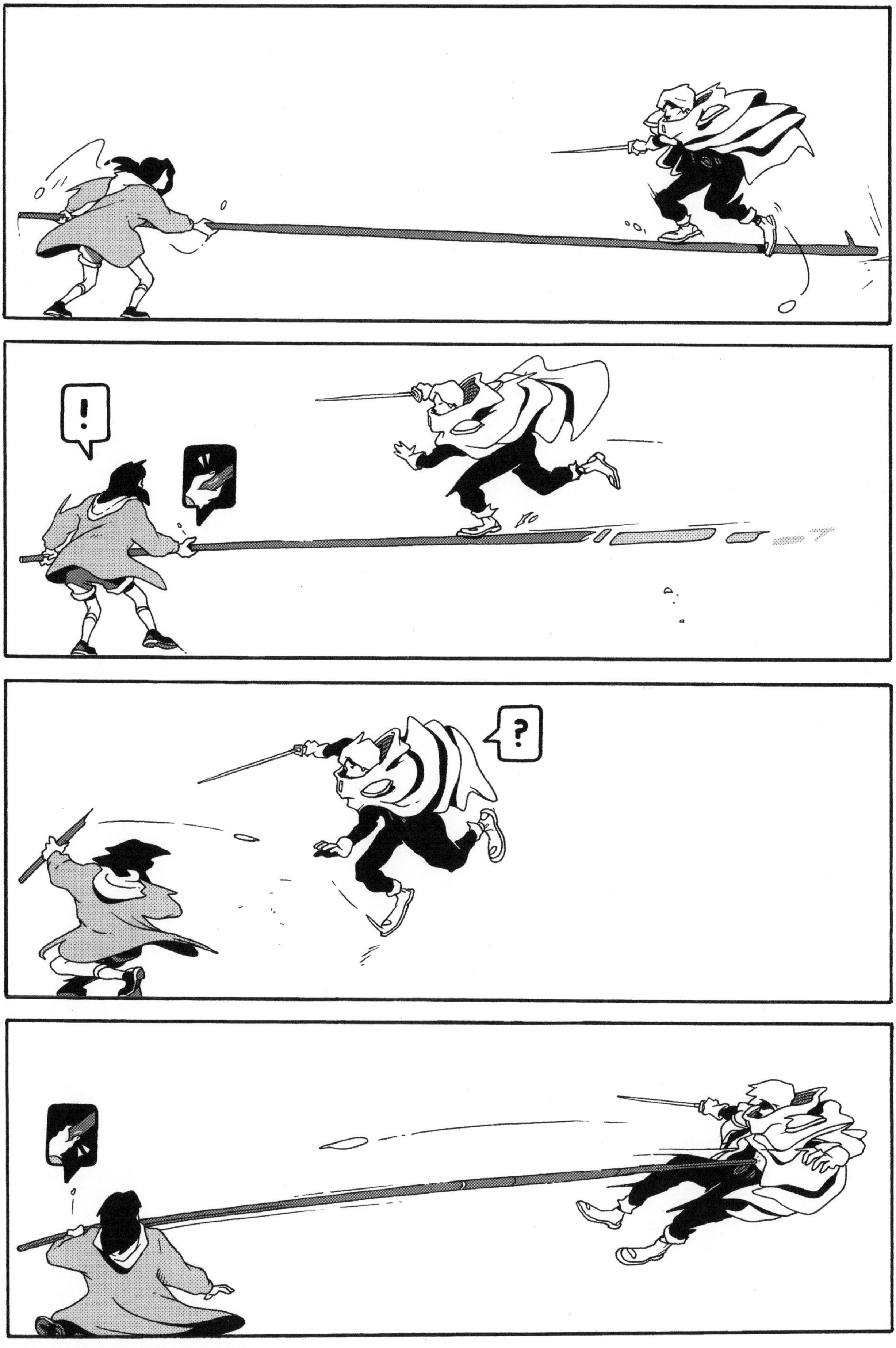
!
?

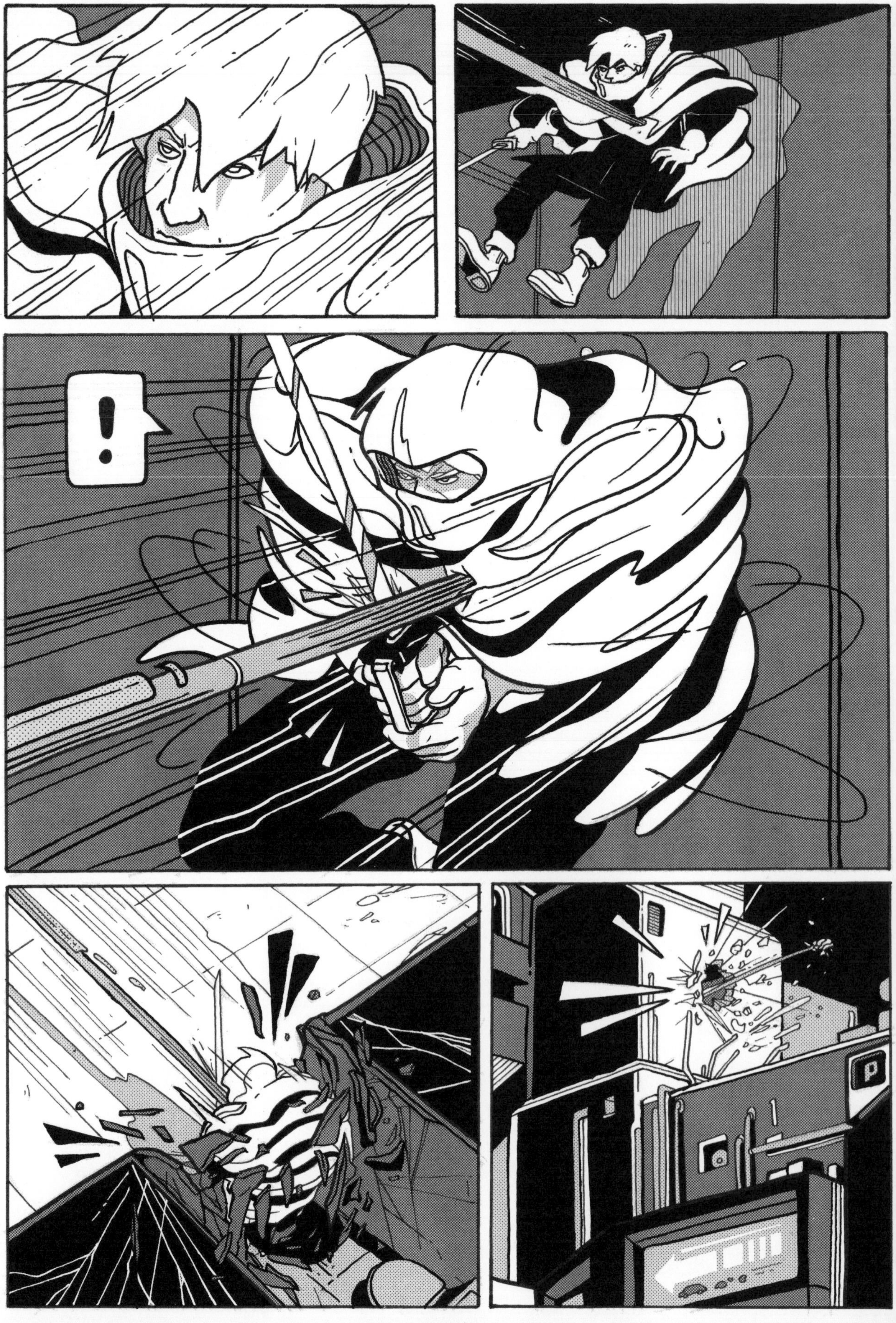
!
P

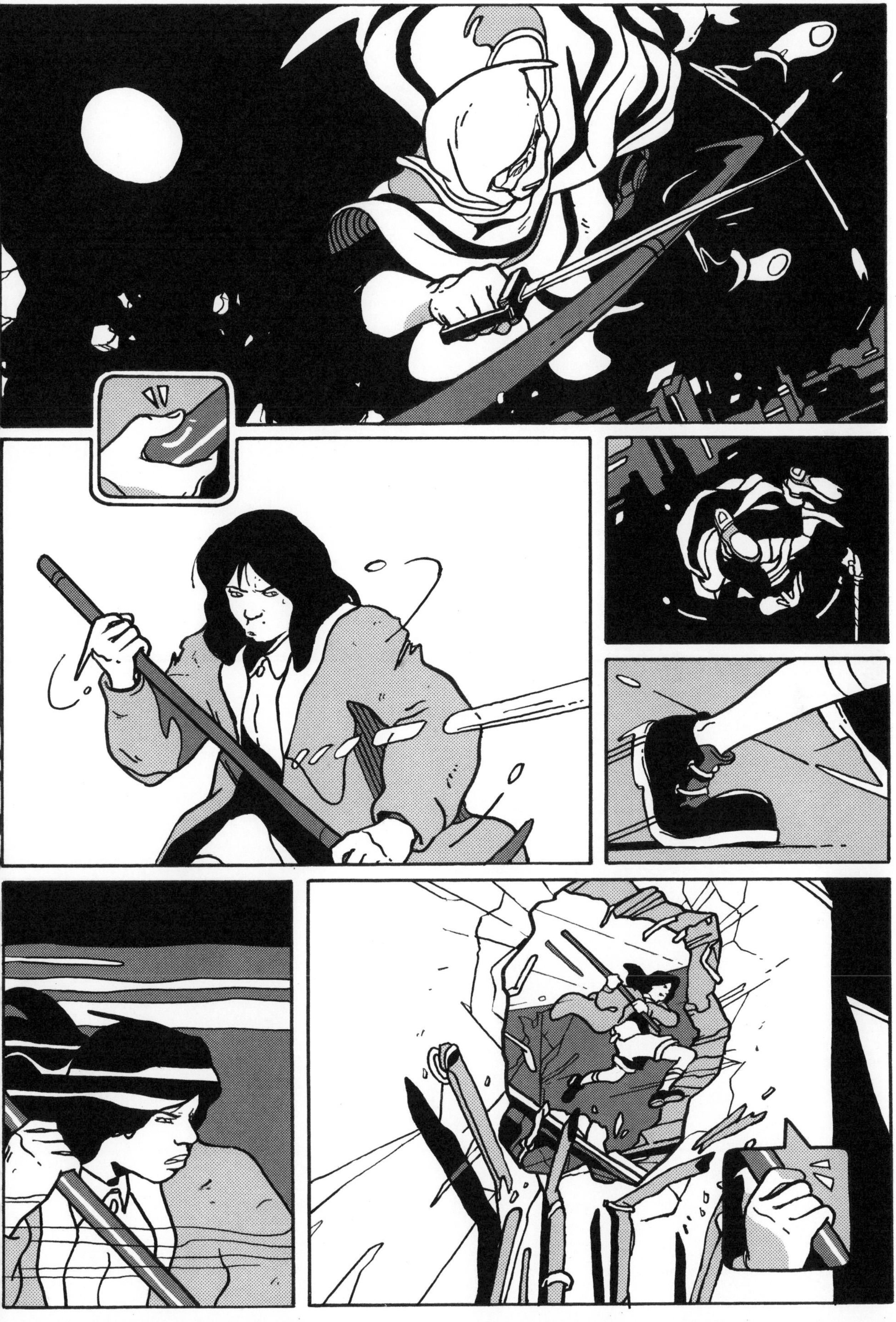

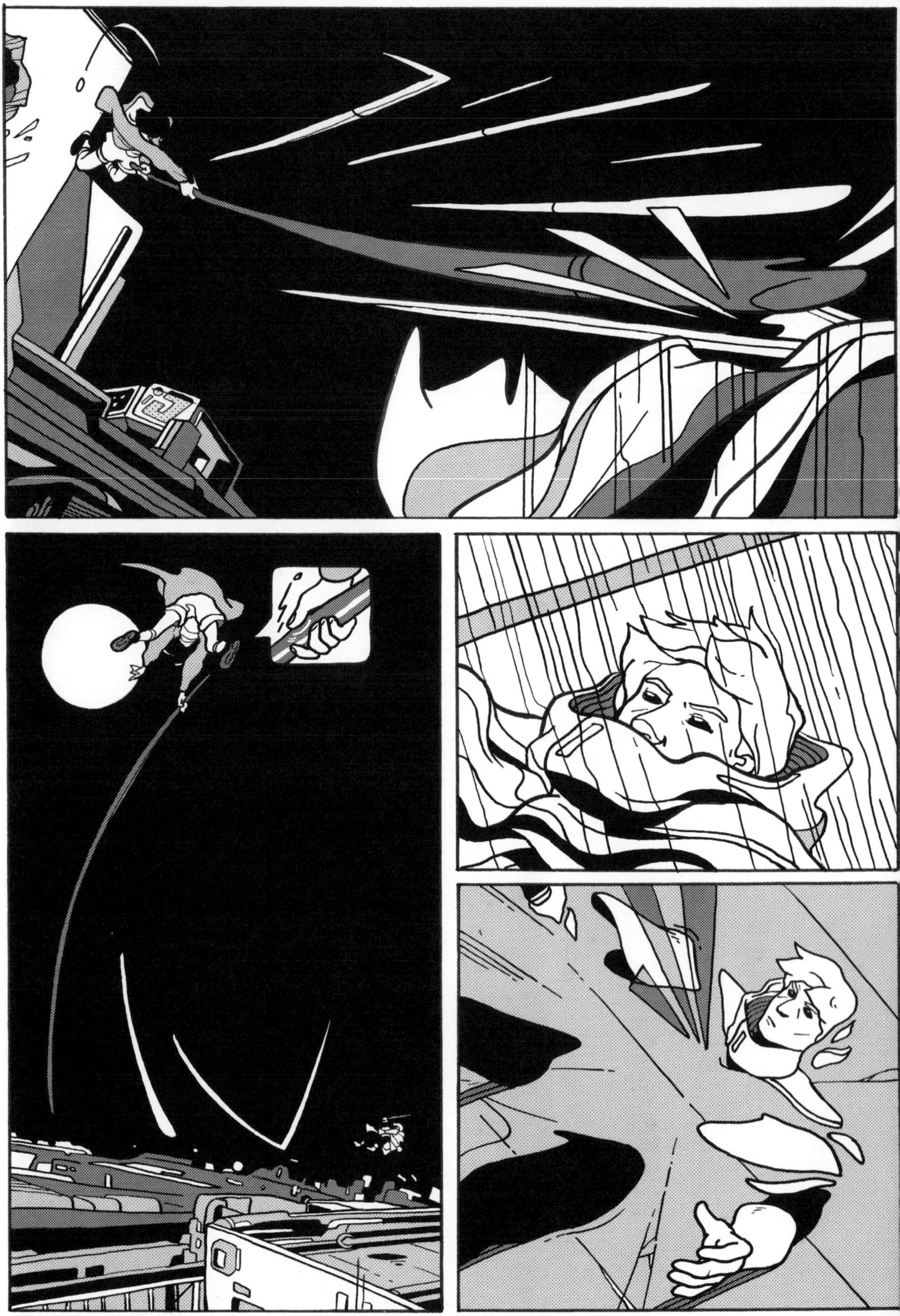

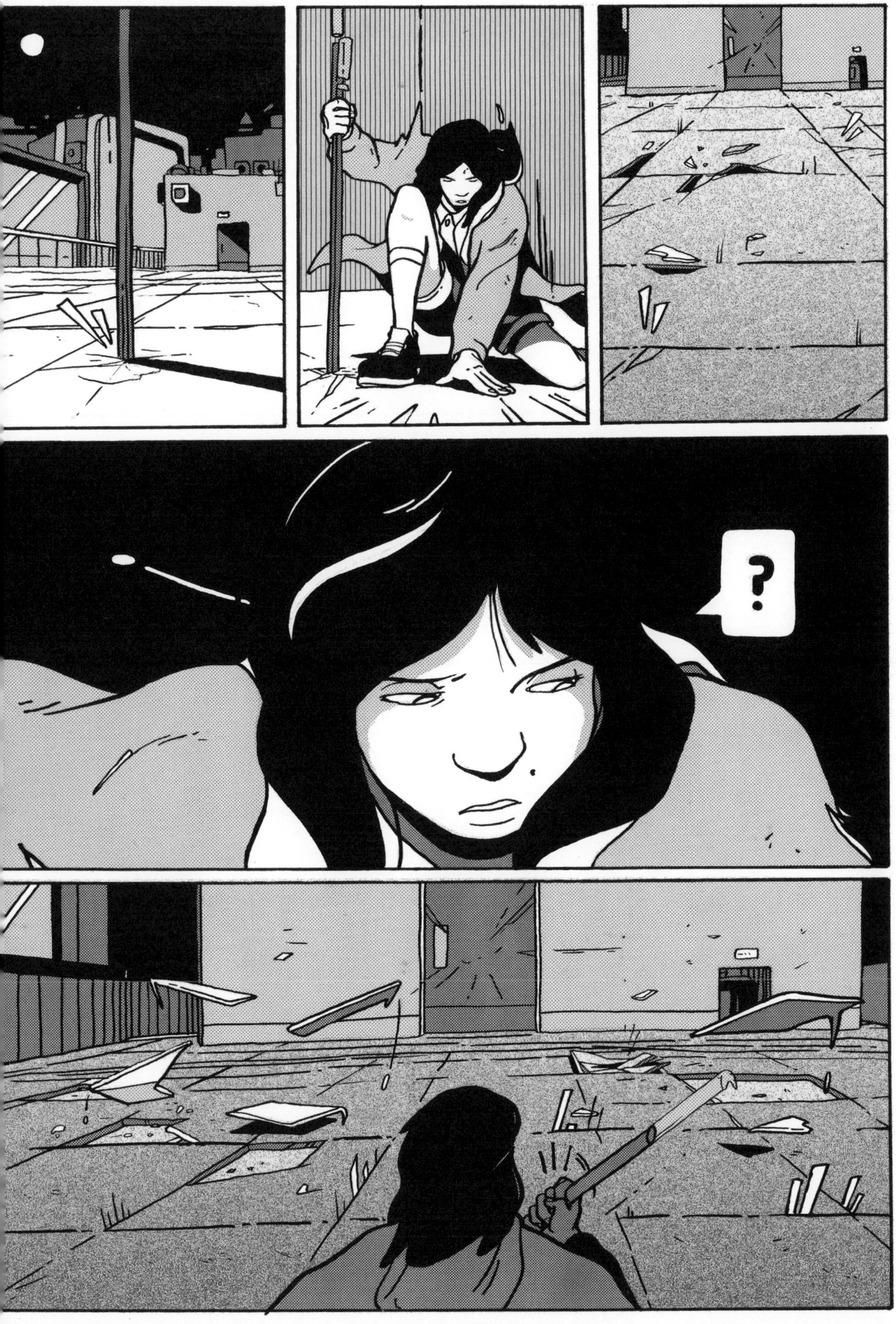
?

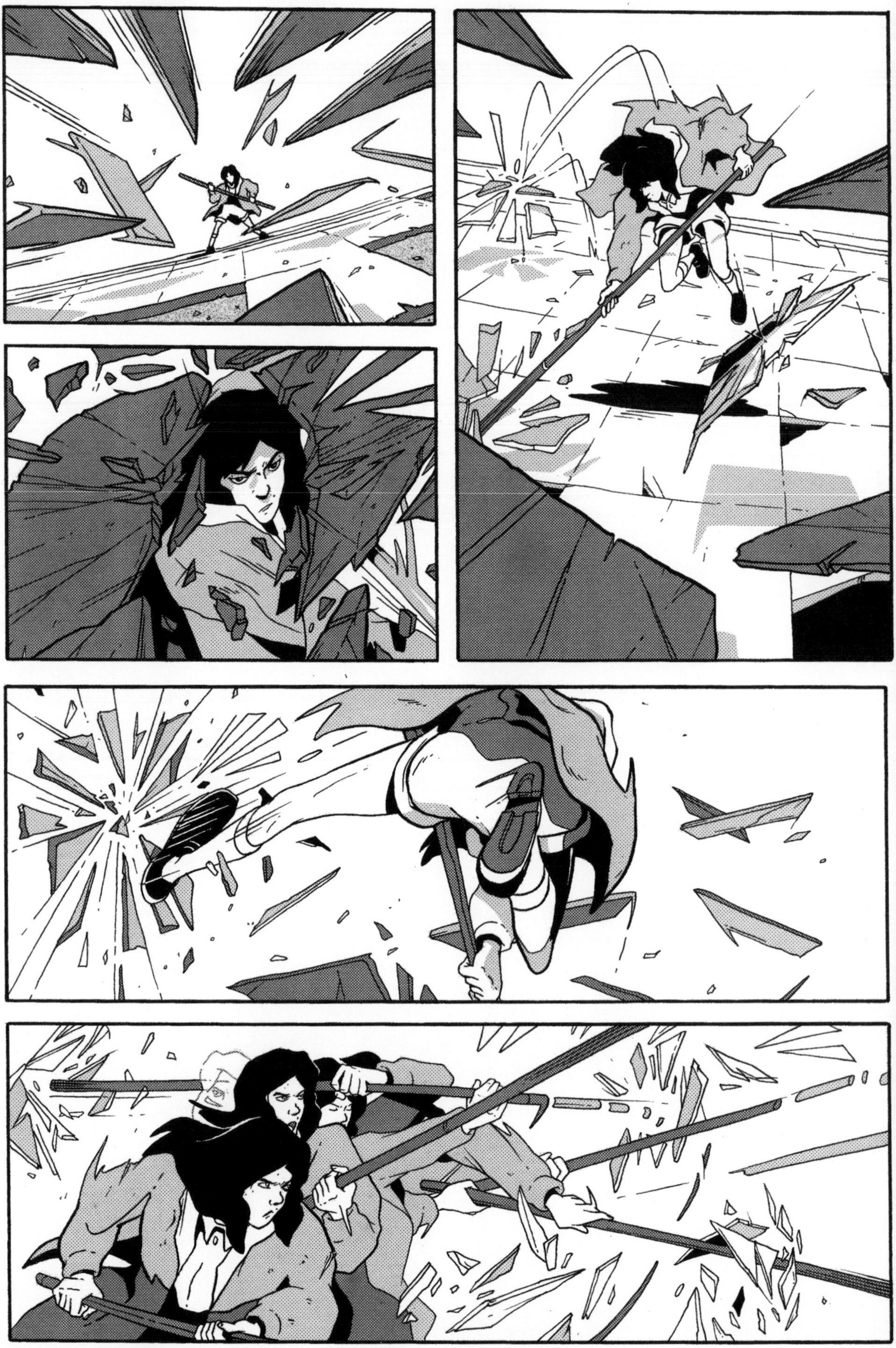

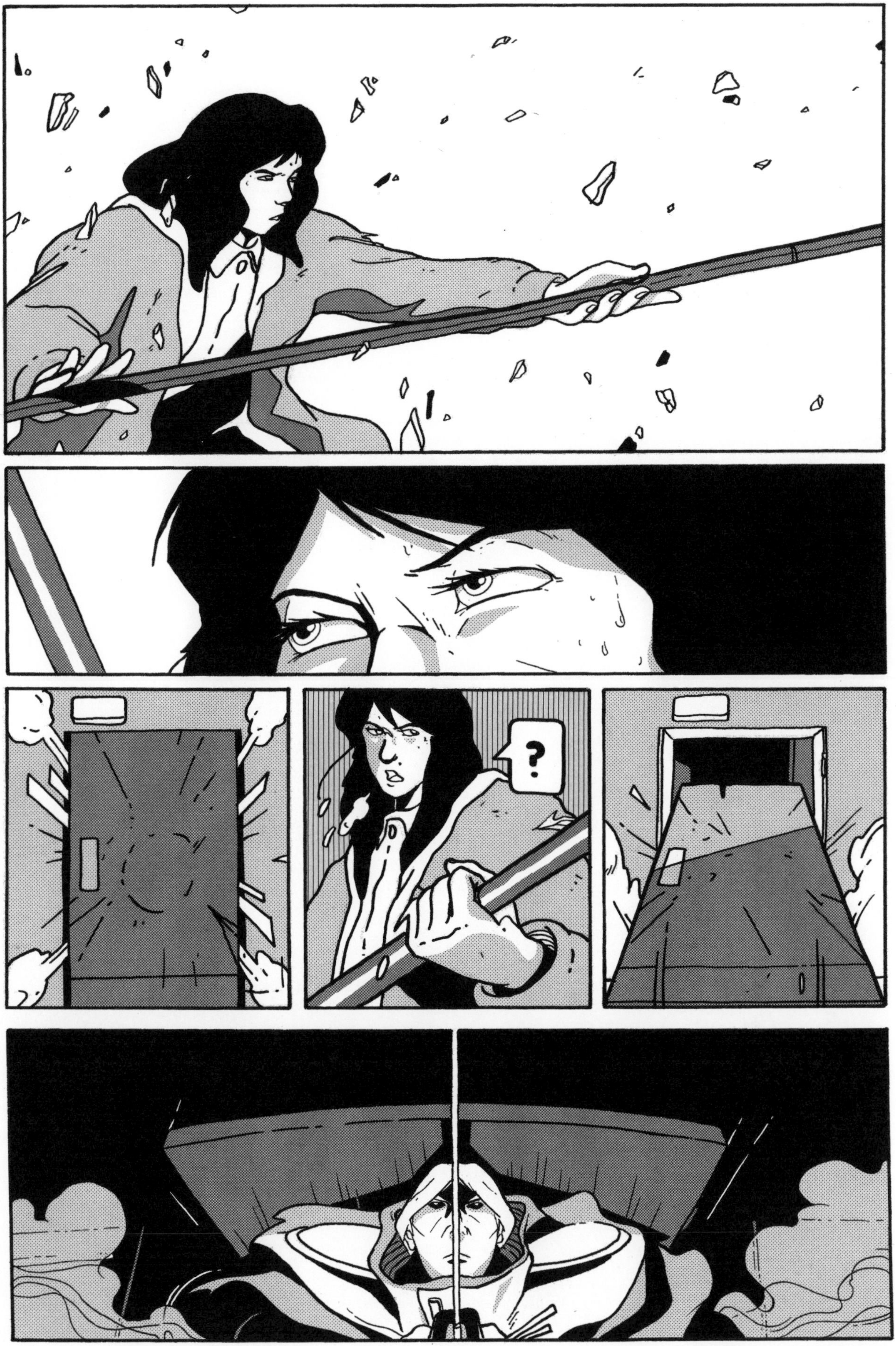
?

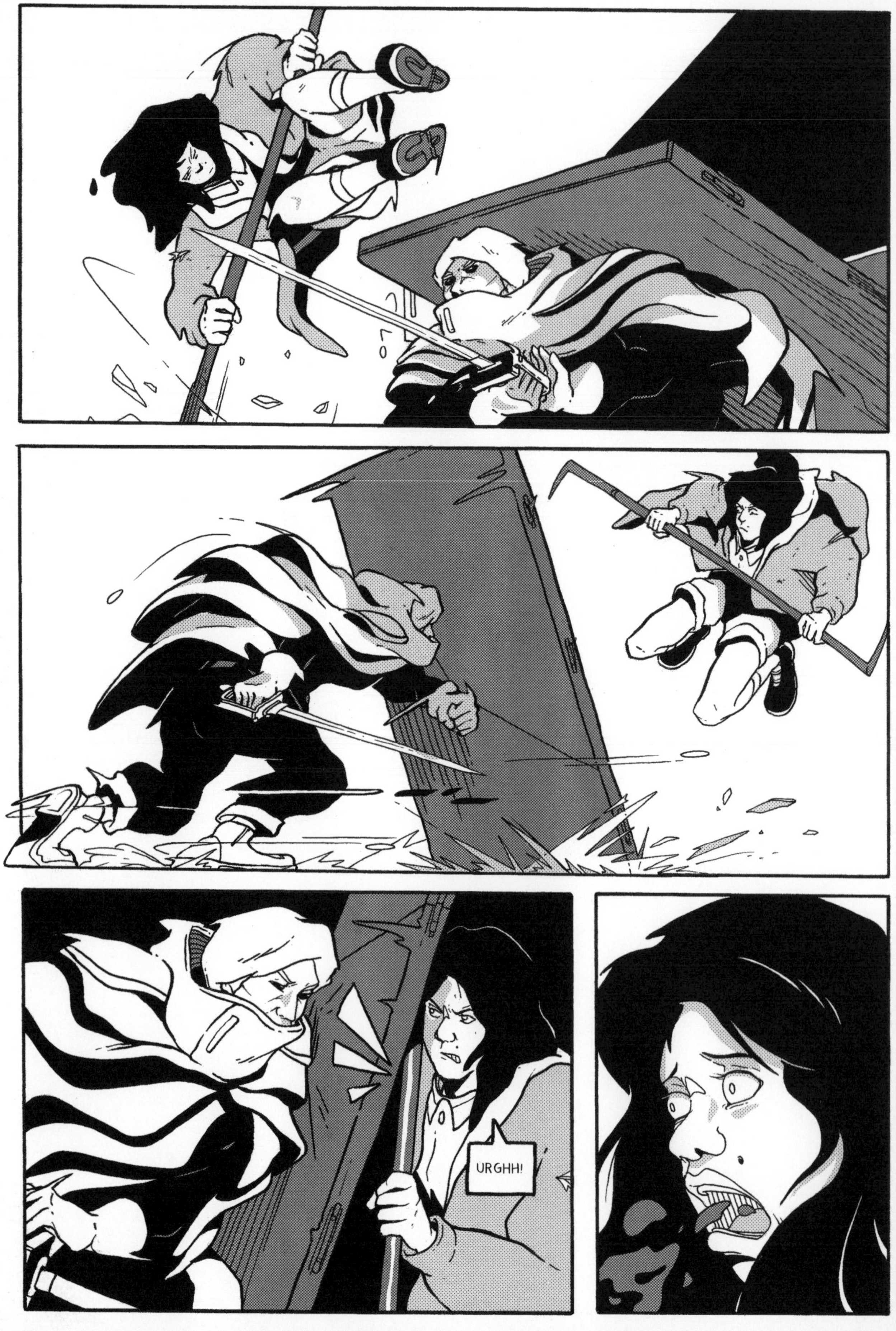
URGHH!

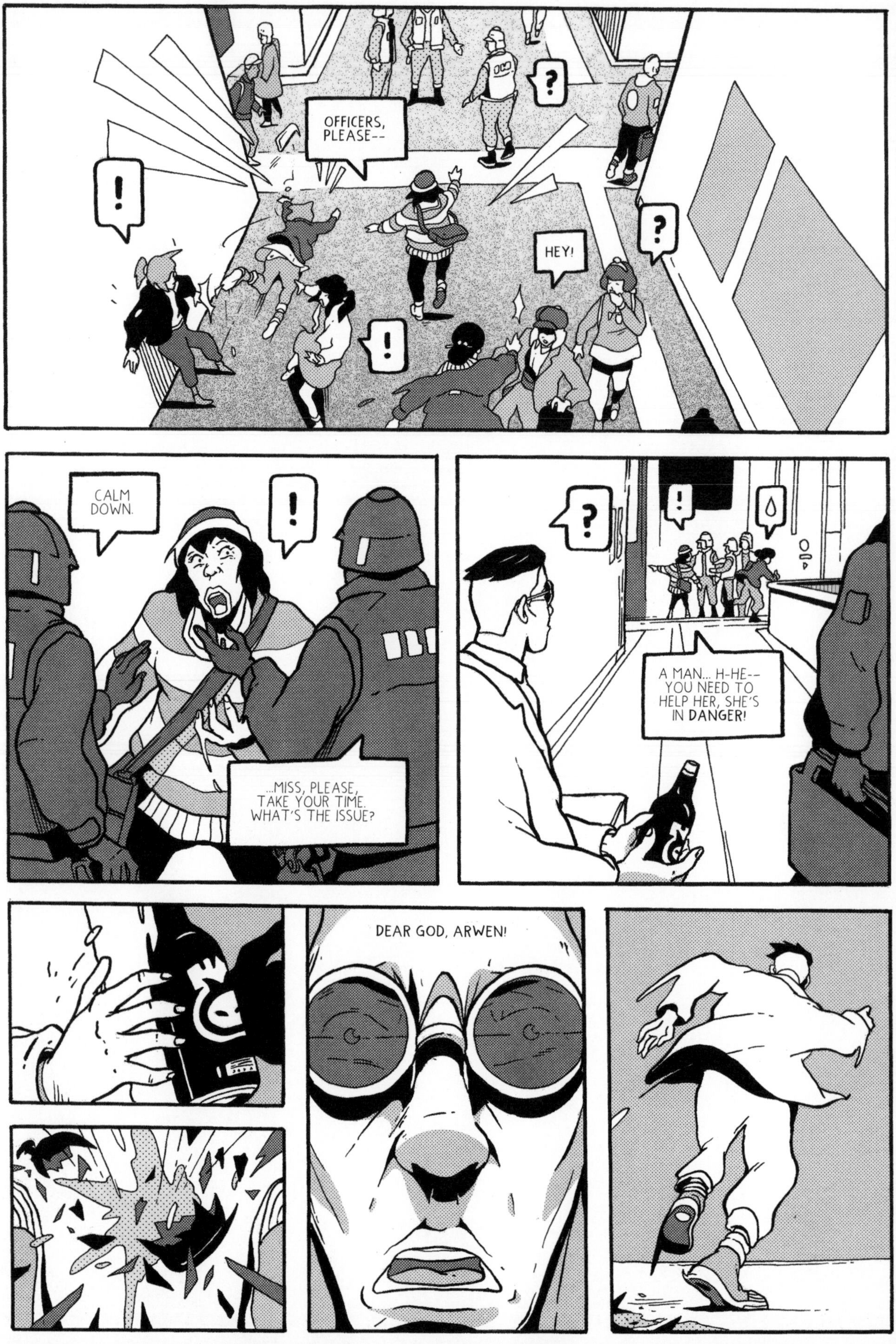

!
OFFICERS, PLEASE--
?
?
HEY!
!
CALM DOWN.
!
...MISS, PLEASE, TAKE YOUR TIME. WHAT'S THE ISSUE?
?
!
A MAN... H-HE-- YOU NEED TO HELP HER, SHE'S IN DANGER!
DEAR GOD, ARWEN!

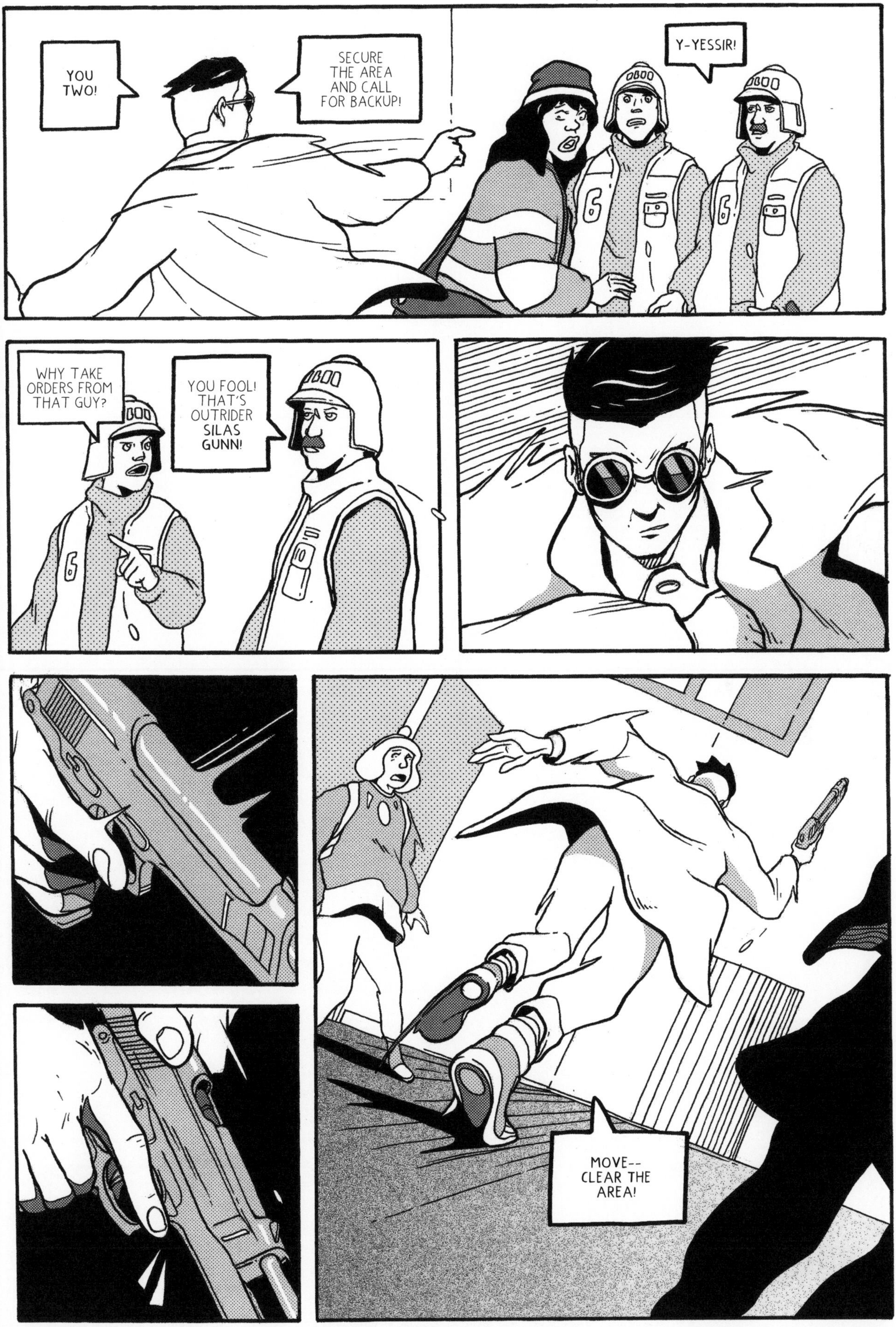
YOU TWO!
SECURE THE AREA AND CALL FOR BACKUP!
Y-YESSIR!
WHY TAKE ORDERS FROM THAT GUY?
YOU FOOL! THAT'S OUTRIDER **SILAS GUNN!**
MOVE-- CLEAR THE AREA!

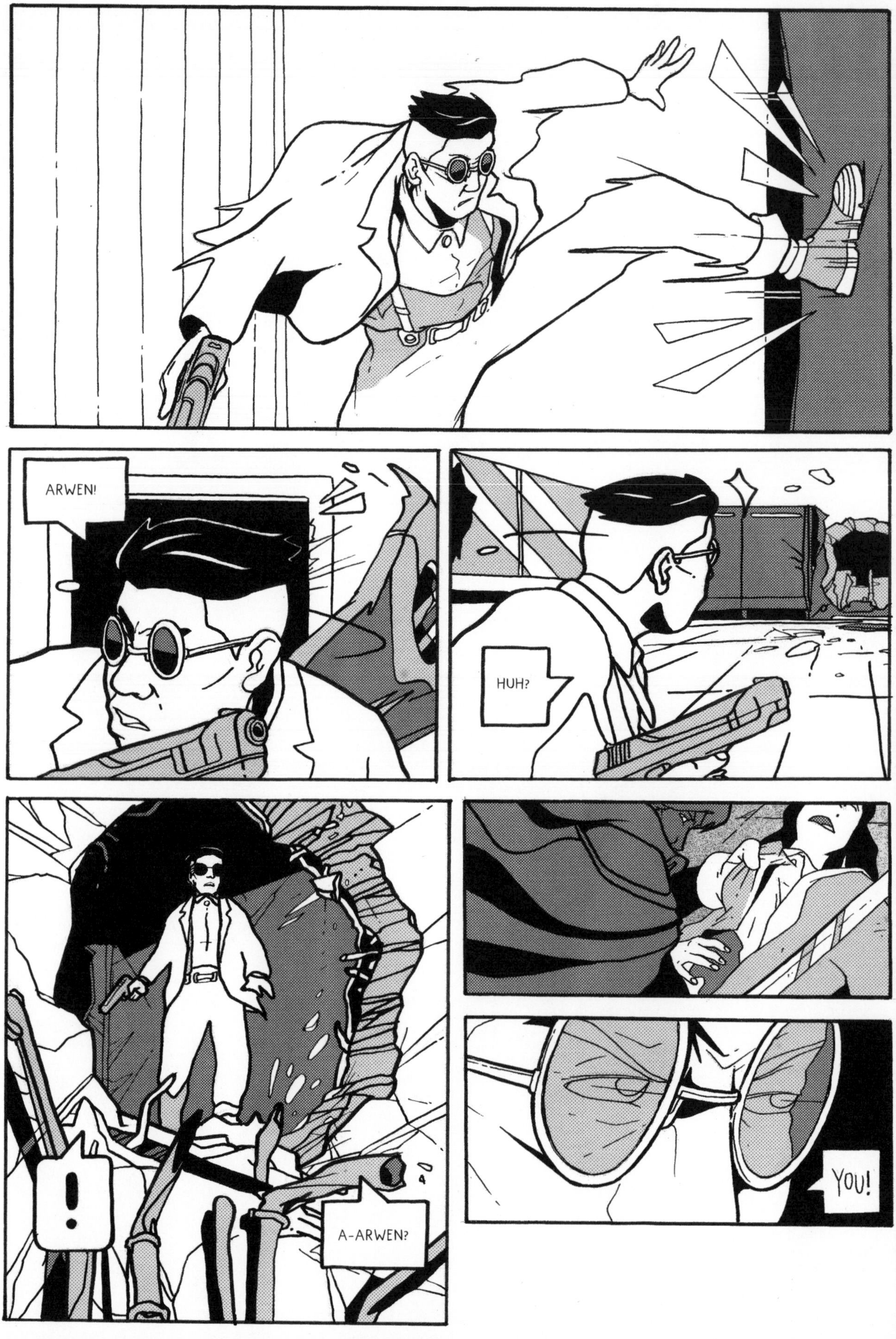
ARWEN!
HUH?
!
A-ARWEN?
YOU!

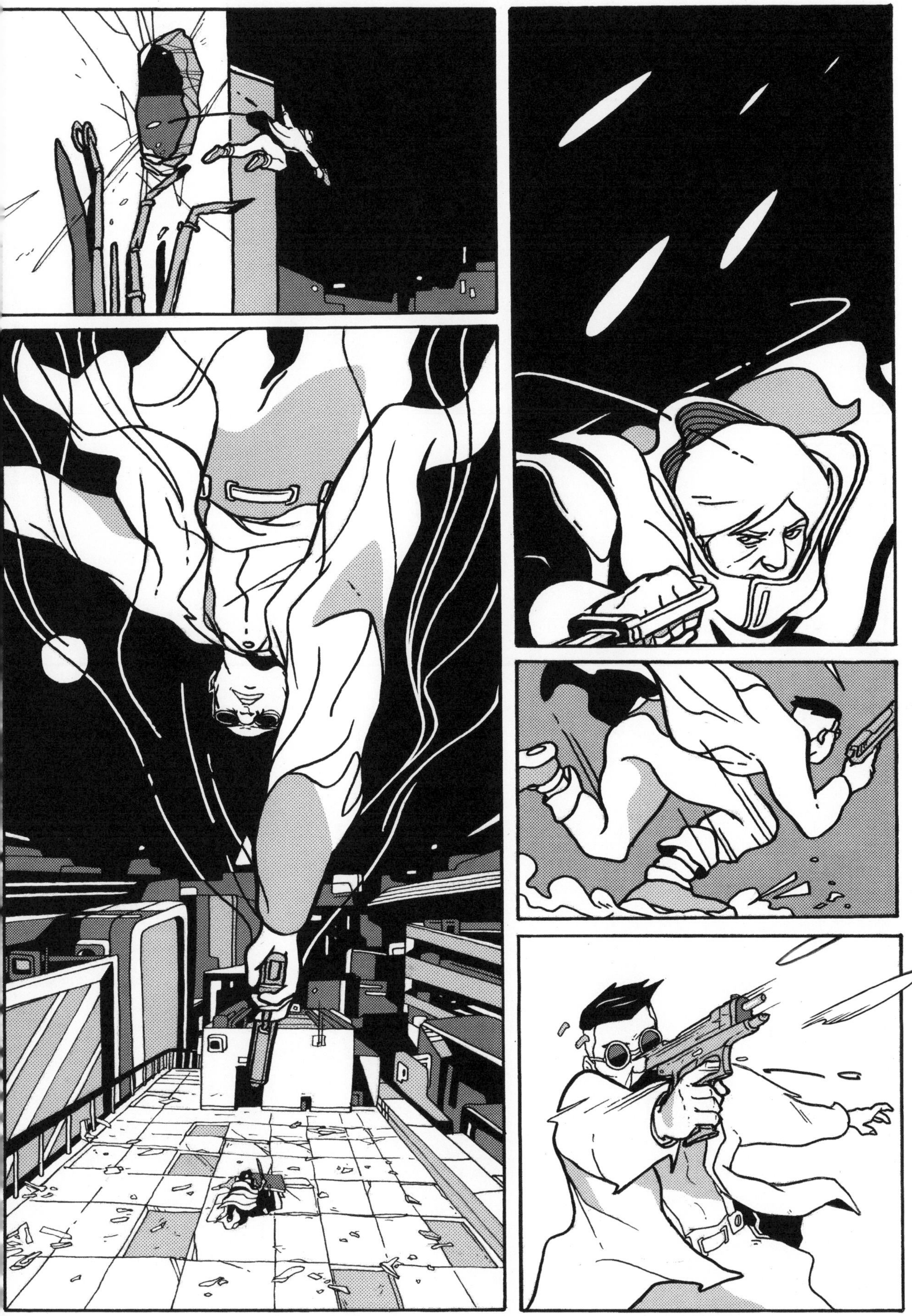

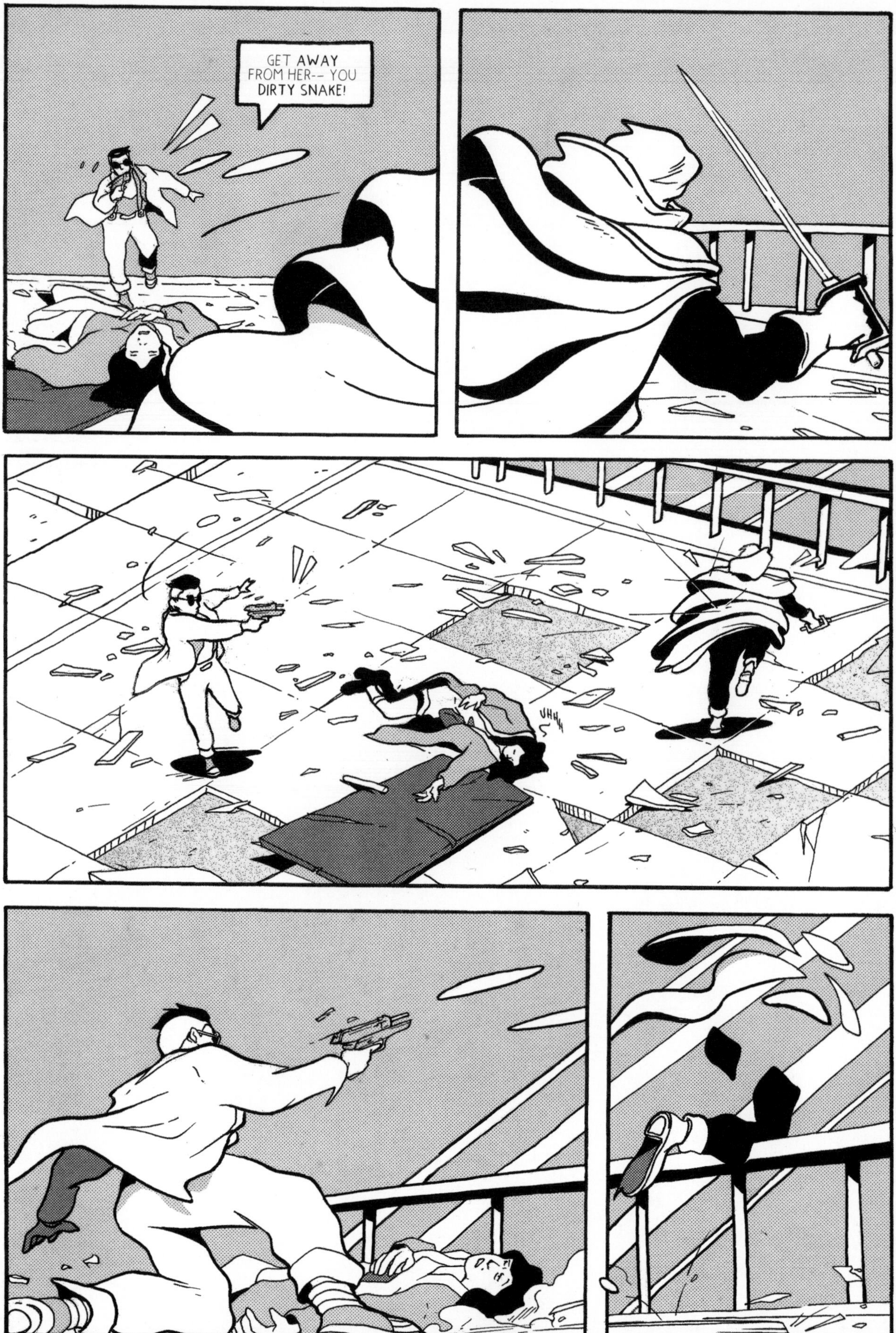
GET AWAY FROM HER-- YOU DIRTY SNAKE!
UHHH

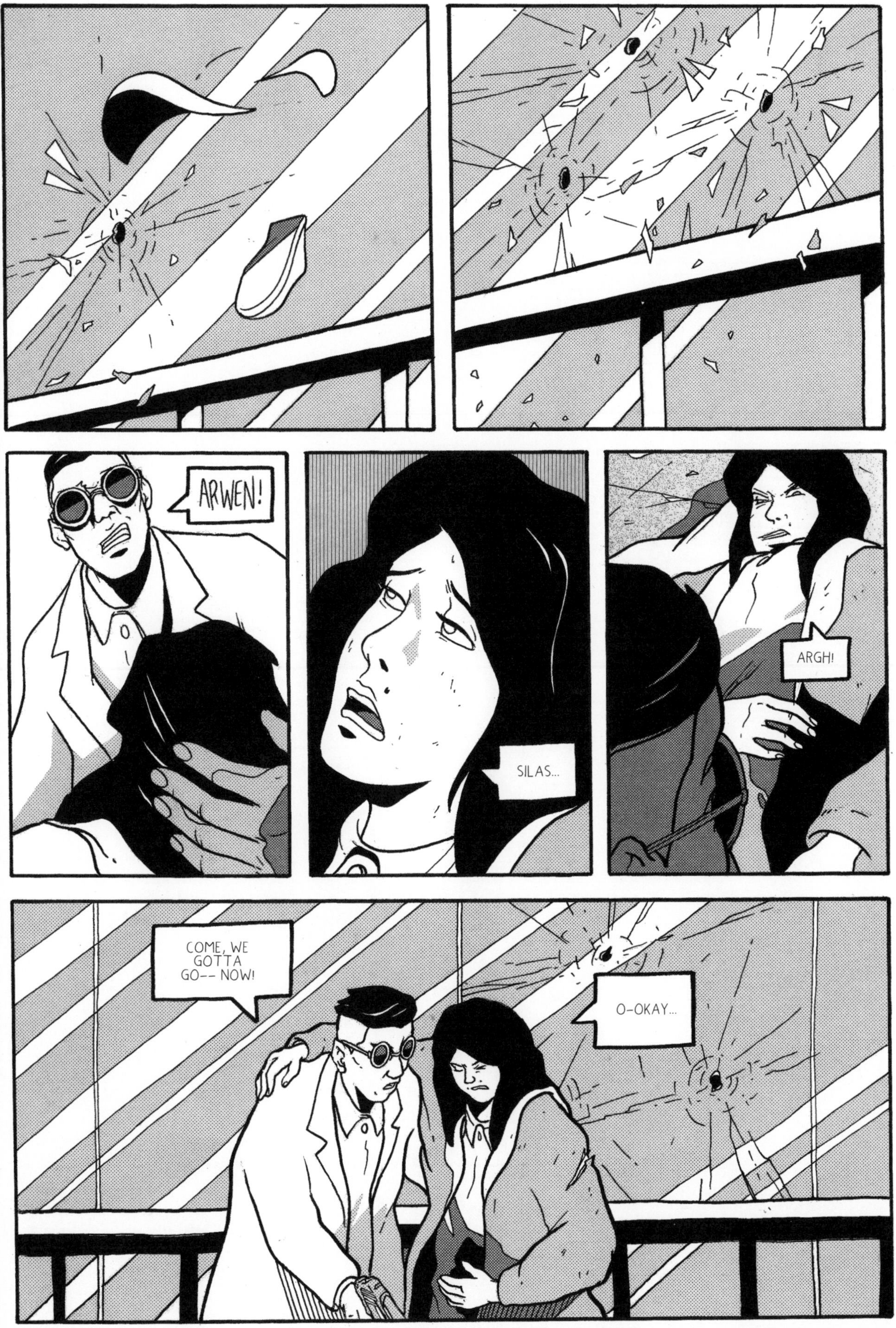
ARWEN!
SILAS...
ARGH!
COME, WE GOTTA GO-- NOW!
O-OKAY...

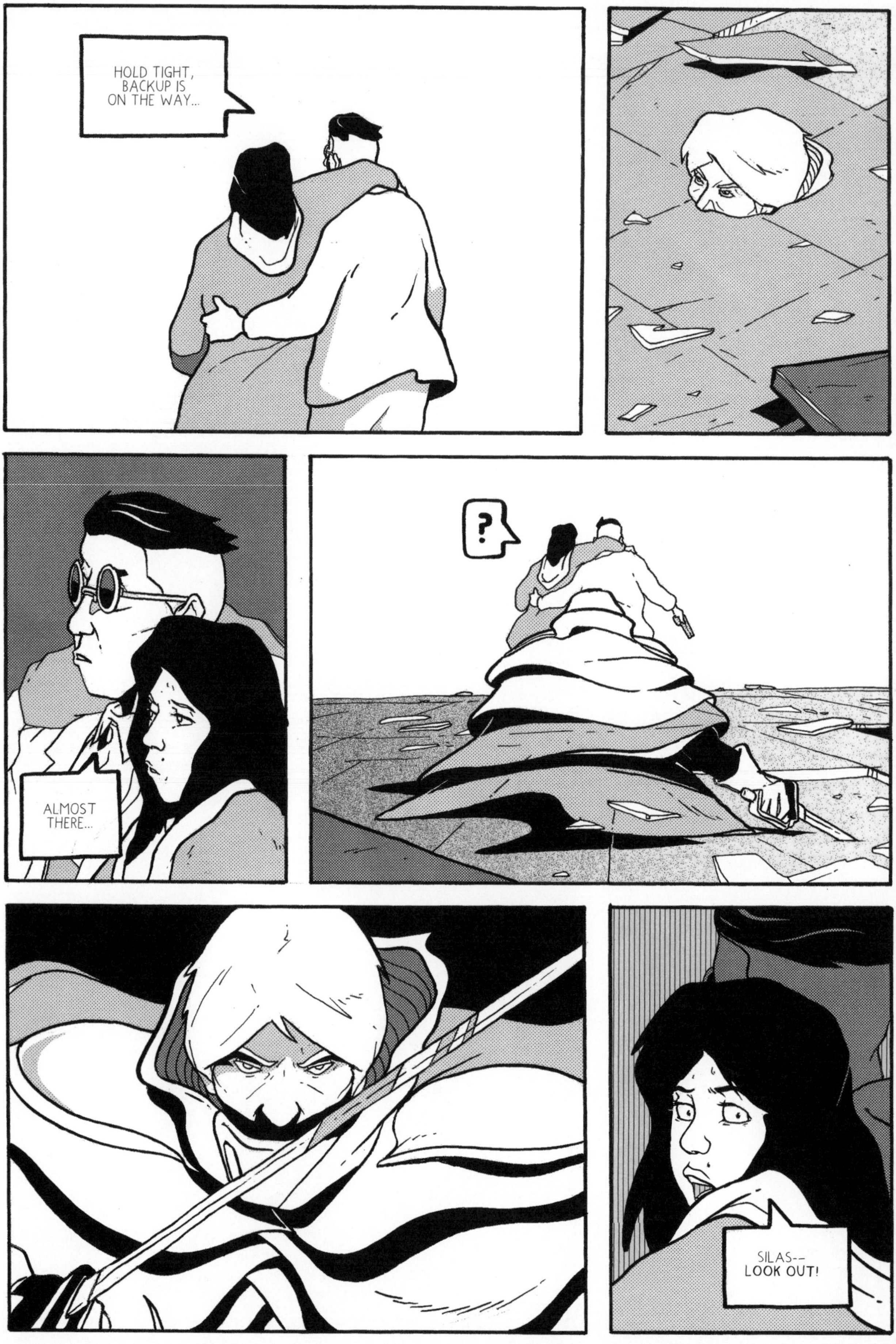
HOLD TIGHT, BACKUP IS ON THE WAY...
ALMOST THERE...
?
SILAS-- LOOK OUT!

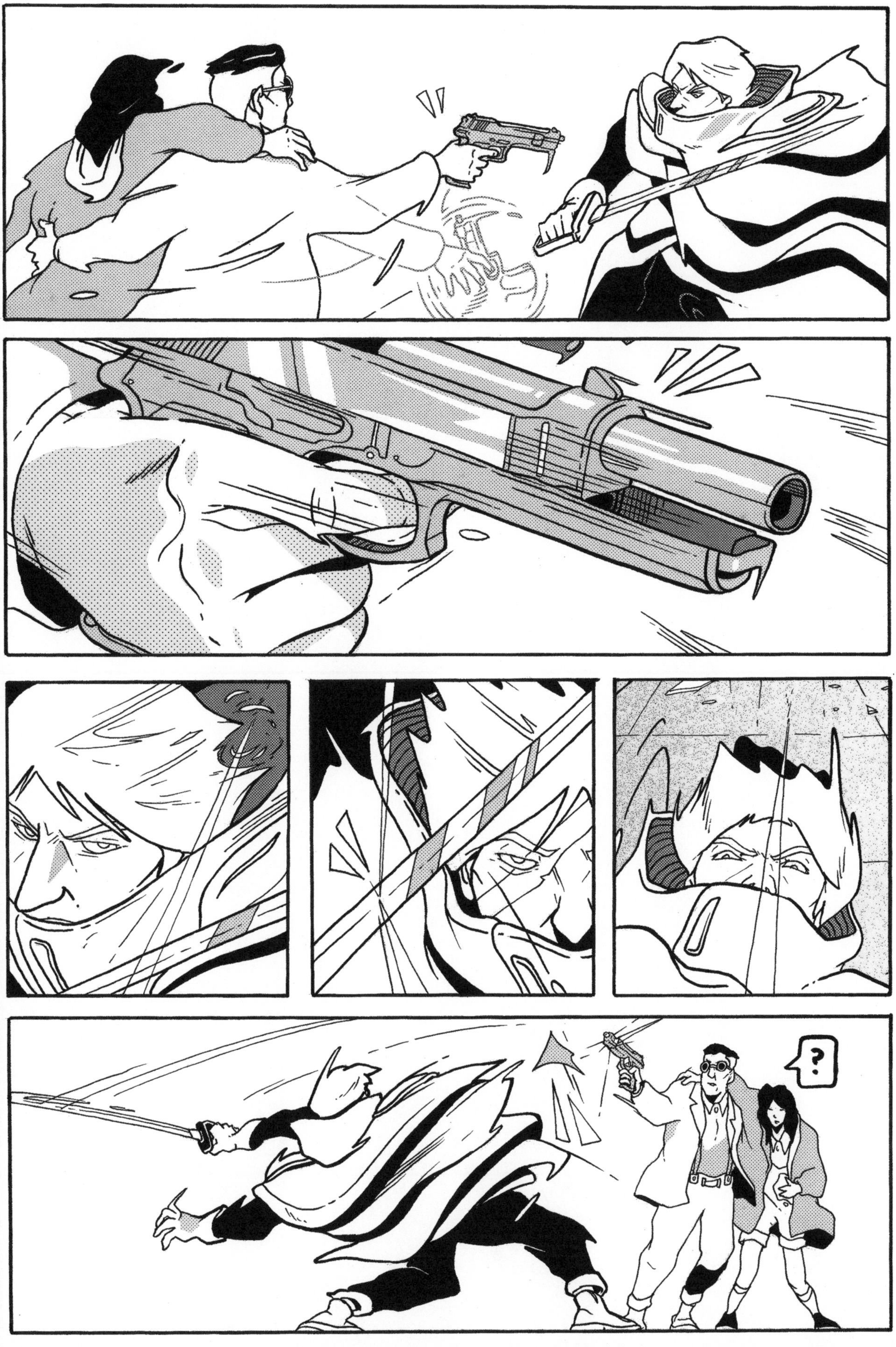
?

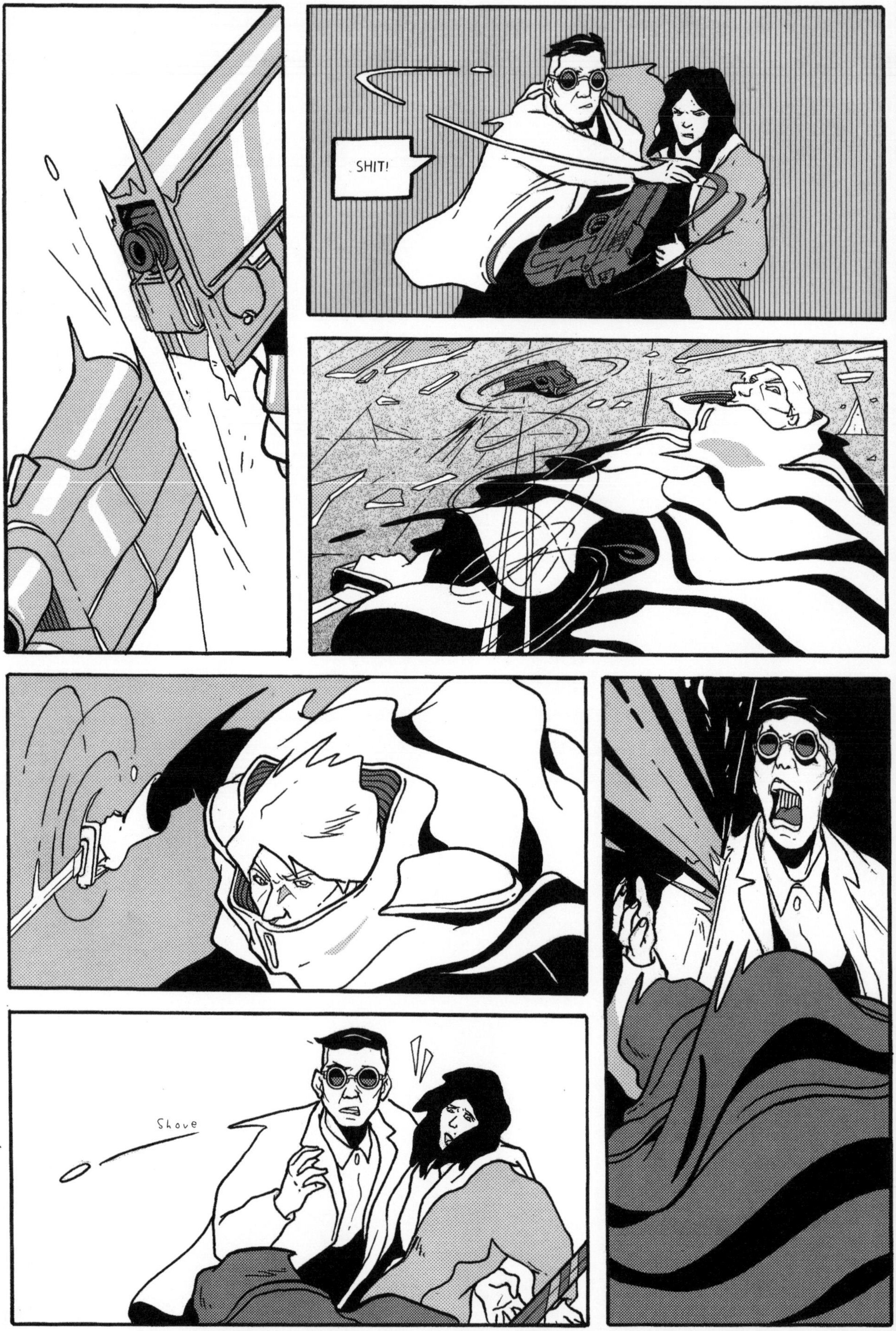
SHIT!
Shove

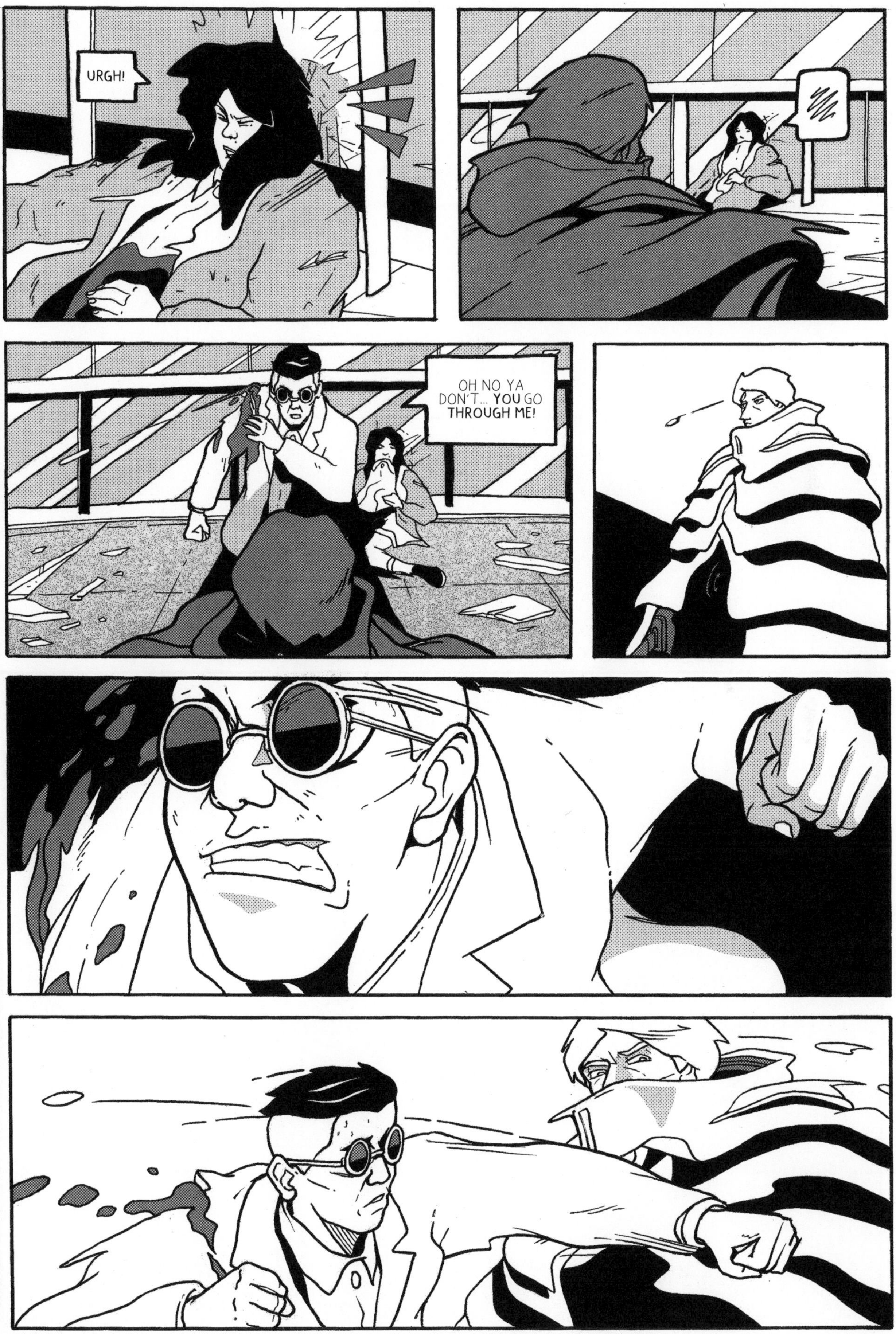
URGH!
OH NO YA DON'T... **YOU** GO **THROUGH ME!**

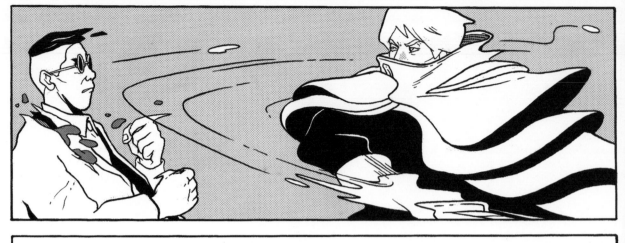

EH!

GRAH!

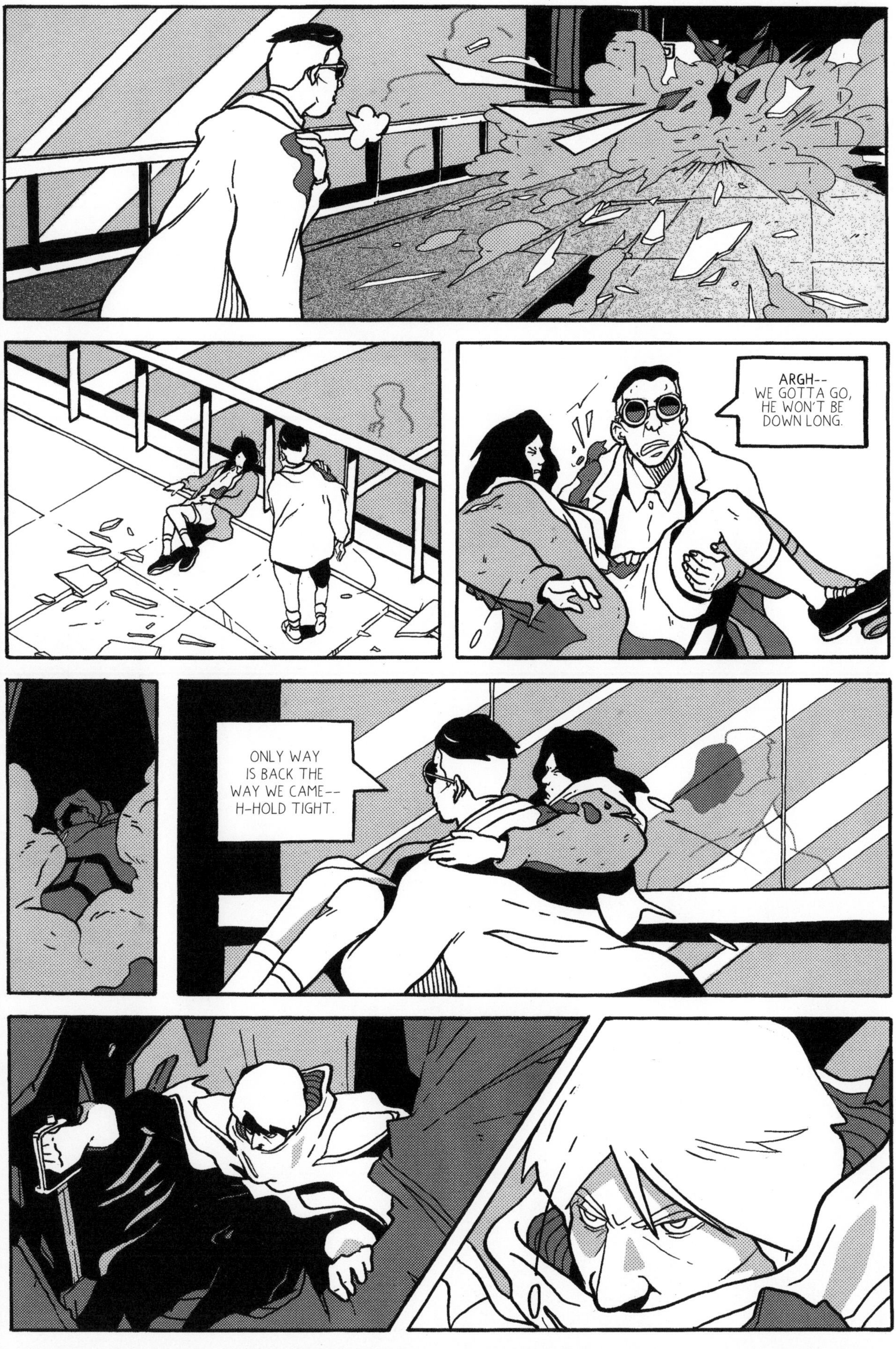
ARGH--
WE GOTTA GO, HE WON'T BE DOWN LONG.
ONLY WAY IS BACK THE WAY WE CAME-- H-HOLD TIGHT.

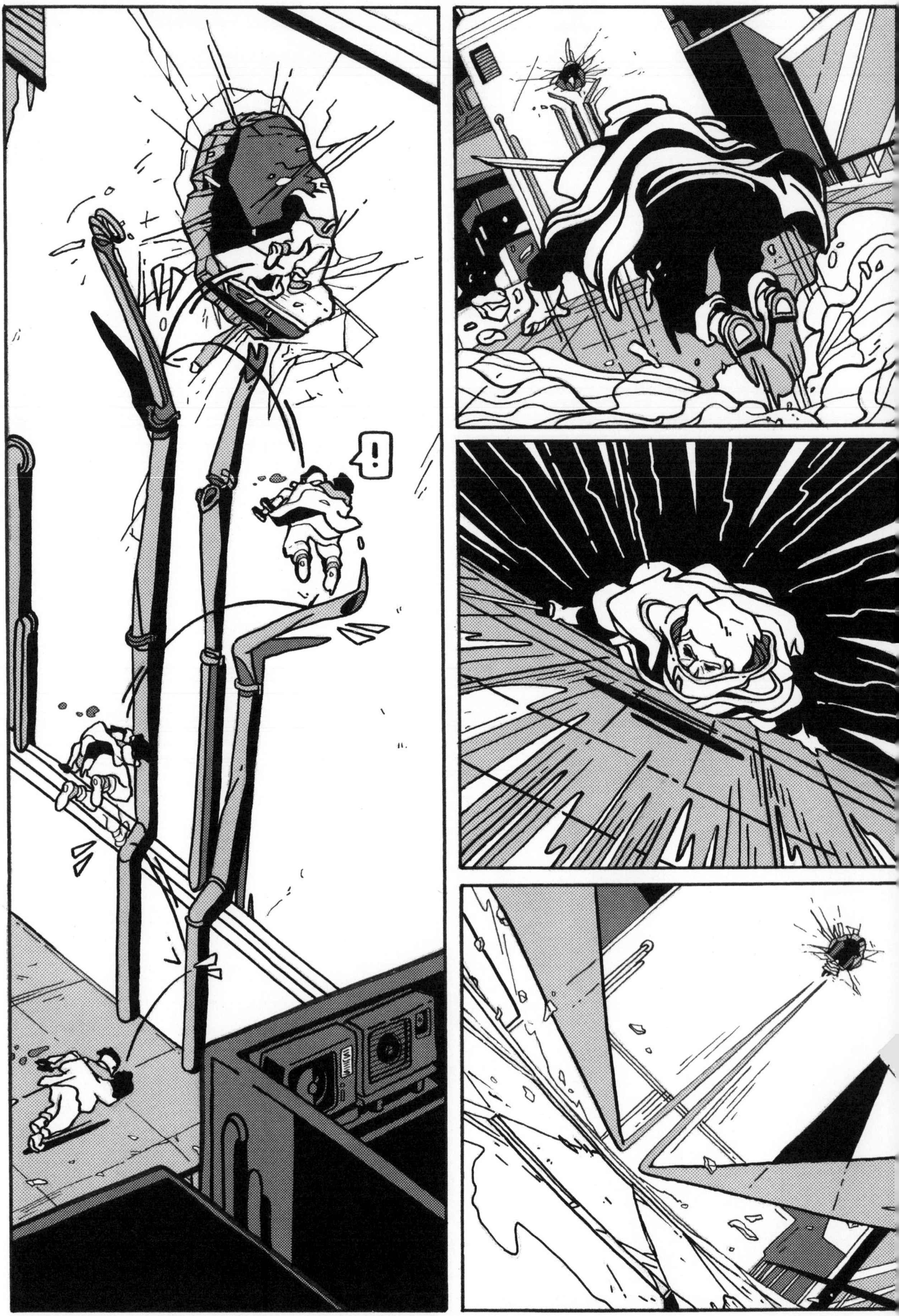
!

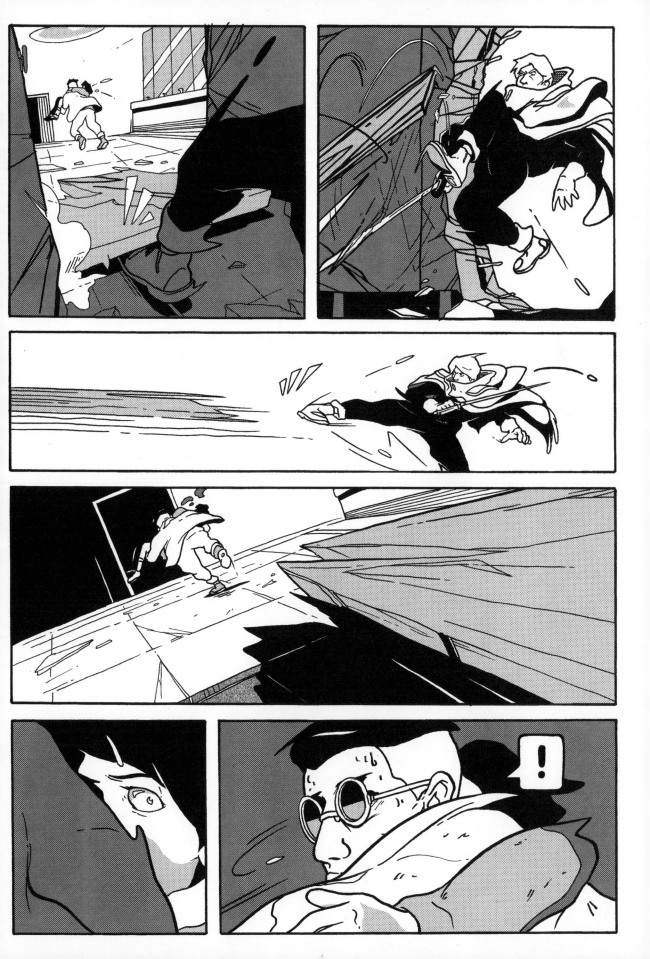

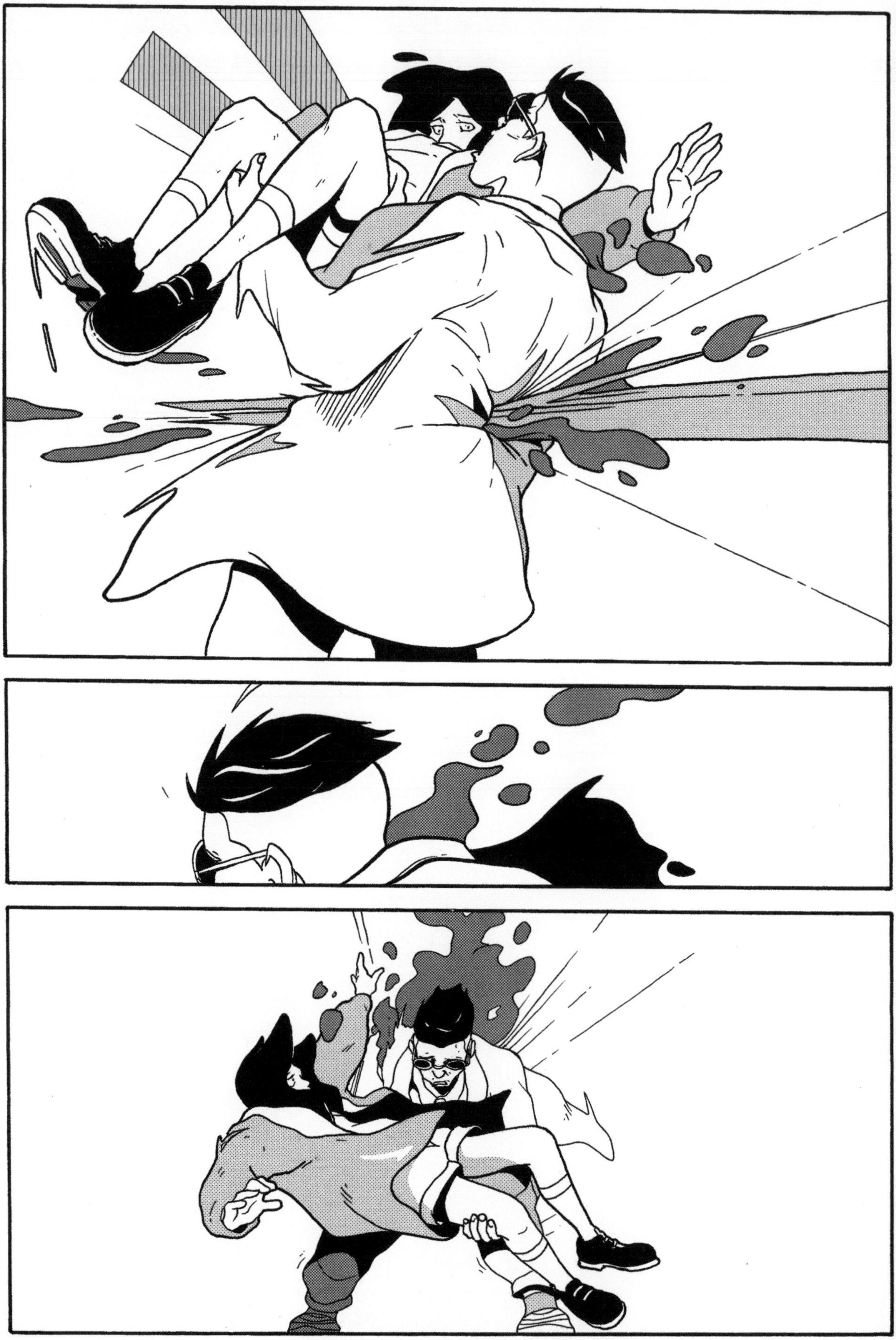

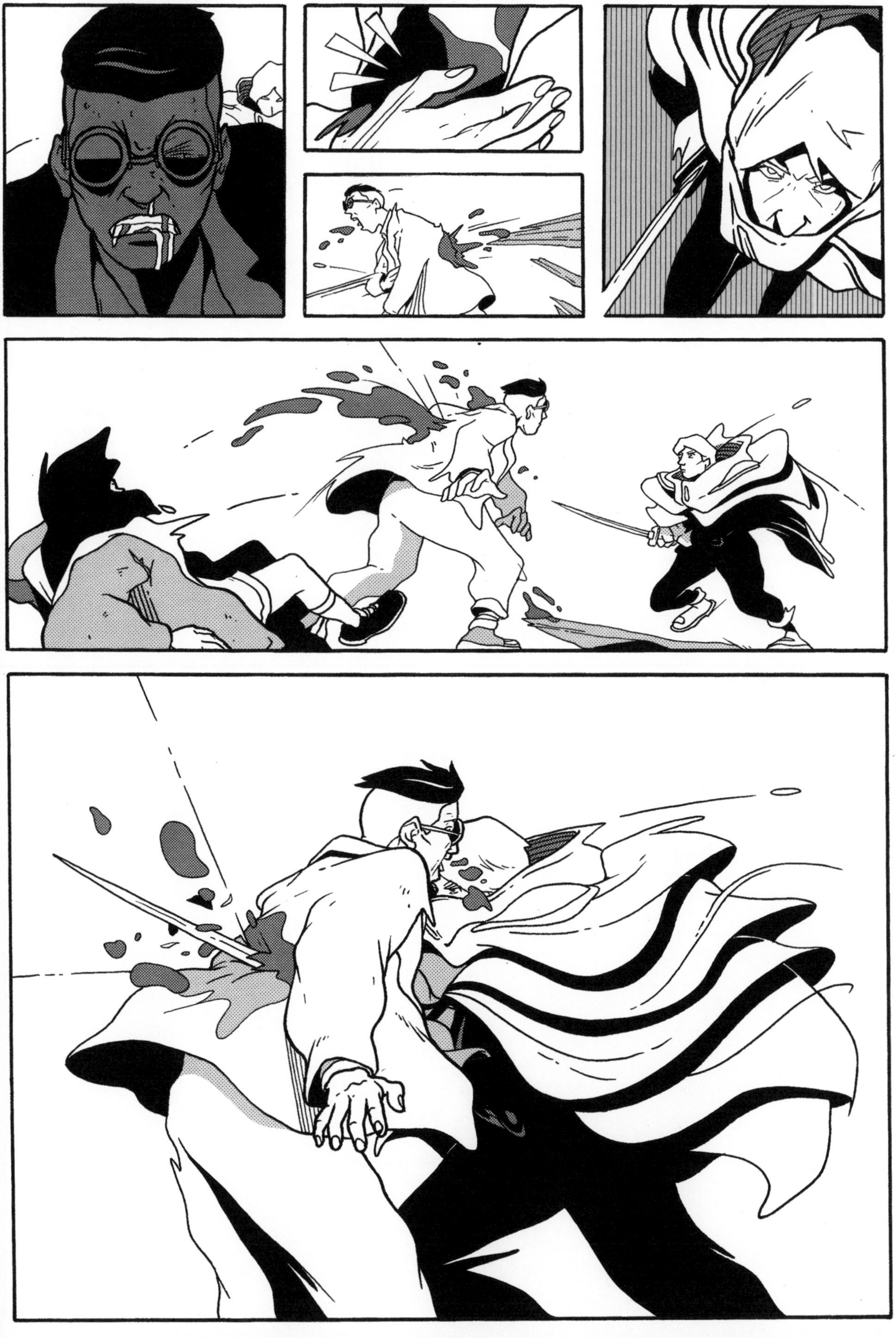

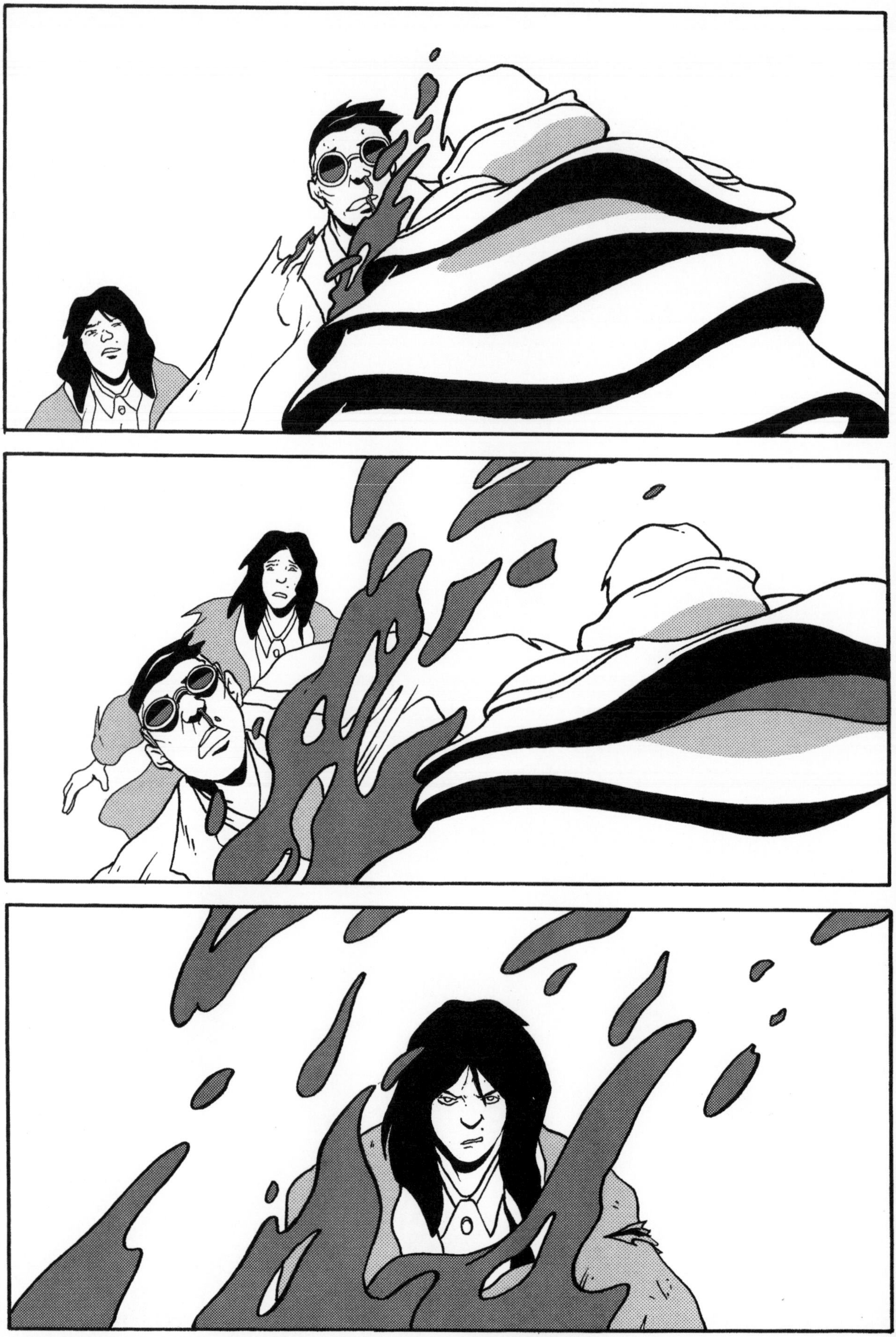

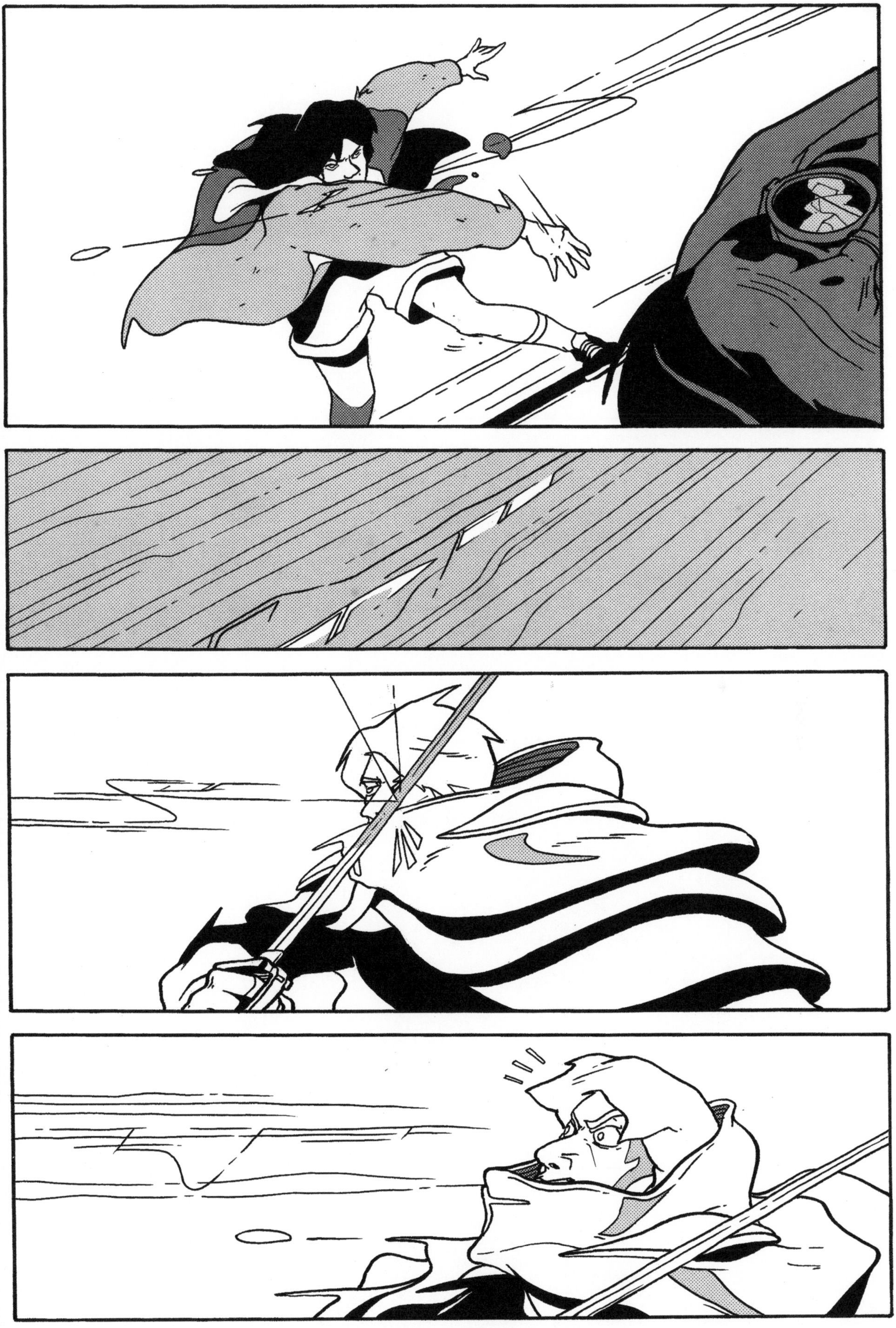

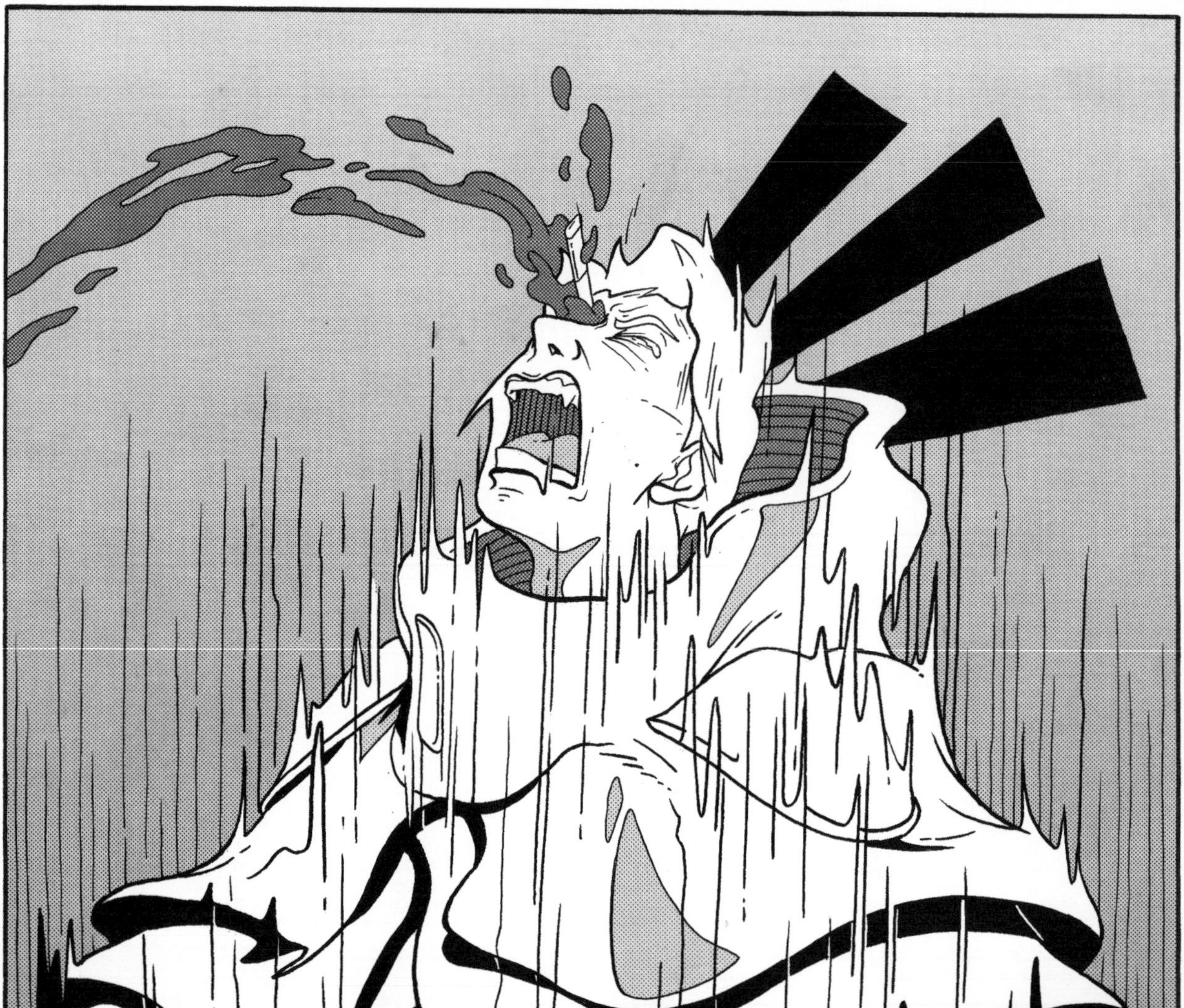
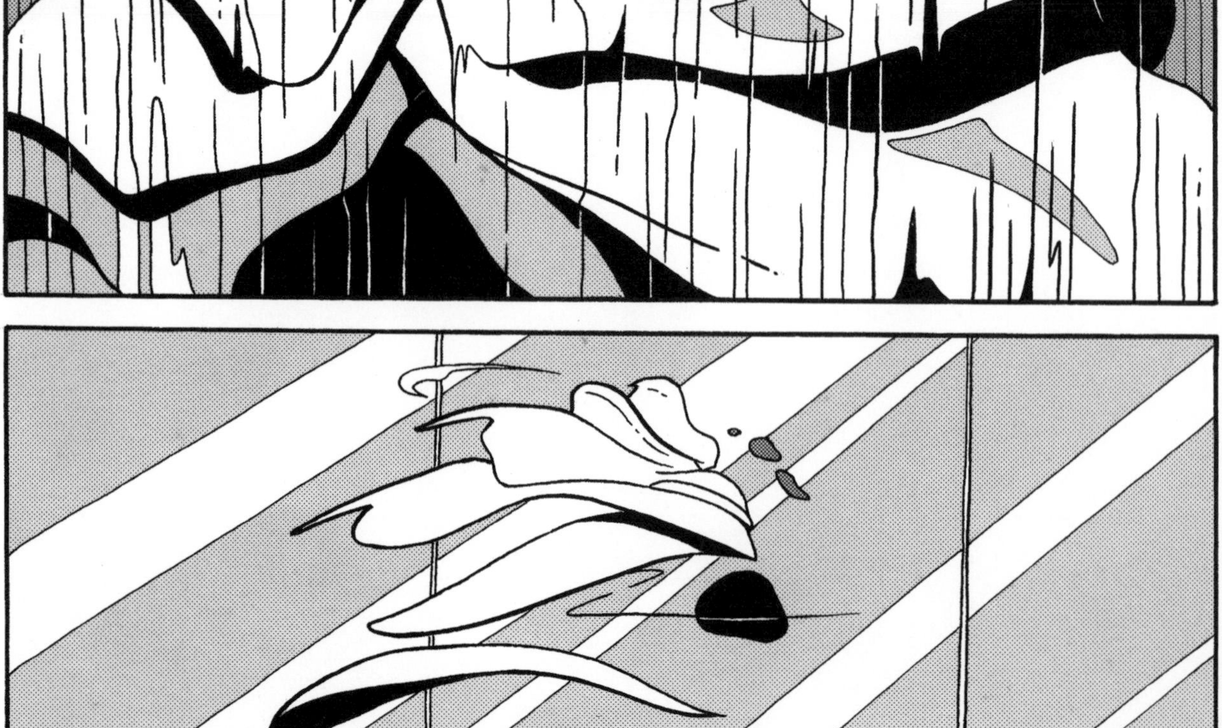

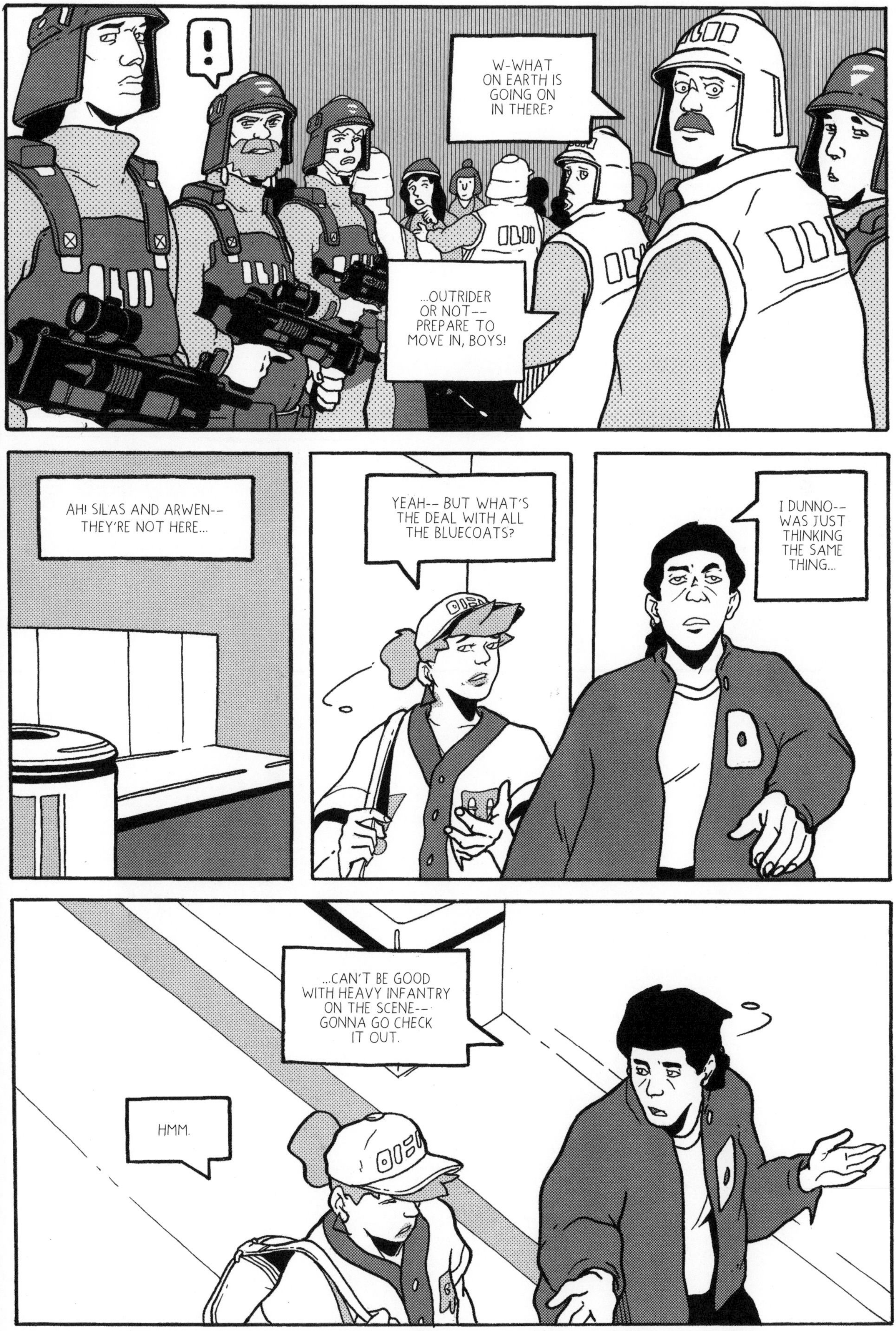
!
W-WHAT ON EARTH IS GOING ON IN THERE?
...OUTRIDER OR NOT-- PREPARE TO MOVE IN, BOYS!
AH! SILAS AND ARWEN-- THEY'RE NOT HERE...
YEAH-- BUT WHAT'S THE DEAL WITH ALL THE BLUECOATS?
I DUNNO-- WAS JUST THINKING THE SAME THING...
...CAN'T BE GOOD WITH HEAVY INFANTRY ON THE SCENE-- GONNA GO CHECK IT OUT.
HMM.

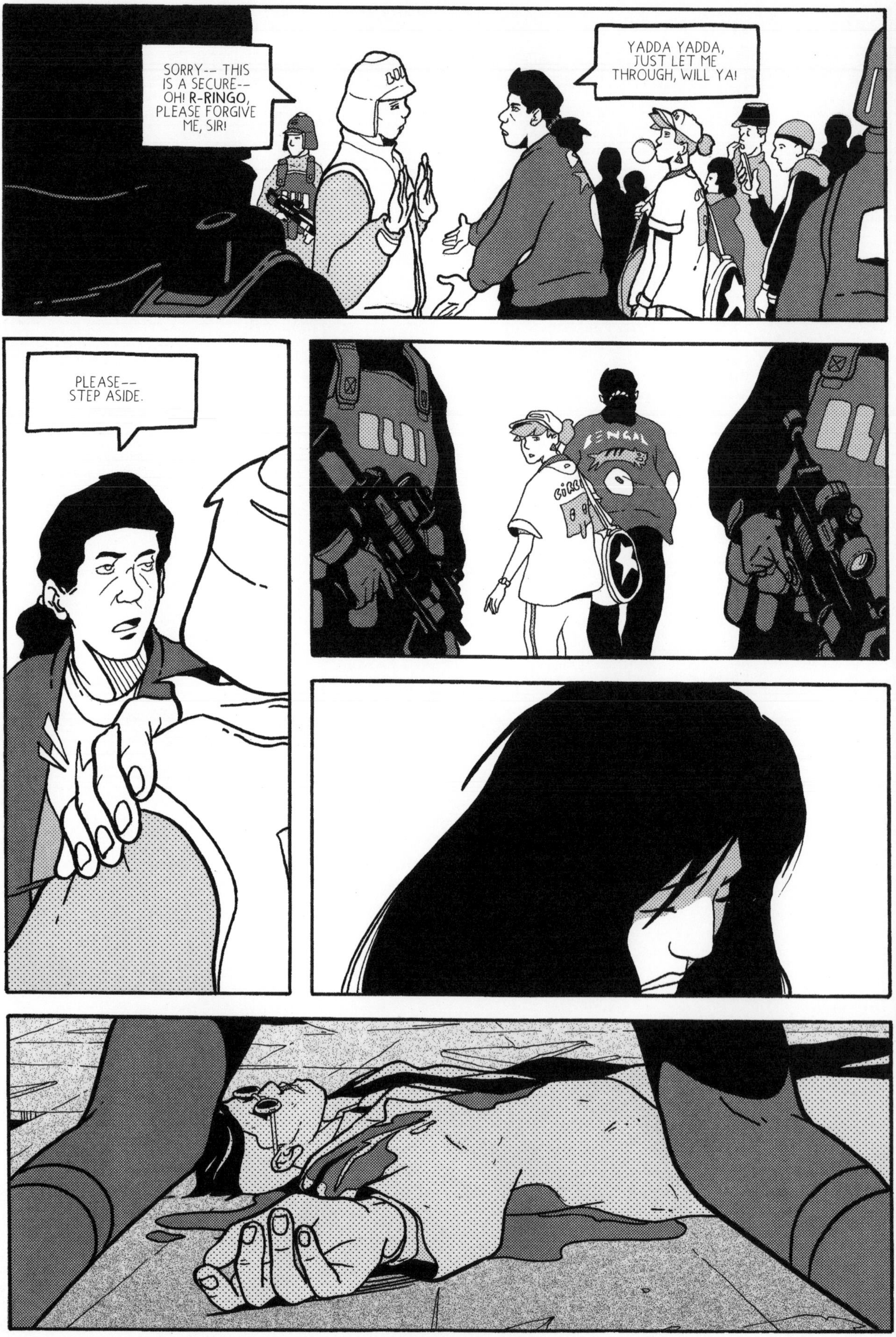
SORRY-- THIS IS A SECURE-- OH! R-RINGO, PLEASE FORGIVE ME, SIR!
YADDA YADDA, JUST LET ME THROUGH, WILL YA!
PLEASE-- STEP ASIDE.

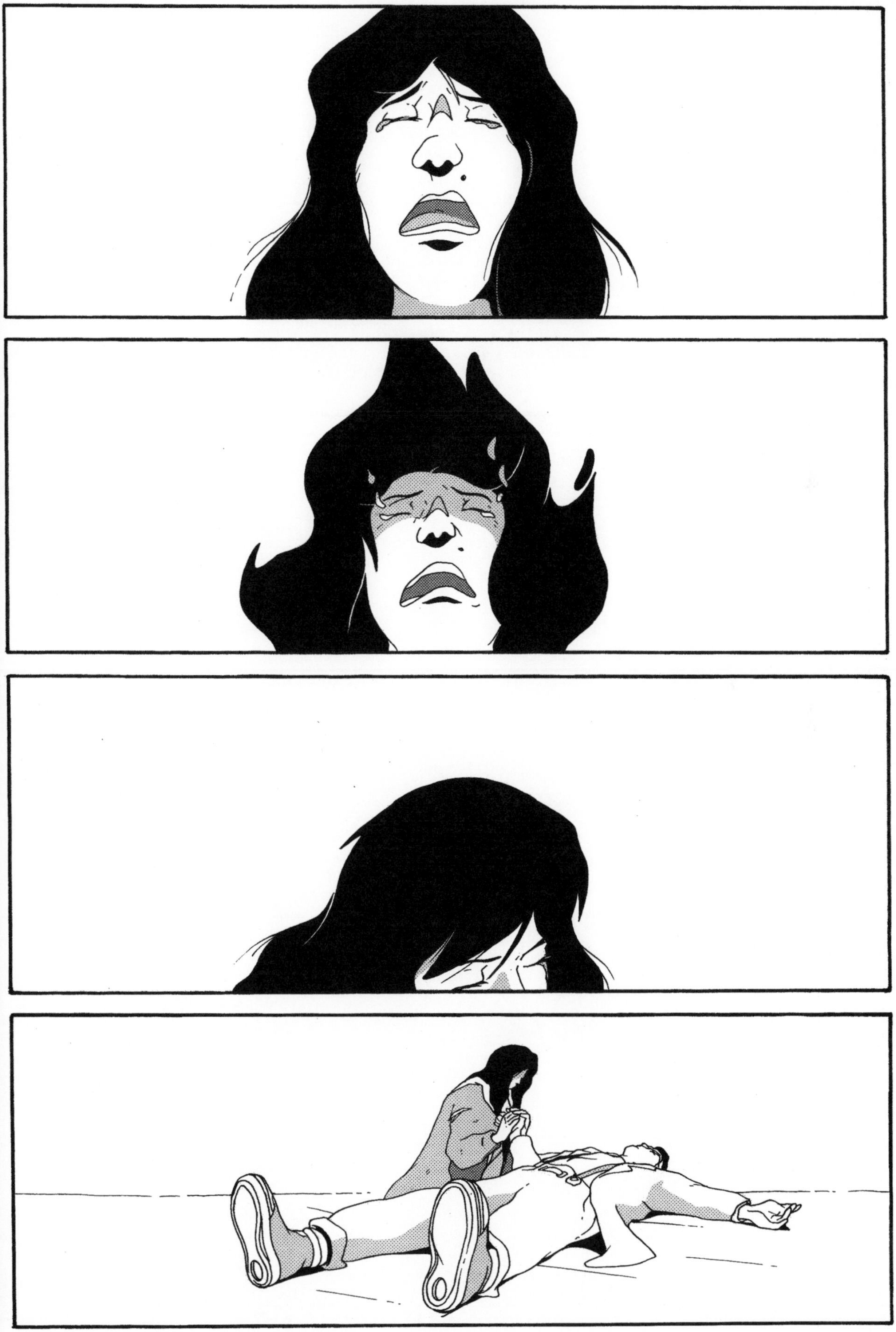

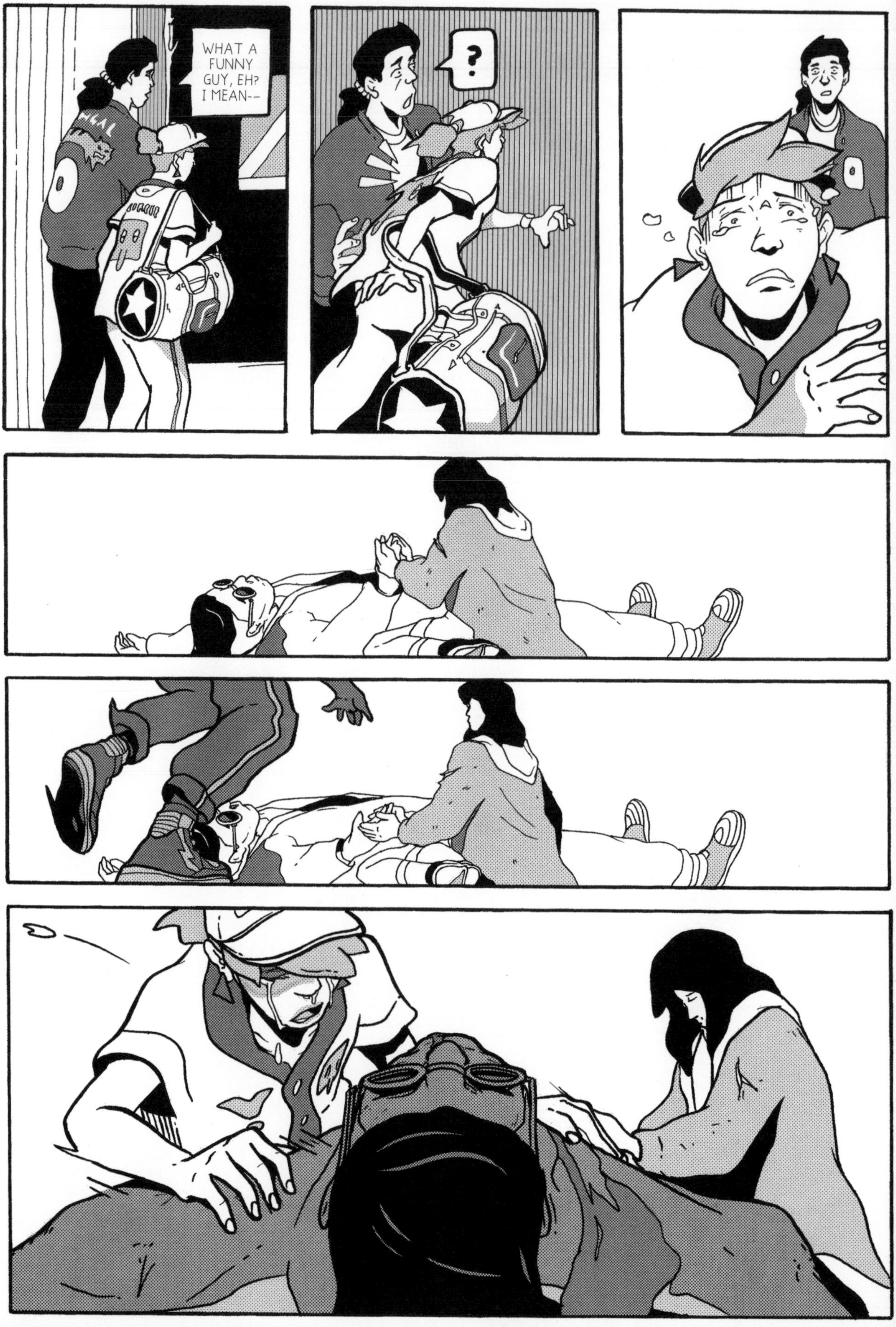
WHAT A FUNNY GUY, EH? I MEAN--
?

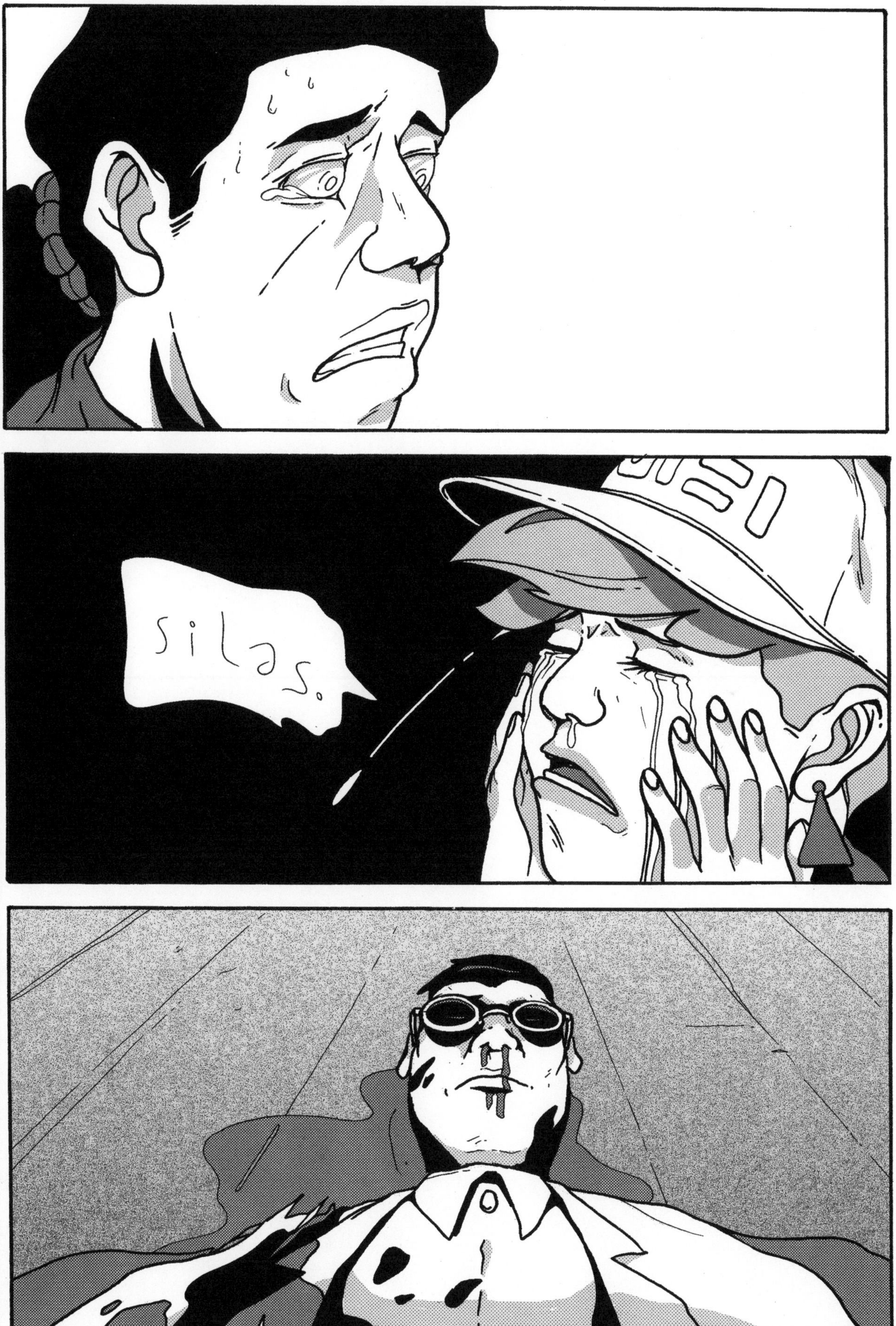
silas.

AMBULANCE

6

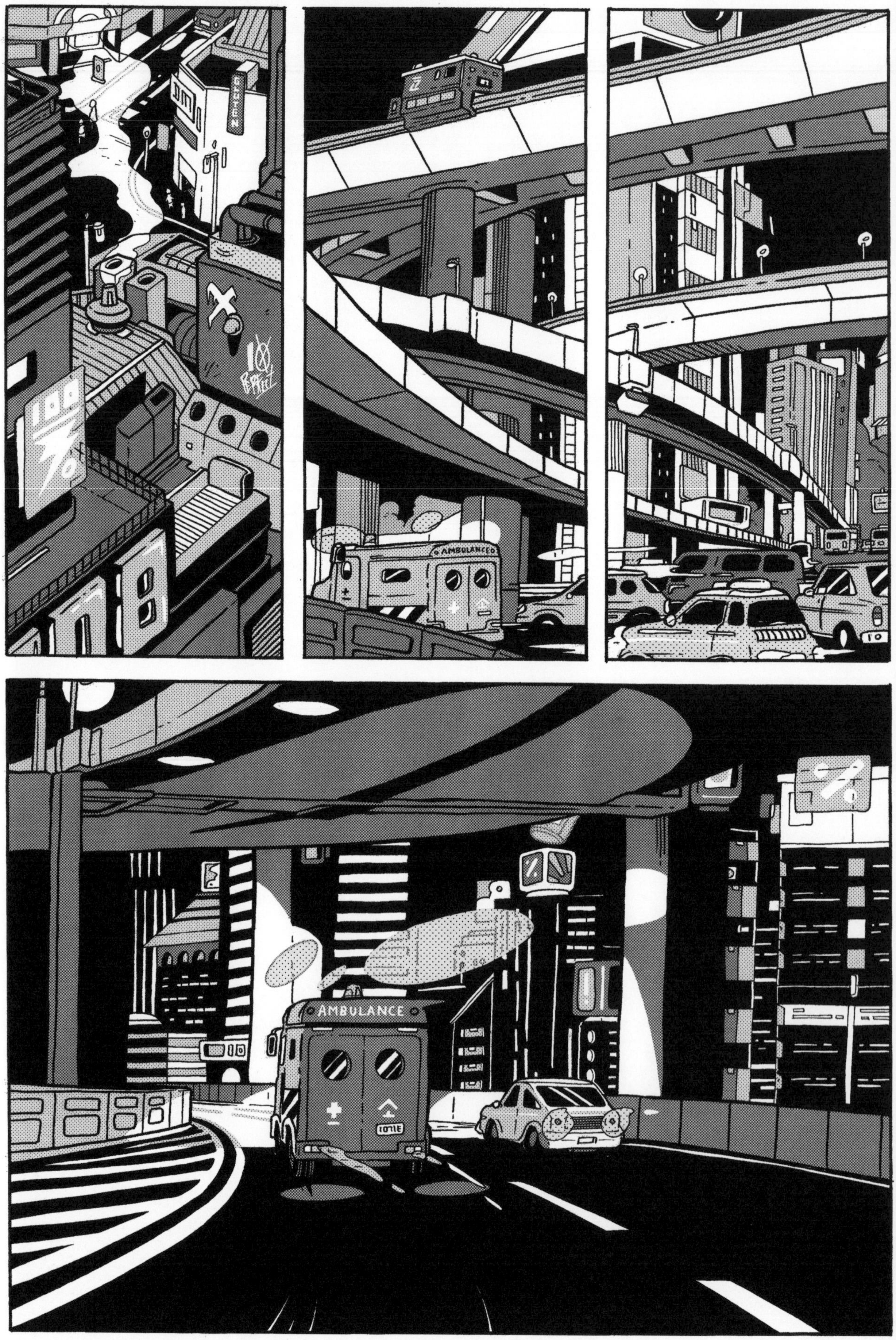
AMBULANCE
AMBULANCE

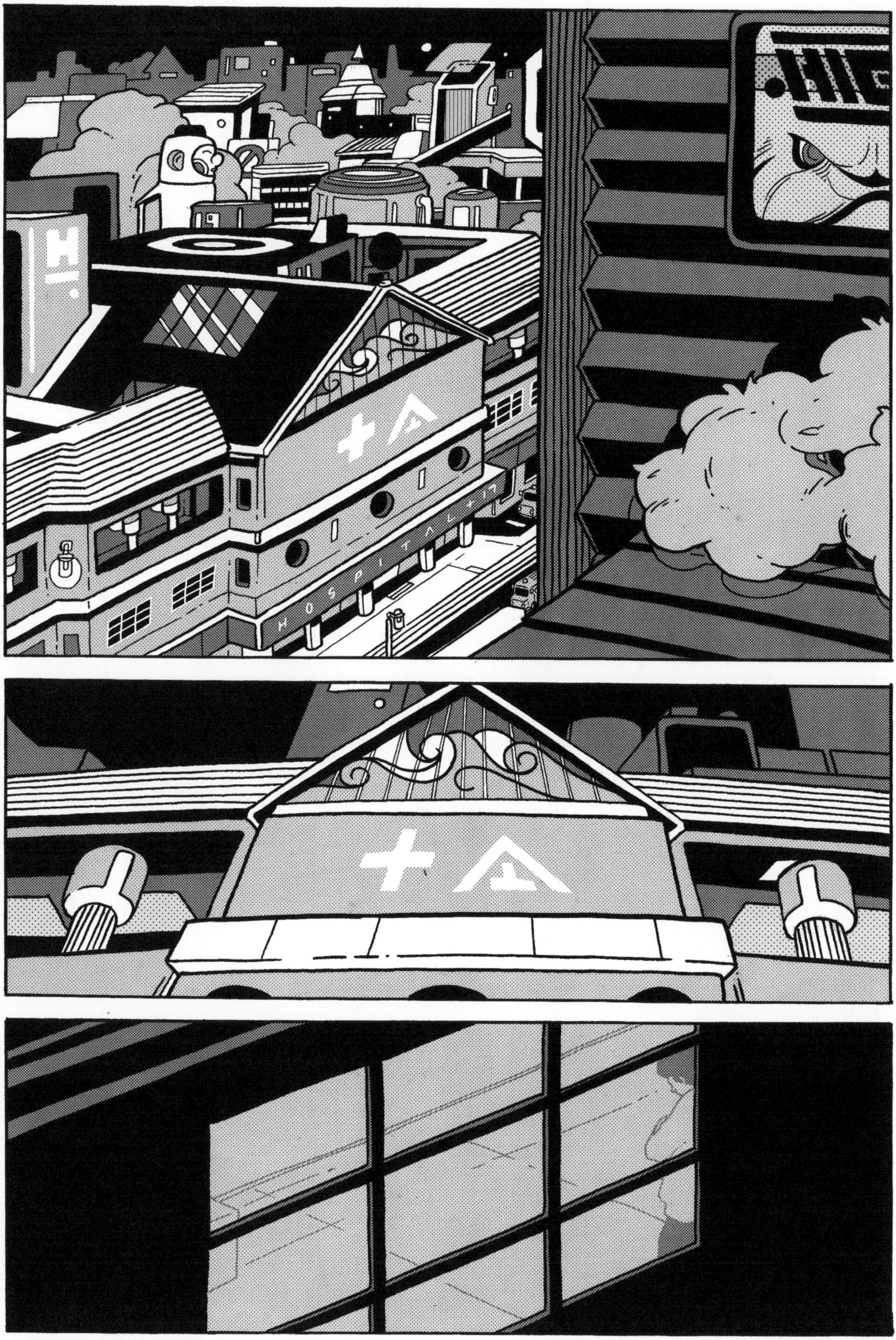

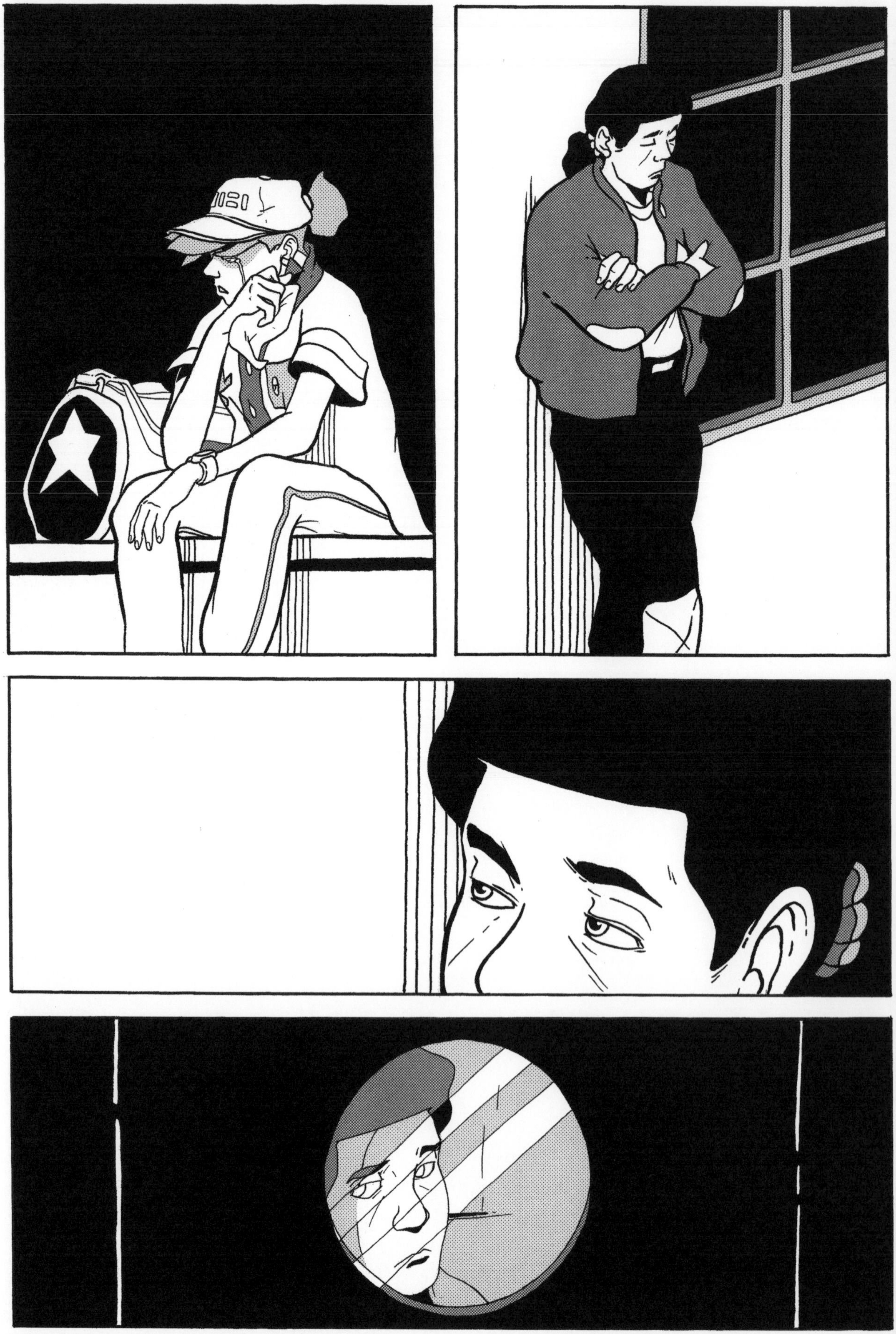

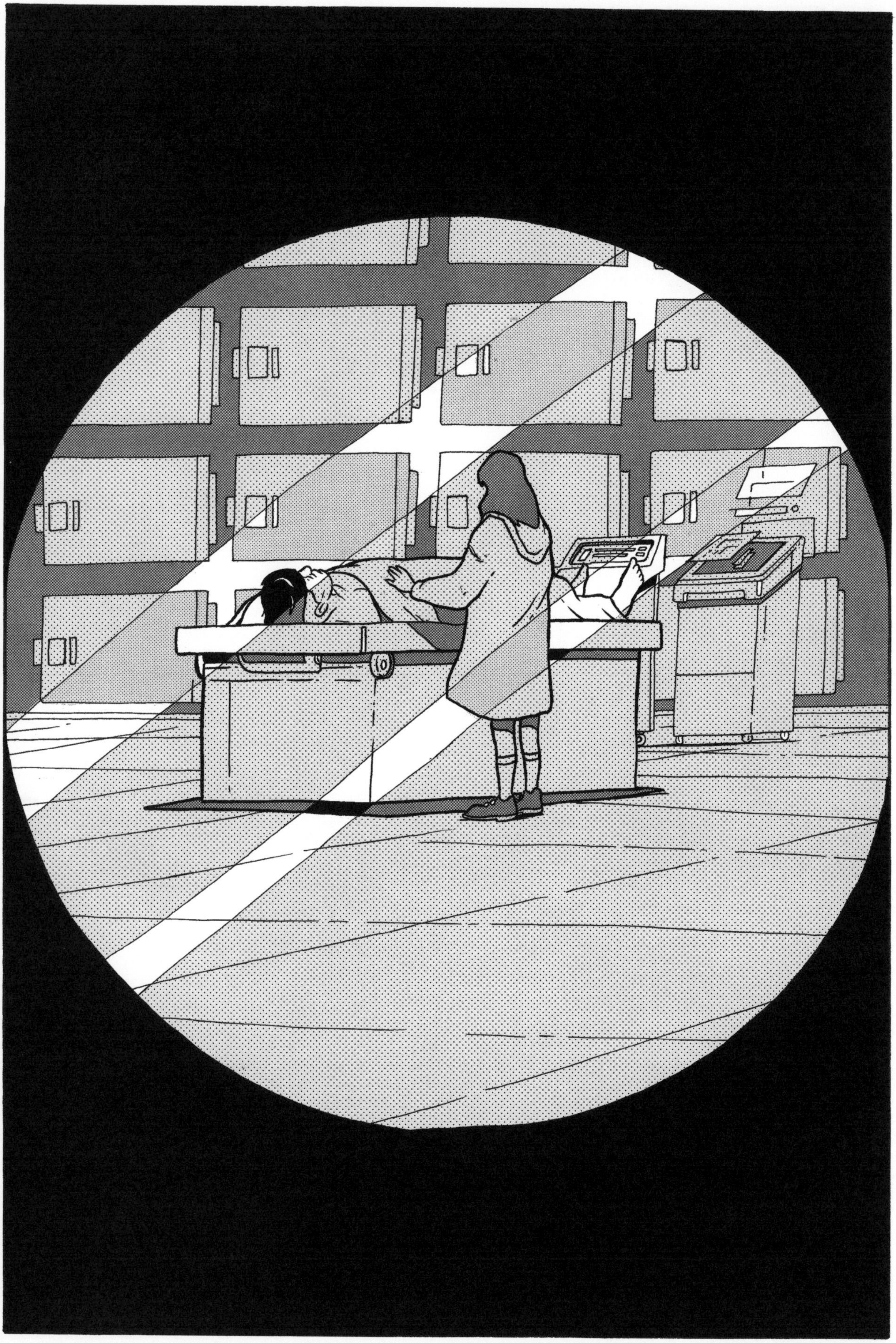

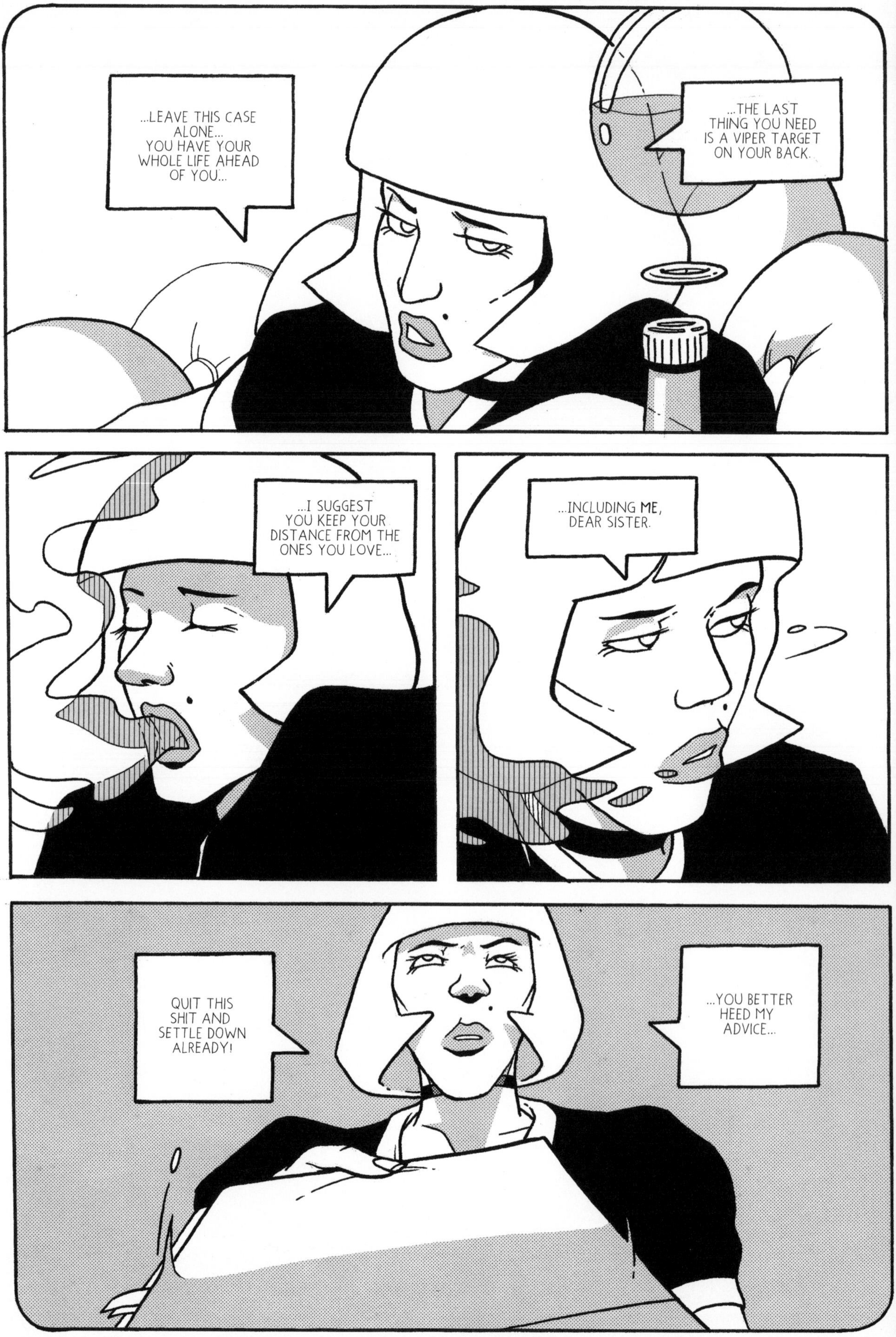
...LEAVE THIS CASE ALONE... YOU HAVE YOUR WHOLE LIFE AHEAD OF YOU...
...THE LAST THING YOU NEED IS A VIPER TARGET ON YOUR BACK.
...I SUGGEST YOU KEEP YOUR DISTANCE FROM THE ONES YOU LOVE...
...INCLUDING ME, DEAR SISTER.
QUIT THIS SHIT AND SETTLE DOWN ALREADY!
...YOU BETTER HEED MY ADVICE...

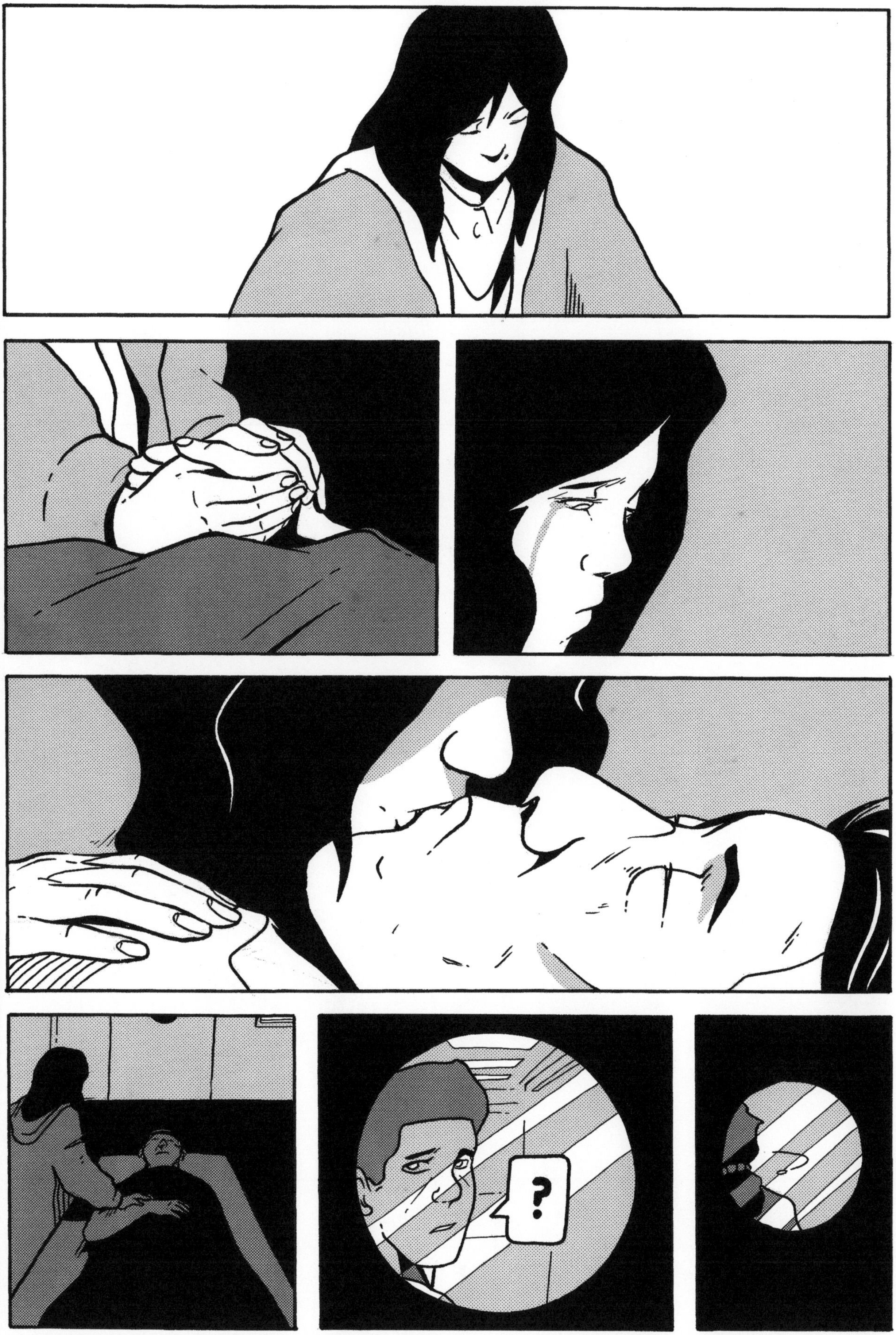
?

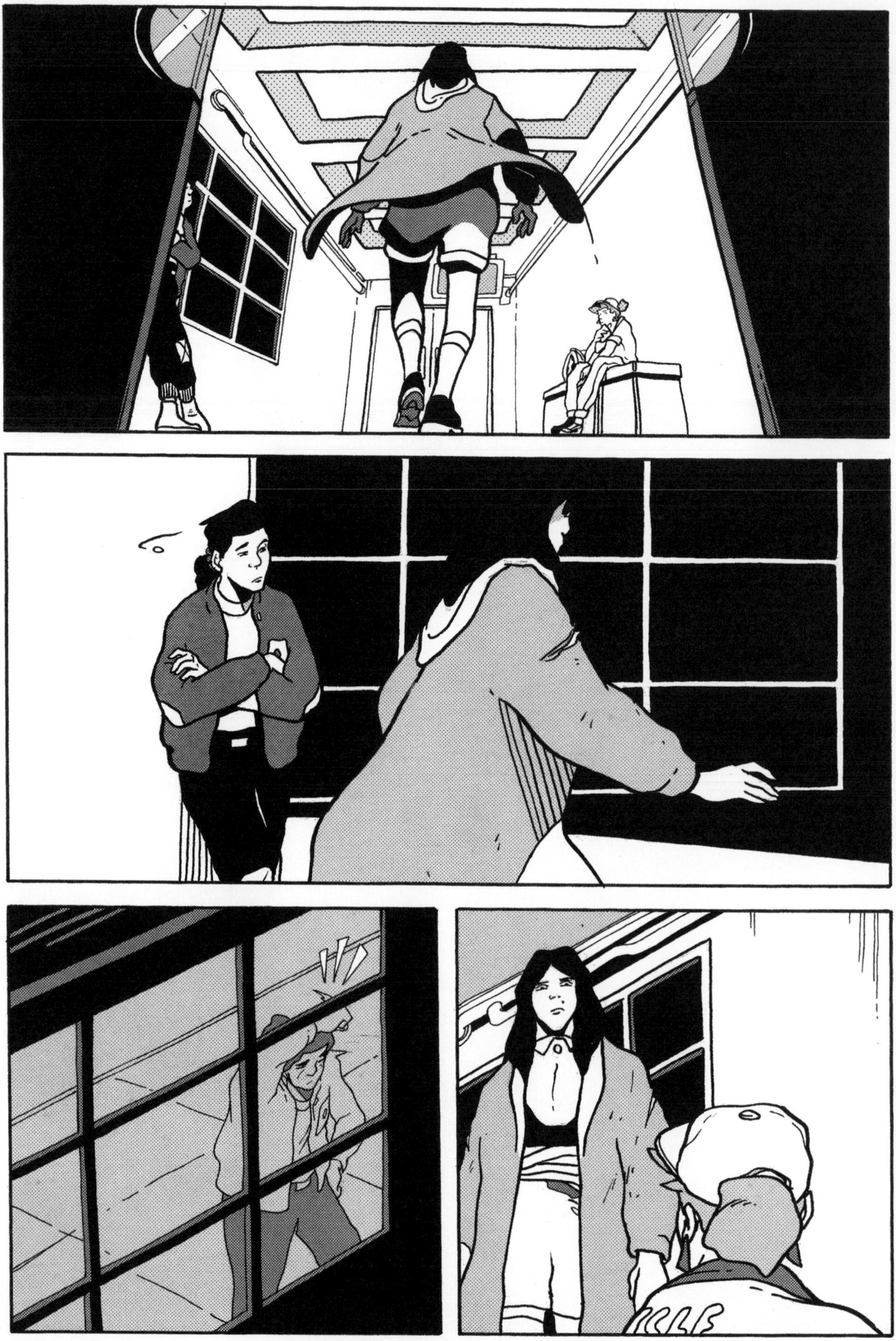

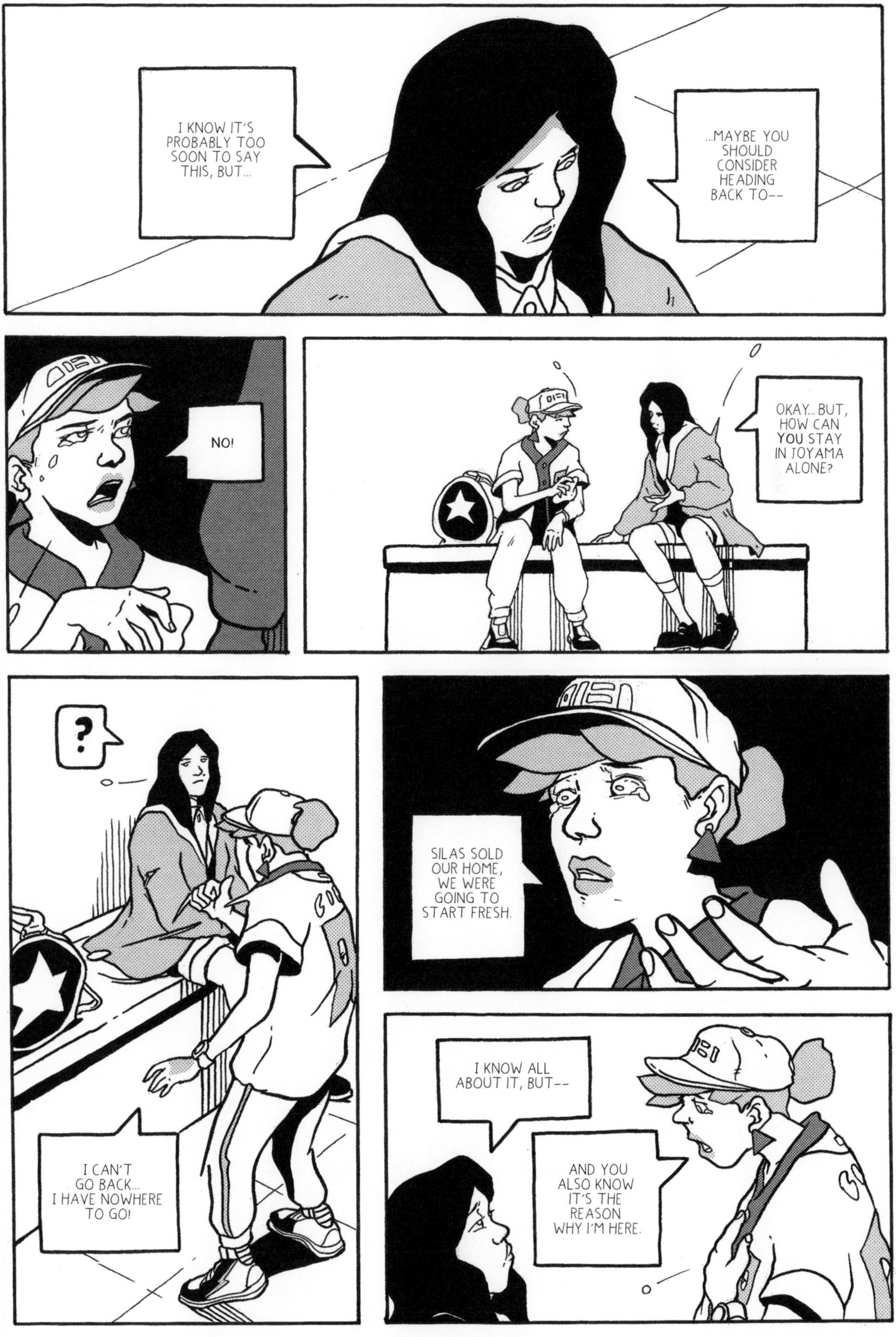
I KNOW IT'S PROBABLY TOO SOON TO SAY THIS, BUT...
...MAYBE YOU SHOULD CONSIDER HEADING BACK TO--
NO!
OKAY... BUT, HOW CAN YOU STAY IN JOYAMA ALONE?
?
I CAN'T GO BACK... I HAVE NOWHERE TO GO!
SILAS SOLD OUR HOME, WE WERE GOING TO START FRESH.
I KNOW ALL ABOUT IT, BUT--
AND YOU ALSO KNOW IT'S THE REASON WHY I'M HERE.

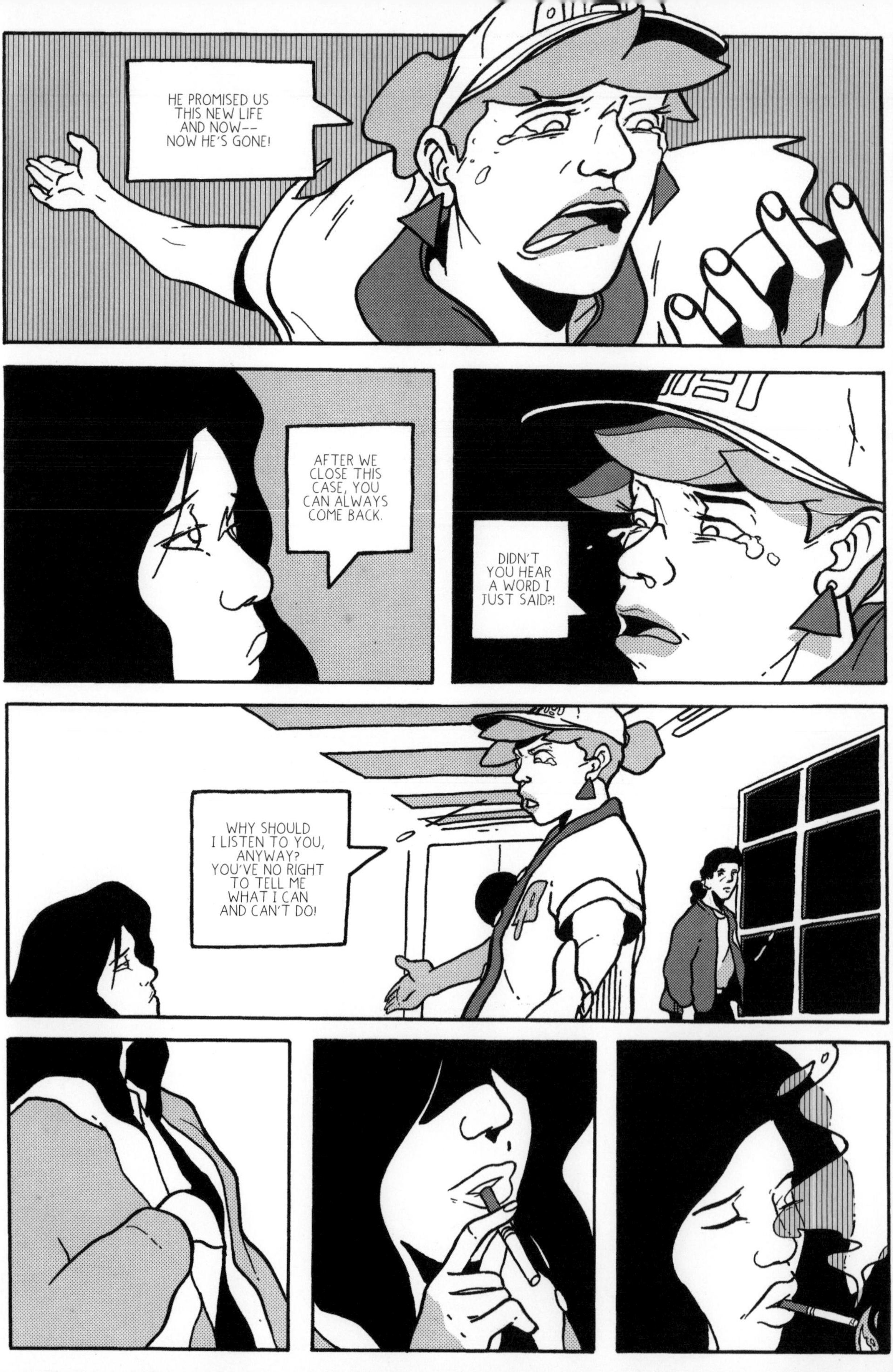
HE PROMISED US THIS NEW LIFE AND NOW-- NOW HE'S GONE!
AFTER WE CLOSE THIS CASE, YOU CAN ALWAYS COME BACK.
DIDN'T YOU HEAR A WORD I JUST SAID?!
WHY SHOULD I LISTEN TO YOU, ANYWAY? YOU'VE NO RIGHT TO TELL ME WHAT I CAN AND CAN'T DO!

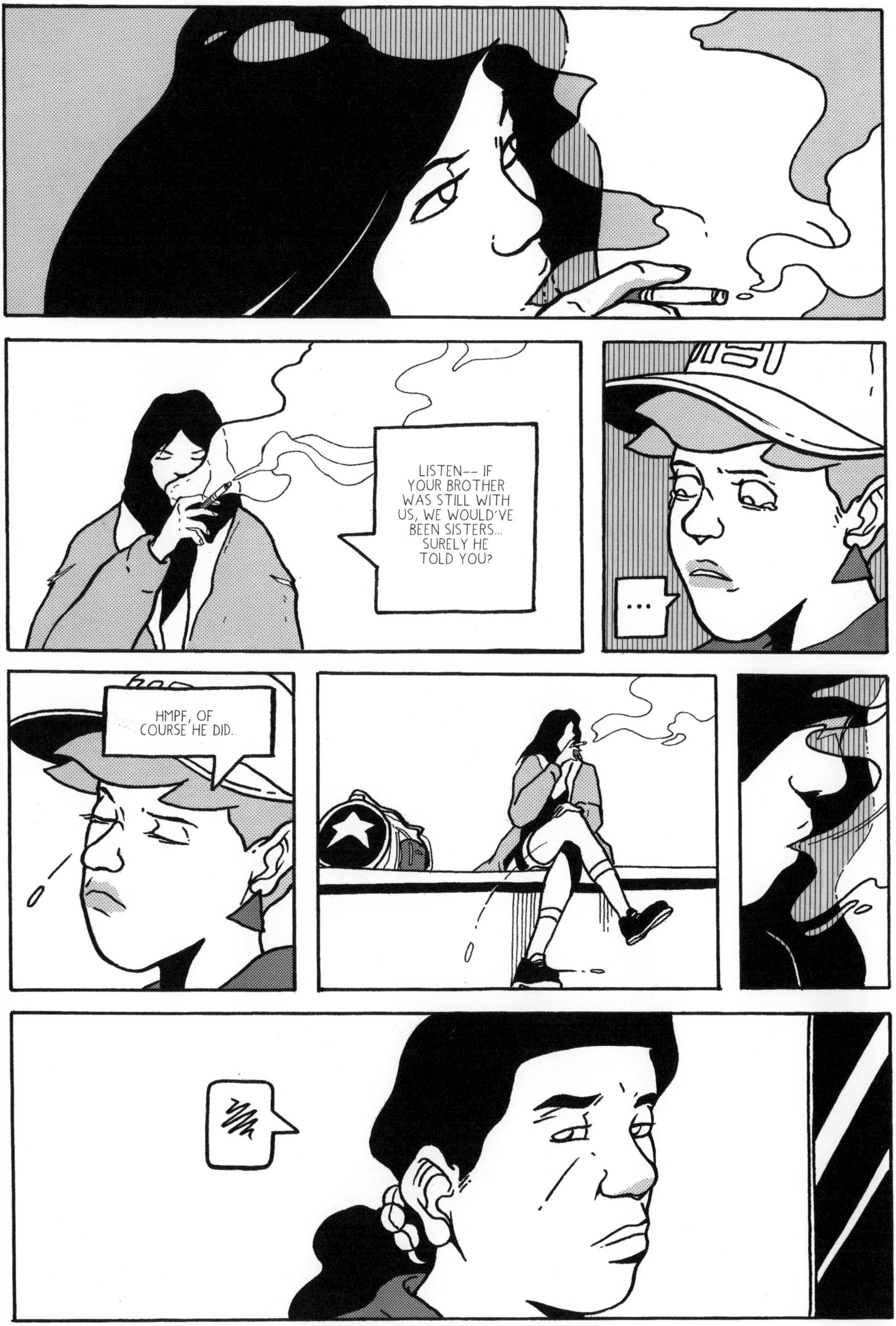
LISTEN-- IF YOUR BROTHER WAS STILL WITH US, WE WOULD'VE BEEN SISTERS... SURELY HE TOLD YOU?
...
HMPF, OF COURSE HE DID.

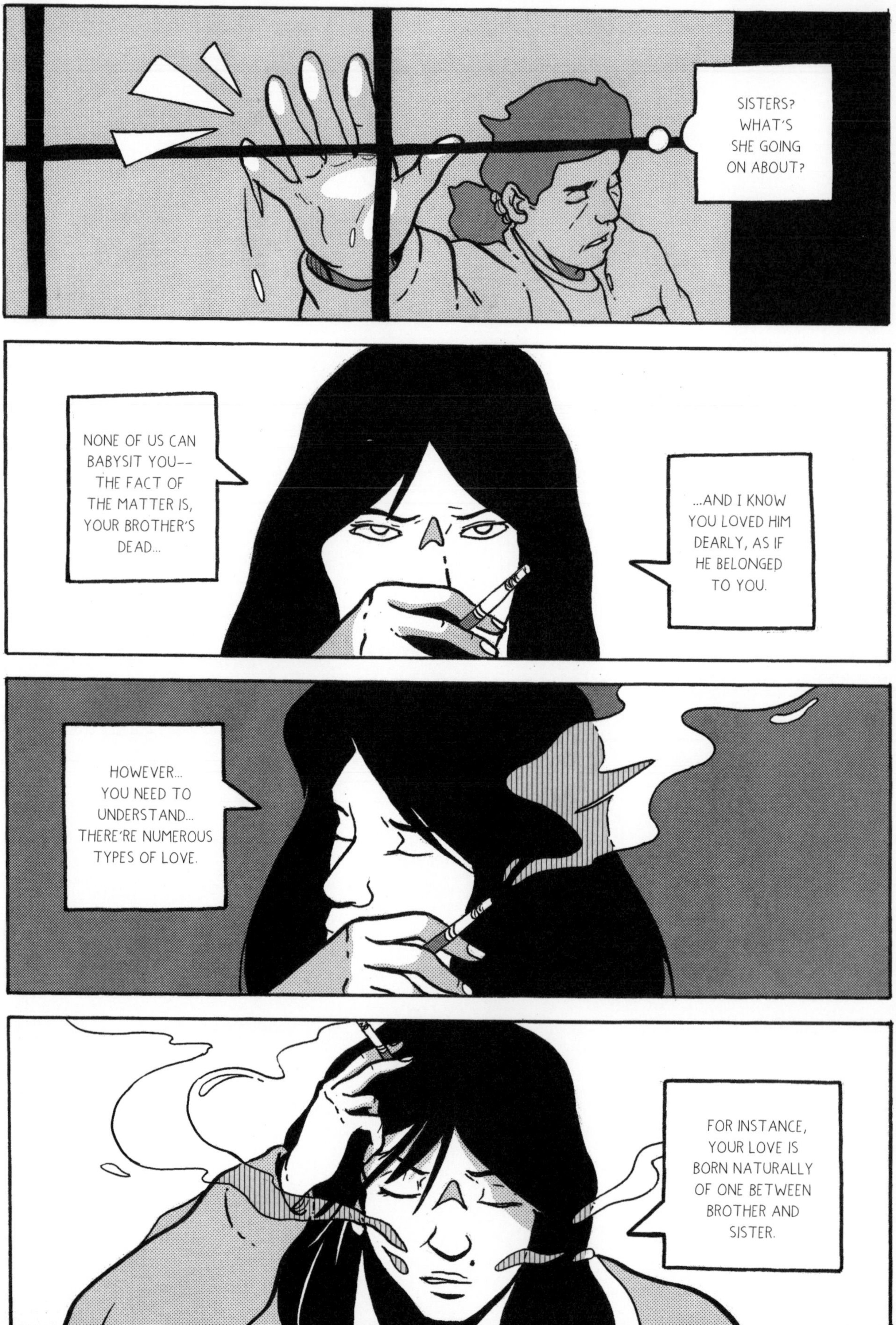
SISTERS? WHAT'S SHE GOING ON ABOUT?
NONE OF US CAN BABYSIT YOU-- THE FACT OF THE MATTER IS, YOUR BROTHER'S DEAD...
...AND I KNOW YOU LOVED HIM DEARLY, AS IF HE BELONGED TO YOU.
HOWEVER... YOU NEED TO UNDERSTAND... THERE'RE NUMEROUS TYPES OF LOVE.
FOR INSTANCE, YOUR LOVE IS BORN NATURALLY OF ONE BETWEEN BROTHER AND SISTER.

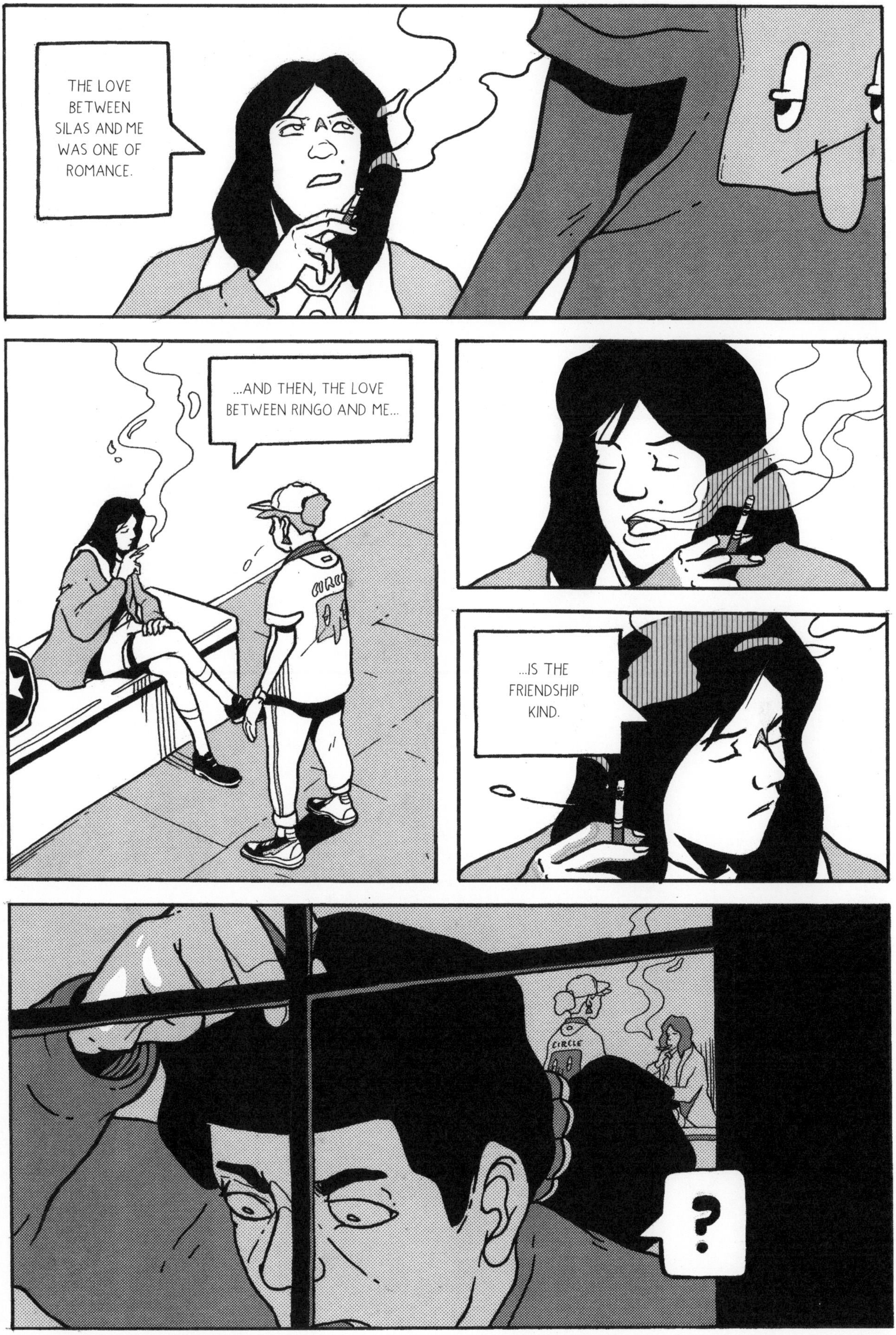
THE LOVE BETWEEN SILAS AND ME WAS ONE OF ROMANCE.
...AND THEN, THE LOVE BETWEEN RINGO AND ME...
...IS THE FRIENDSHIP KIND.
CIRCLE
?

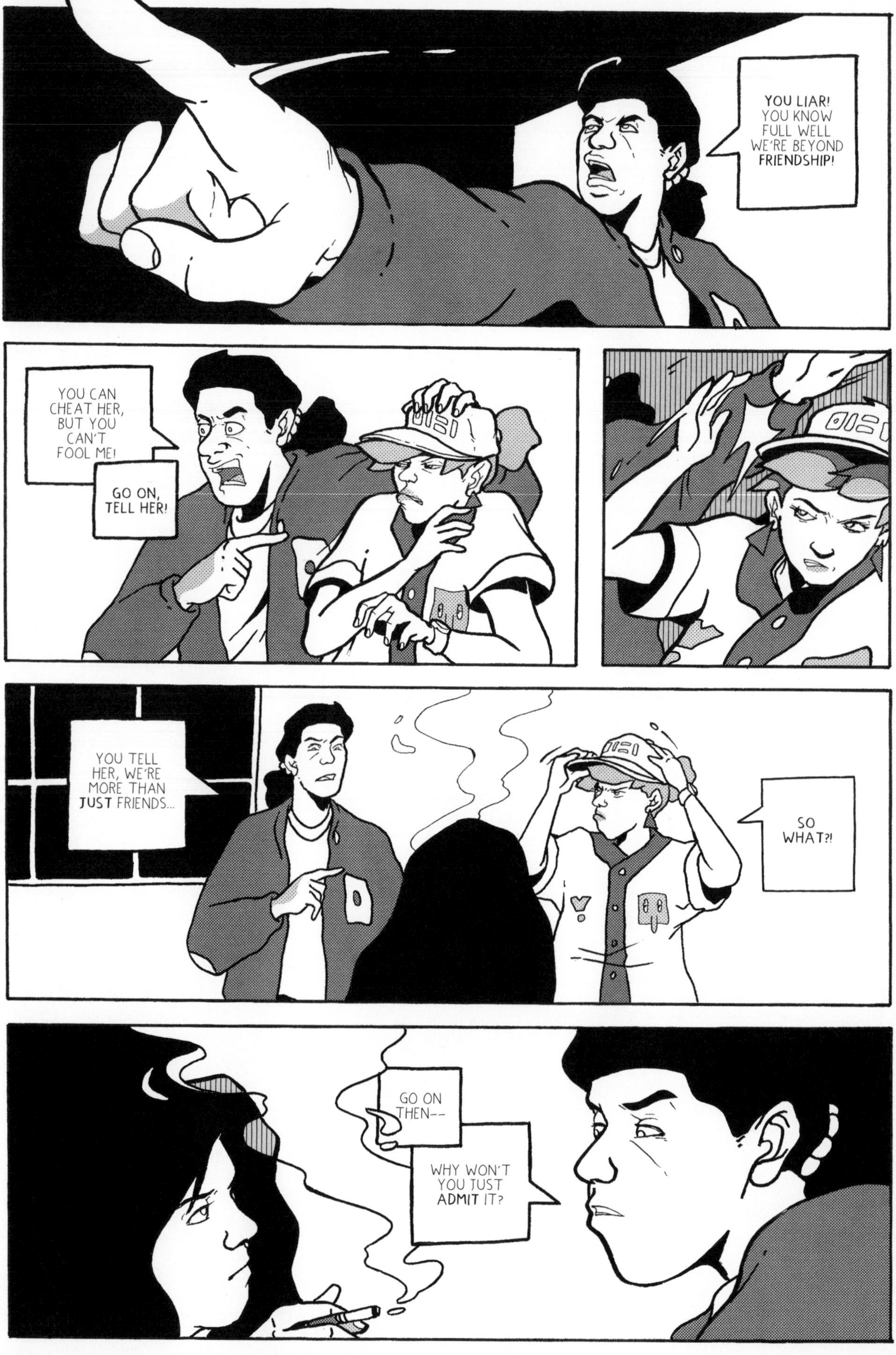
YOU LIAR! YOU KNOW FULL WELL WE'RE BEYOND FRIENDSHIP!
YOU CAN CHEAT HER, BUT YOU CAN'T FOOL ME!
GO ON, TELL HER!
YOU TELL HER, WE'RE MORE THAN JUST FRIENDS...
SO WHAT?!
GO ON THEN--
WHY WON'T YOU JUST ADMIT IT?

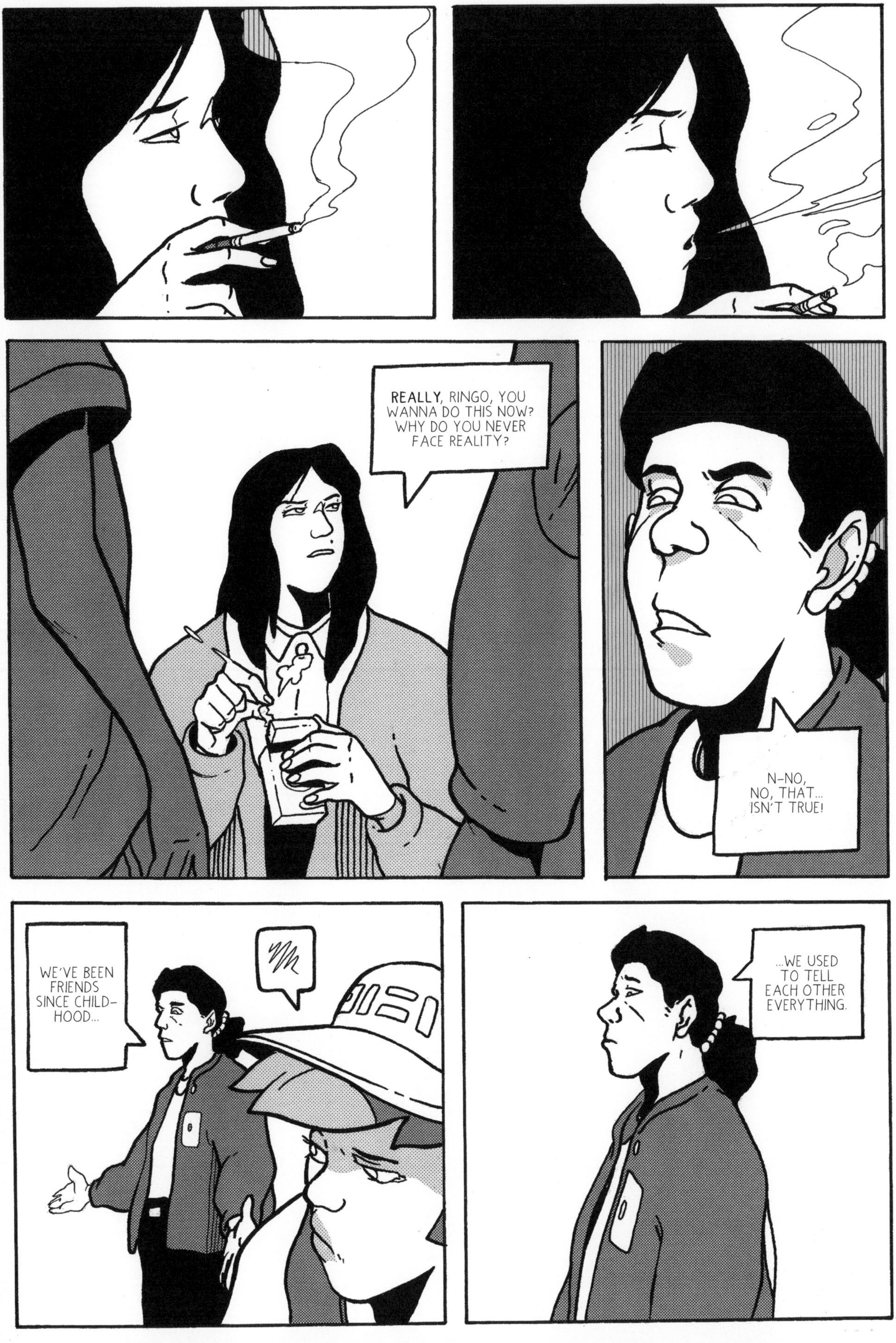

REALLY, RINGO, YOU WANNA DO THIS NOW? WHY DO YOU NEVER FACE REALITY?
N-NO, NO, THAT... ISN'T TRUE!
WE'VE BEEN FRIENDS SINCE CHILD-HOOD...
...WE USED TO TELL EACH OTHER EVERYTHING.

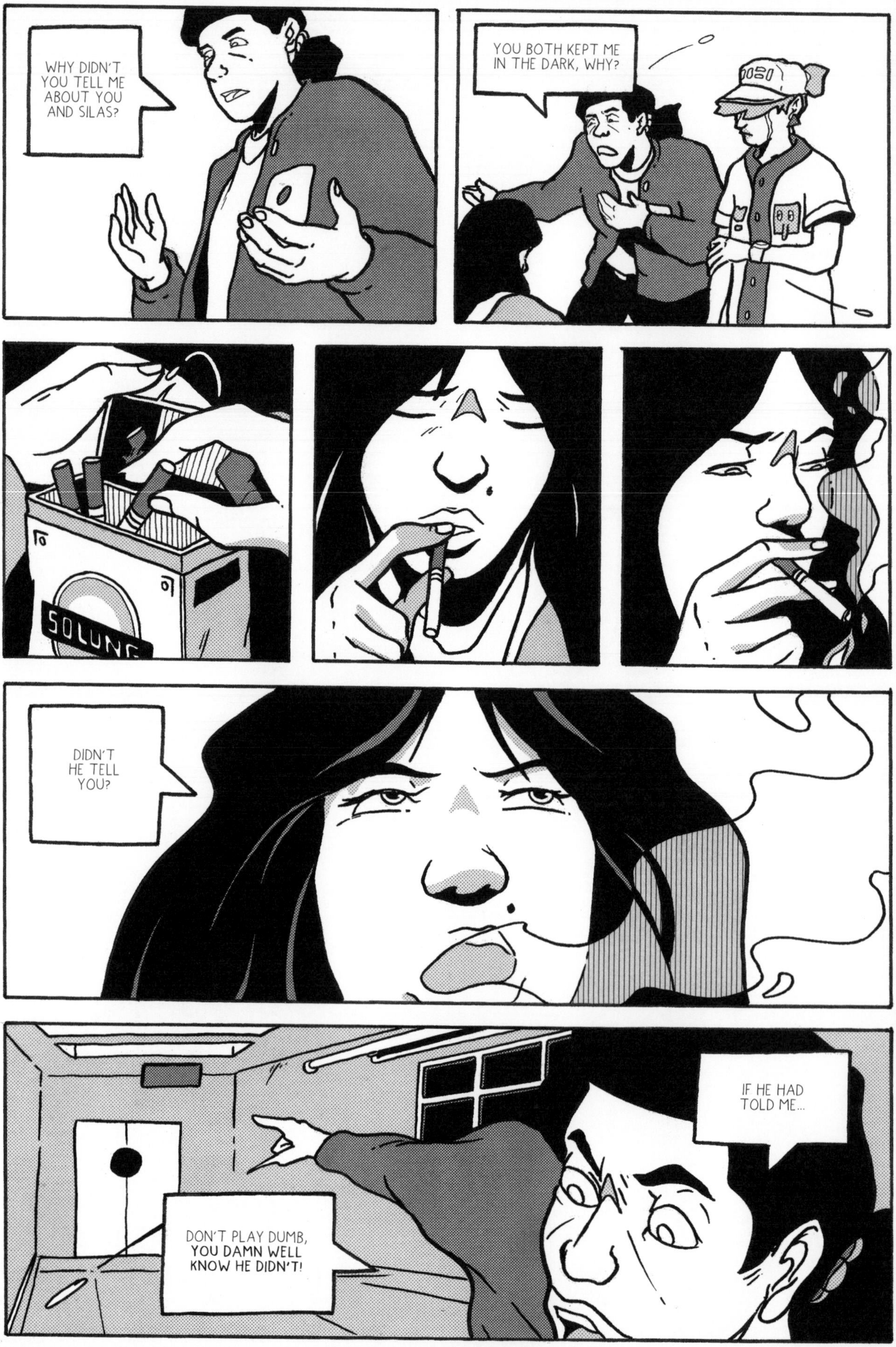
WHY DIDN'T YOU TELL ME ABOUT YOU AND SILAS?
YOU BOTH KEPT ME IN THE DARK, WHY?
SOLUNG
DIDN'T HE TELL YOU?
IF HE HAD TOLD ME...
DON'T PLAY DUMB, **YOU DAMN WELL KNOW HE DIDN'T!**

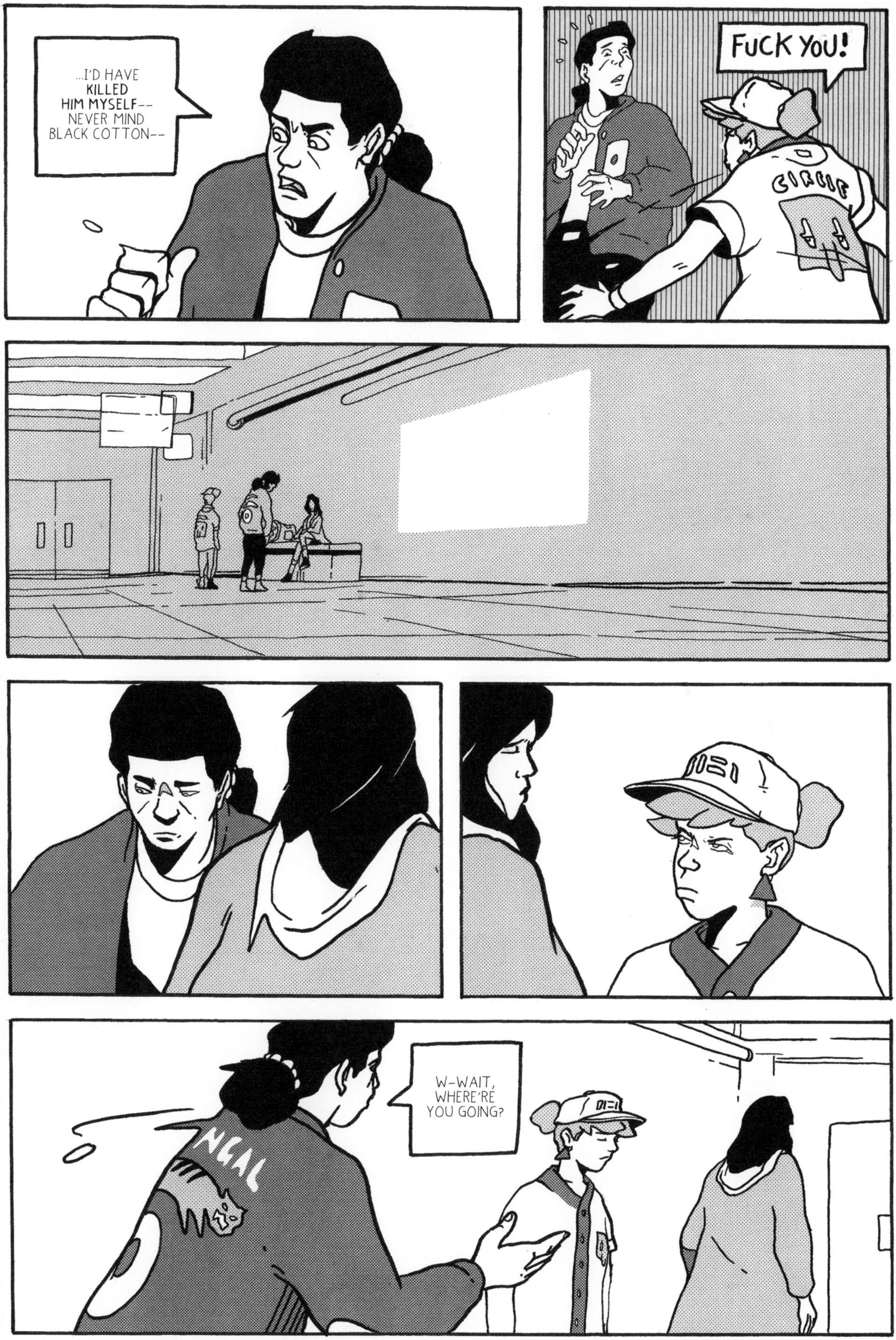

...I'D HAVE KILLED HIM MYSELF-- NEVER MIND BLACK COTTON--
FUCK YOU!
W-WAIT, WHERE'RE YOU GOING?

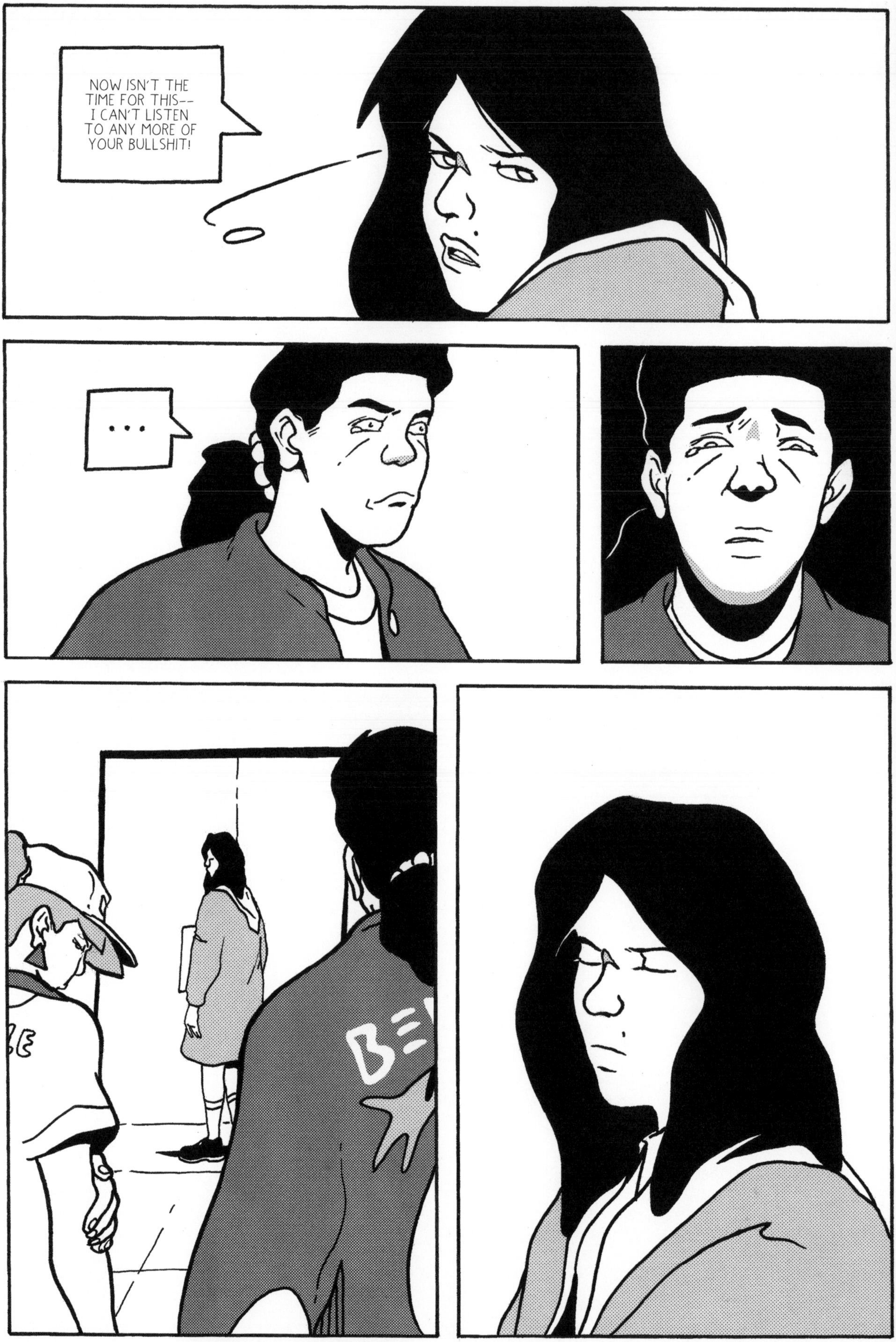
NOW ISN'T THE TIME FOR THIS-- I CAN'T LISTEN TO ANY MORE OF YOUR BULLSHIT!
...

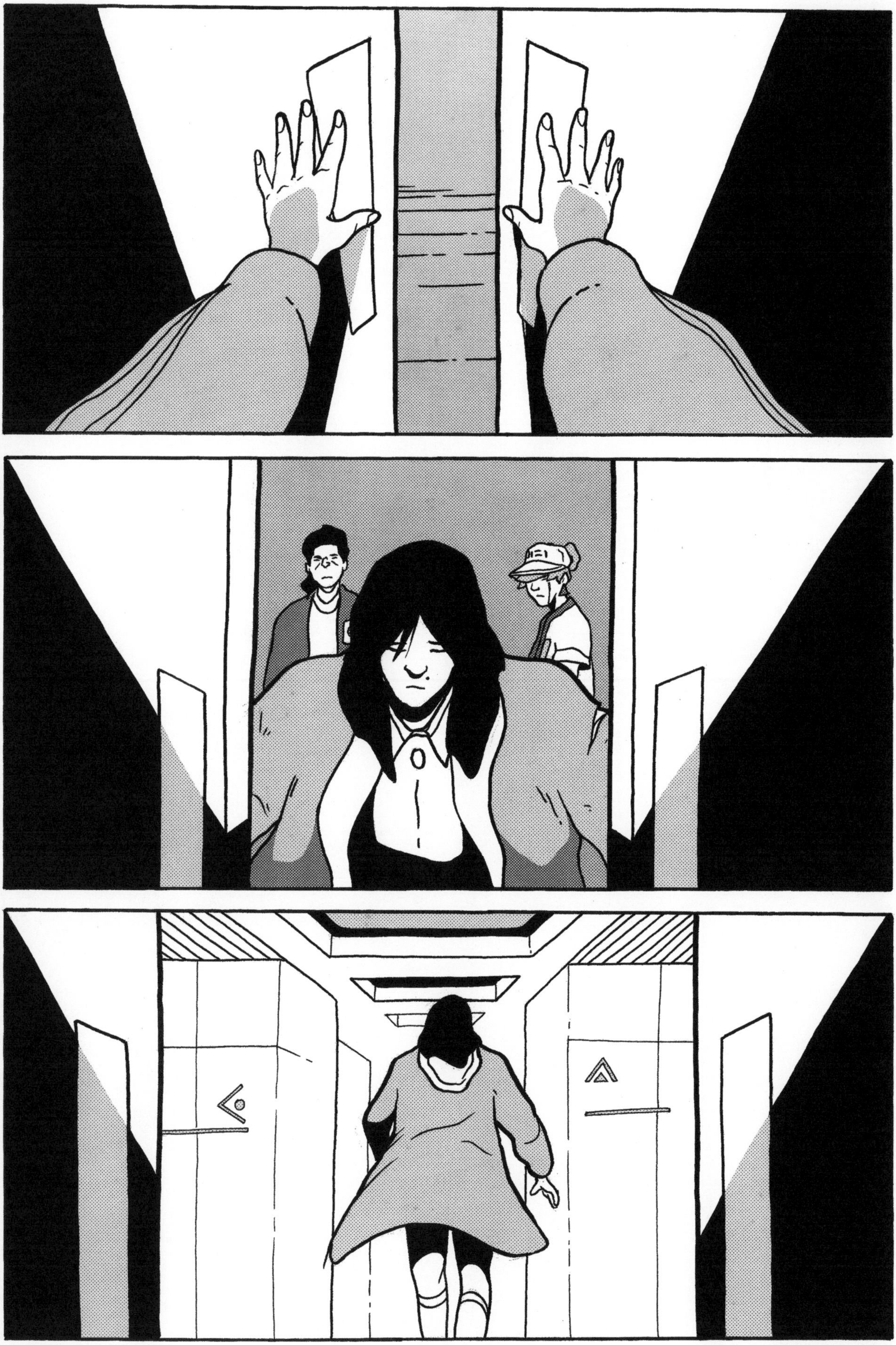

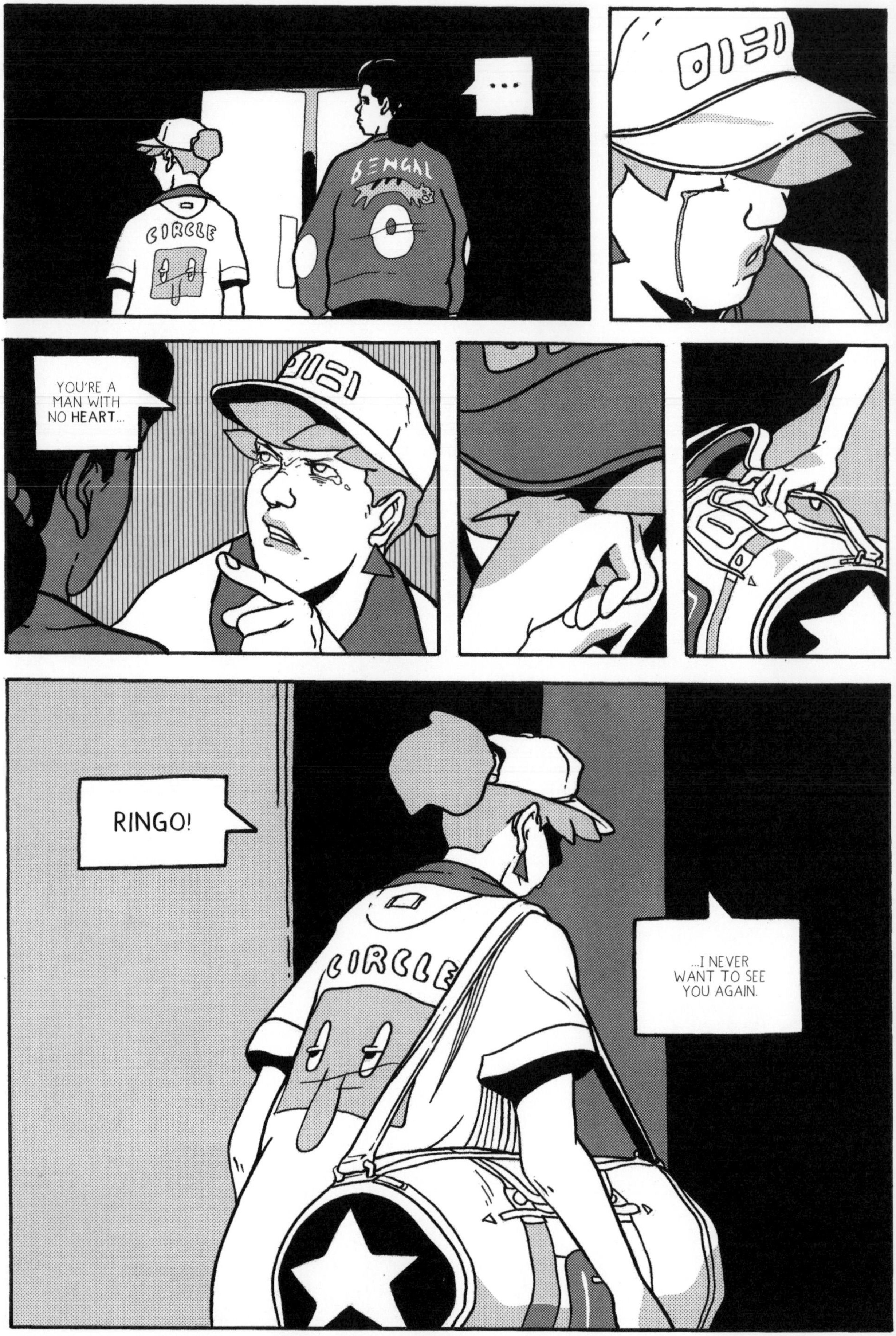
...
YOU'RE A MAN WITH NO HEART...
RINGO!
...I NEVER WANT TO SEE YOU AGAIN.

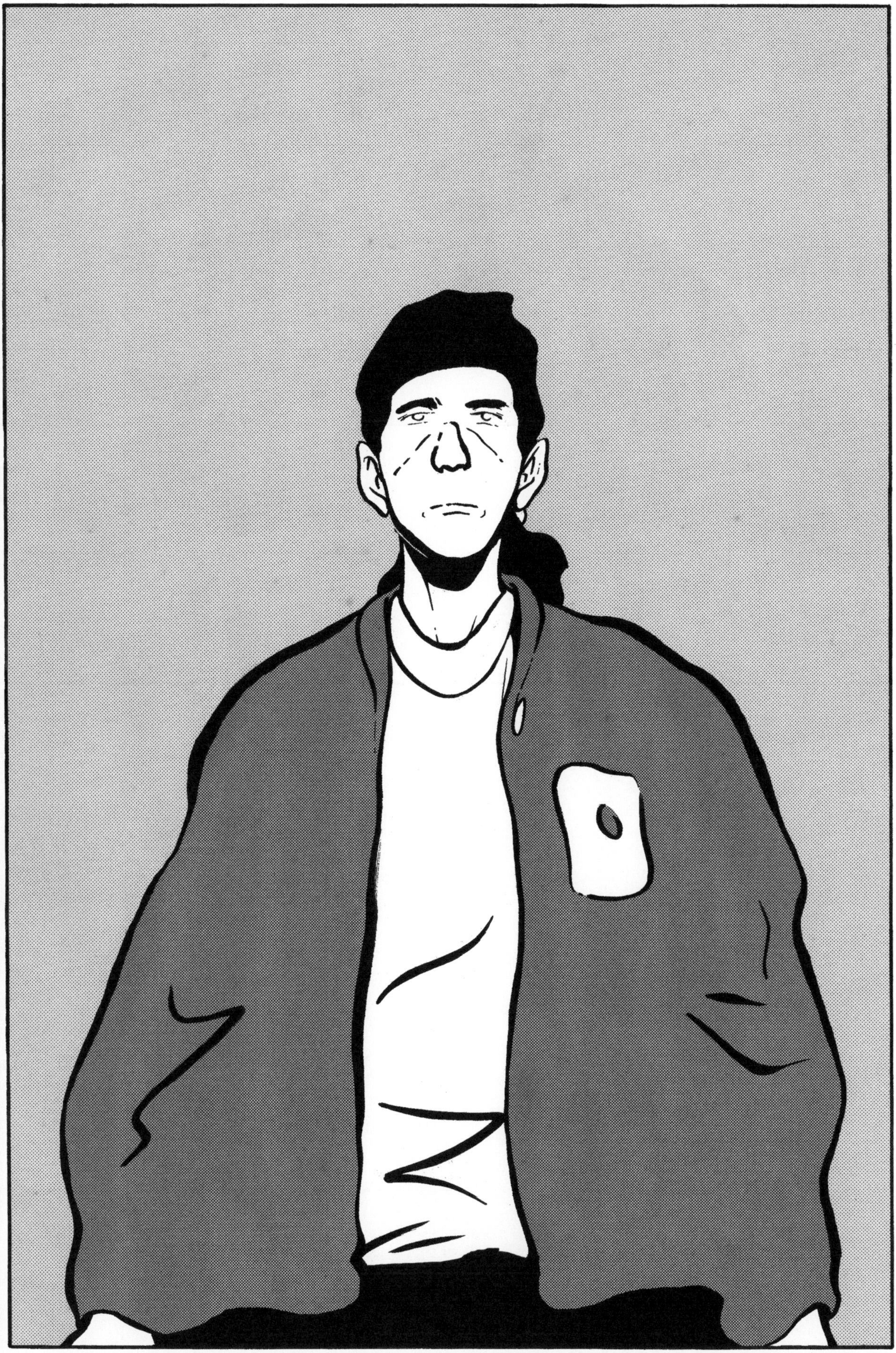

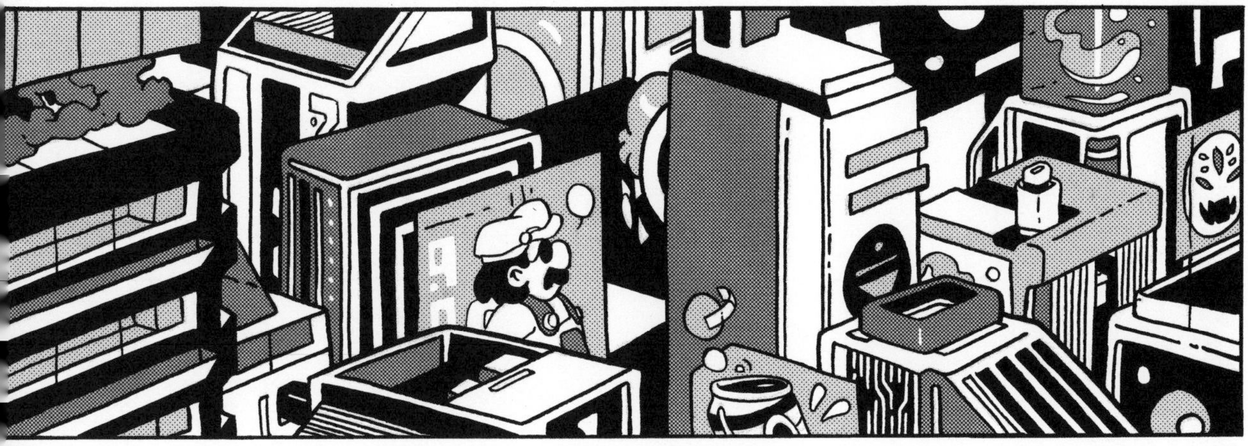

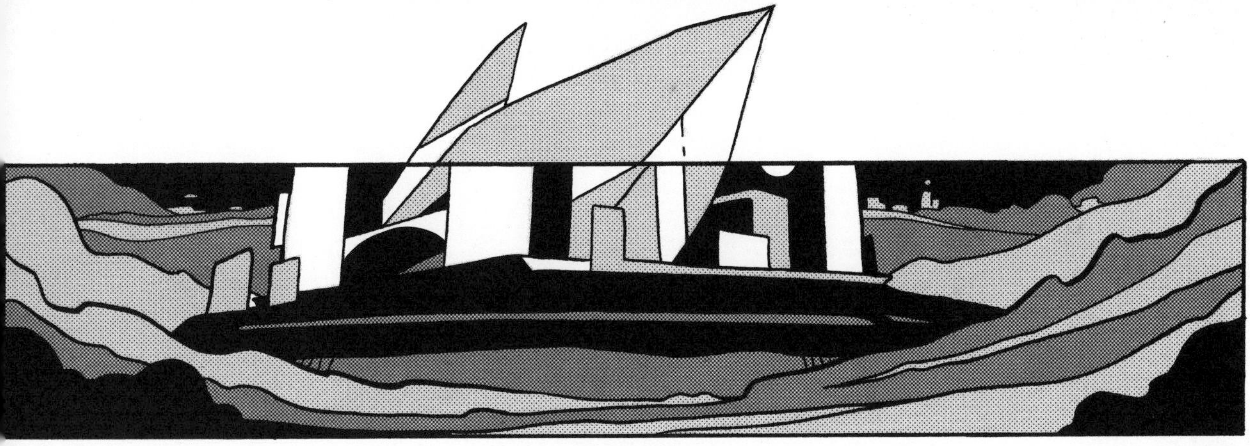

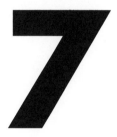

7

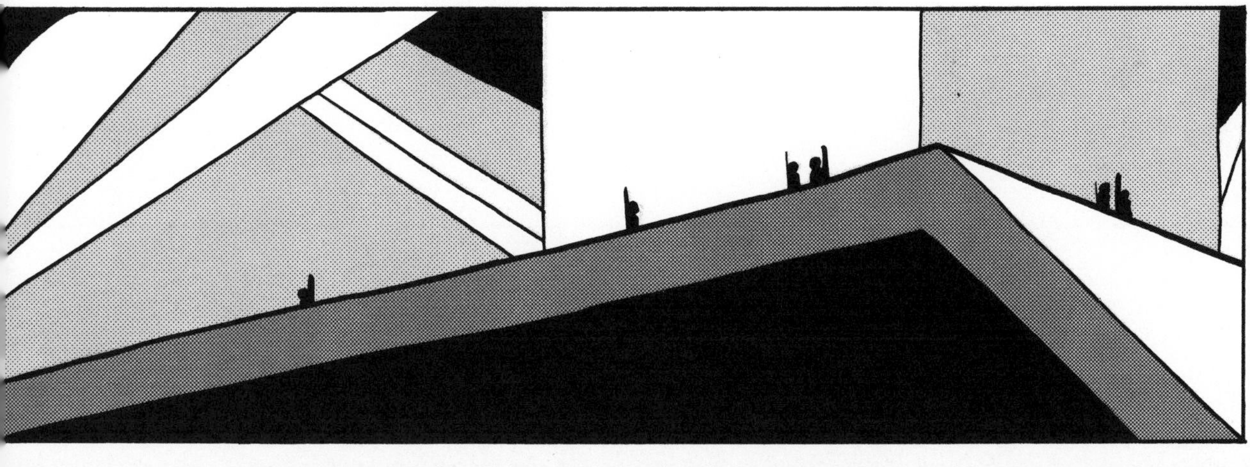

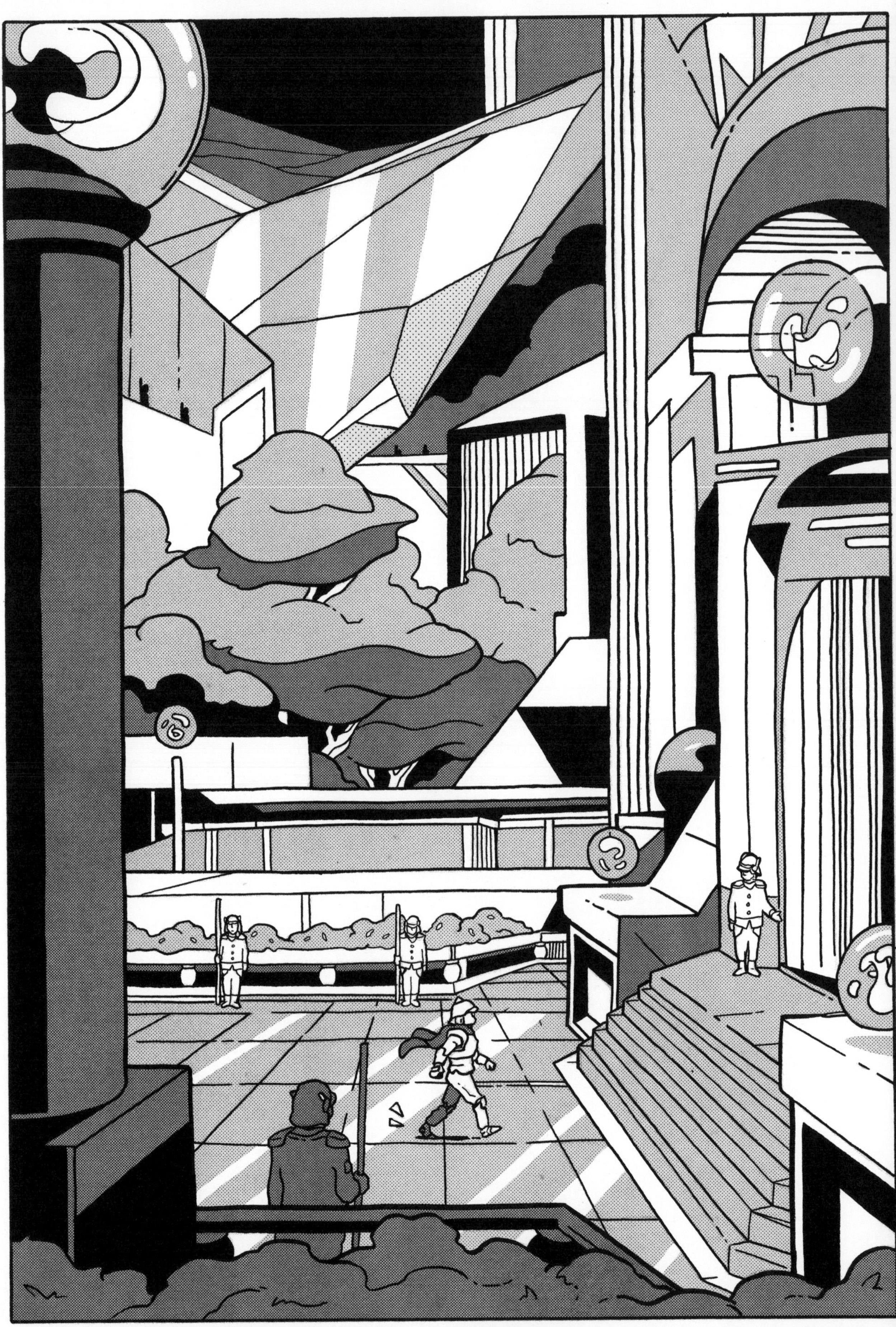

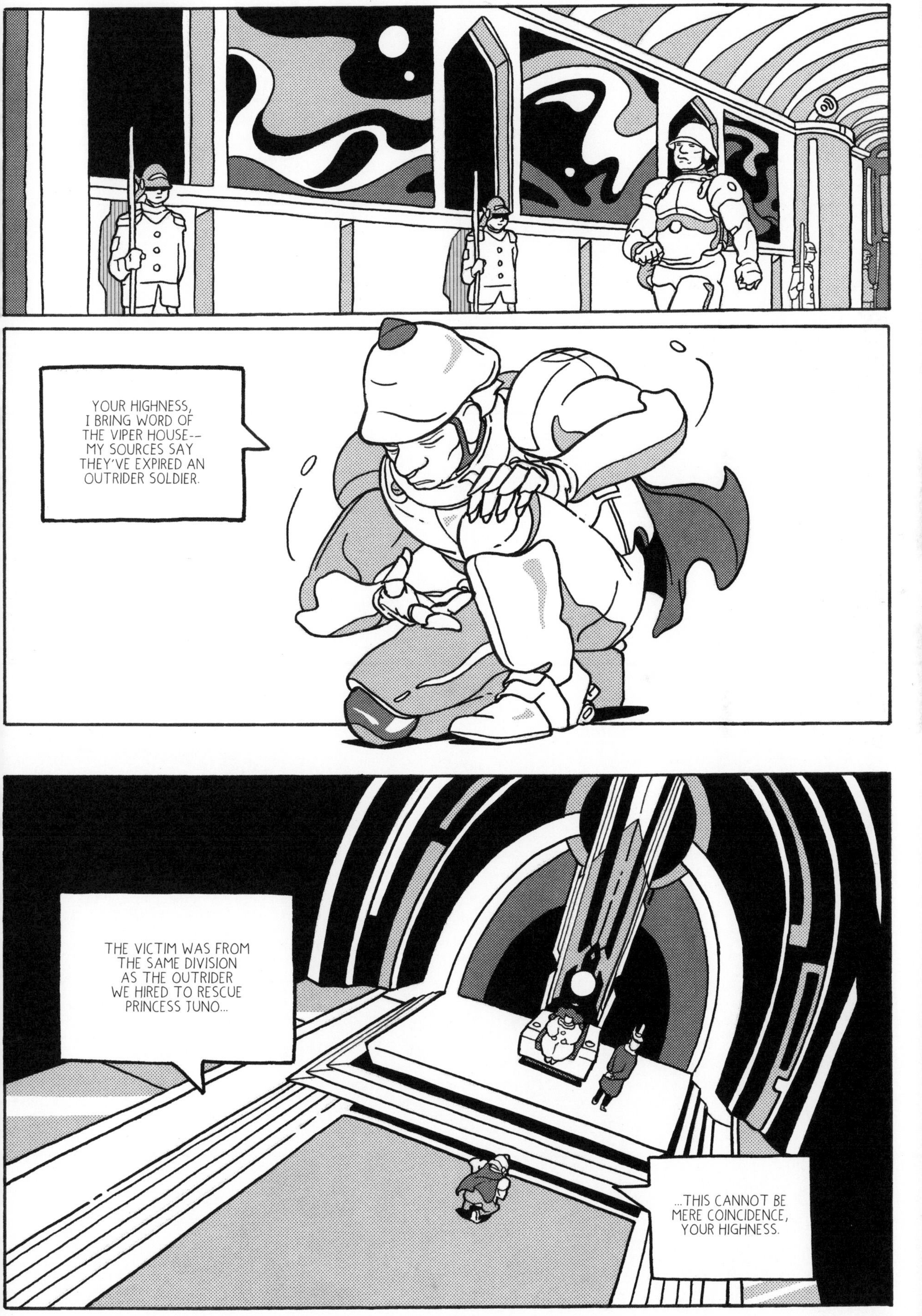
YOUR HIGHNESS, I BRING WORD OF THE VIPER HOUSE-- MY SOURCES SAY THEY'VE EXPIRED AN OUTRIDER SOLDIER.
THE VICTIM WAS FROM THE SAME DIVISION AS THE OUTRIDER WE HIRED TO RESCUE PRINCESS JUNO...
...THIS CANNOT BE MERE COINCIDENCE, YOUR HIGHNESS.

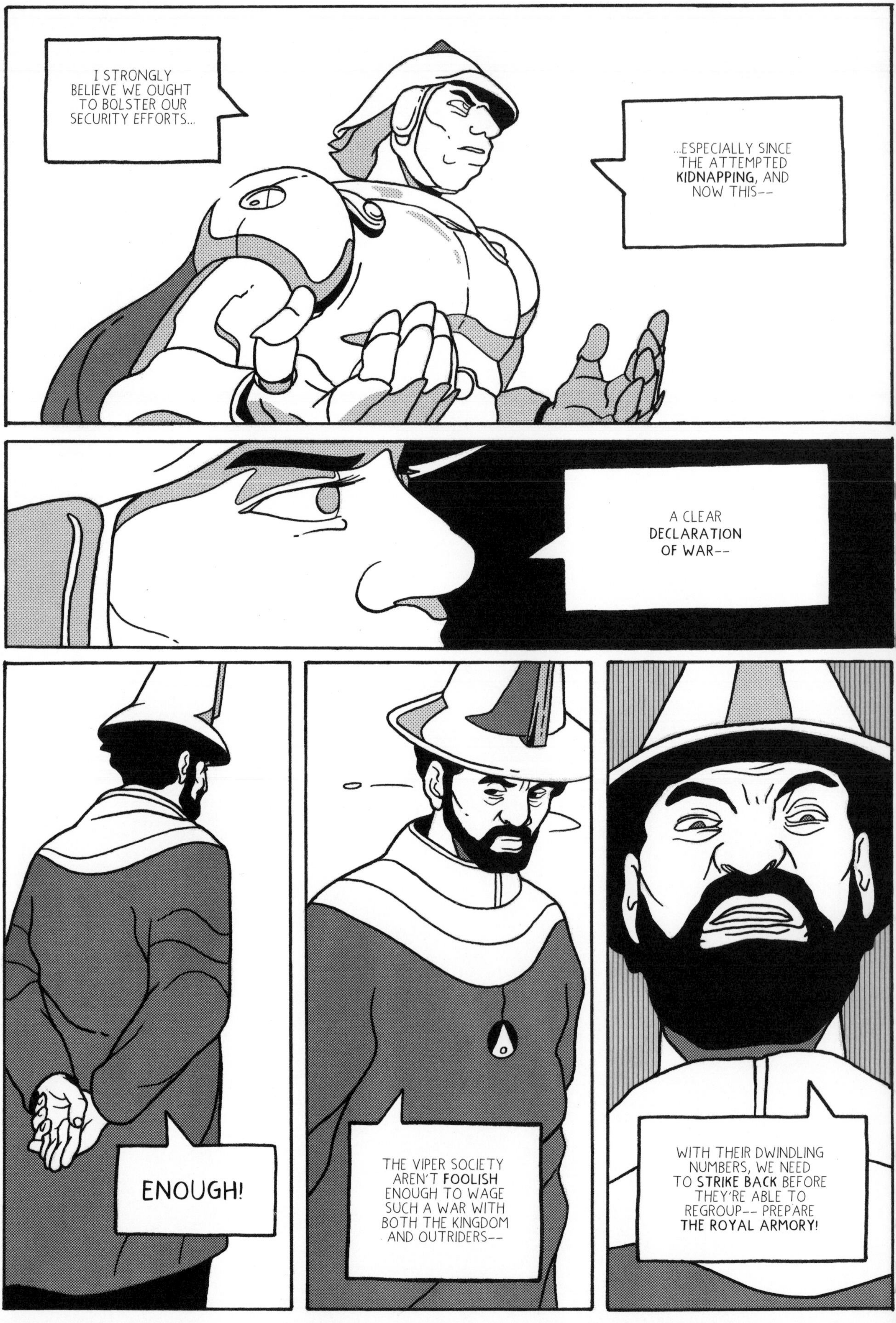
I STRONGLY BELIEVE WE OUGHT TO BOLSTER OUR SECURITY EFFORTS...
...ESPECIALLY SINCE THE ATTEMPTED **KIDNAPPING**, AND NOW THIS--
A CLEAR **DECLARATION** OF WAR--
ENOUGH!
THE VIPER SOCIETY AREN'T **FOOLISH** ENOUGH TO WAGE SUCH A WAR WITH BOTH THE KINGDOM AND OUTRIDERS--
WITH THEIR DWINDLING NUMBERS, WE NEED TO **STRIKE BACK** BEFORE THEY'RE ABLE TO REGROUP-- PREPARE **THE ROYAL ARMORY!**

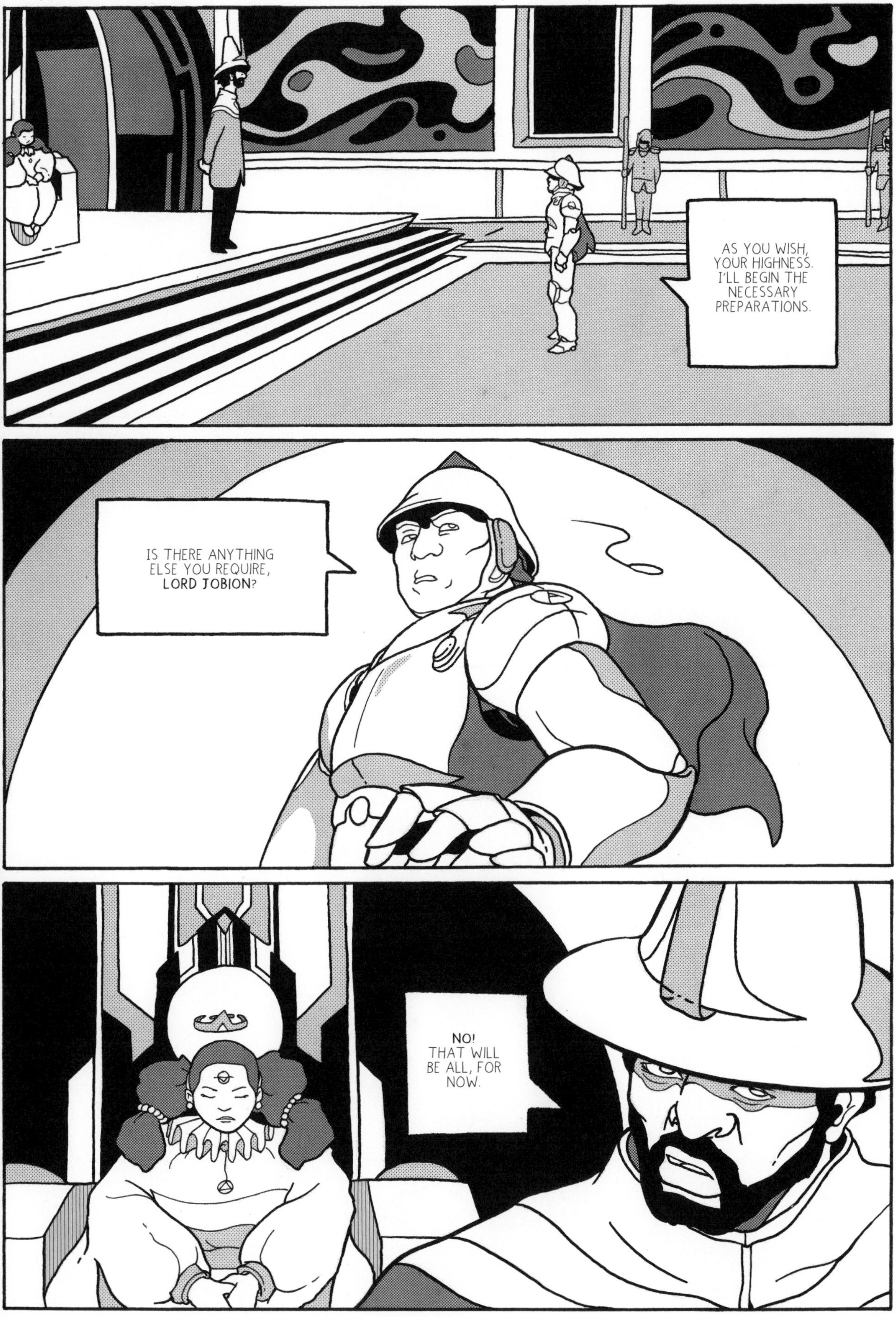
AS YOU WISH, YOUR HIGHNESS. I'LL BEGIN THE NECESSARY PREPARATIONS.
IS THERE ANYTHING ELSE YOU REQUIRE, LORD JOBION?
NO! THAT WILL BE ALL, FOR NOW.

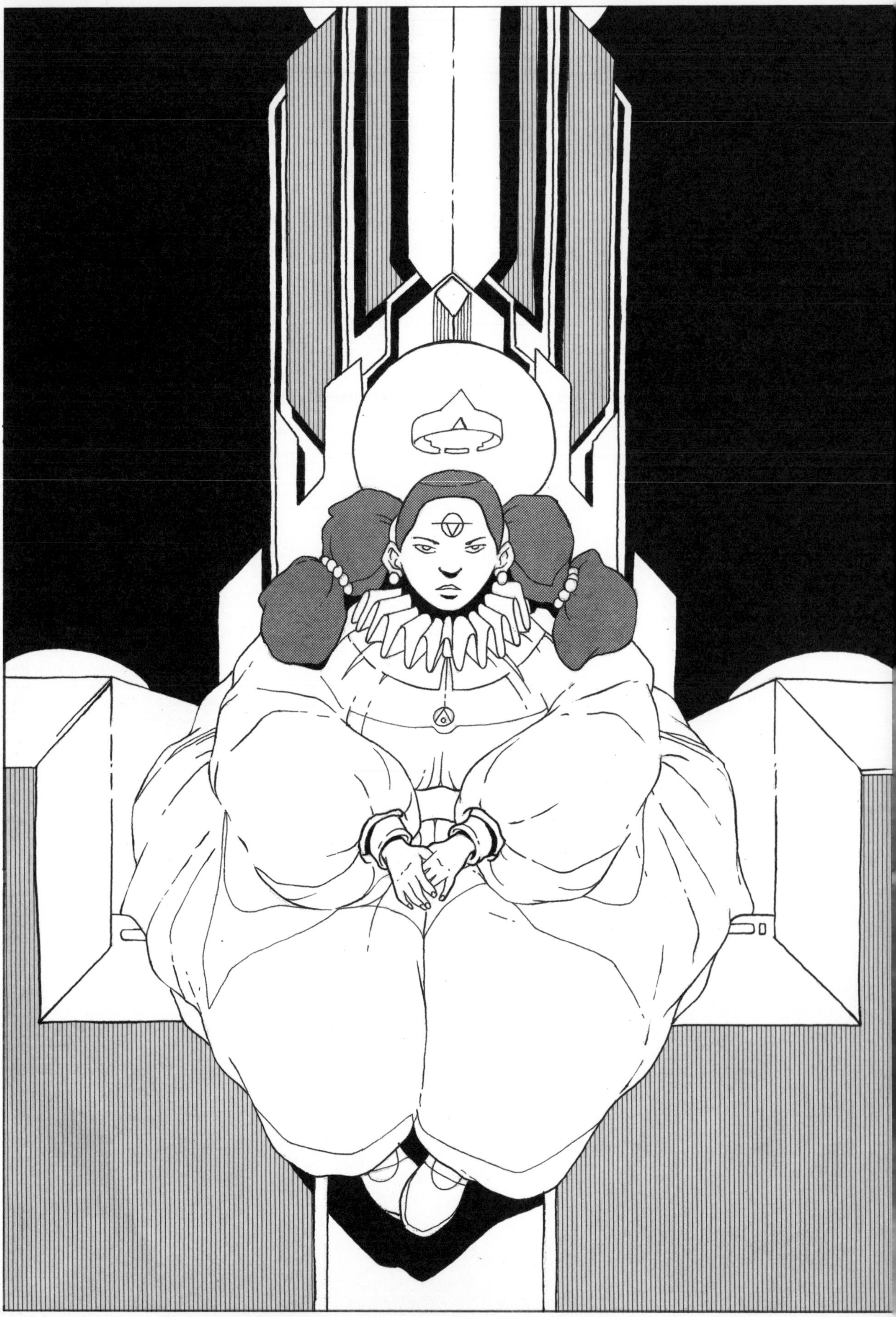

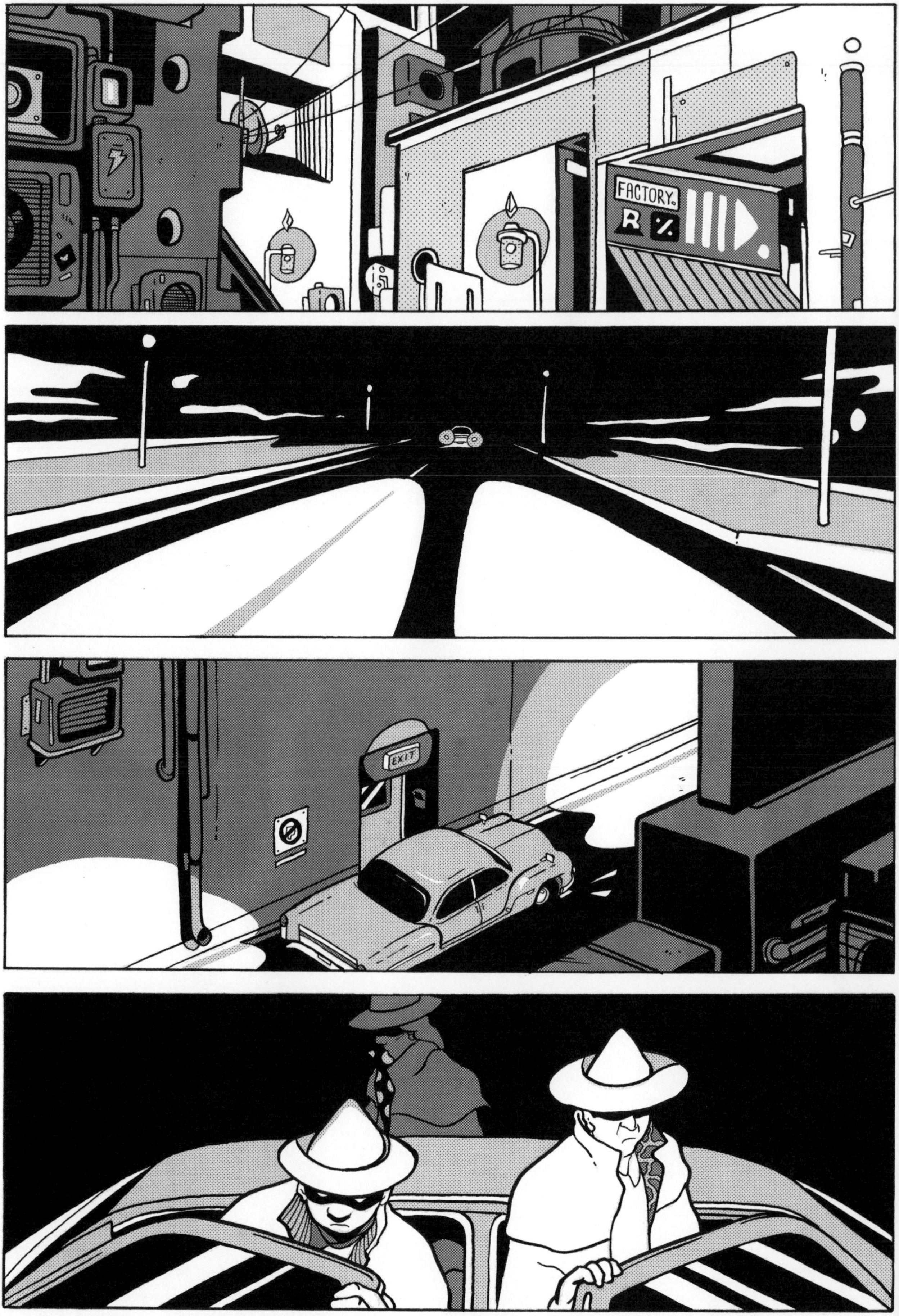
FACTORY
EXIT

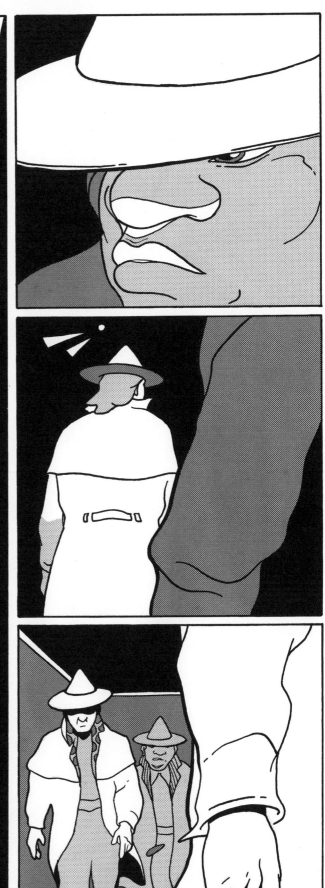

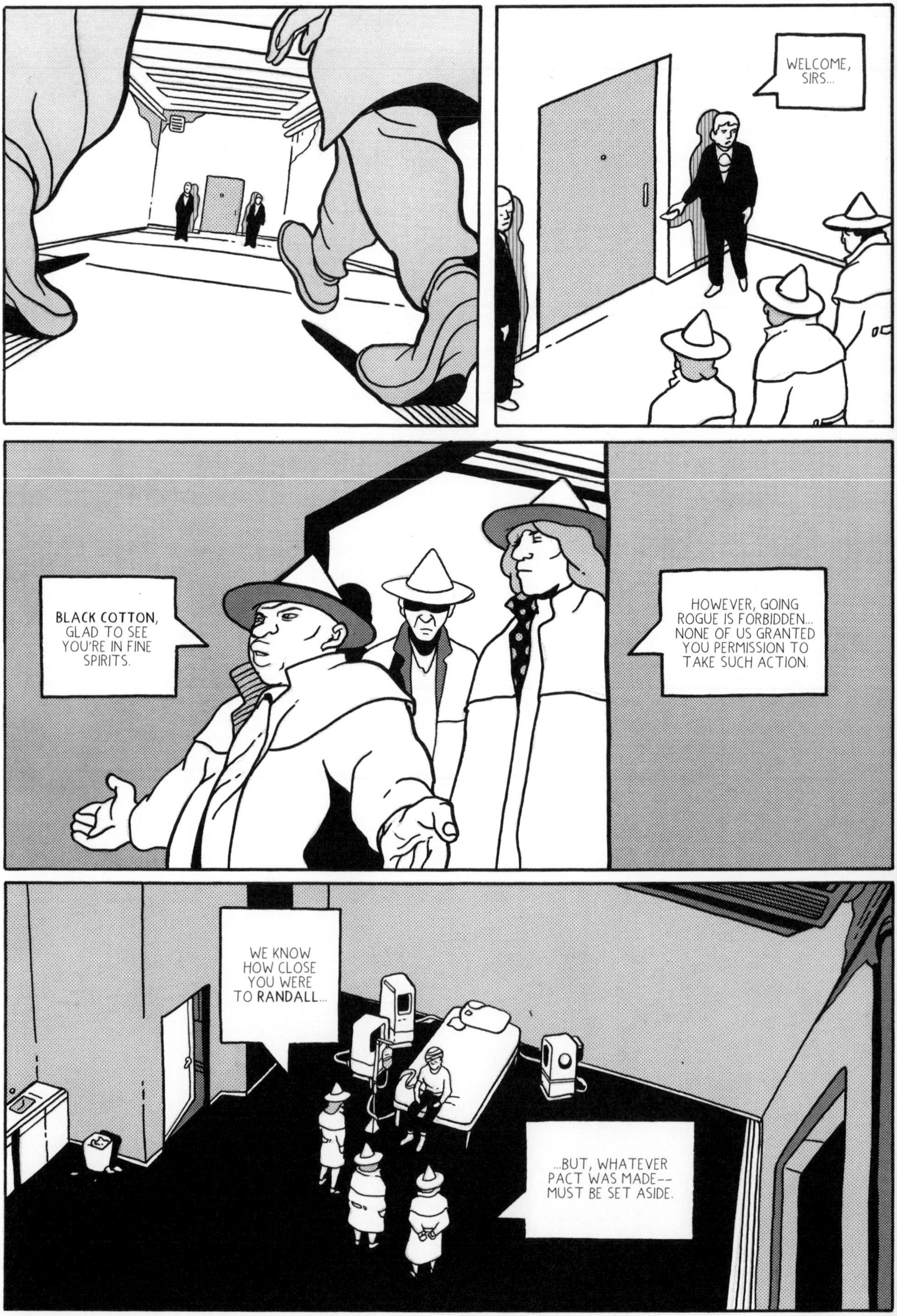
WELCOME, SIRS...
BLACK COTTON, GLAD TO SEE YOU'RE IN FINE SPIRITS.
HOWEVER, GOING ROGUE IS FORBIDDEN... NONE OF US GRANTED YOU PERMISSION TO TAKE SUCH ACTION.
WE KNOW HOW CLOSE YOU WERE TO RANDALL...
...BUT, WHATEVER PACT WAS MADE-- MUST BE SET ASIDE.

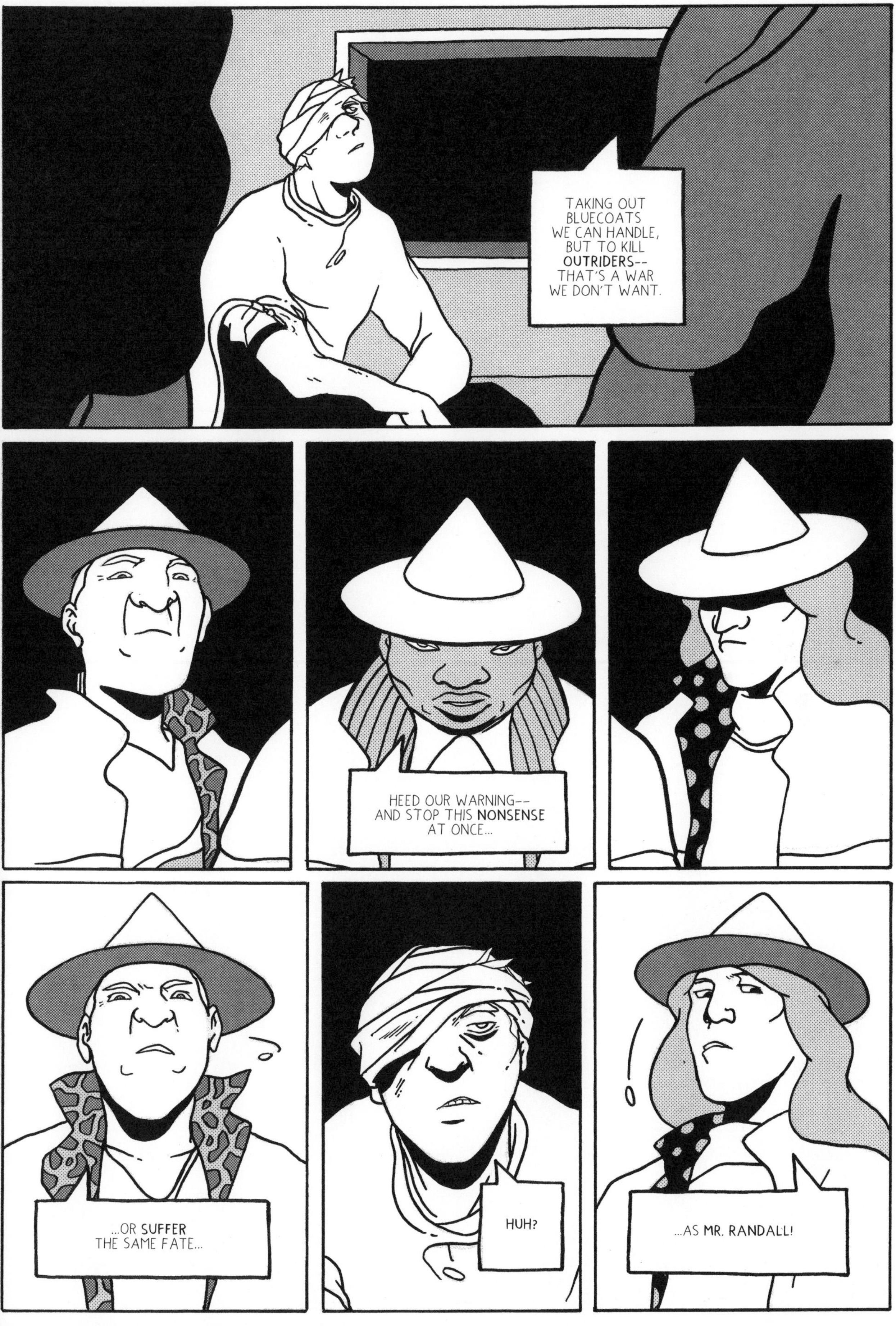
TAKING OUT BLUECOATS WE CAN HANDLE, BUT TO KILL **OUTRIDERS**-- THAT'S A WAR WE DON'T WANT.
HEED OUR WARNING-- AND STOP THIS **NONSENSE** AT ONCE...
...OR **SUFFER** THE SAME FATE...
HUH?
...AS **MR. RANDALL**!

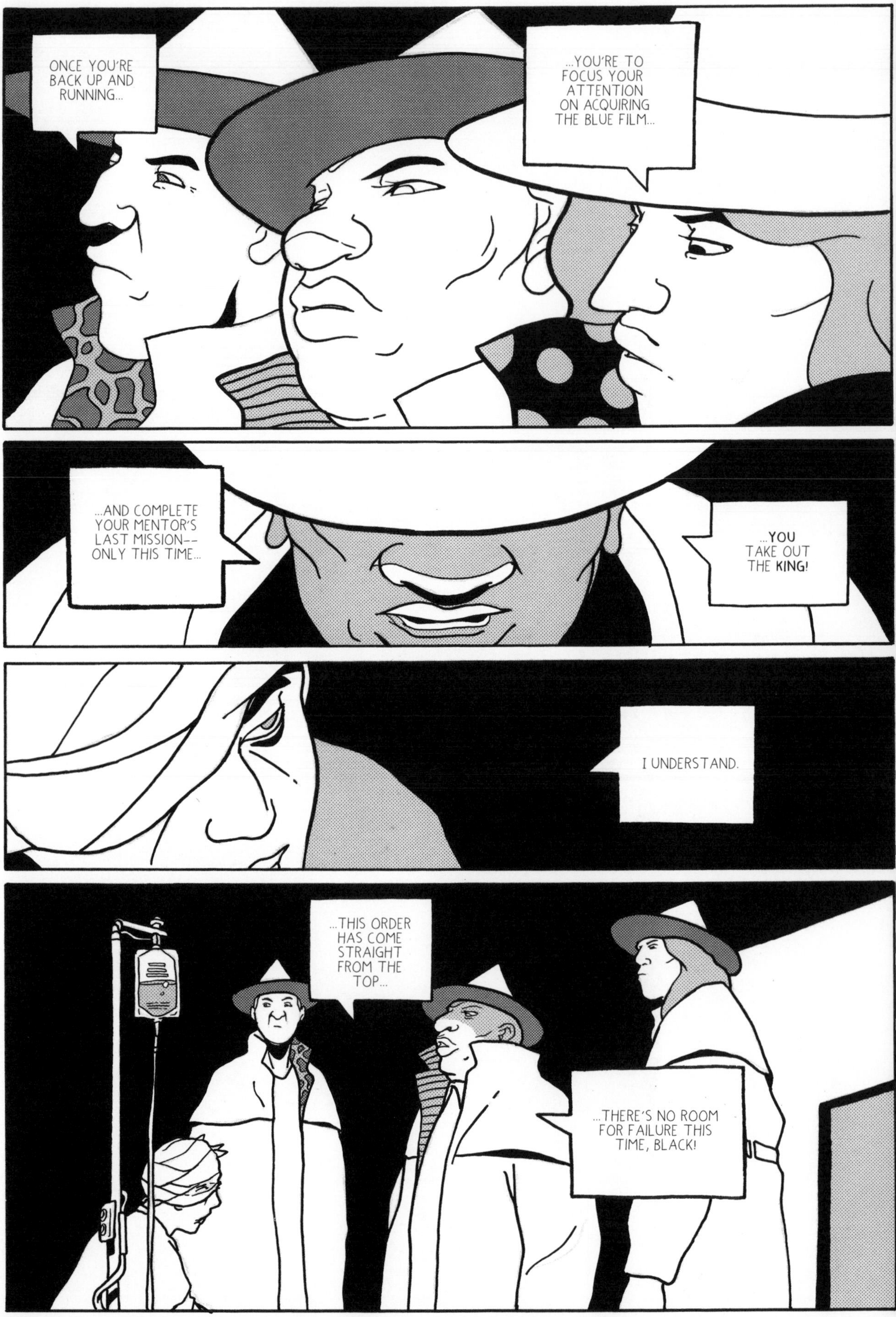

ONCE YOU'RE BACK UP AND RUNNING...
...YOU'RE TO FOCUS YOUR ATTENTION ON ACQUIRING THE BLUE FILM...
...AND COMPLETE YOUR MENTOR'S LAST MISSION-- ONLY THIS TIME...
...YOU TAKE OUT THE KING!
I UNDERSTAND.
...THIS ORDER HAS COME STRAIGHT FROM THE TOP...
...THERE'S NO ROOM FOR FAILURE THIS TIME, BLACK!

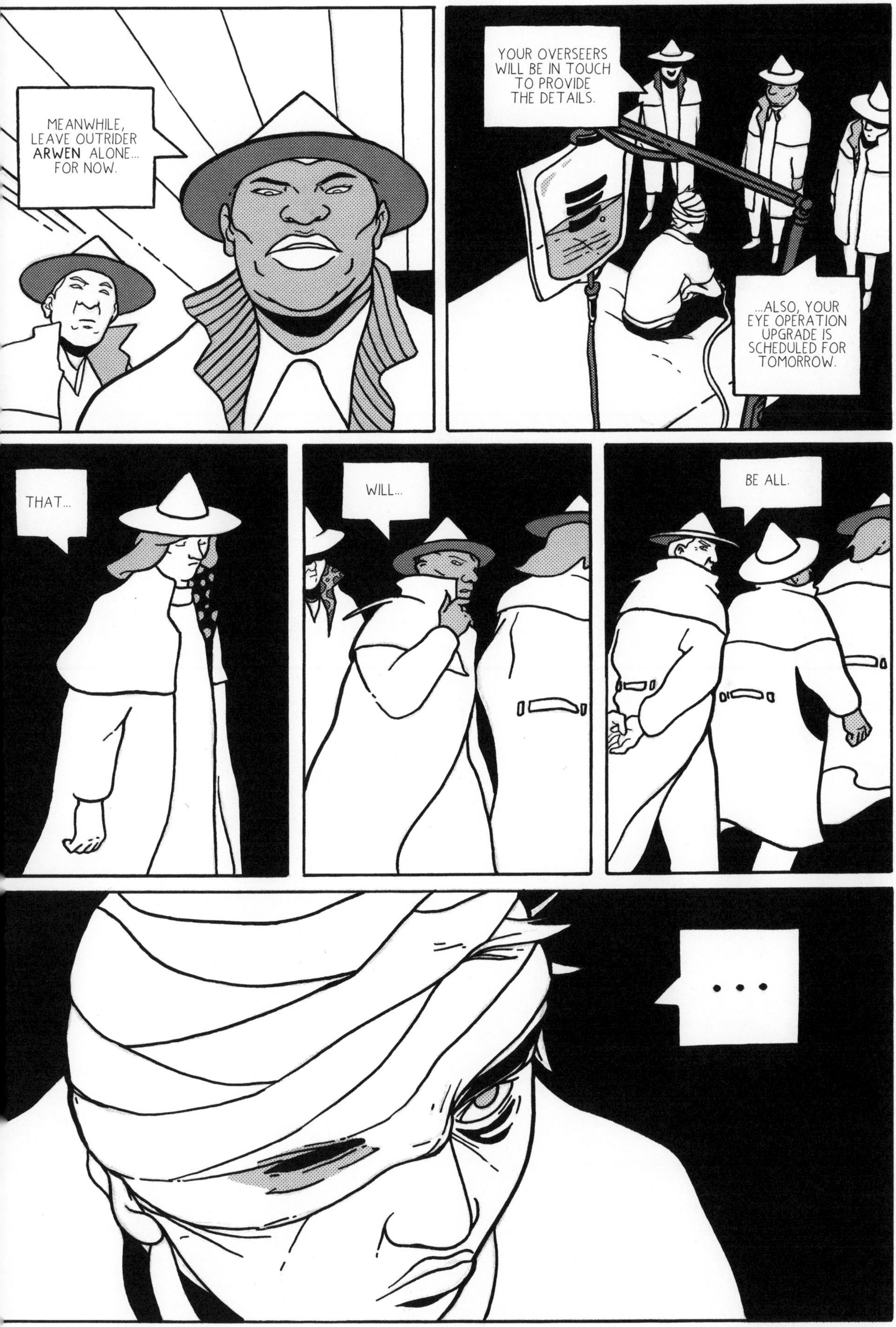
MEANWHILE, LEAVE OUTRIDER **ARWEN** ALONE... FOR NOW.
YOUR OVERSEERS WILL BE IN TOUCH TO PROVIDE THE DETAILS.
...ALSO, YOUR EYE OPERATION UPGRADE IS SCHEDULED FOR TOMORROW.
THAT...
WILL...
BE ALL.
• • •

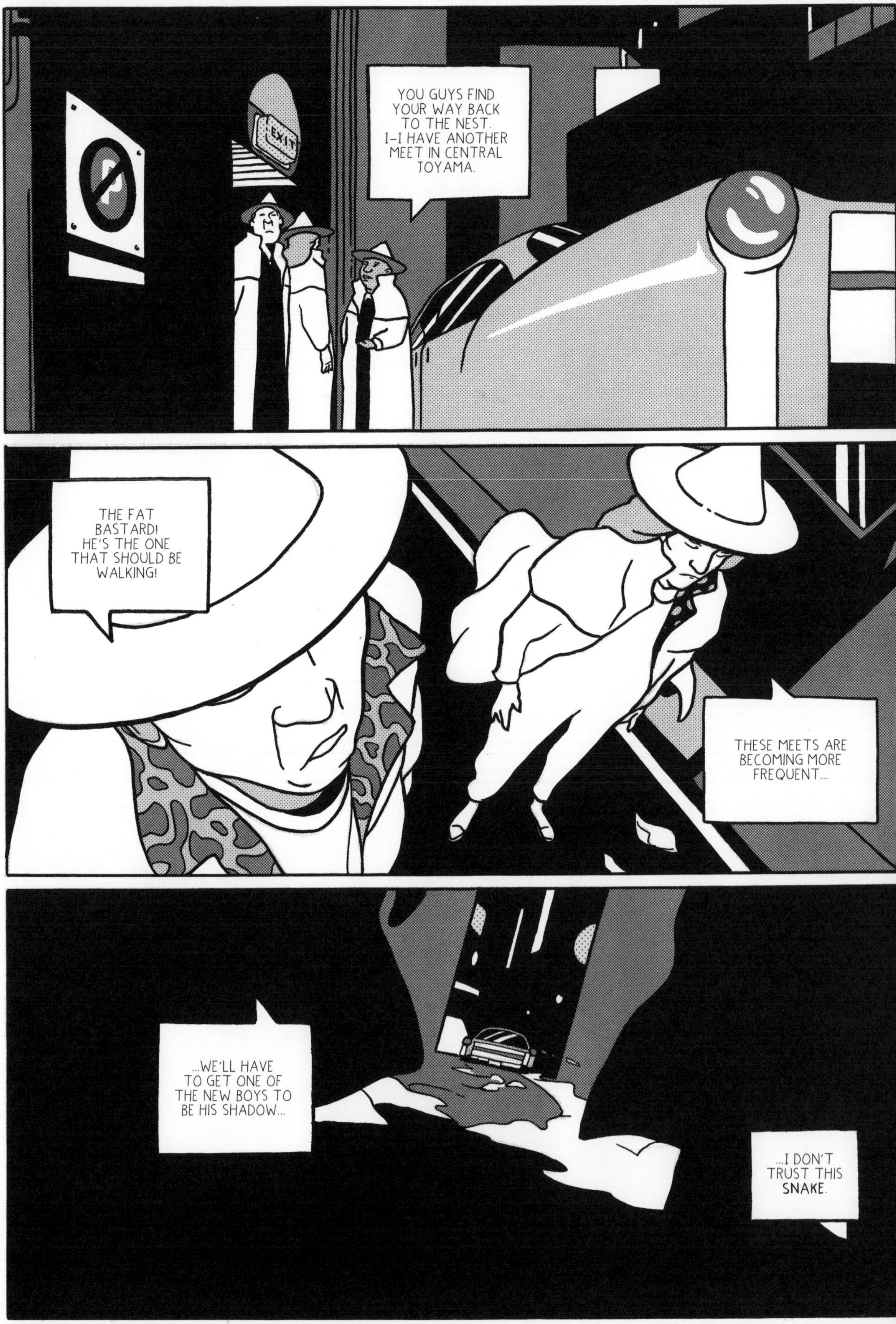
EXIT
YOU GUYS FIND YOUR WAY BACK TO THE NEST. I-I HAVE ANOTHER MEET IN CENTRAL JOYAMA.
THE FAT BASTARD! HE'S THE ONE THAT SHOULD BE WALKING!
THESE MEETS ARE BECOMING MORE FREQUENT...
...WE'LL HAVE TO GET ONE OF THE NEW BOYS TO BE HIS SHADOW...
...I DON'T TRUST THIS **SNAKE**.

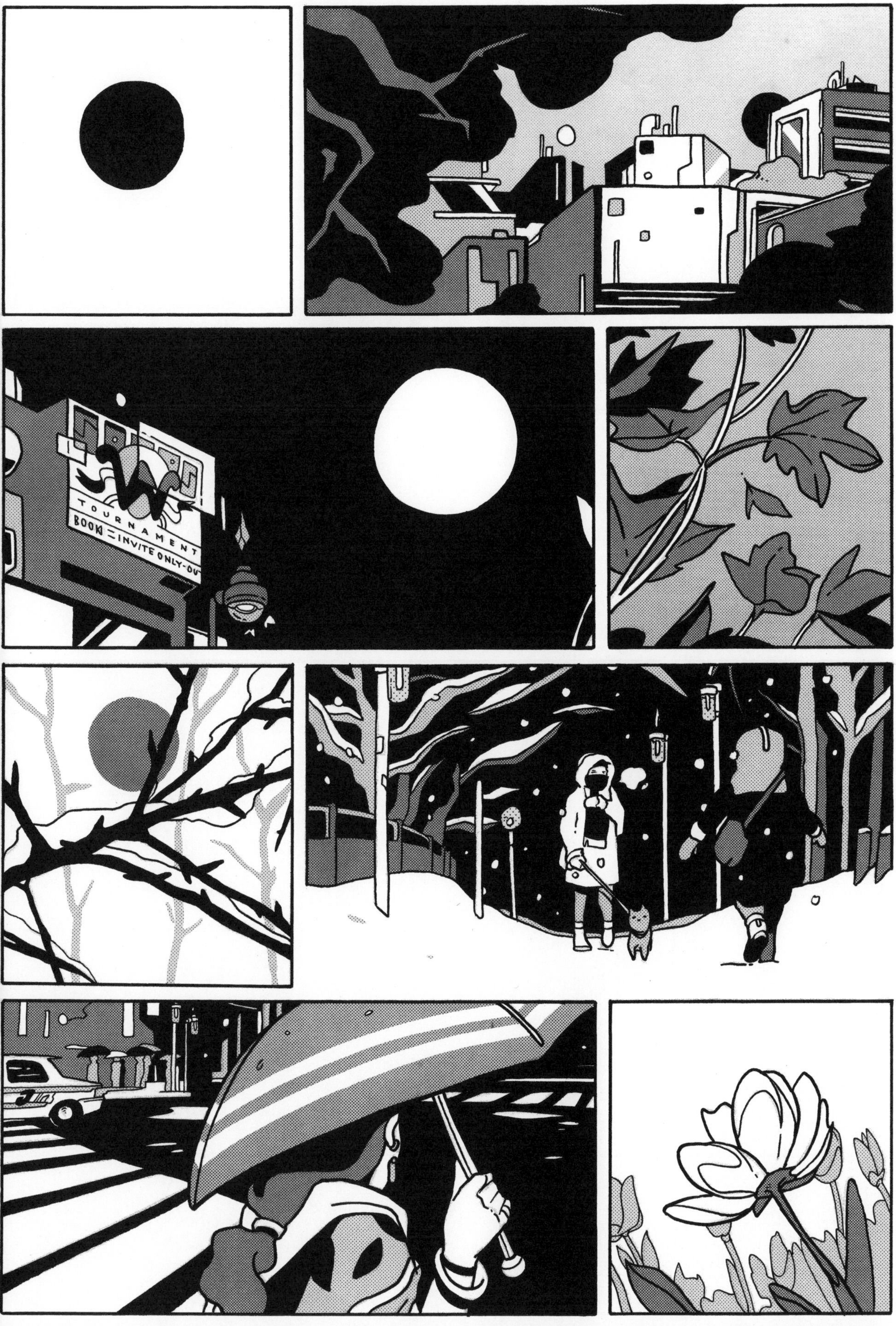
TOURNAMENT
BOOK = INVITE ONLY-OU

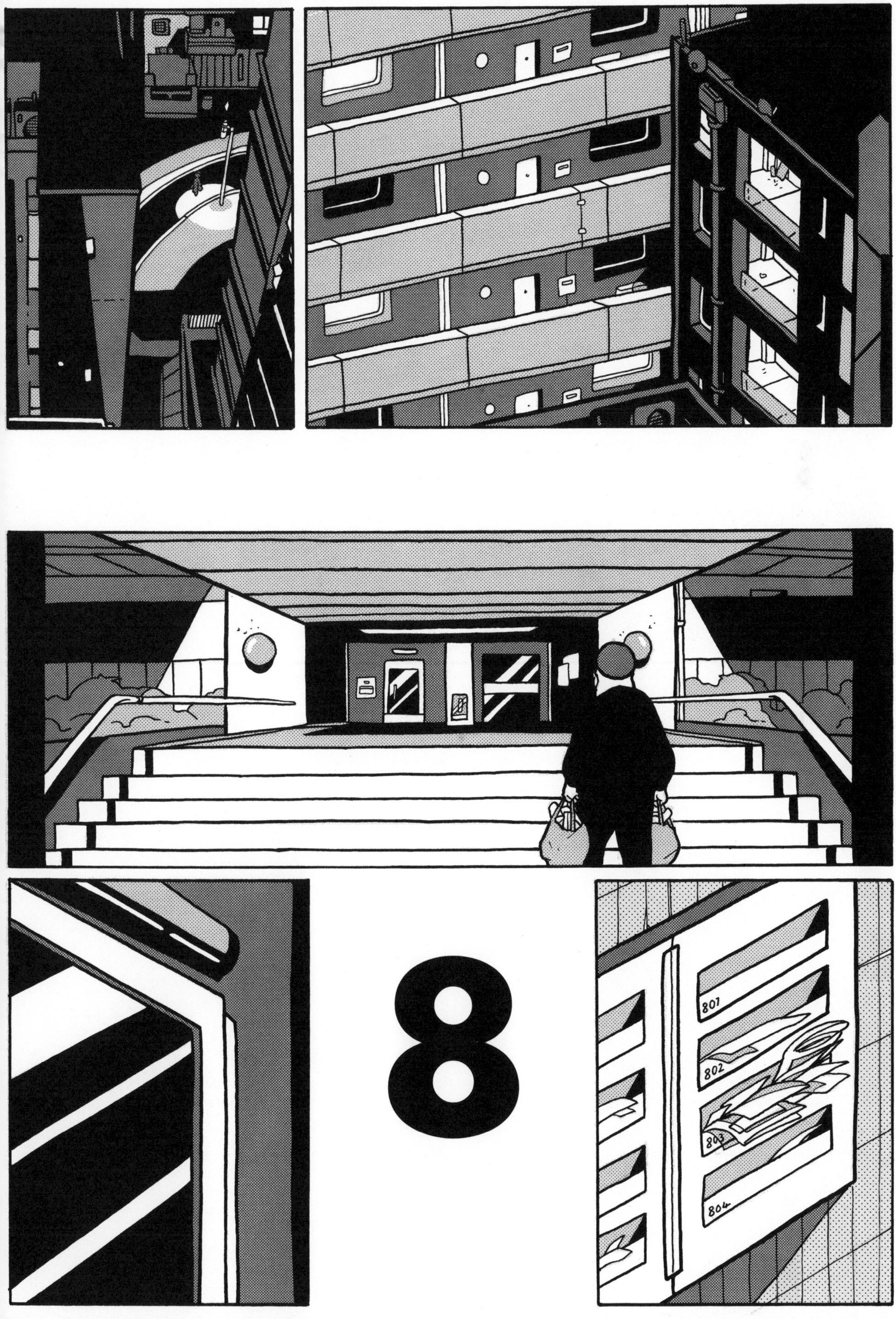
8
801
802
803
804

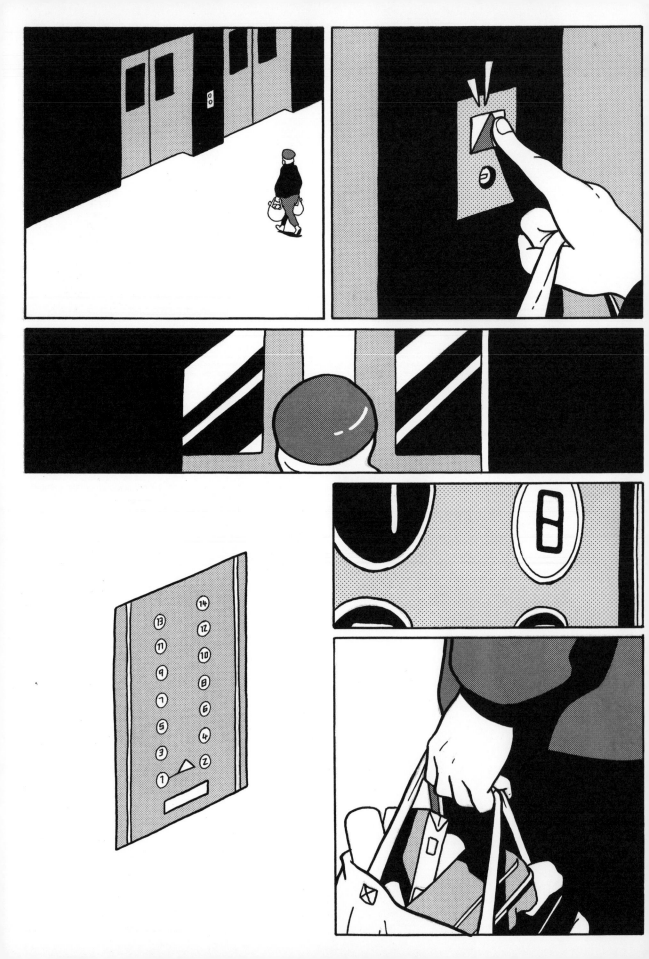

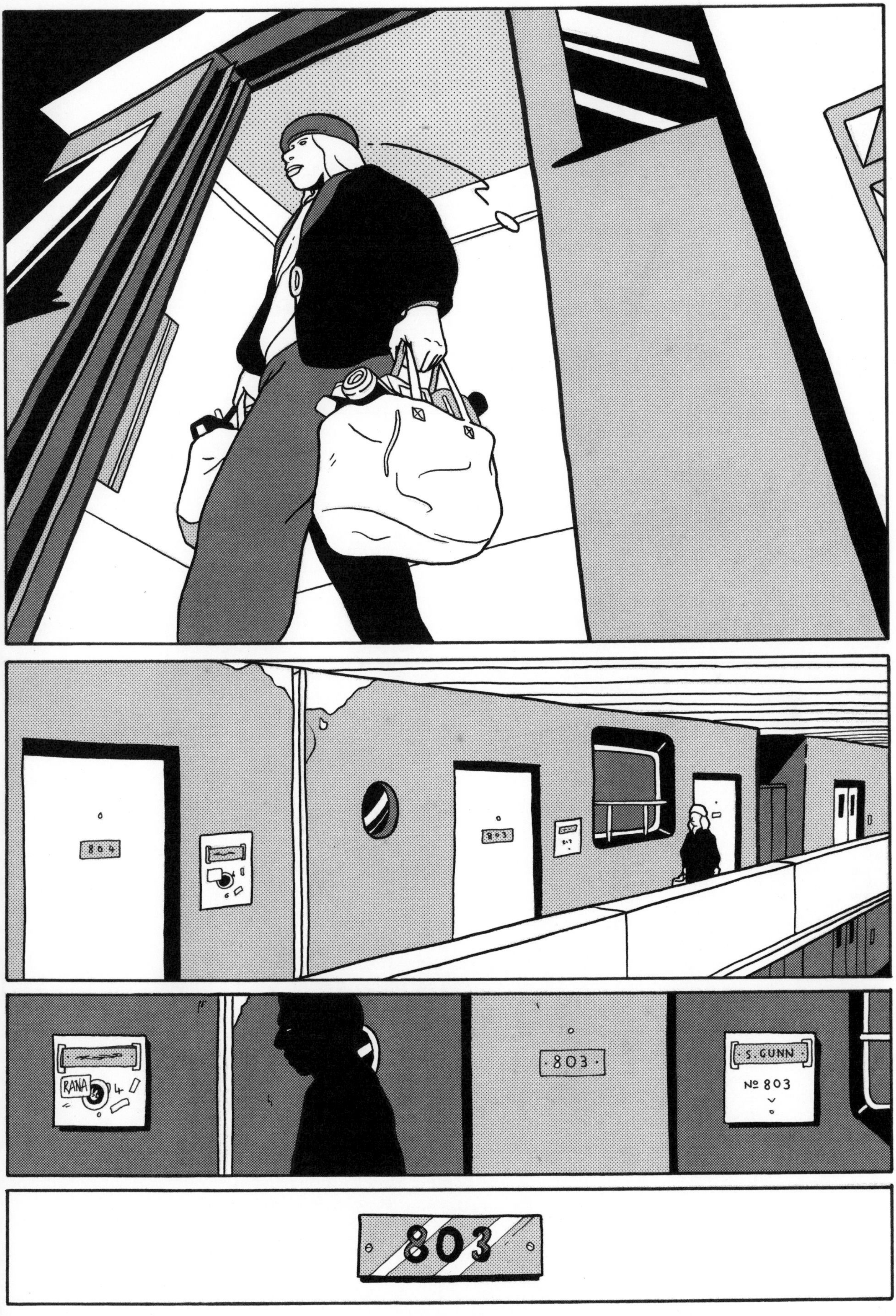
804
803
RANA
803
S. GUNN
№ 803
803

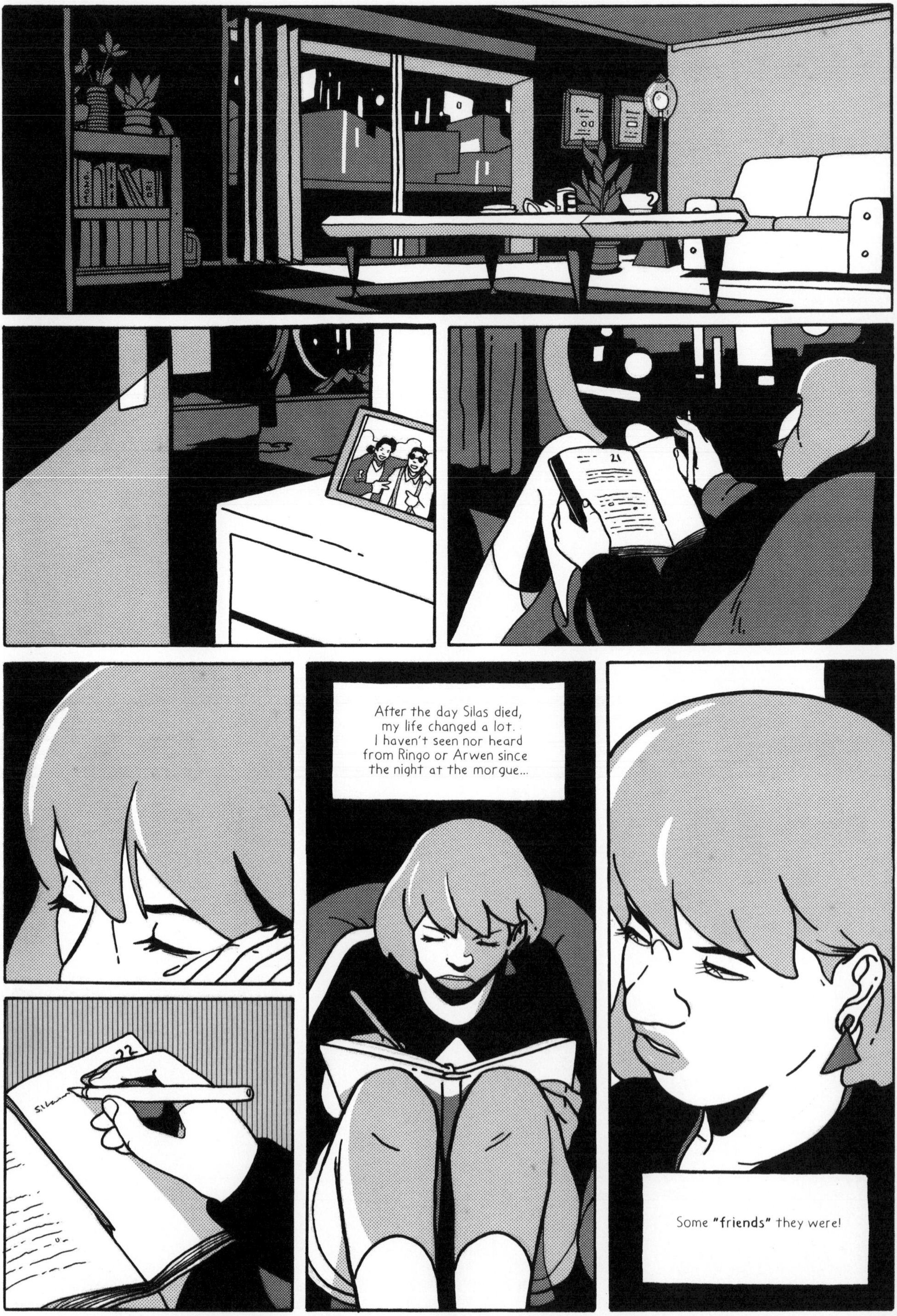
After the day Silas died, my life changed a lot. I haven't seen nor heard from Ringo or Arwen since the night at the morgue...
Some **"friends"** they were!

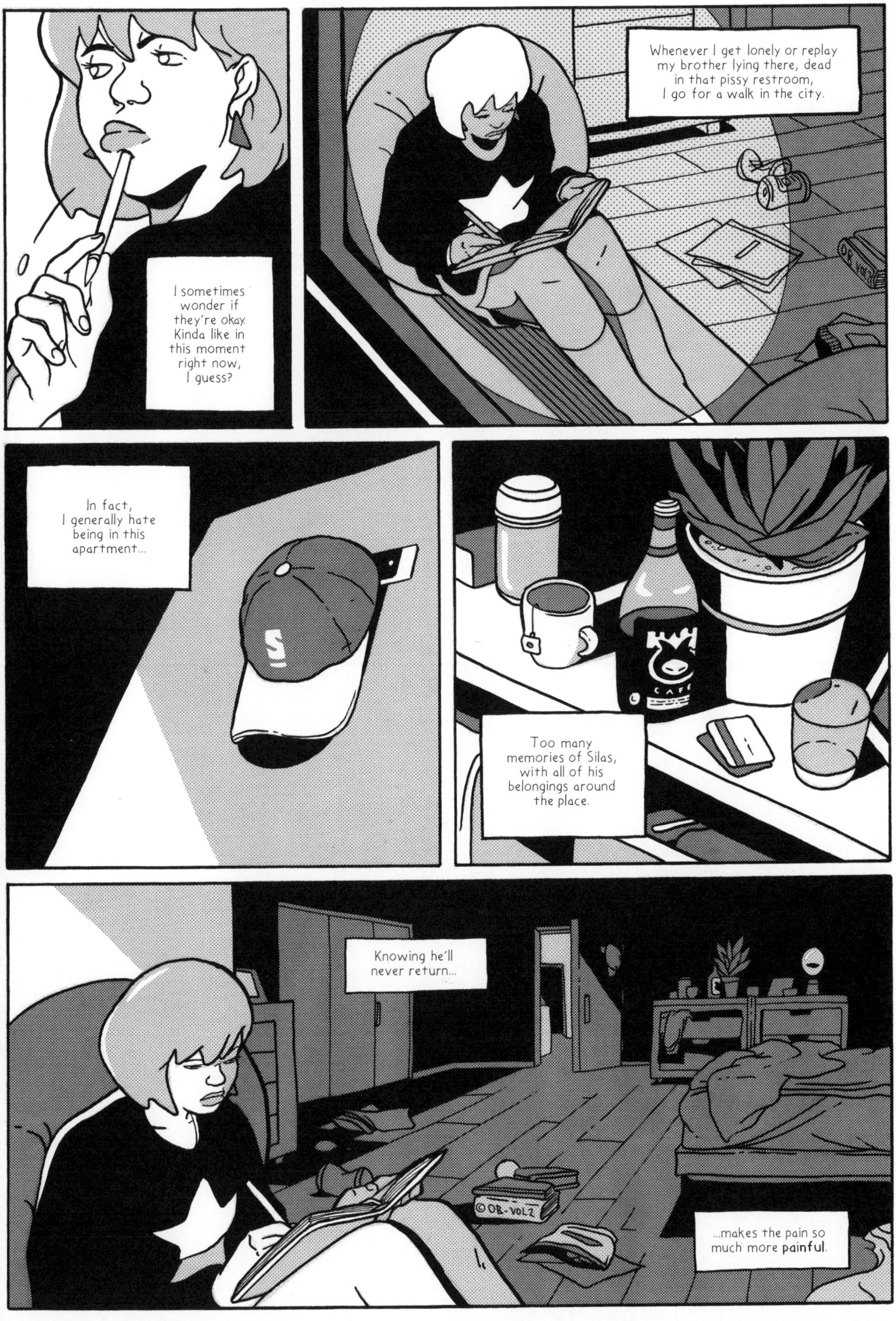
I sometimes wonder if they're okay. Kinda like in this moment right now, I guess?
Whenever I get lonely or replay my brother lying there, dead in that pissy restroom, I go for a walk in the city.
In fact, I generally hate being in this apartment...
CAFE
Too many memories of Silas, with all of his belongings around the place.
Knowing he'll never return...
OB-VOL2
...makes the pain so much more **painful**.

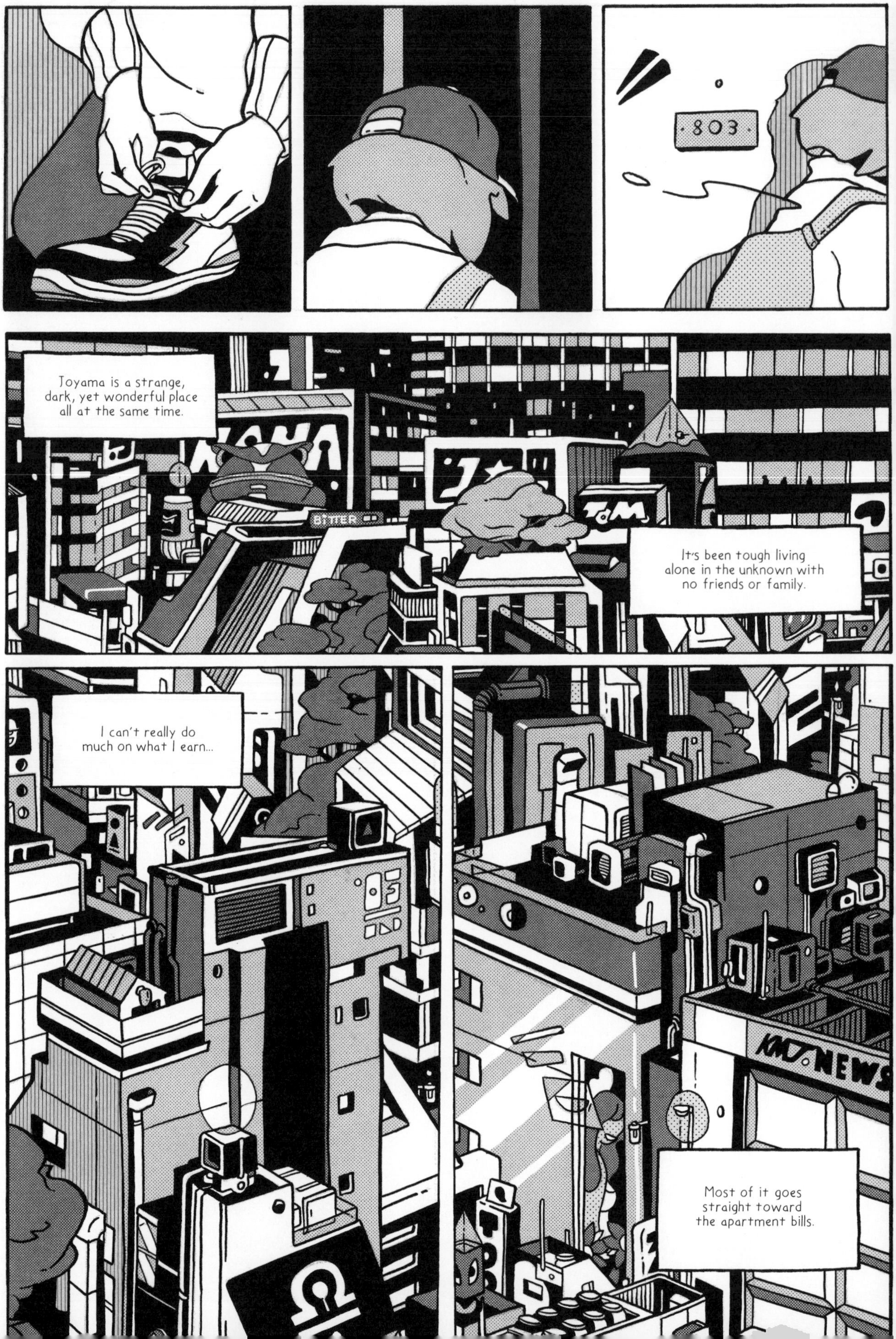
803
Toyama is a strange, dark, yet wonderful place all at the same time.
BITTER
It's been tough living alone in the unknown with no friends or family.
I can't really do much on what I earn...
NEWS
Most of it goes straight toward the apartment bills.

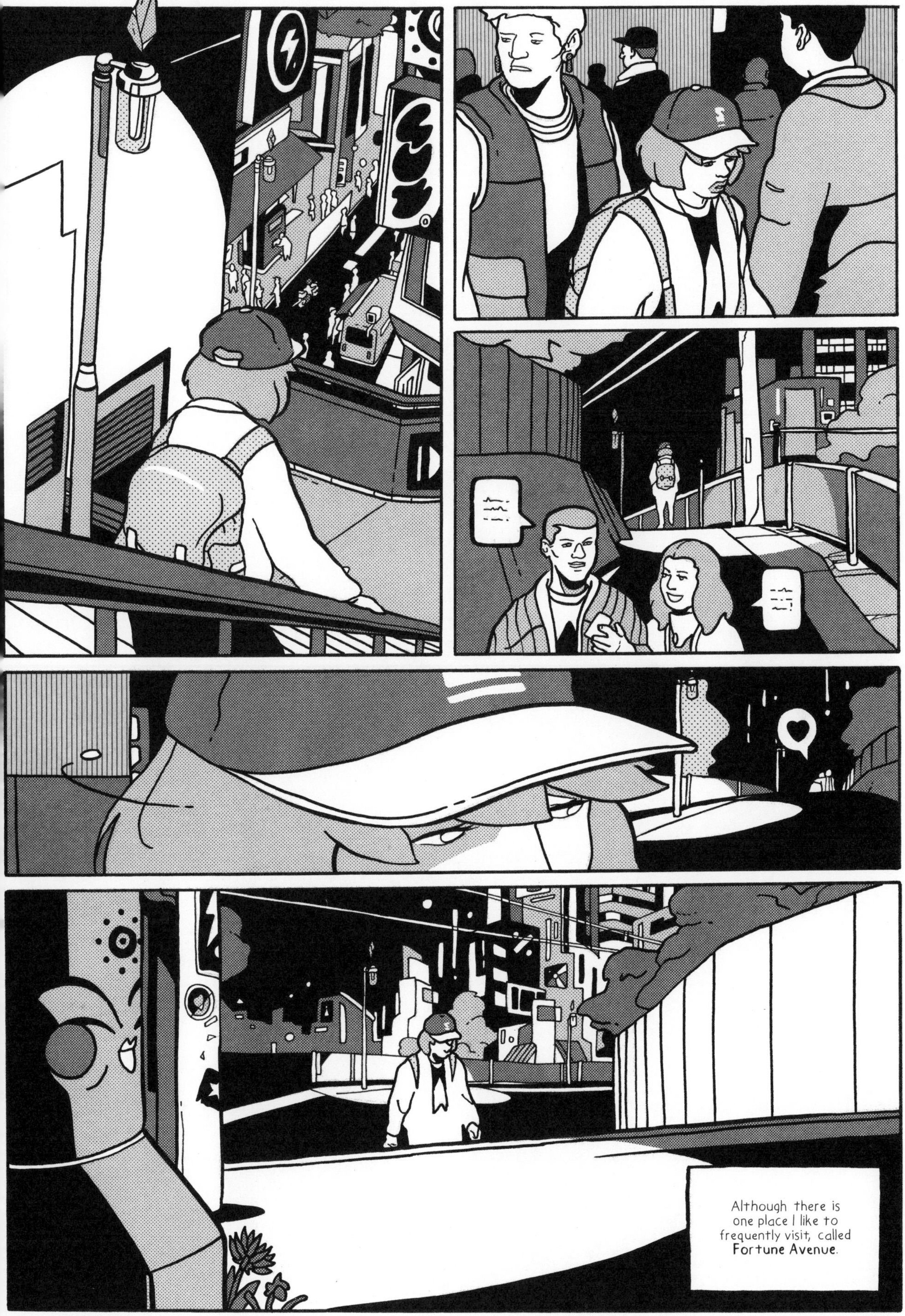
Although there is one place I like to frequently visit, called Fortune Avenue.

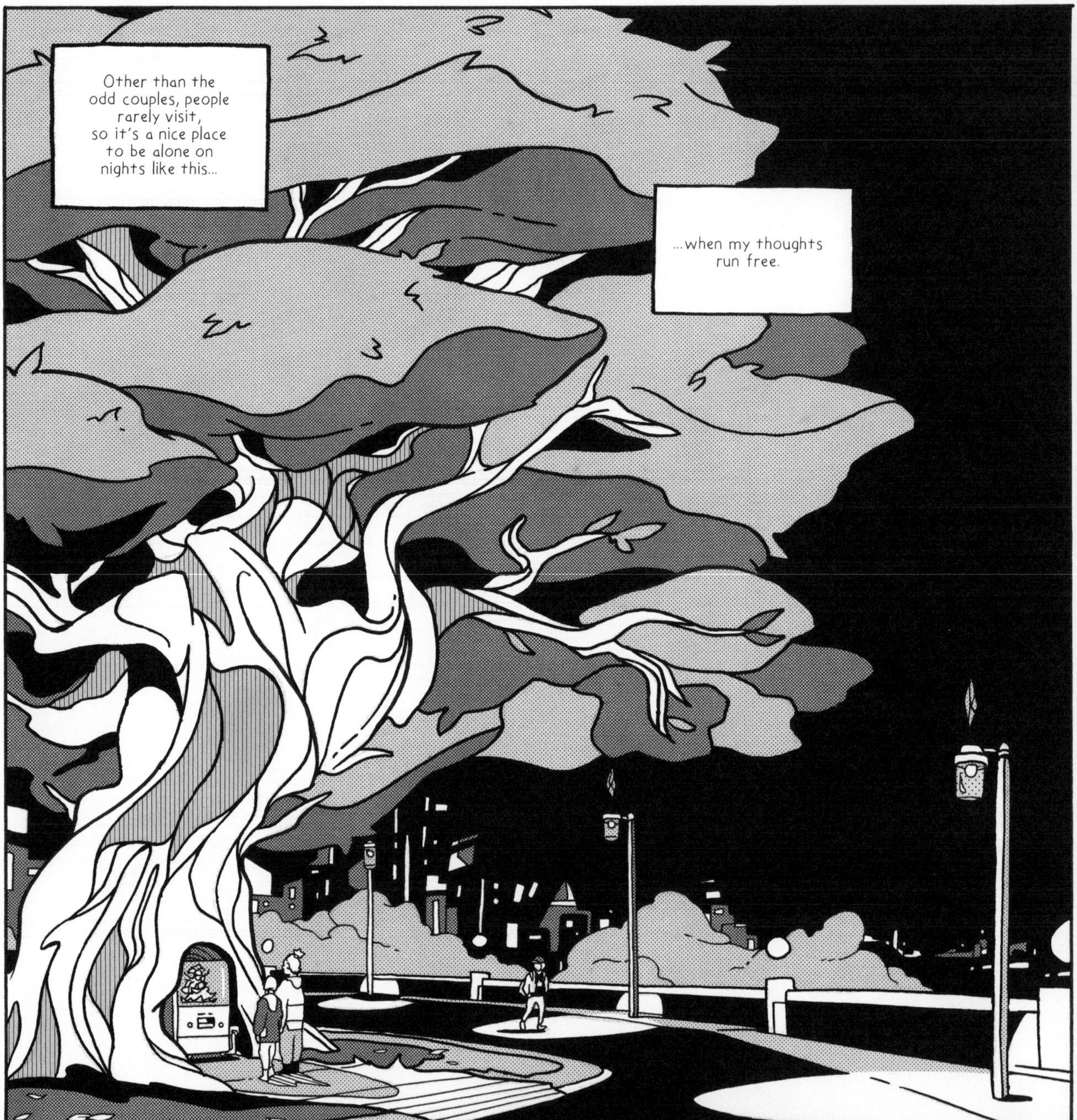
Other than the odd couples, people rarely visit, so it's a nice place to be alone on nights like this...
...when my thoughts run free.

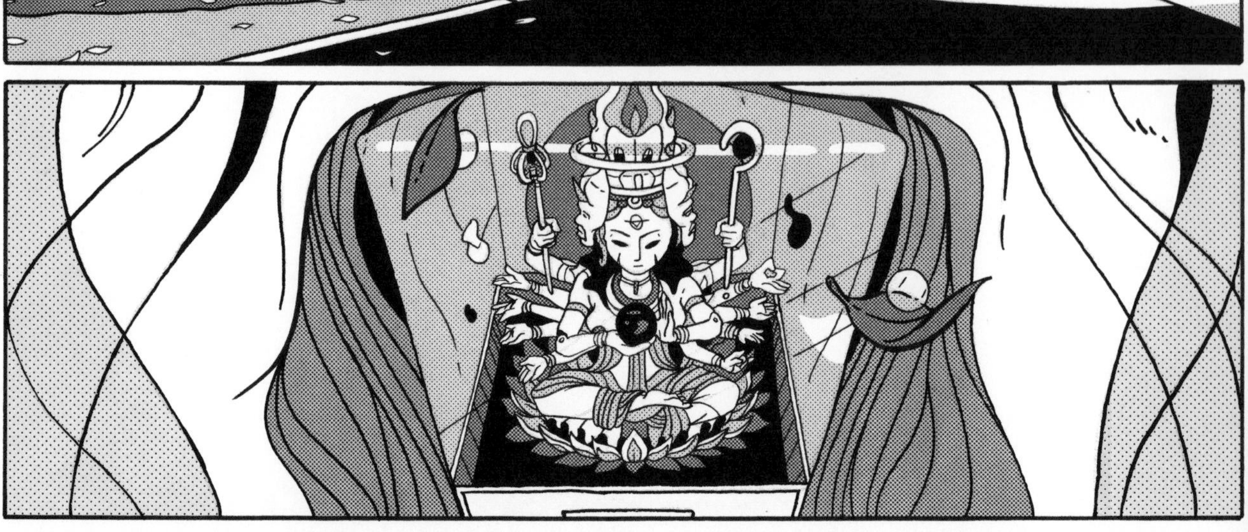

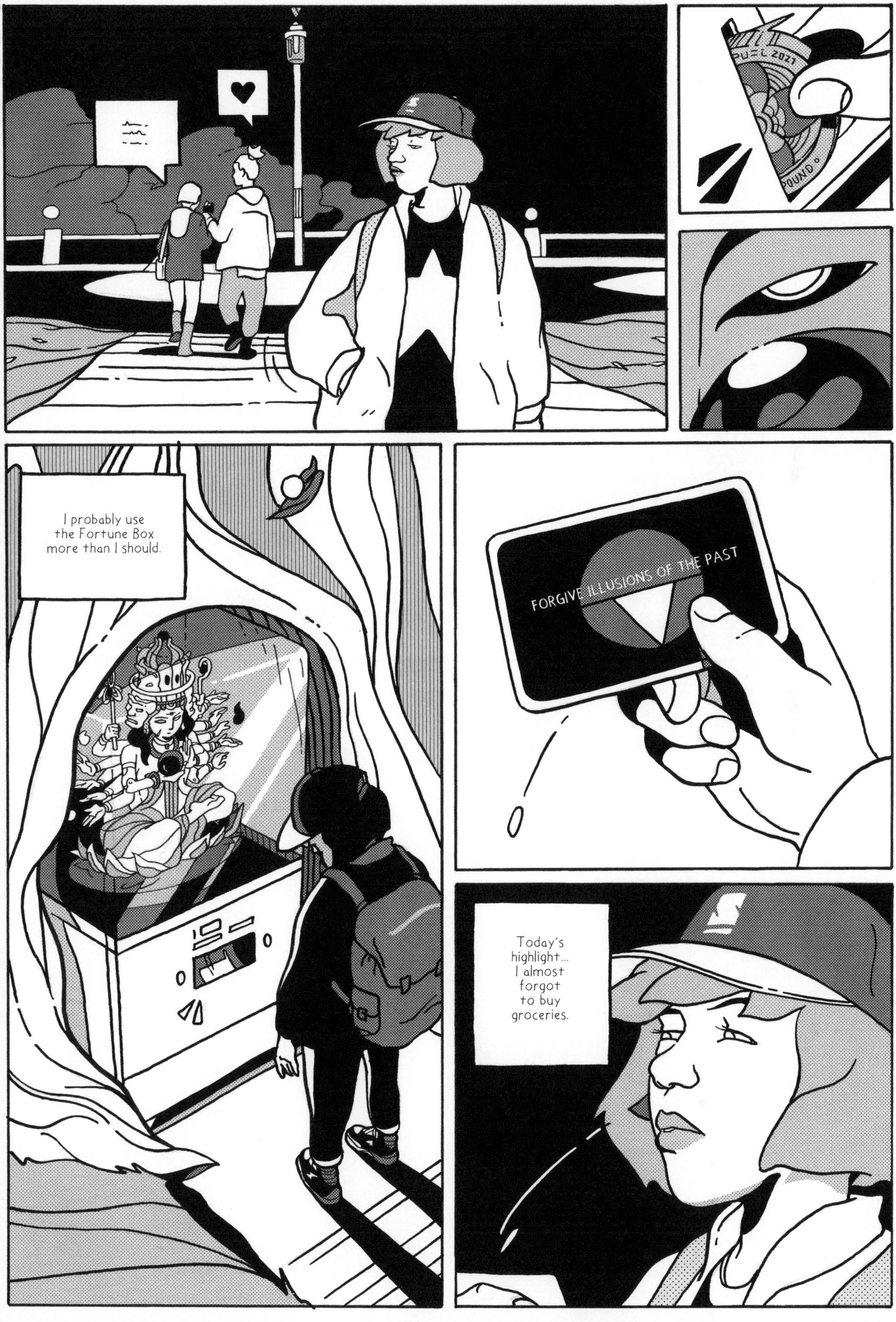
I probably use the Fortune Box more than I should.
FORGIVE ILLUSIONS OF THE PAST
Today's highlight... I almost forgot to buy groceries.

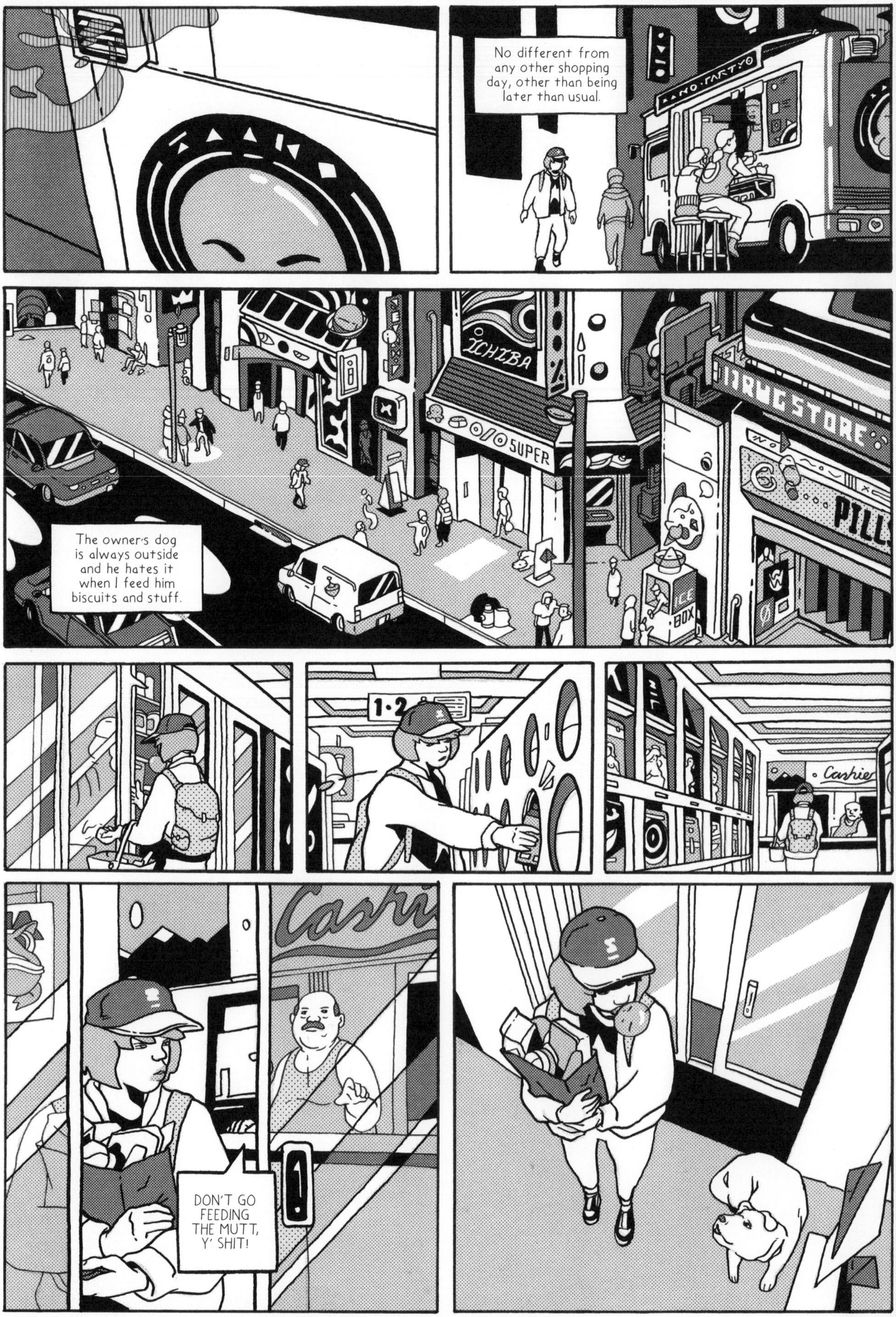
No different from any other shopping day, other than being later than usual.
ICHIBA
SUPER
DRUG STORE
PILLS
ICE BOX
The owner's dog is always outside and he hates it when I feed him biscuits and stuff.
1·2
Cashier
DON'T GO FEEDING THE MUTT, Y' SHIT!

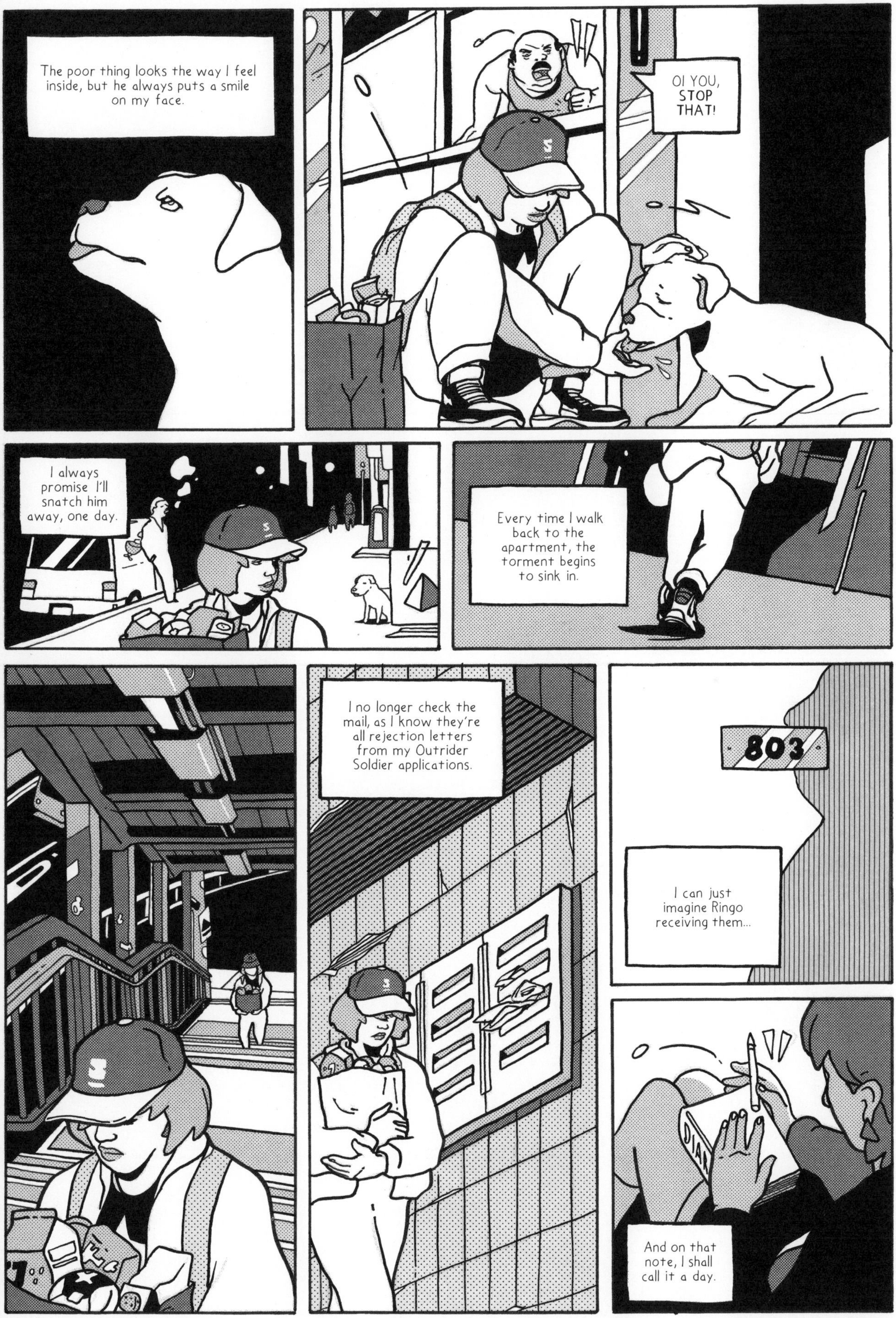
The poor thing looks the way I feel inside, but he always puts a smile on my face.
OI YOU, STOP THAT!
I always promise I'll snatch him away, one day.
Every time I walk back to the apartment, the torment begins to sink in.
I no longer check the mail, as I know they're all rejection letters from my Outrider Soldier applications.
803
I can just imagine Ringo receiving them...
And on that note, I shall call it a day.

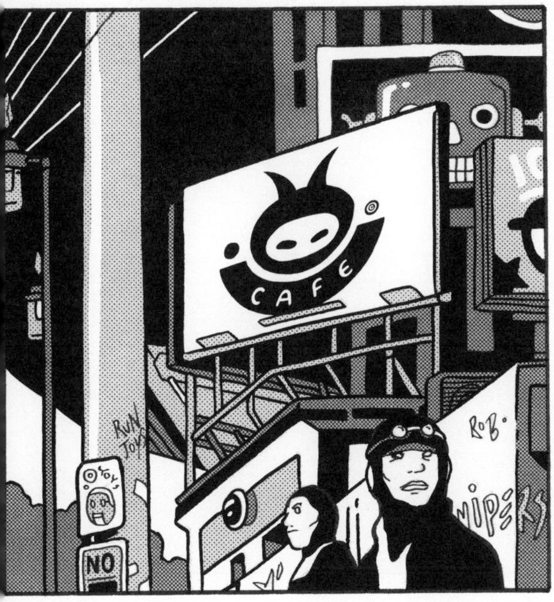
CAFE
NO

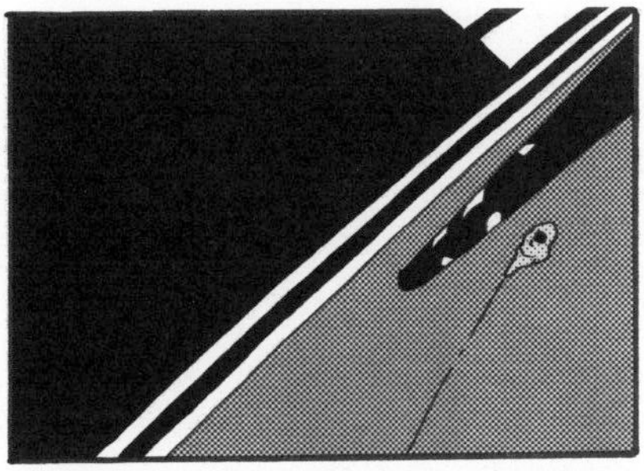

9

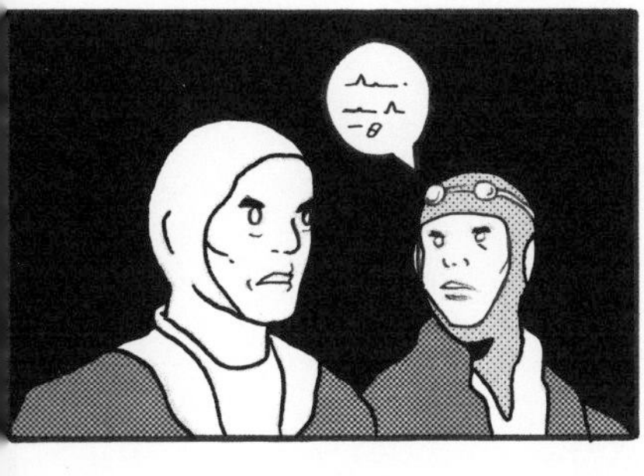

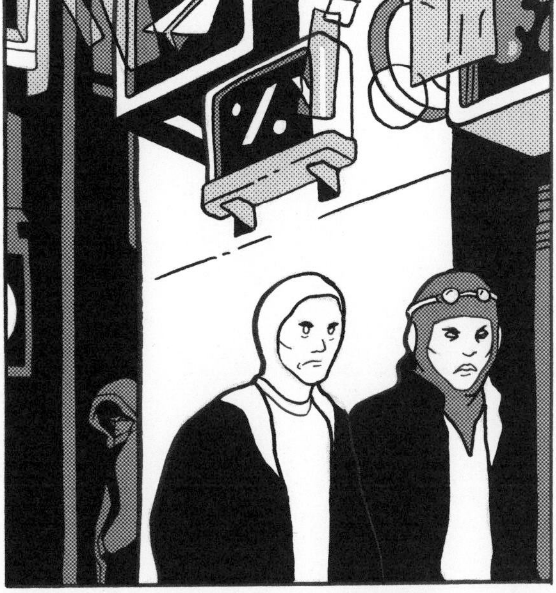

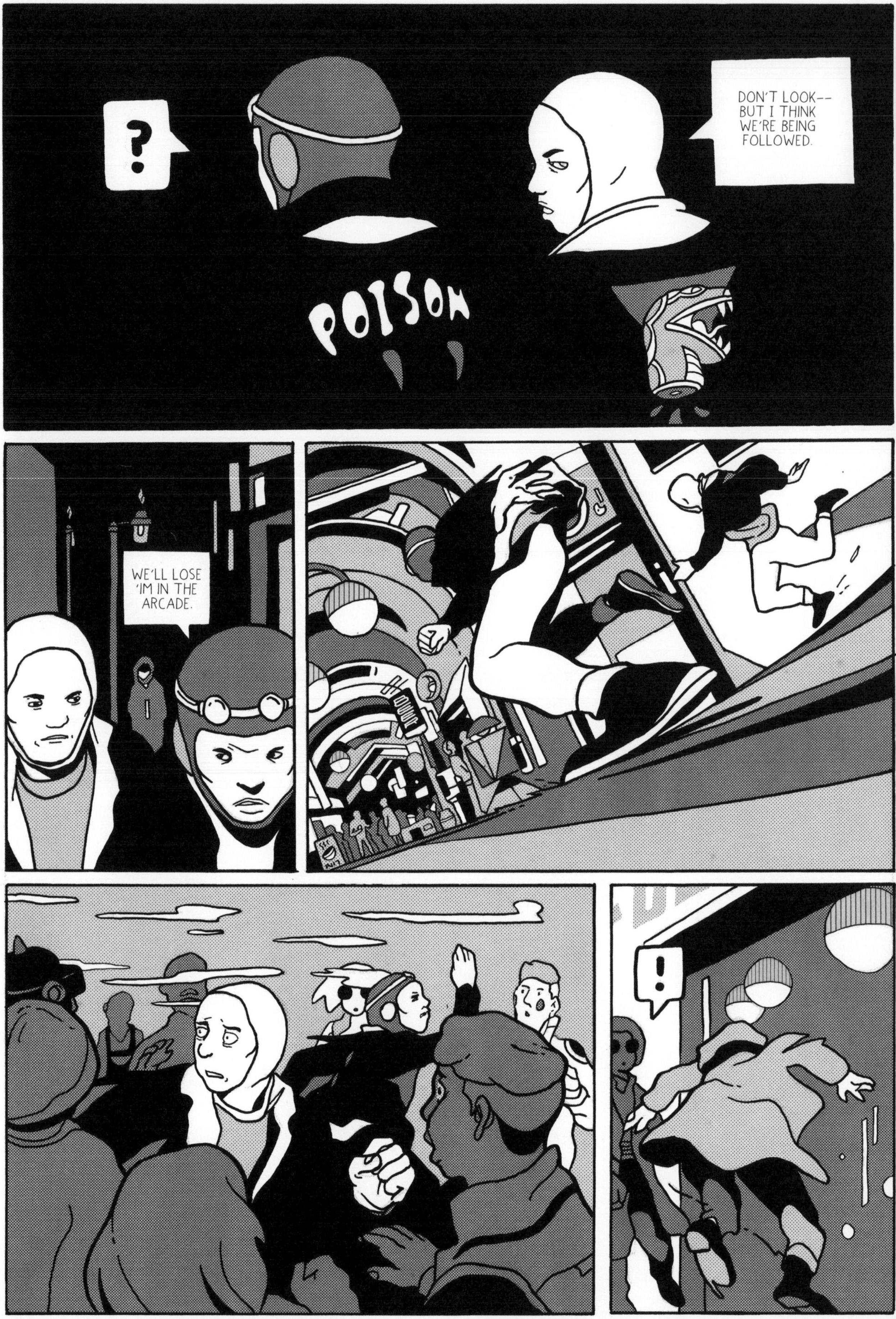
?
DON'T LOOK-- BUT I THINK WE'RE BEING FOLLOWED.
POISON
WE'LL LOSE 'IM IN THE ARCADE.
!

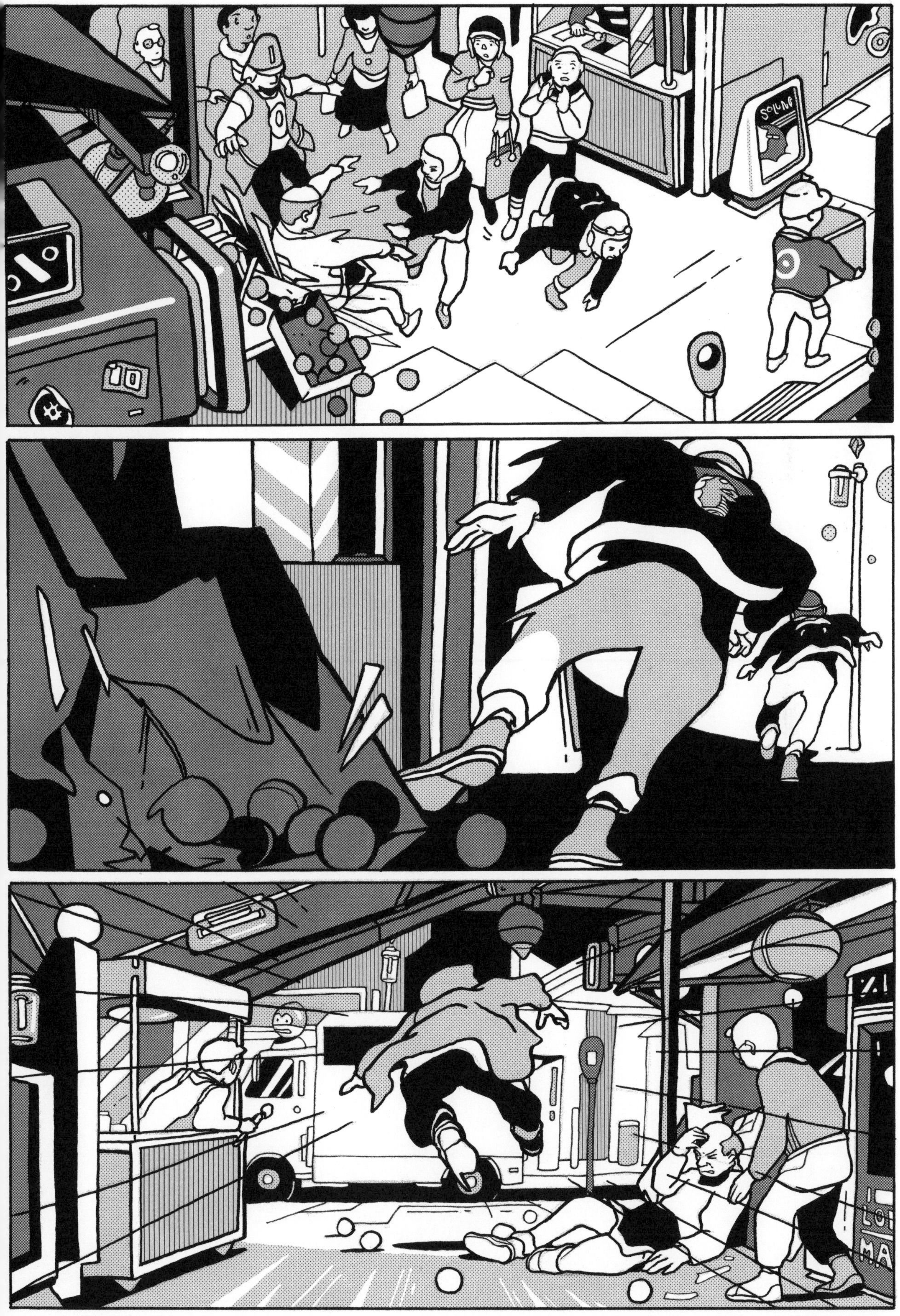

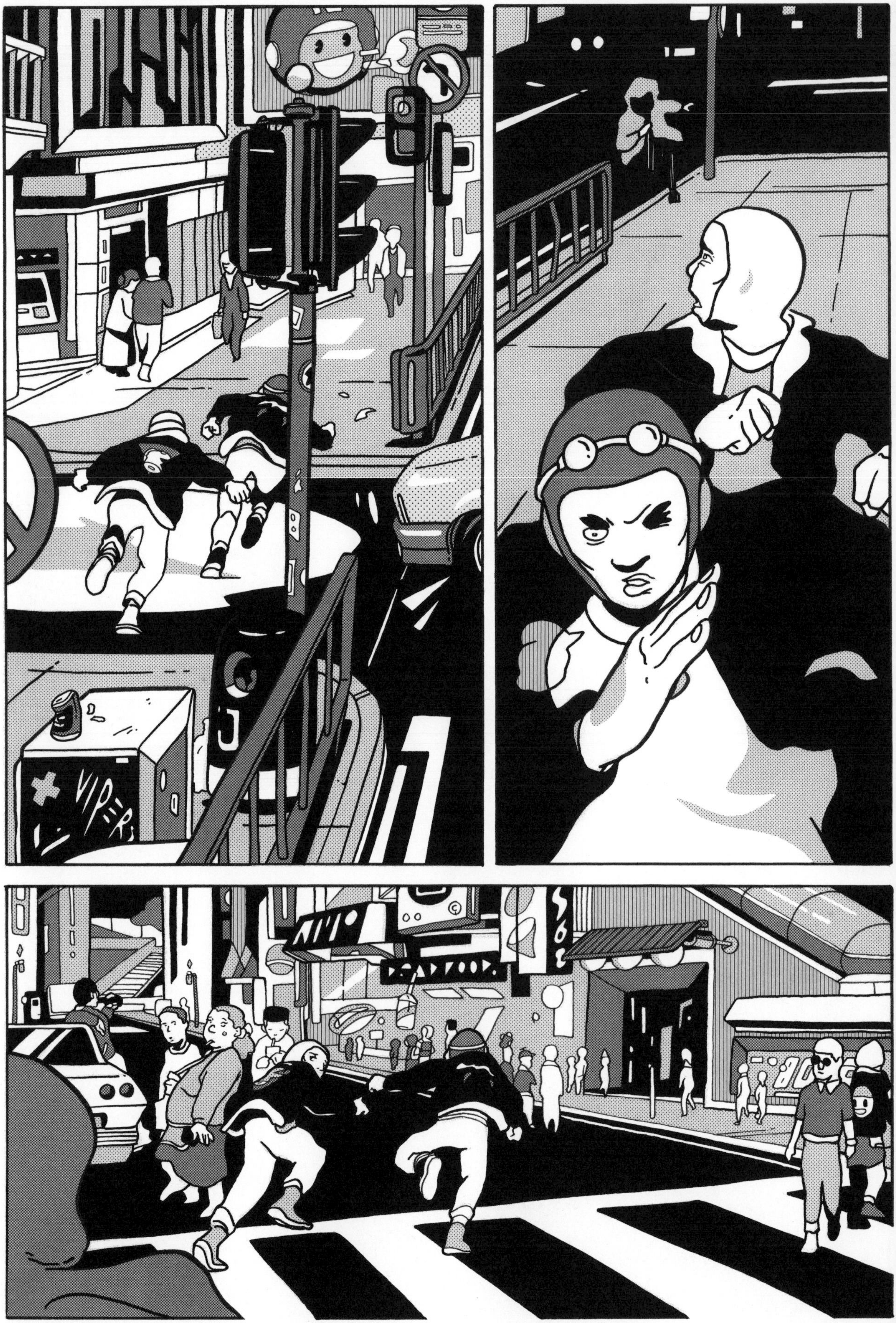

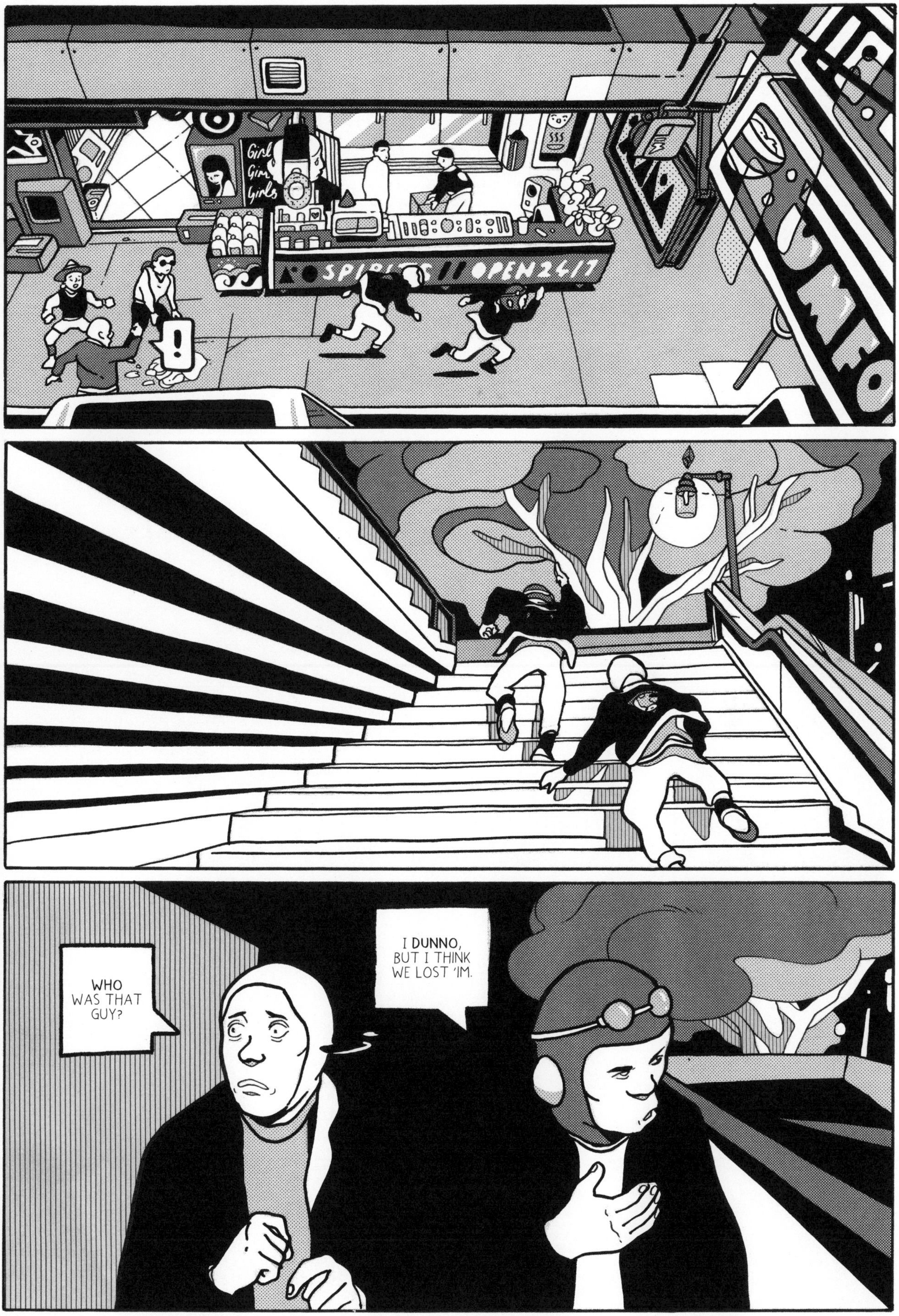
OPEN 24/7
!
WHO WAS THAT GUY?
I DUNNO, BUT I THINK WE LOST 'IM.

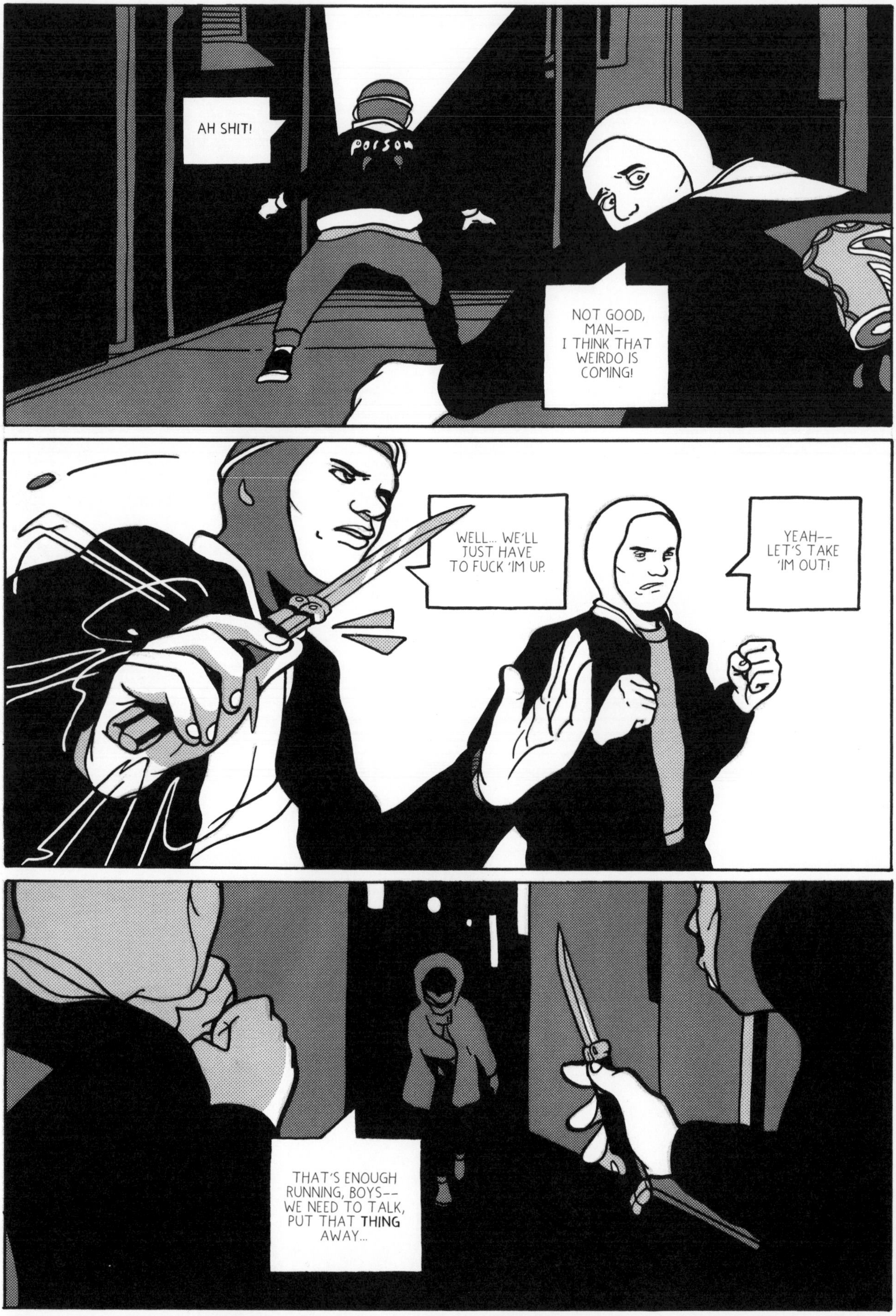
POISON
AH SHIT!
NOT GOOD, MAN-- I THINK THAT WEIRDO IS COMING!
WELL... WE'LL JUST HAVE TO FUCK 'IM UP.
YEAH-- LET'S TAKE 'IM OUT!
THAT'S ENOUGH RUNNING, BOYS-- WE NEED TO TALK, PUT THAT THING AWAY...

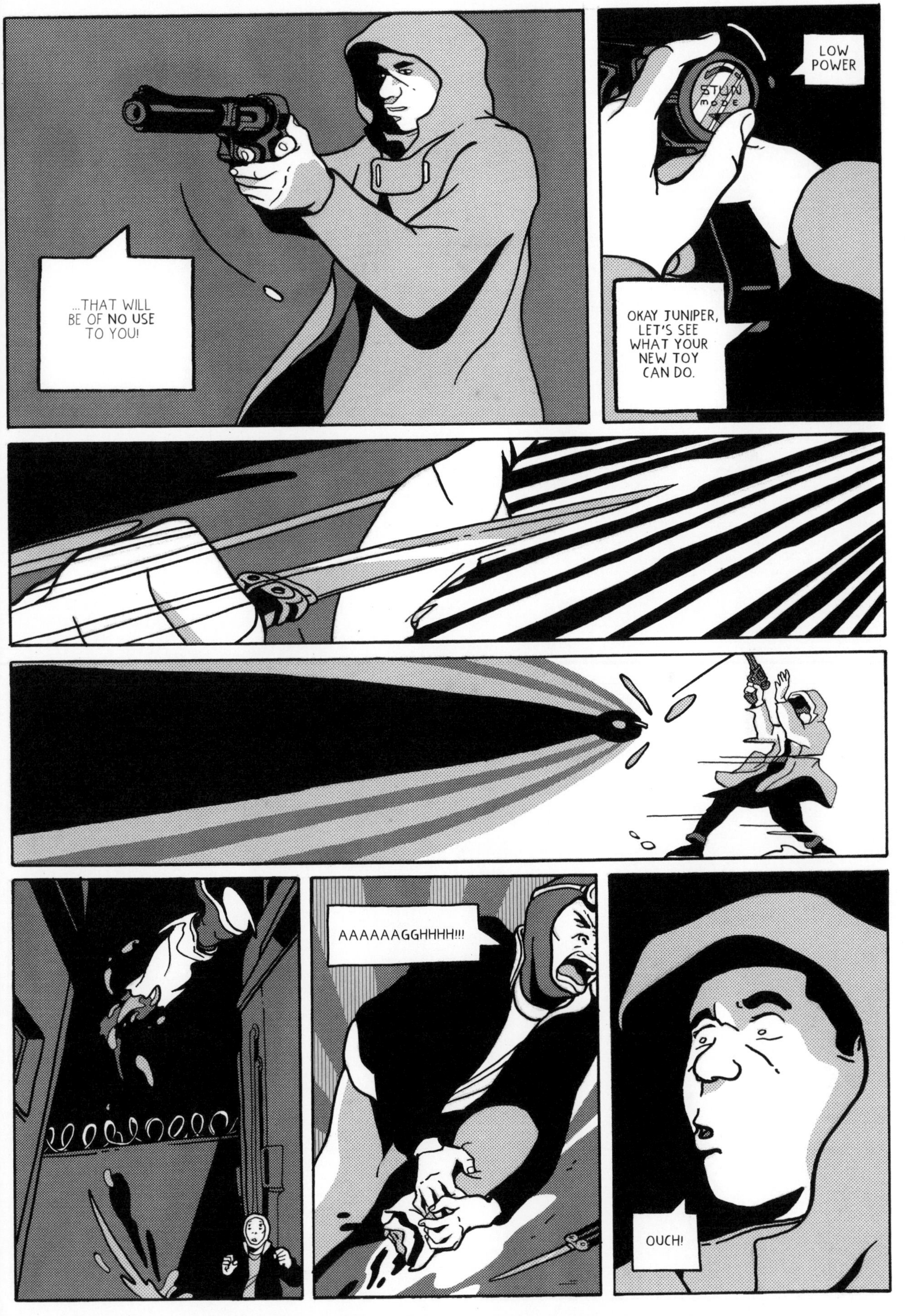
...THAT WILL BE OF NO USE TO YOU!
LOW POWER
STUN MODE
OKAY JUNIPER, LET'S SEE WHAT YOUR NEW TOY CAN DO.
AAAAAAGGHHHH!!!
OUCH!

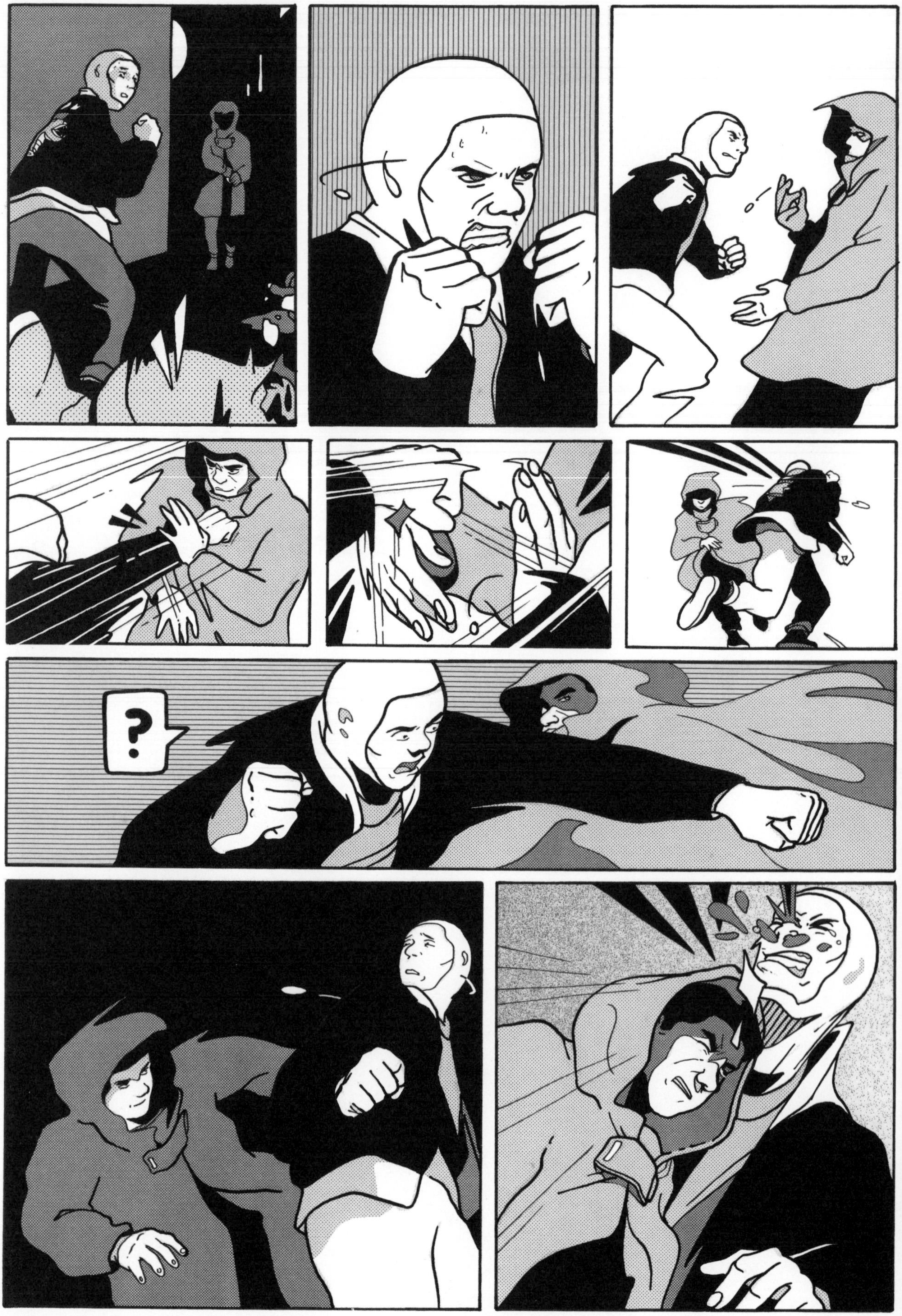
?

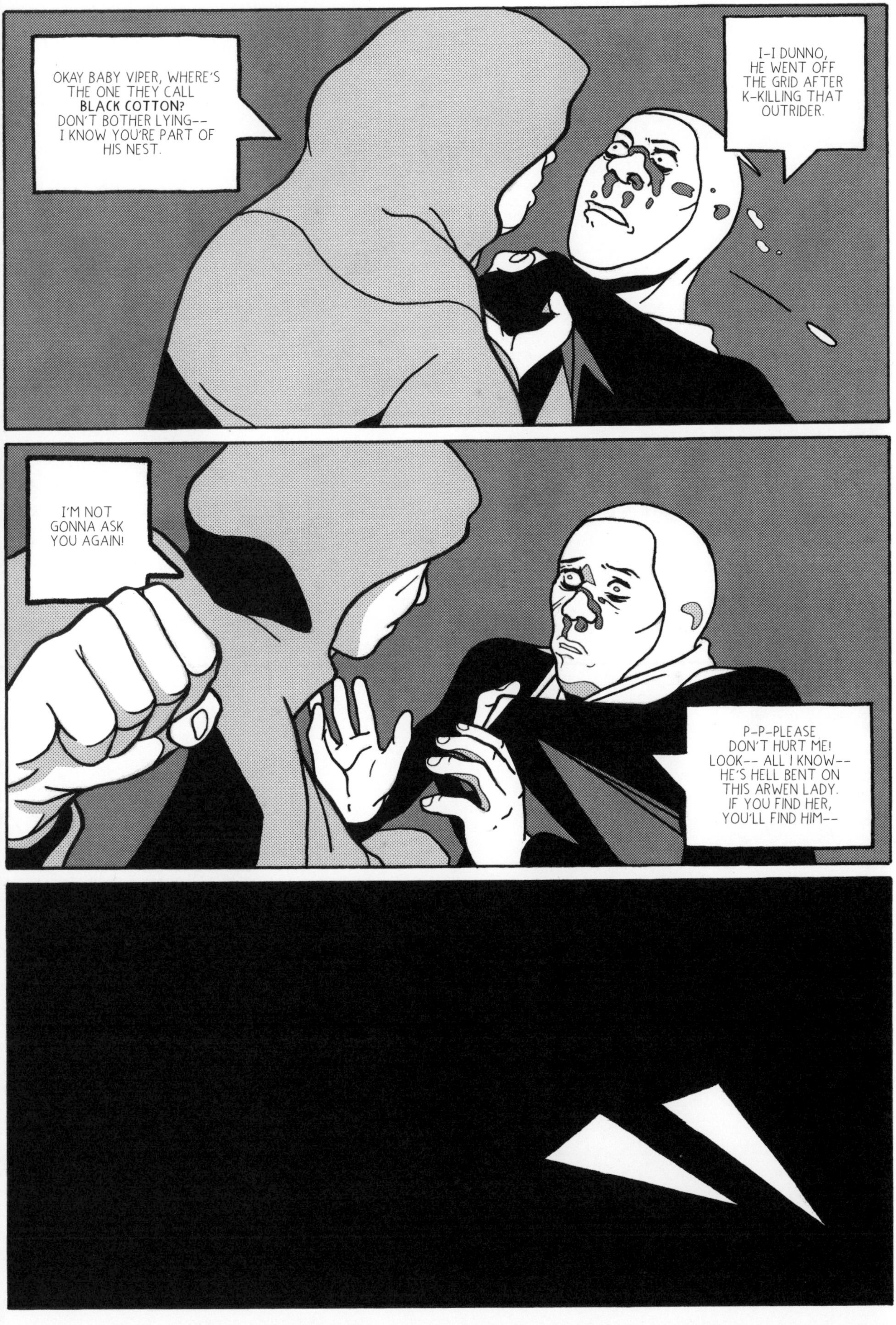
OKAY BABY VIPER, WHERE'S THE ONE THEY CALL **BLACK COTTON?** DON'T BOTHER LYING-- I KNOW YOU'RE PART OF HIS NEST.
I-I DUNNO, HE WENT OFF THE GRID AFTER K-KILLING THAT OUTRIDER.
I'M NOT GONNA ASK YOU AGAIN!
P-P-PLEASE DON'T HURT ME! LOOK-- ALL I KNOW-- HE'S HELL BENT ON THIS ARWEN LADY. IF YOU FIND HER, YOU'LL FIND HIM--

STUPID **JUNIPA**-- SHODDY WORK.

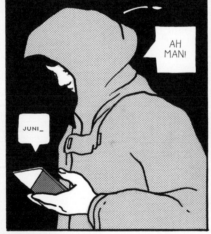

AH MAN!

JUNI_

JUNIPA

PIECE O' CRAP GONNA GET US SUSPENDED FOR SURE-- ANYWAY, HERE GOES... PFFF!

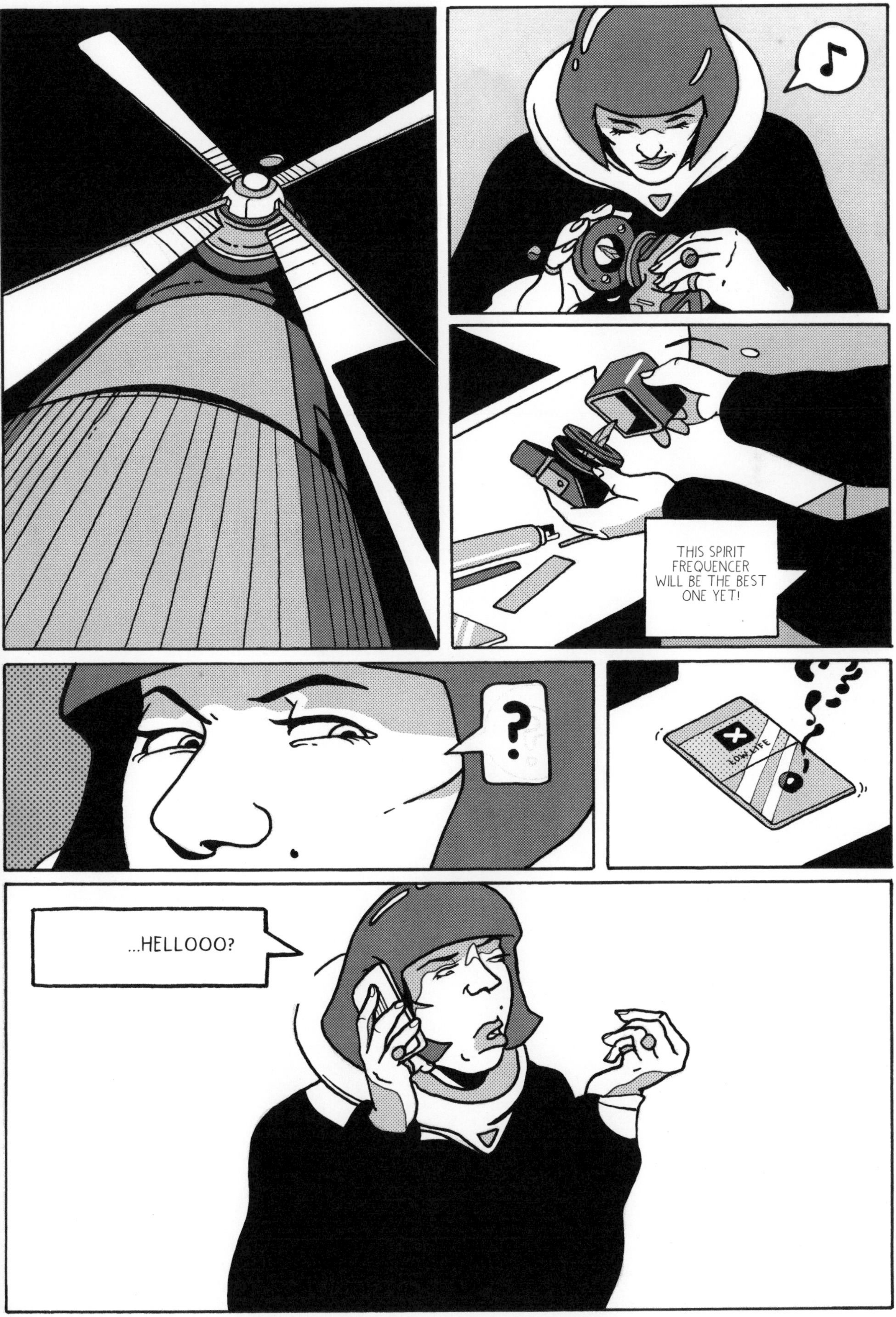
♪
THIS SPIRIT FREQUENCER WILL BE THE BEST ONE YET!
?
LOW LIFE
...HELLOOO?

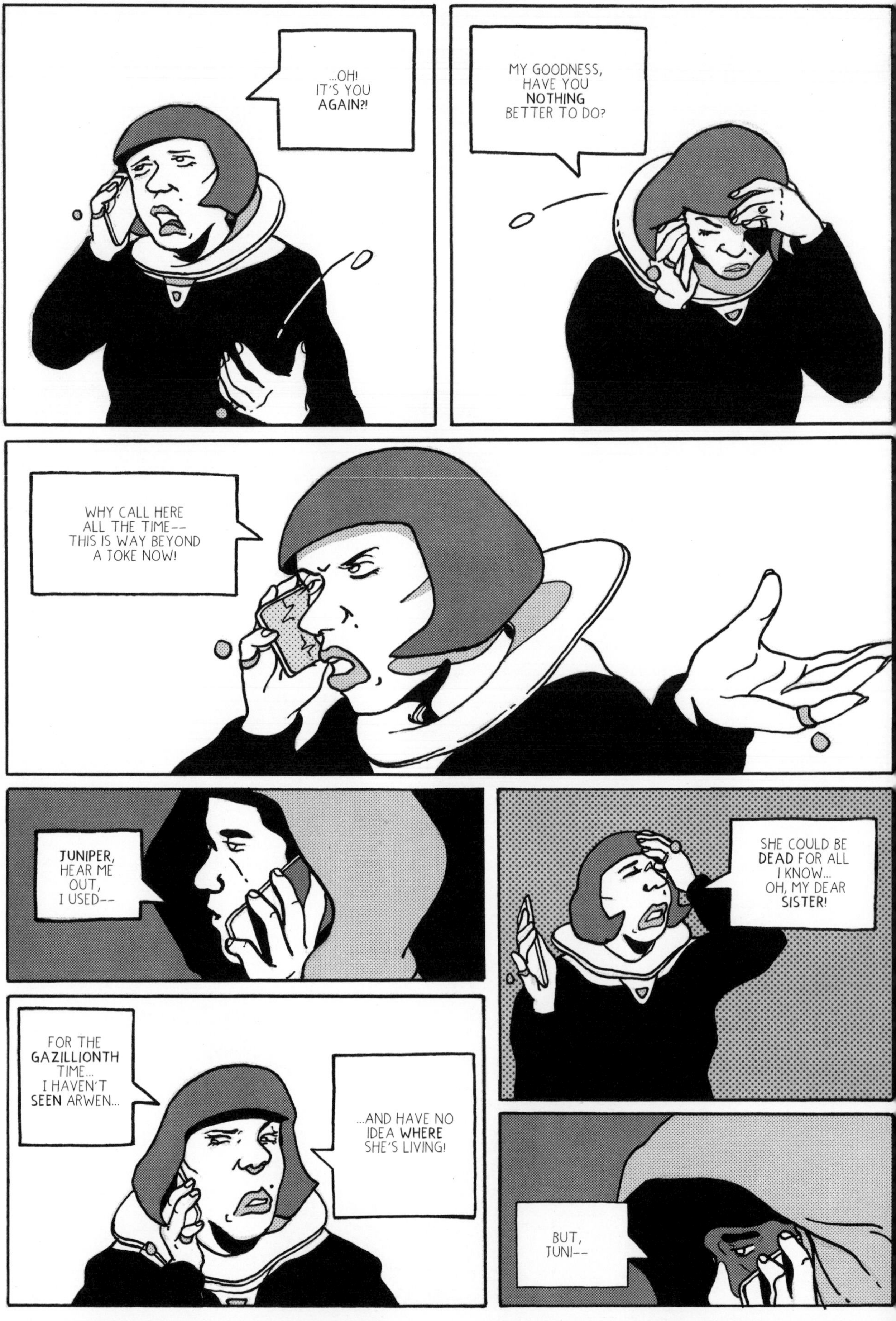
...OH! IT'S YOU **AGAIN?!**
MY GOODNESS, HAVE YOU **NOTHING** BETTER TO DO?
WHY CALL HERE ALL THE TIME-- THIS IS WAY BEYOND A JOKE NOW!
JUNIPER, HEAR ME OUT, I USED--
SHE COULD BE **DEAD** FOR ALL I KNOW... OH, MY DEAR **SISTER!**
FOR THE **GAZILLIONTH** TIME... I HAVEN'T **SEEN** ARWEN...
...AND HAVE NO IDEA **WHERE** SHE'S LIVING!
BUT, JUNI--

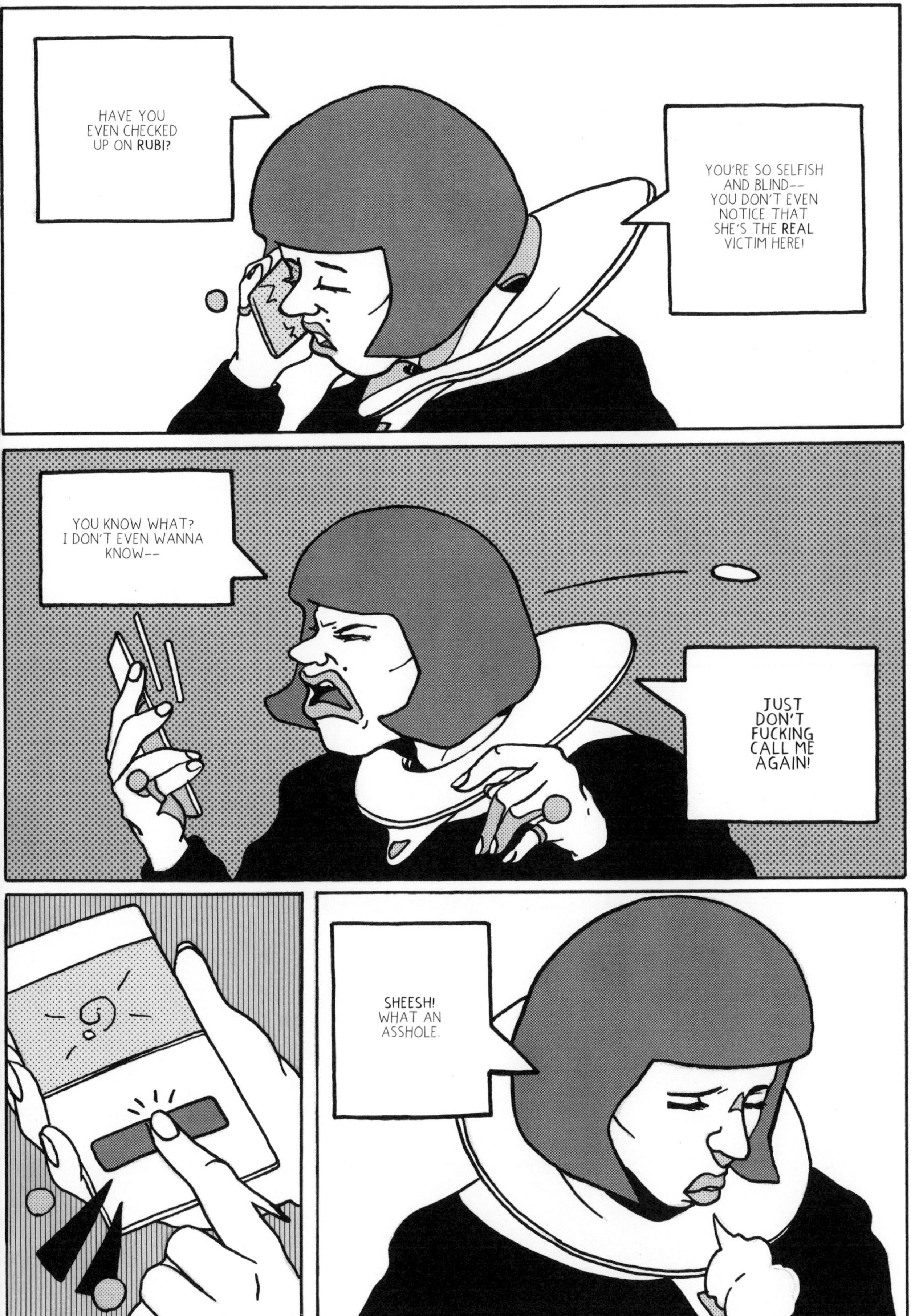
HAVE YOU EVEN CHECKED UP ON **RUBI**?
YOU'RE SO SELFISH AND BLIND-- YOU DON'T EVEN NOTICE THAT SHE'S THE **REAL** VICTIM HERE!
YOU KNOW WHAT? I DON'T EVEN WANNA KNOW--
JUST DON'T FUCKING CALL ME AGAIN!
SHEESH! WHAT AN ASSHOLE.

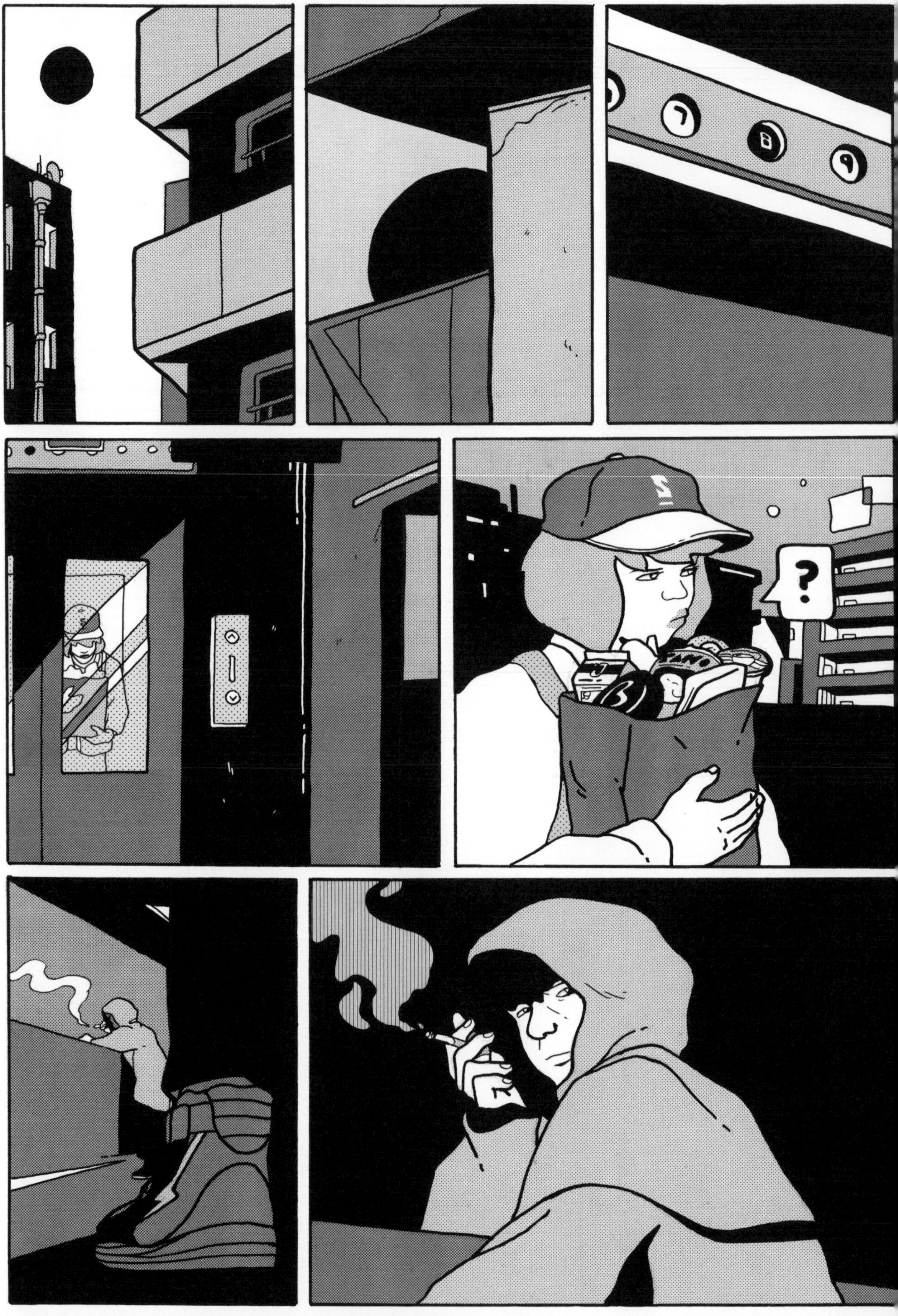
?

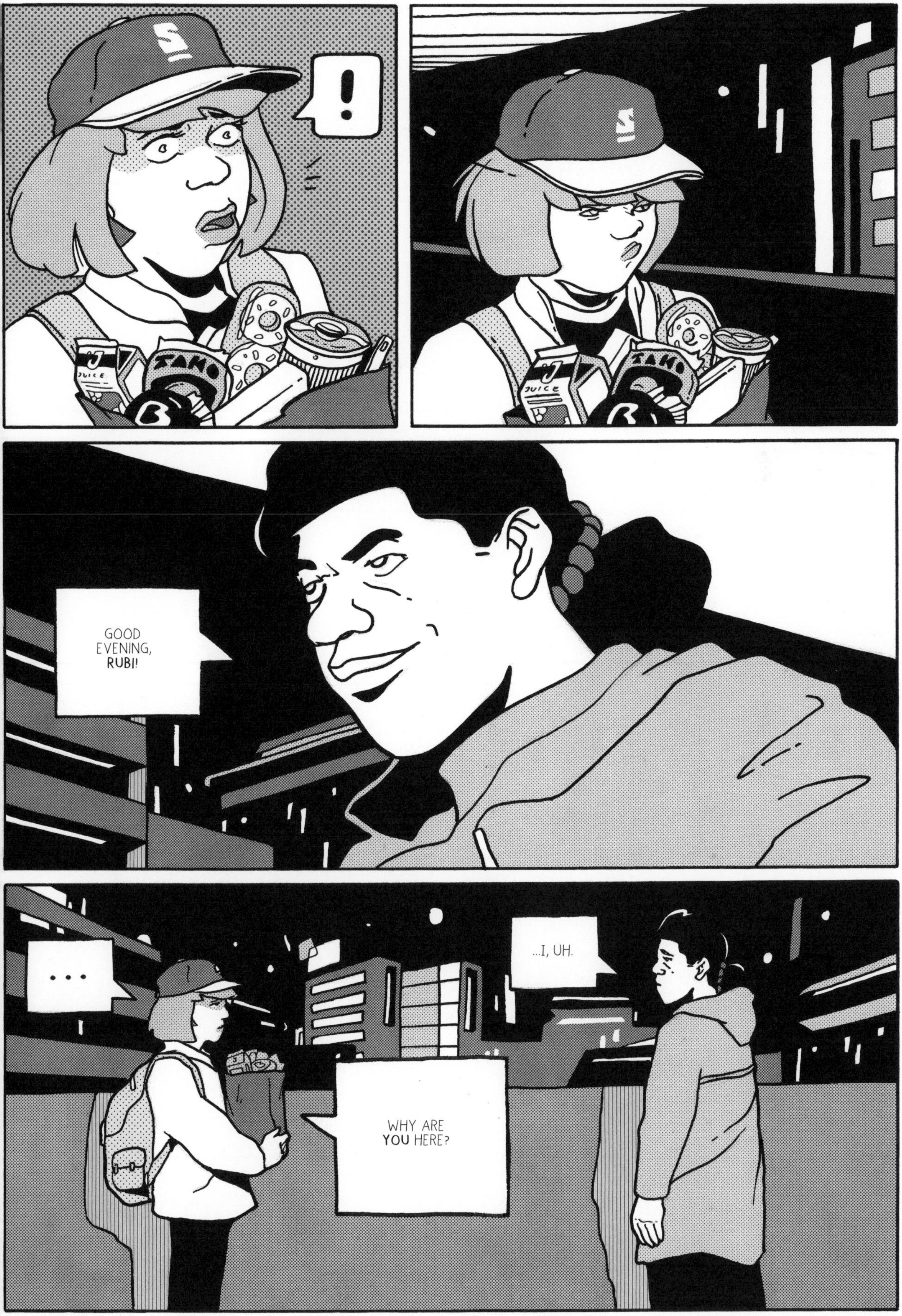
!
GOOD EVENING, RUBI!
...
...I, UH.
WHY ARE YOU HERE?

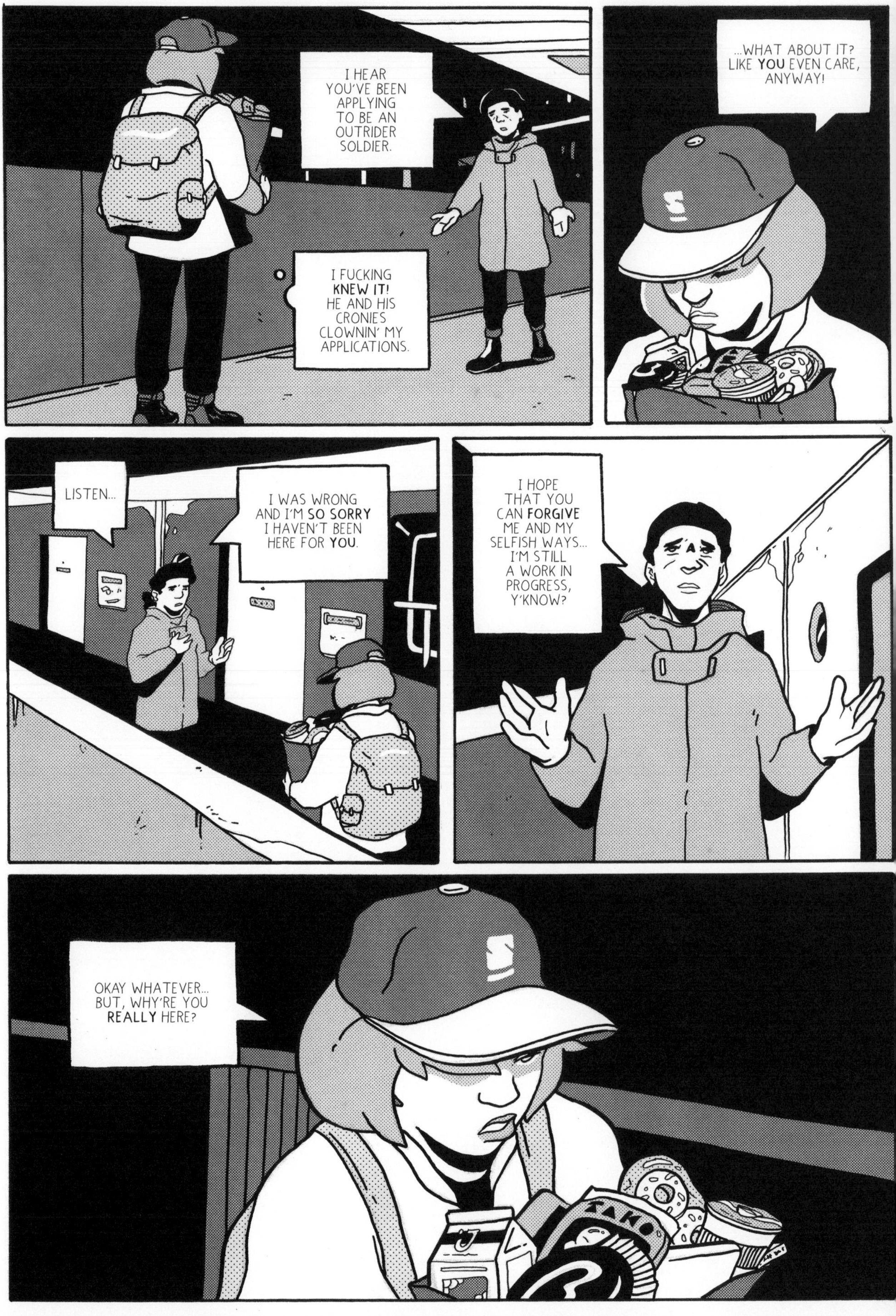
I HEAR YOU'VE BEEN APPLYING TO BE AN OUTRIDER SOLDIER.
I FUCKING KNEW IT! HE AND HIS CRONIES CLOWNIN' MY APPLICATIONS.
...WHAT ABOUT IT? LIKE YOU EVEN CARE, ANYWAY!
LISTEN...
I WAS WRONG AND I'M SO SORRY I HAVEN'T BEEN HERE FOR YOU.
I HOPE THAT YOU CAN FORGIVE ME AND MY SELFISH WAYS... I'M STILL A WORK IN PROGRESS, Y'KNOW?
OKAY WHATEVER... BUT, WHY'RE YOU REALLY HERE?

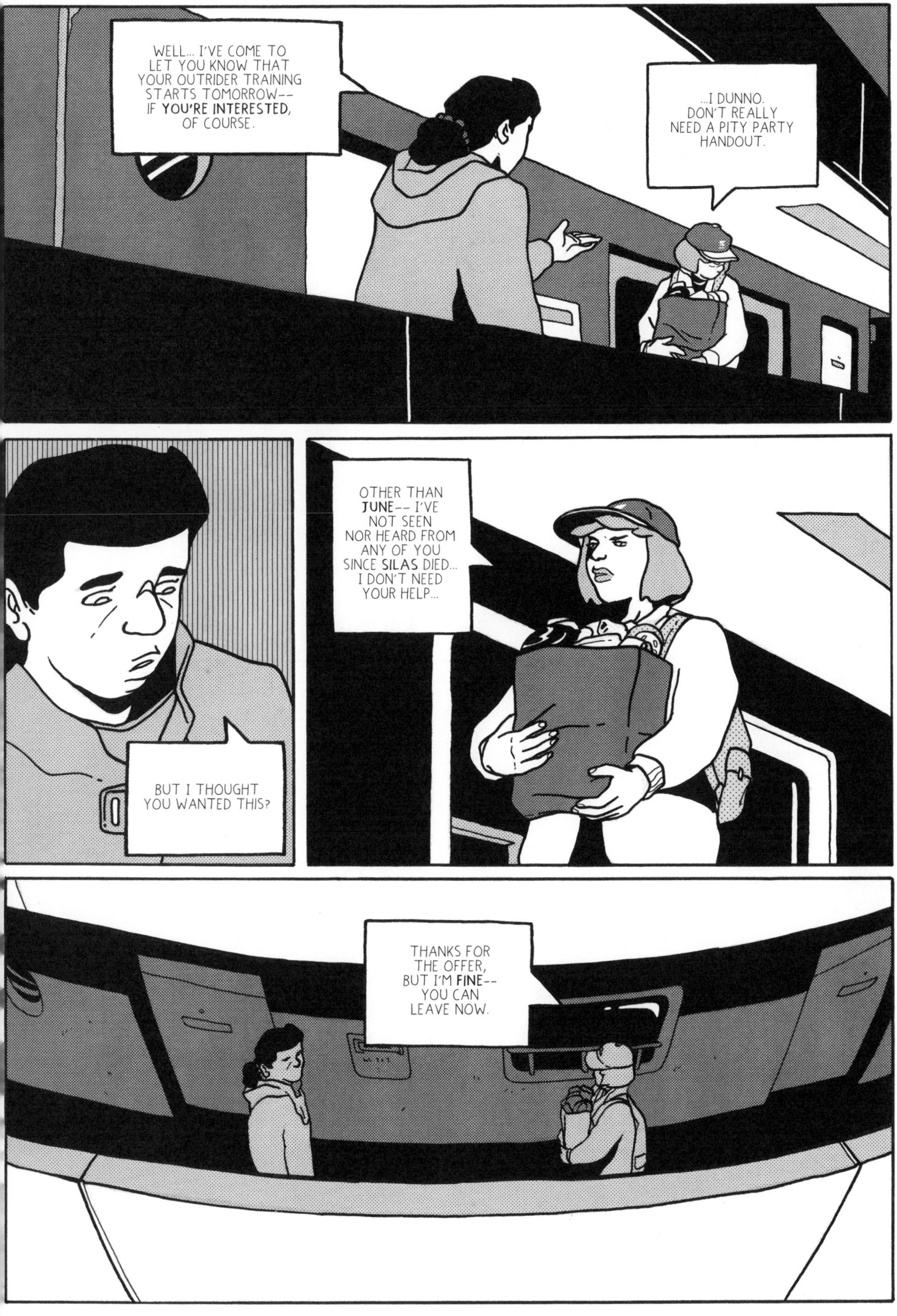
WELL... I'VE COME TO LET YOU KNOW THAT YOUR OUTRIDER TRAINING STARTS TOMORROW-- IF **YOU'RE INTERESTED,** OF COURSE.
...I DUNNO. DON'T REALLY NEED A PITY PARTY HANDOUT.
BUT I THOUGHT YOU WANTED THIS?
OTHER THAN **JUNE**-- I'VE NOT SEEN NOR HEARD FROM ANY OF YOU SINCE **SILAS** DIED... I DON'T NEED YOUR HELP...
THANKS FOR THE OFFER, BUT I'M **FINE**-- YOU CAN LEAVE NOW.

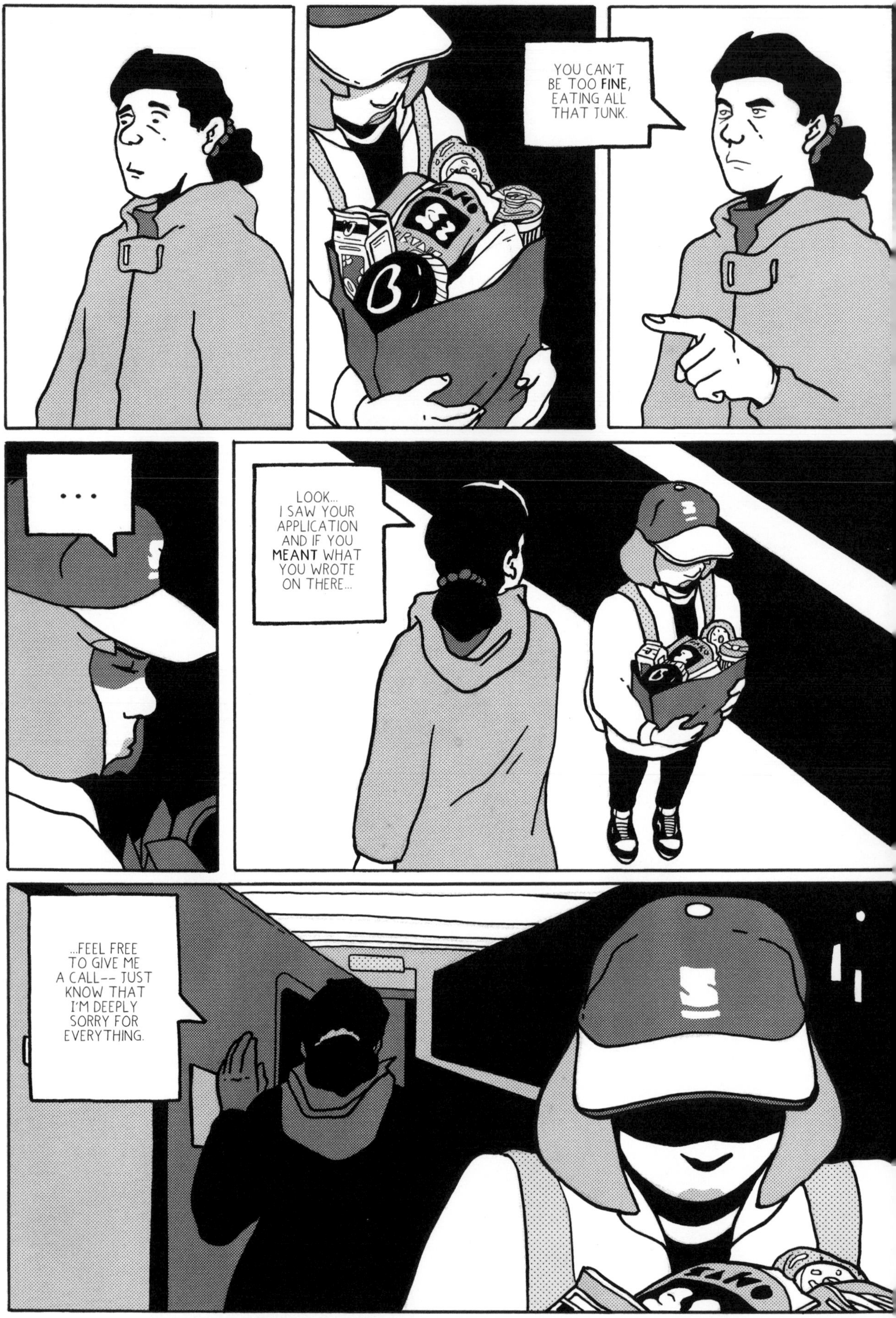
YOU CAN'T BE TOO FINE, EATING ALL THAT JUNK.
...
LOOK... I SAW YOUR APPLICATION AND IF YOU MEANT WHAT YOU WROTE ON THERE...
...FEEL FREE TO GIVE ME A CALL-- JUST KNOW THAT I'M DEEPLY SORRY FOR EVERYTHING.

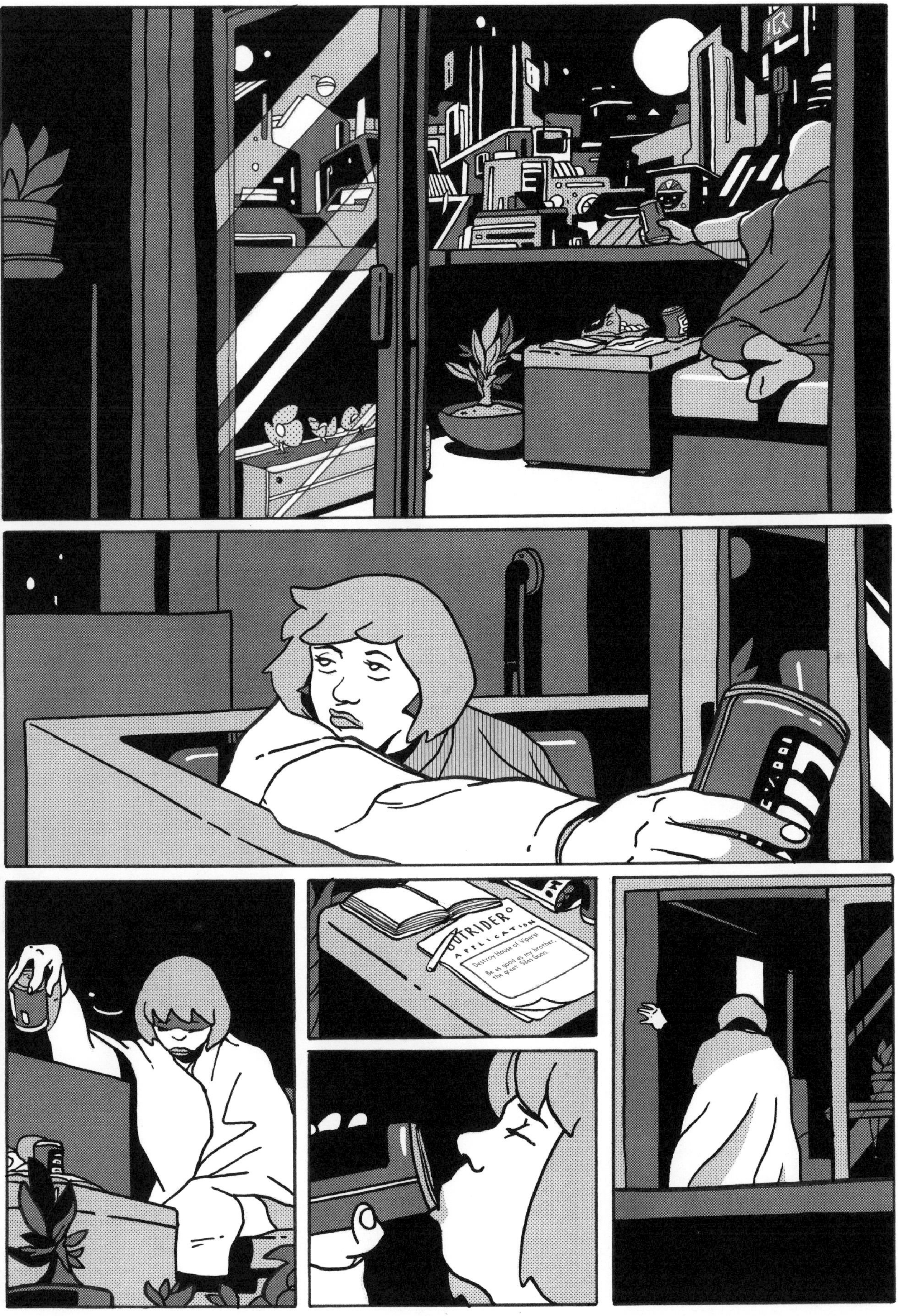
OUTRIDER
APPLICATION
Destroy House of Vipers!
Be as good as my brother, the great Silas Gunn.

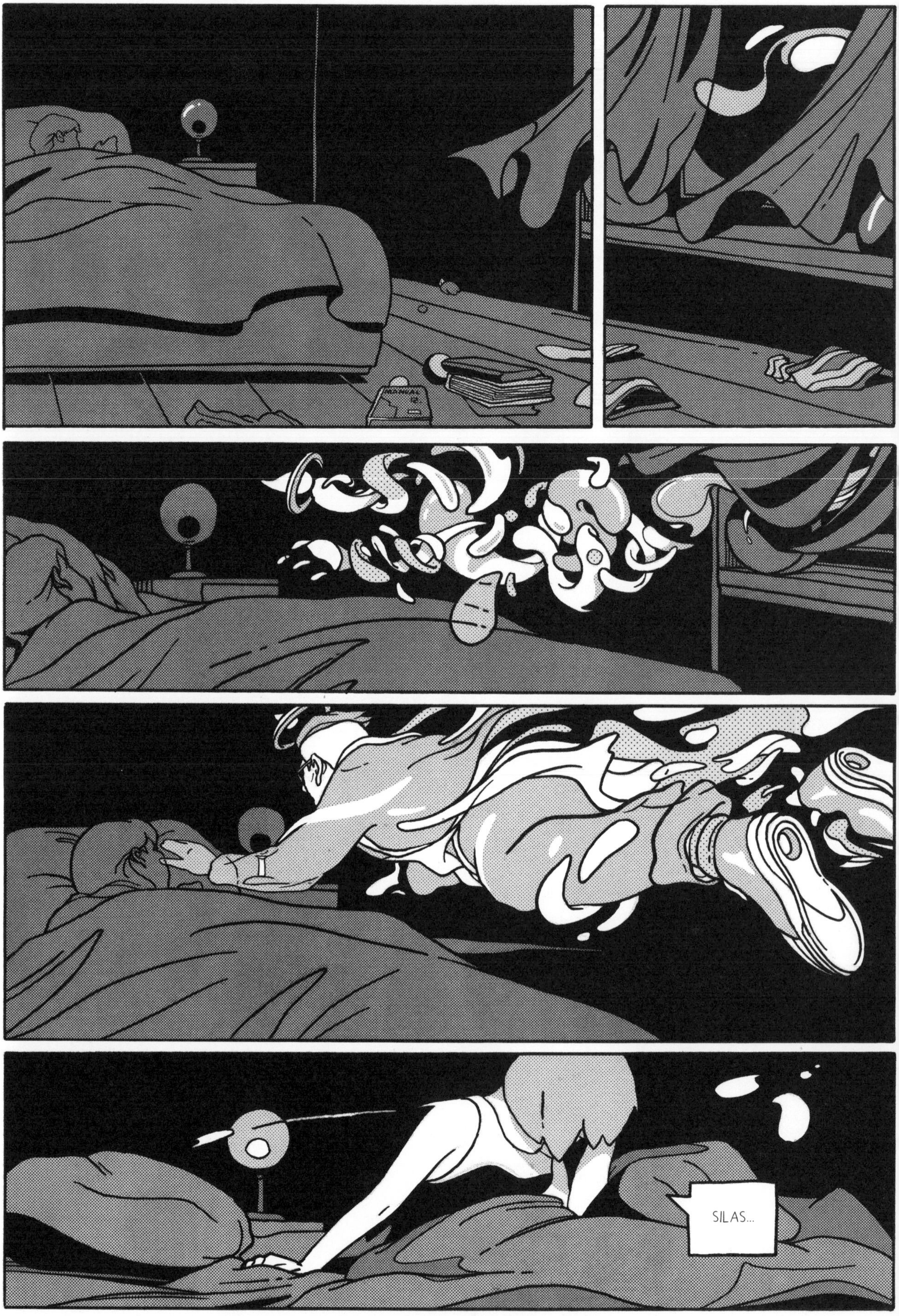
MANUAL
SILAS...

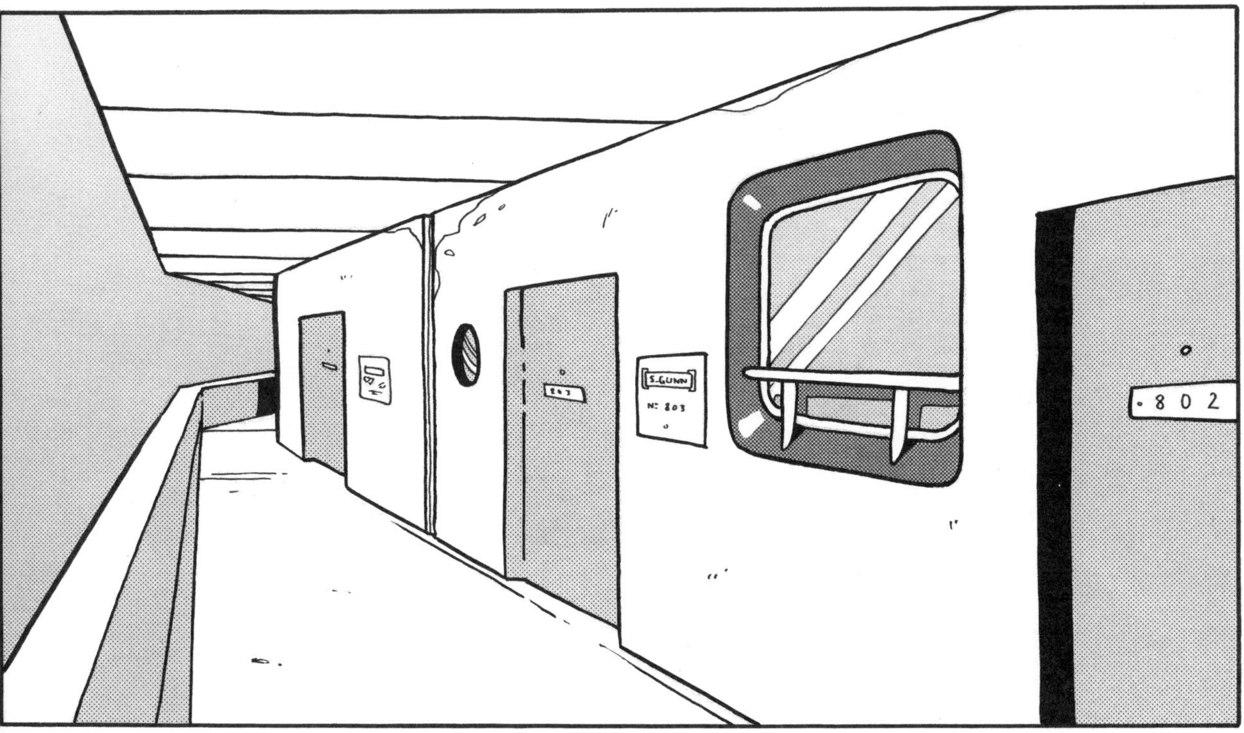
S.GUNN
Nº 803
802

10

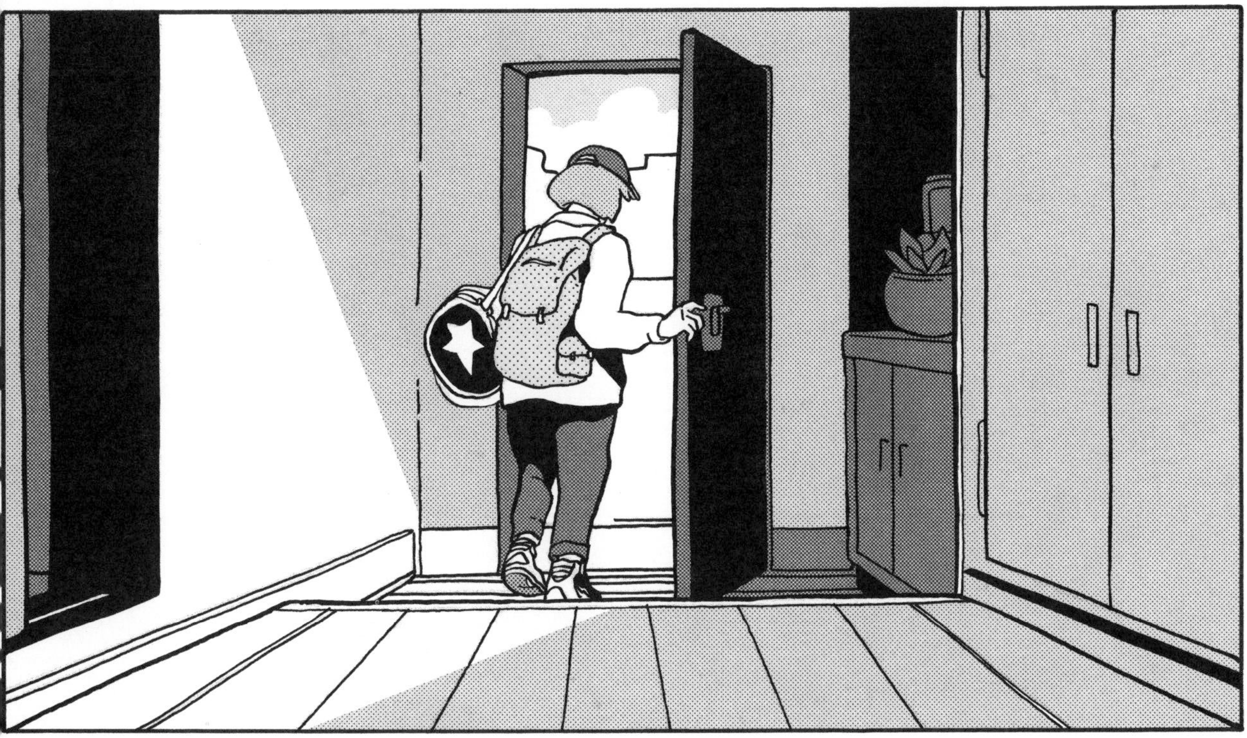

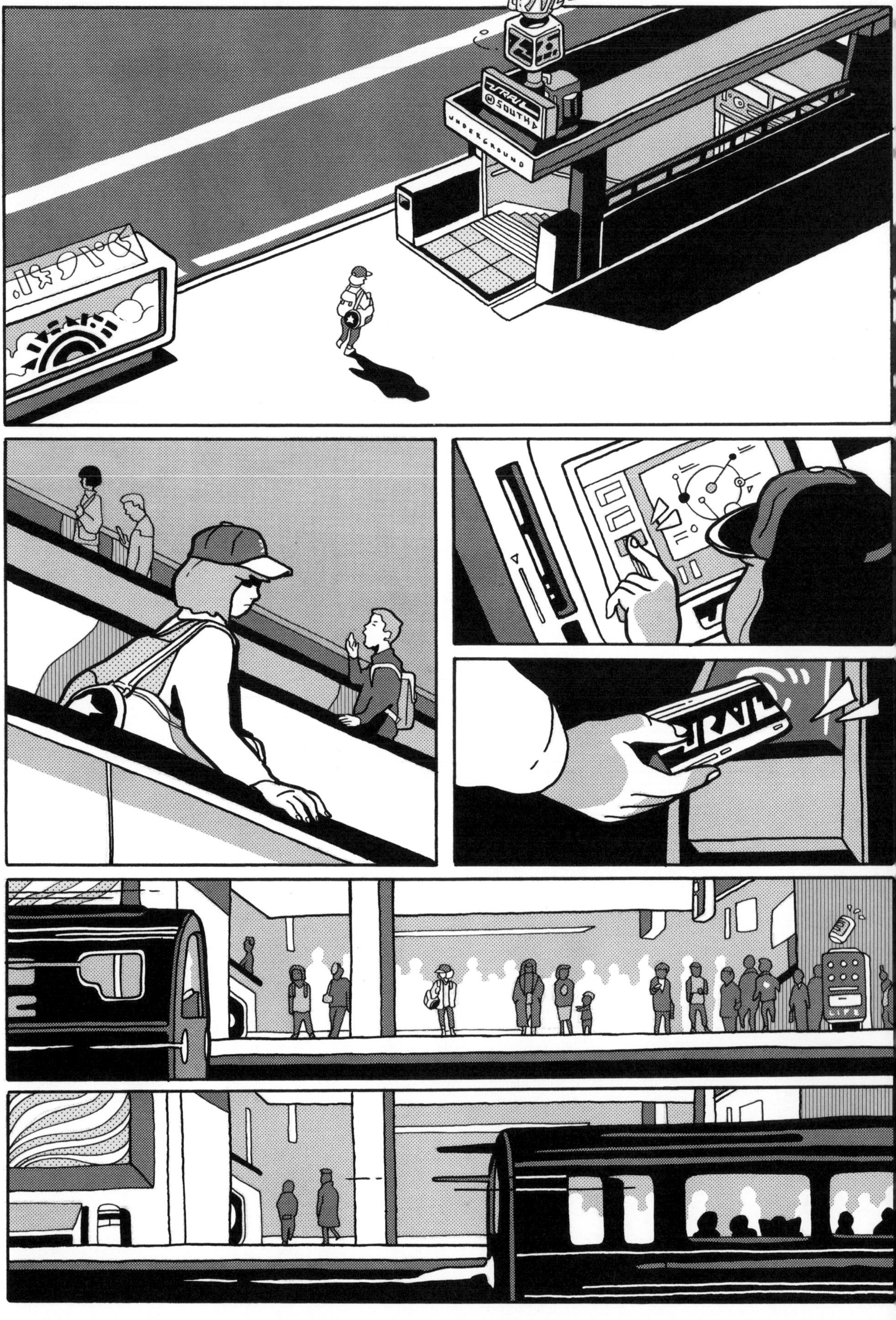
SOUTH
UNDERGROUND

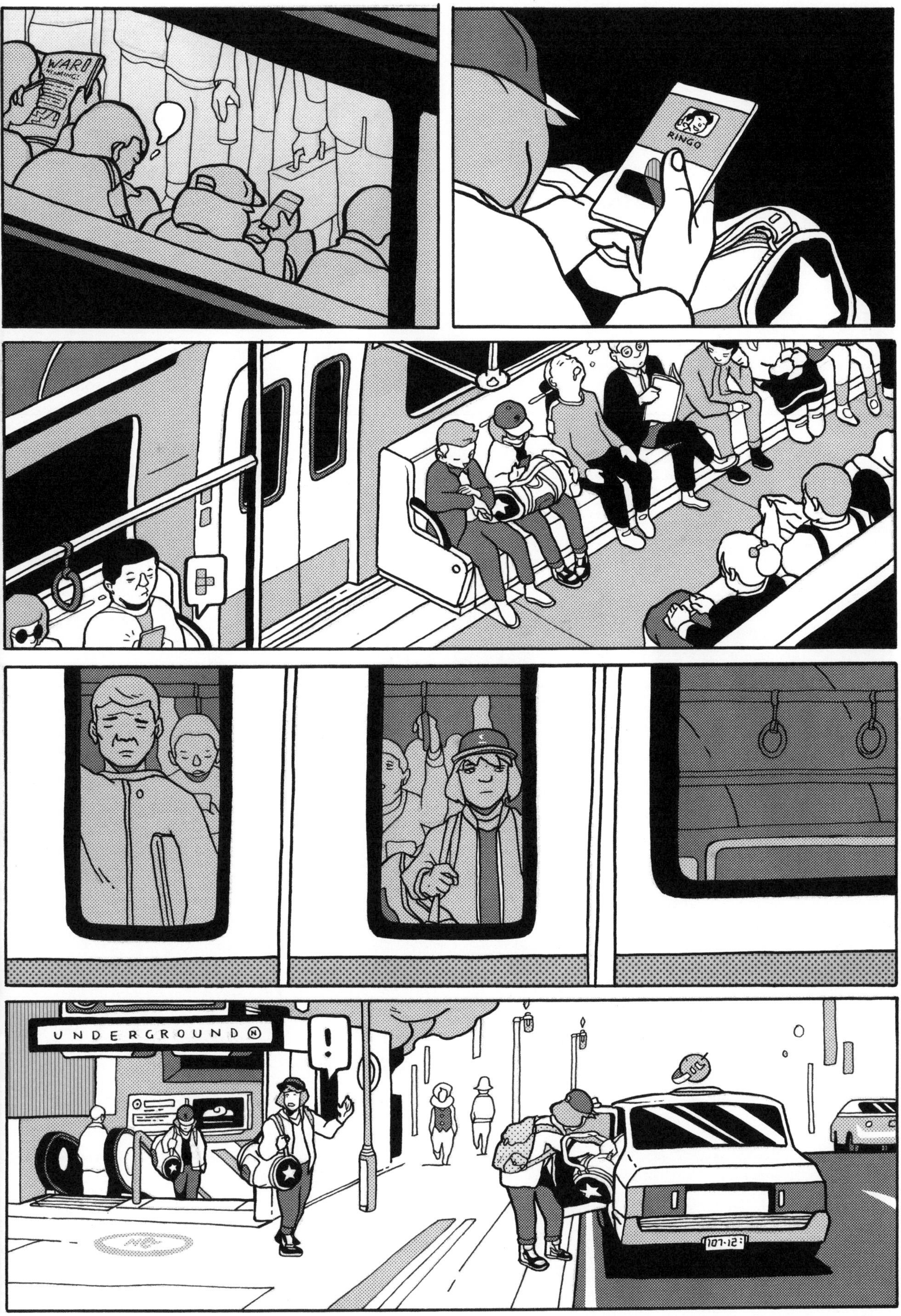
WARD
RINGO
UNDERGROUND
!
107-12

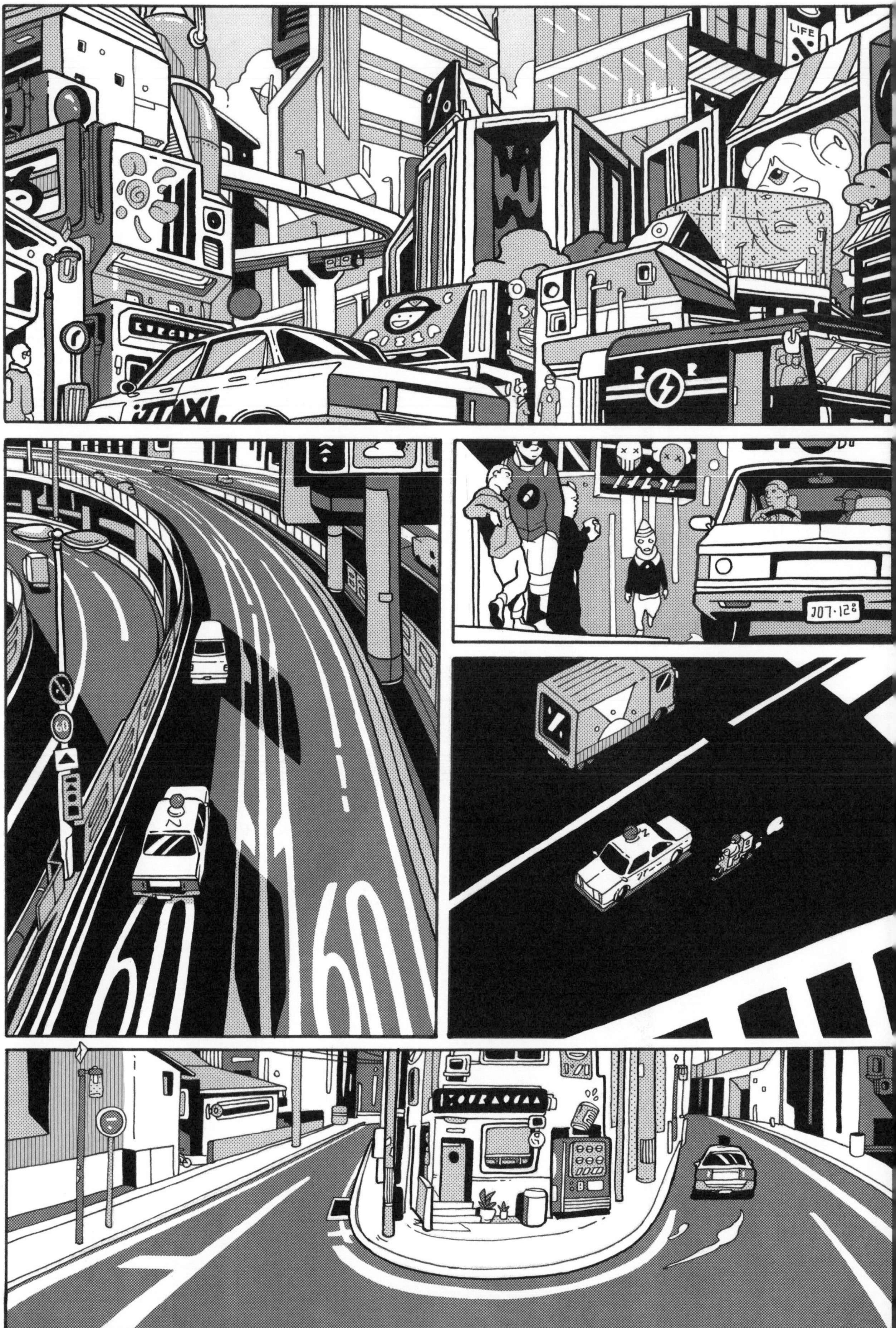
LIFE
60

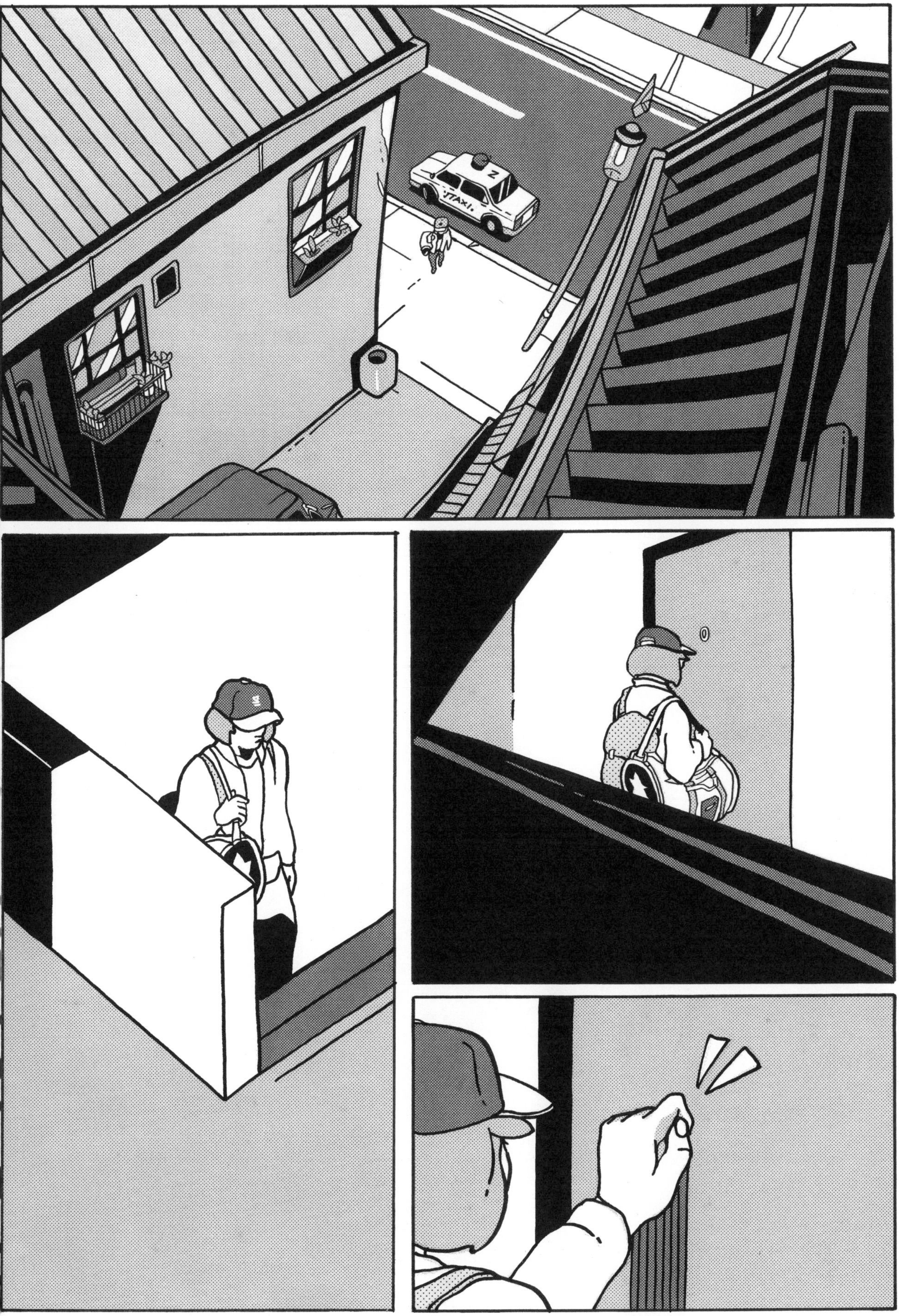
TAXI

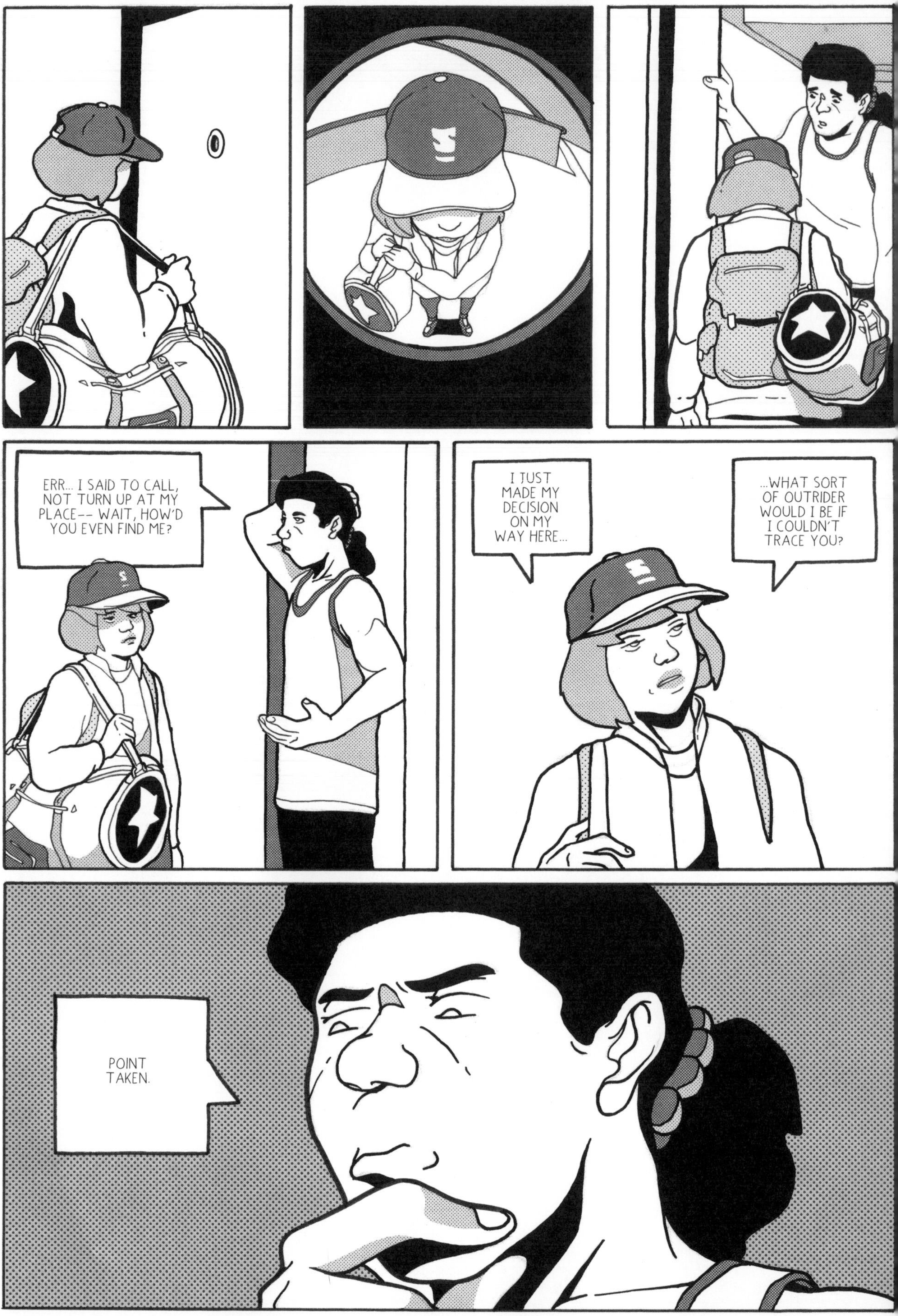
ERR... I SAID TO CALL, NOT TURN UP AT MY PLACE-- WAIT, HOW'D YOU EVEN FIND ME?
I JUST MADE MY DECISION ON MY WAY HERE...
...WHAT SORT OF OUTRIDER WOULD I BE IF I COULDN'T TRACE YOU?
POINT TAKEN.

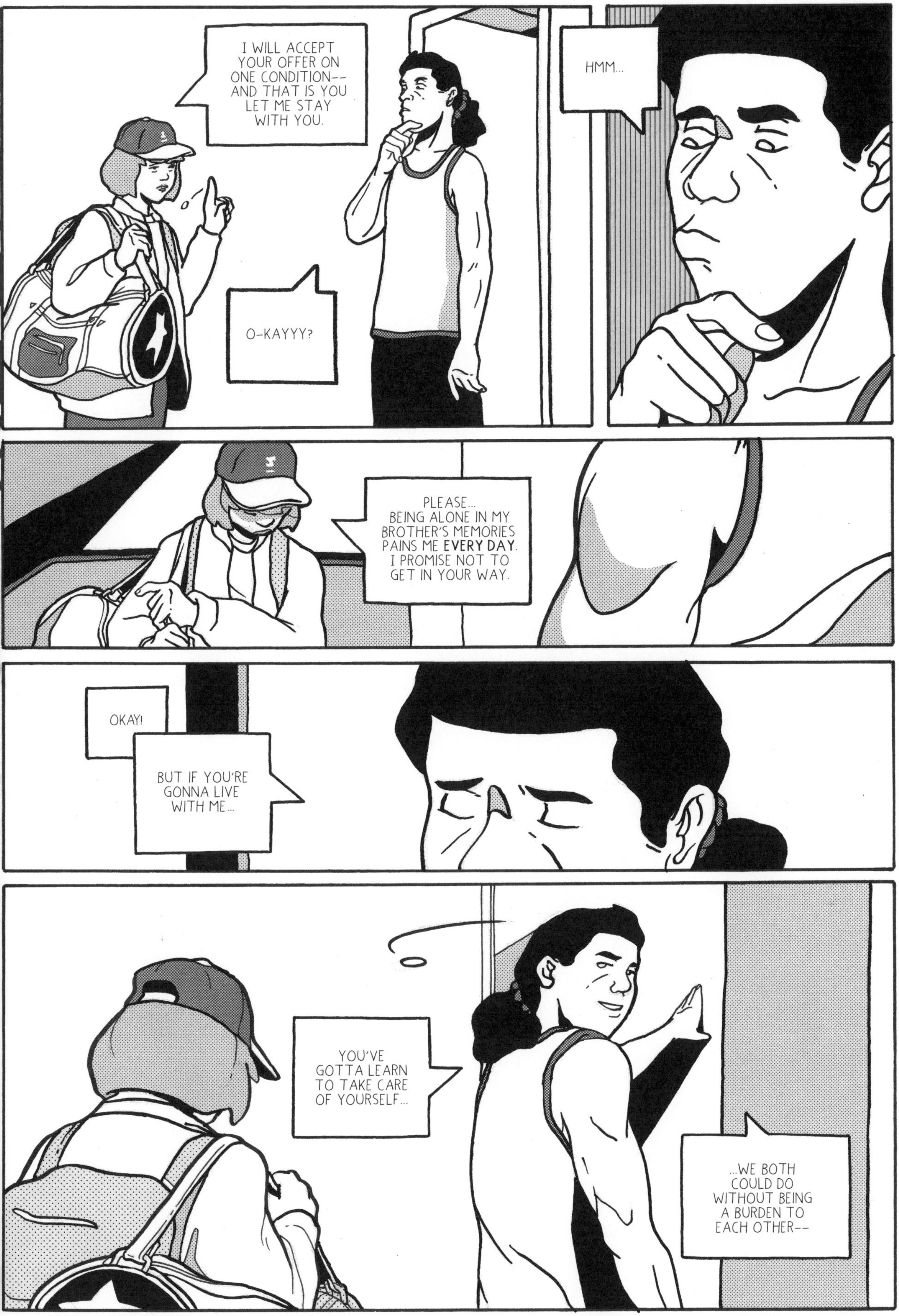
I WILL ACCEPT YOUR OFFER ON ONE CONDITION-- AND THAT IS YOU LET ME STAY WITH YOU.
O-KAYYY?
HMM...
PLEASE... BEING ALONE IN MY BROTHER'S MEMORIES PAINS ME **EVERY DAY**. I PROMISE NOT TO GET IN YOUR WAY.
OKAY!
BUT IF YOU'RE GONNA LIVE WITH ME...
YOU'VE GOTTA LEARN TO TAKE CARE OF YOURSELF...
...WE BOTH COULD DO WITHOUT BEING A BURDEN TO EACH OTHER--

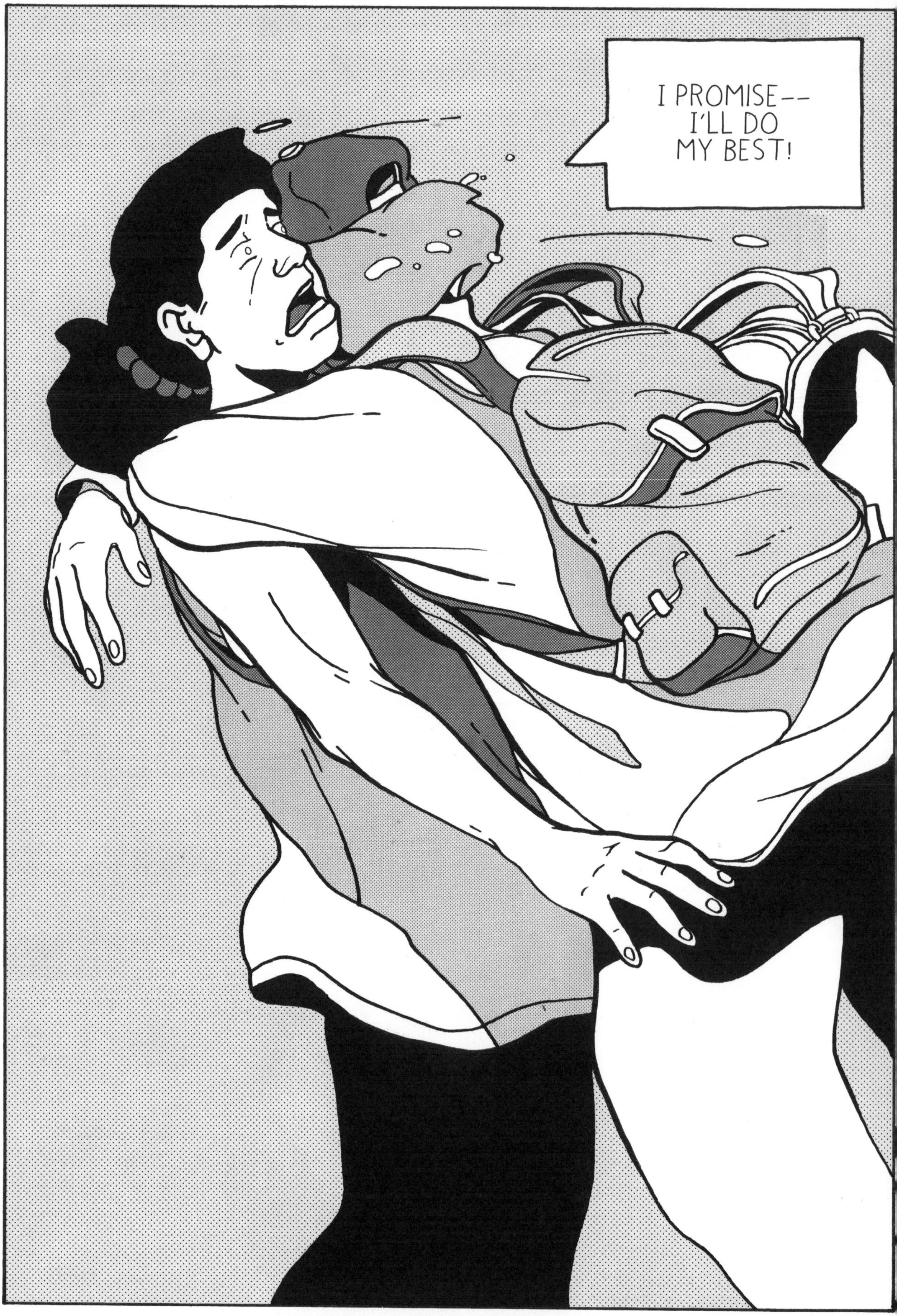
I PROMISE-- I'LL DO MY BEST!

JOYAMA™

VOLUME 1

SKETCHBOOK

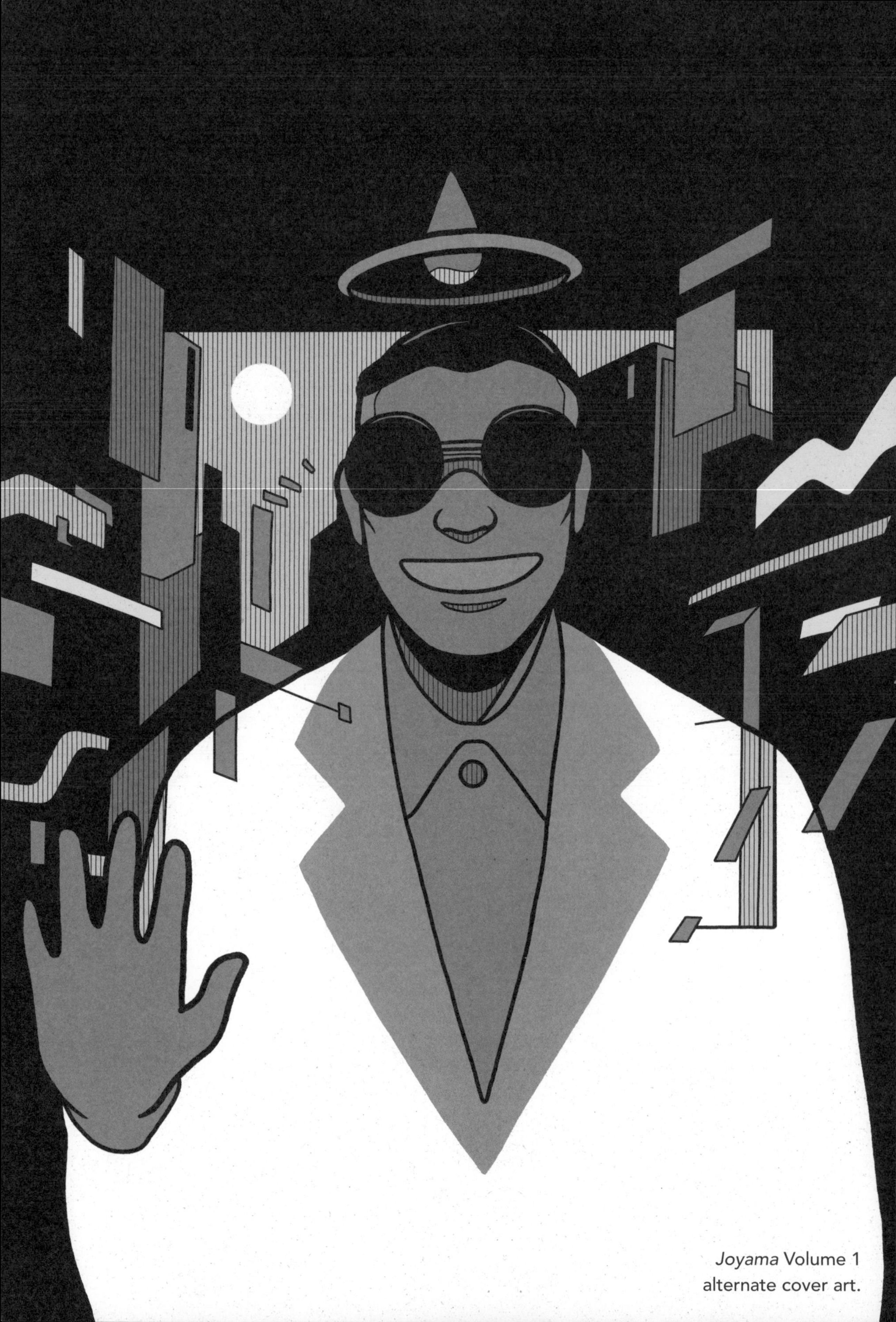

Joyama Volume 1
alternate cover art.

Rana is one of the many fast-food joints around the city and is the most popular among the residents of Joyama, closely followed by the Tako Party and Cool Boy Pizza franchises.

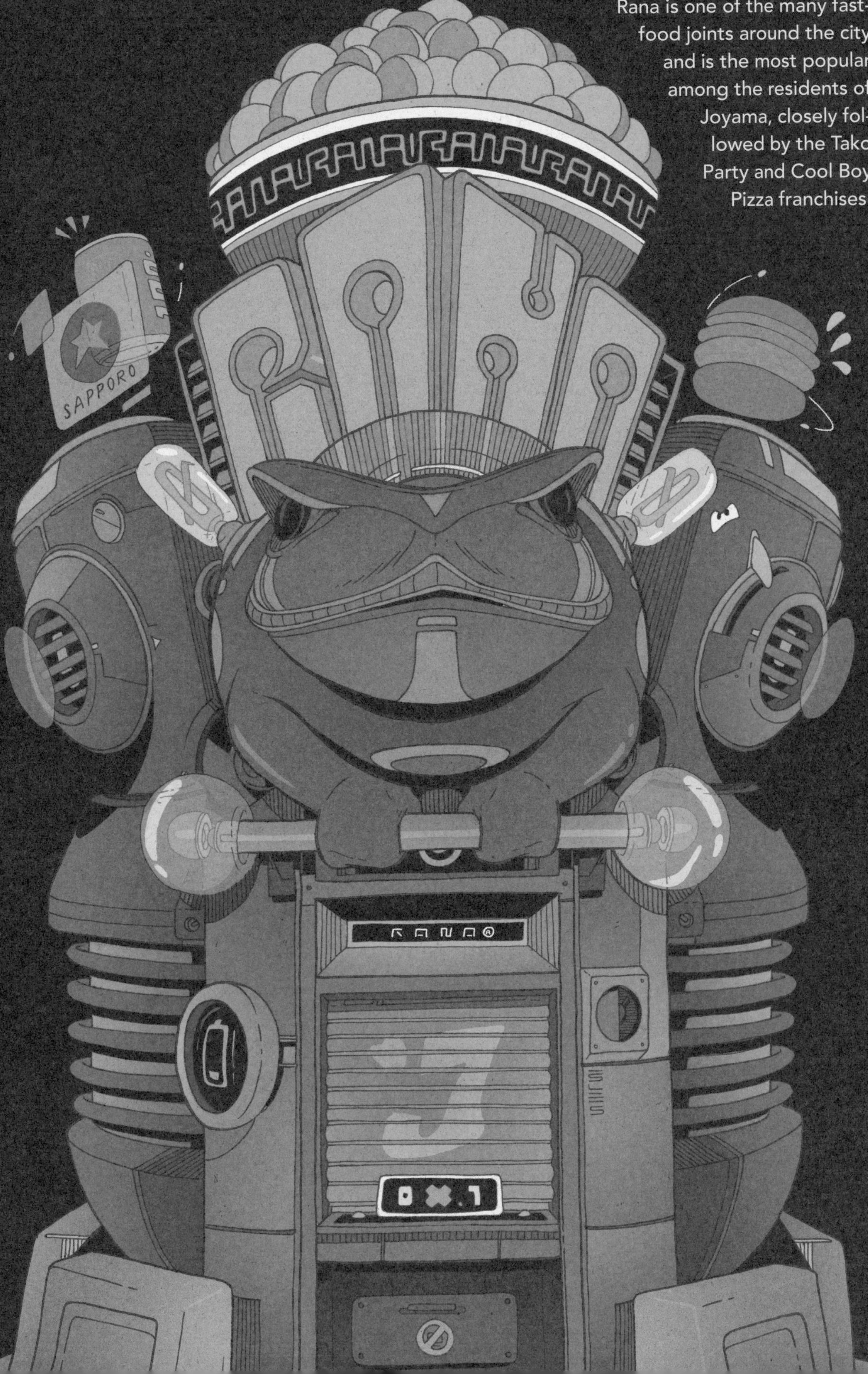
SAPPORO

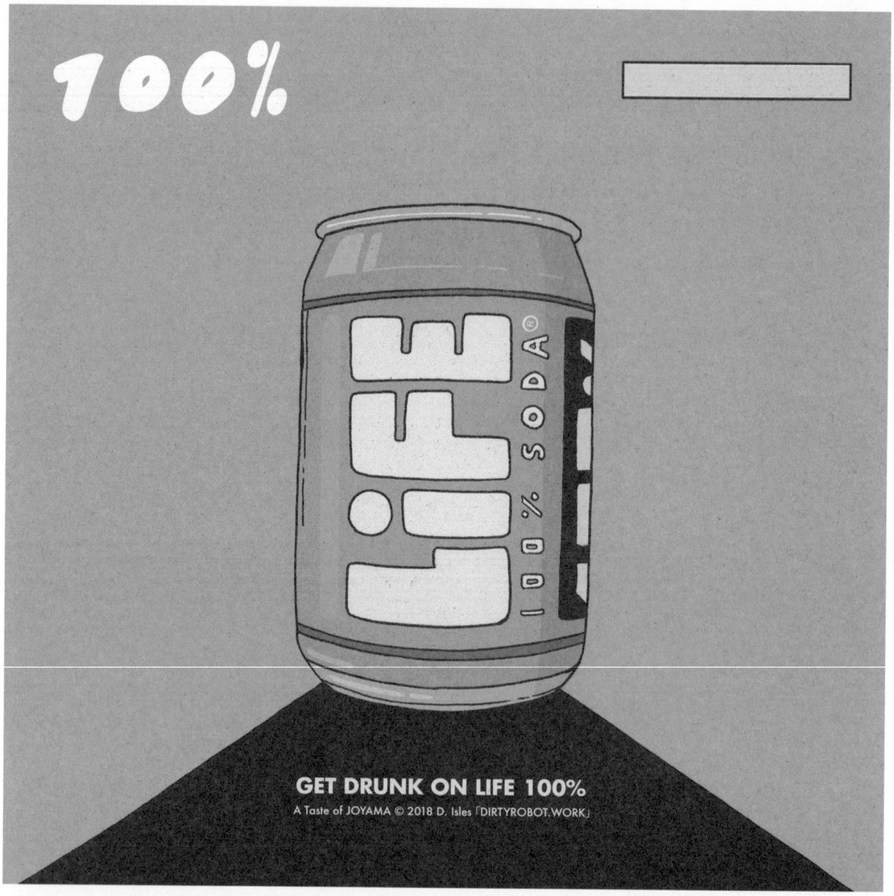
100%
LIFE
100% SODA
GET DRUNK ON LIFE 100%
A Taste of JOYAMA © 2018 D. Isles「DIRTYROBOT.WORK」

In the metropolitan city of Joyama, advertising is featured on almost every corner—from buildings and skyscrapers to public transit centers and local intersections. Here is an ad for the popular soda brand Life, seen enjoyed by the various residents of Joyama.

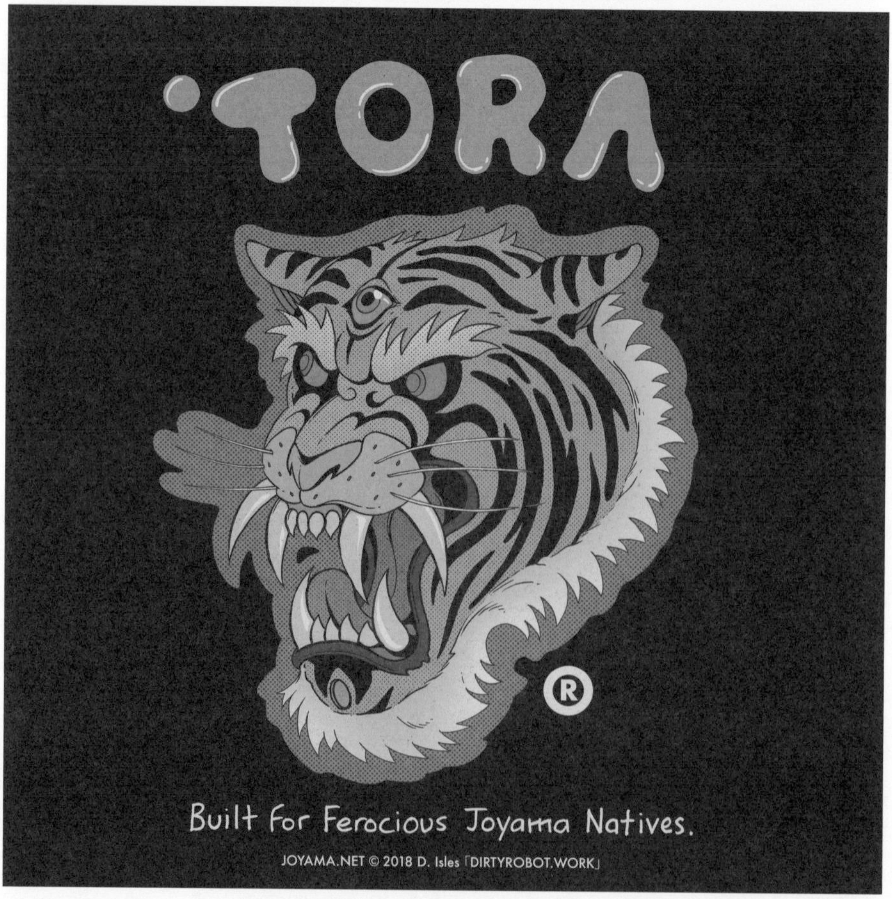
TORA
Built for Ferocious Joyama Natives.
JOYAMA.NET © 2018 D. Isles「DIRTYROBOT.WORK」

Ad for Tora, a clothing brand worn by Ringo.

Character sketches of Ringo.

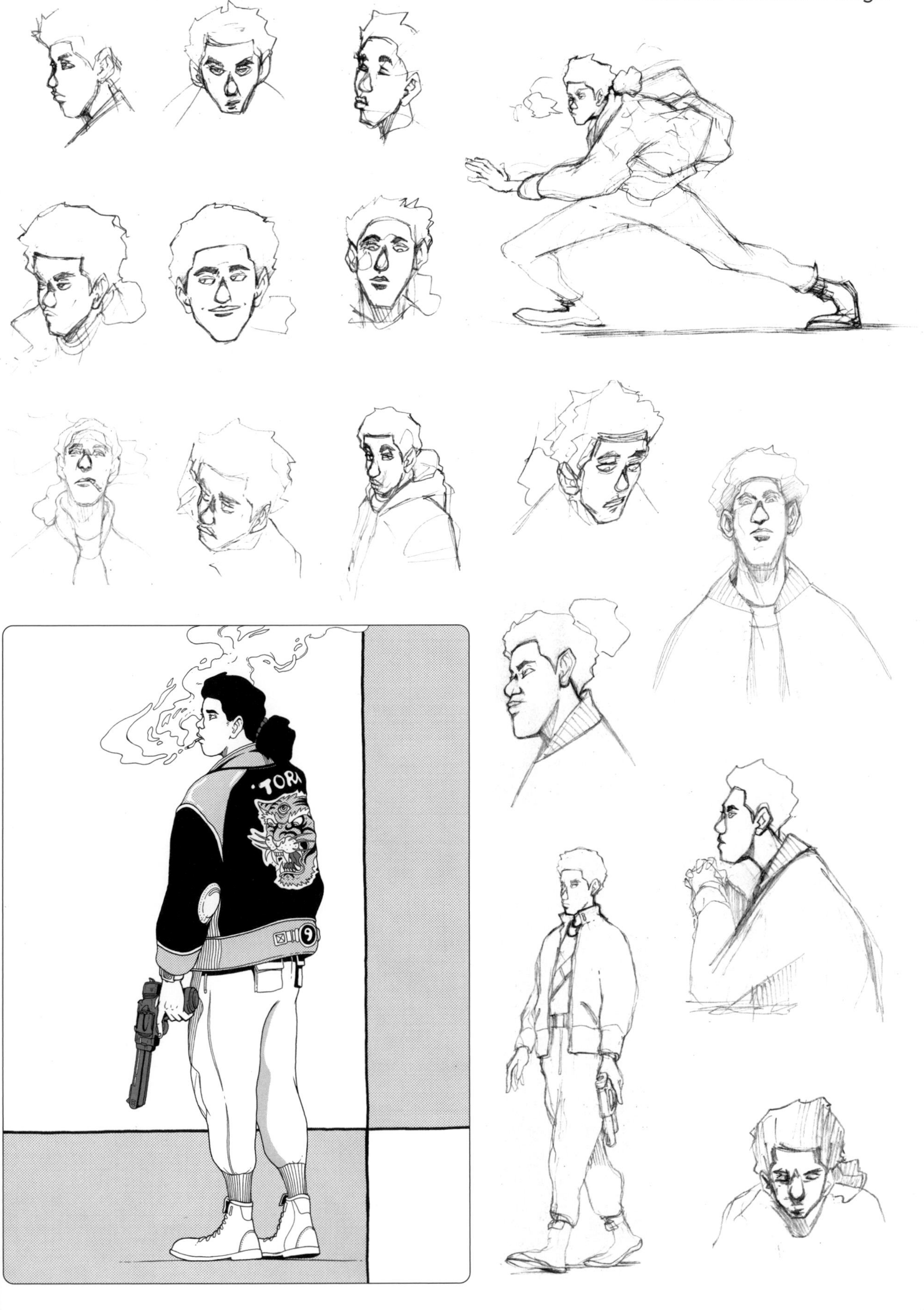

Character sketches of Silas.

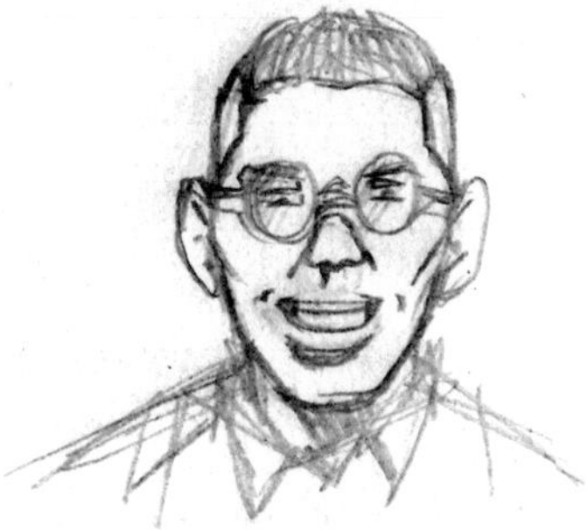

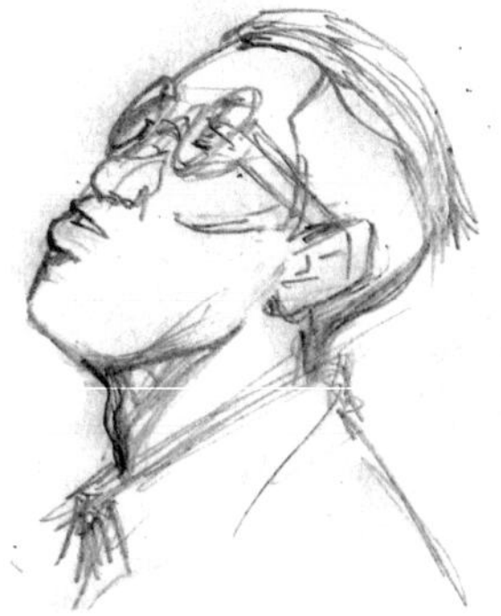

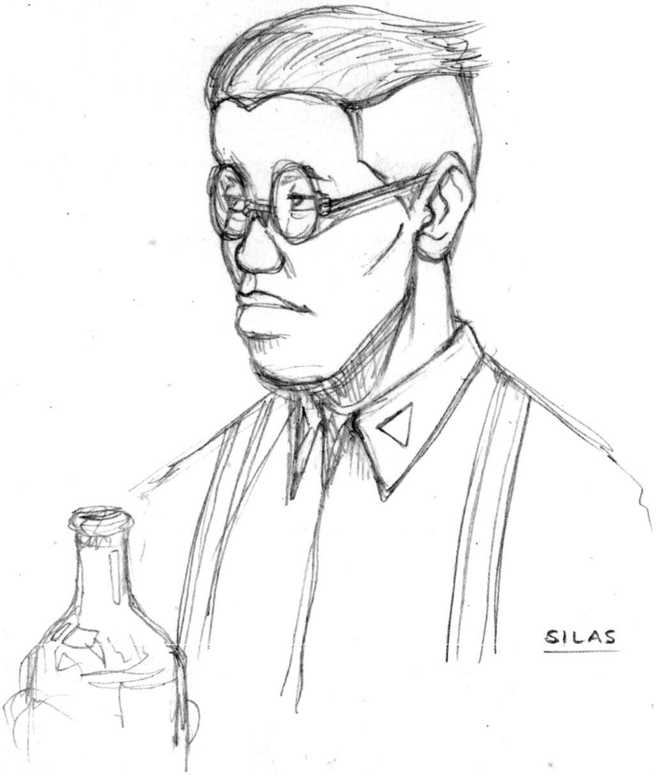
SILAS

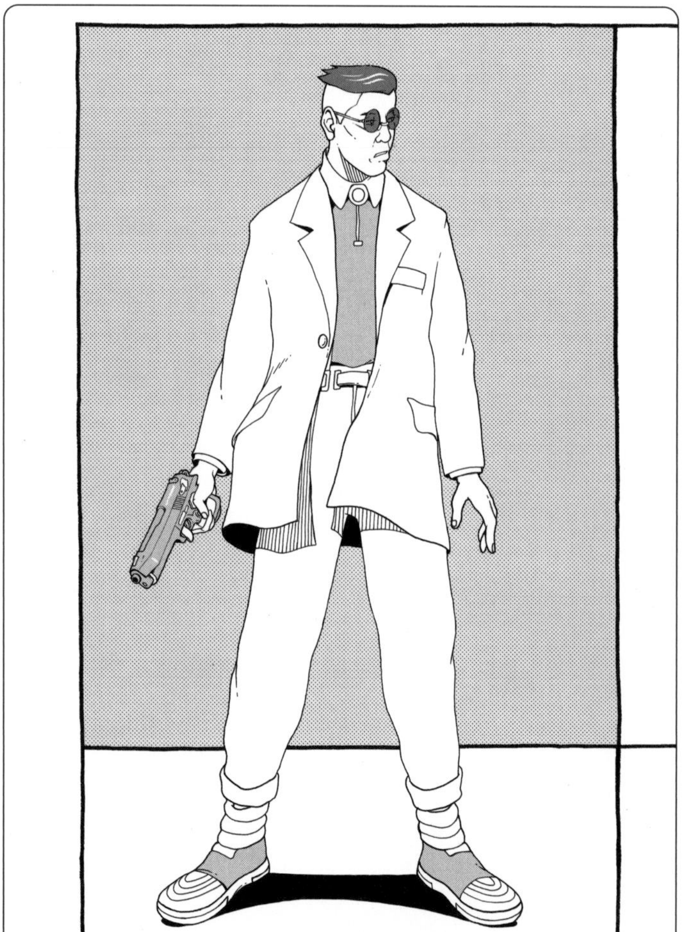

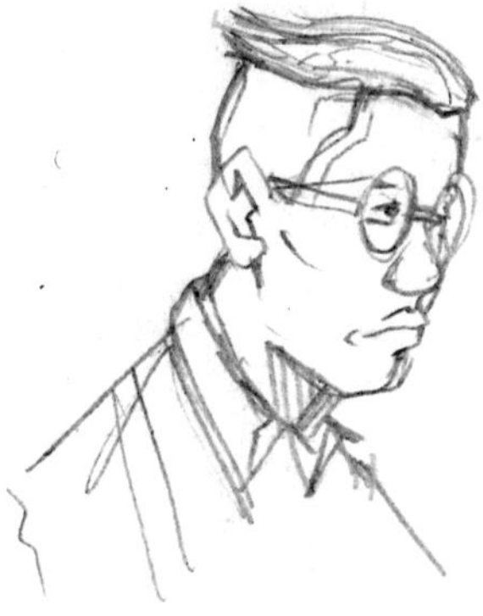

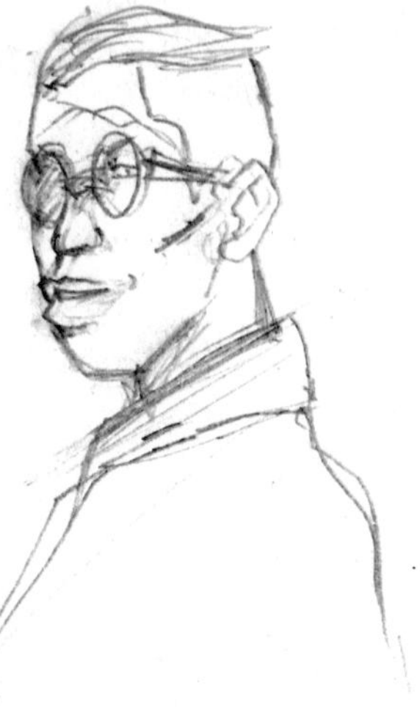

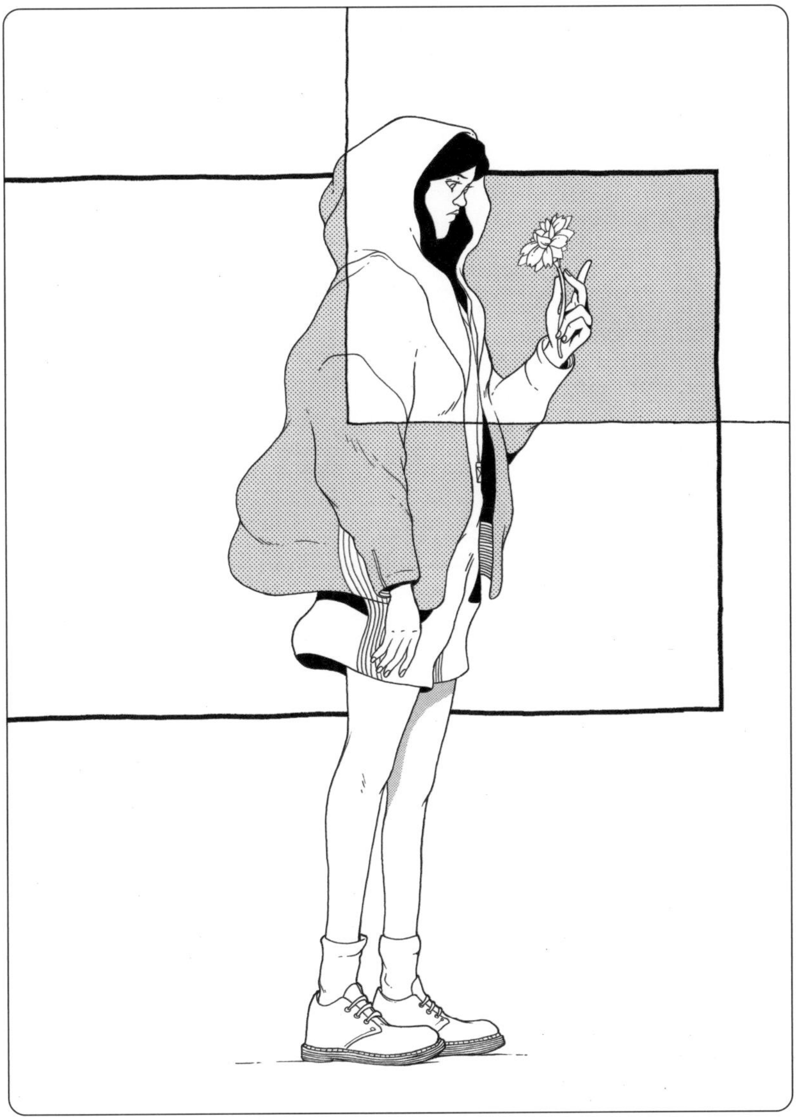

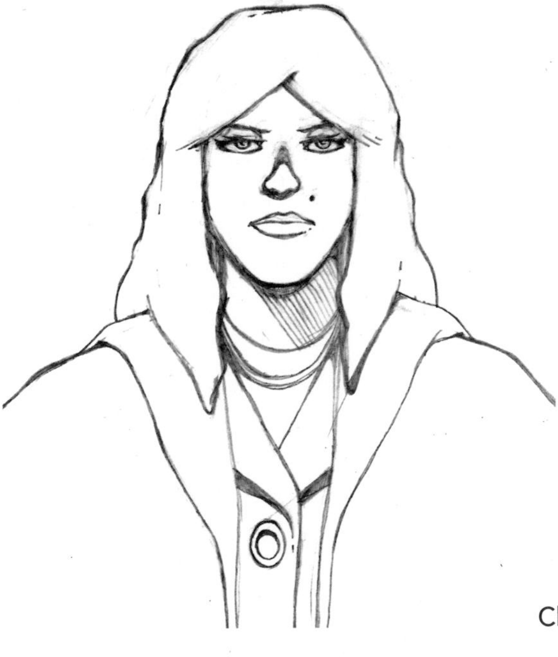

Character sketches of Arwen.

Character sketches of Rubi.

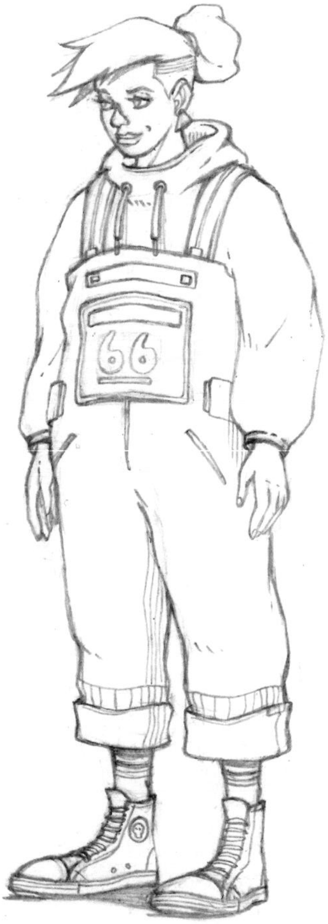
66

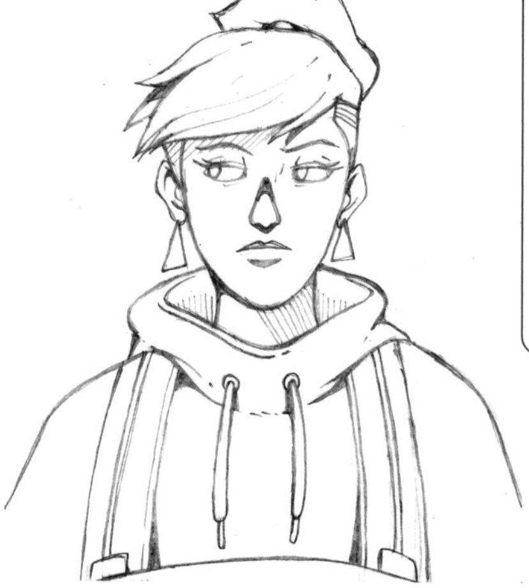

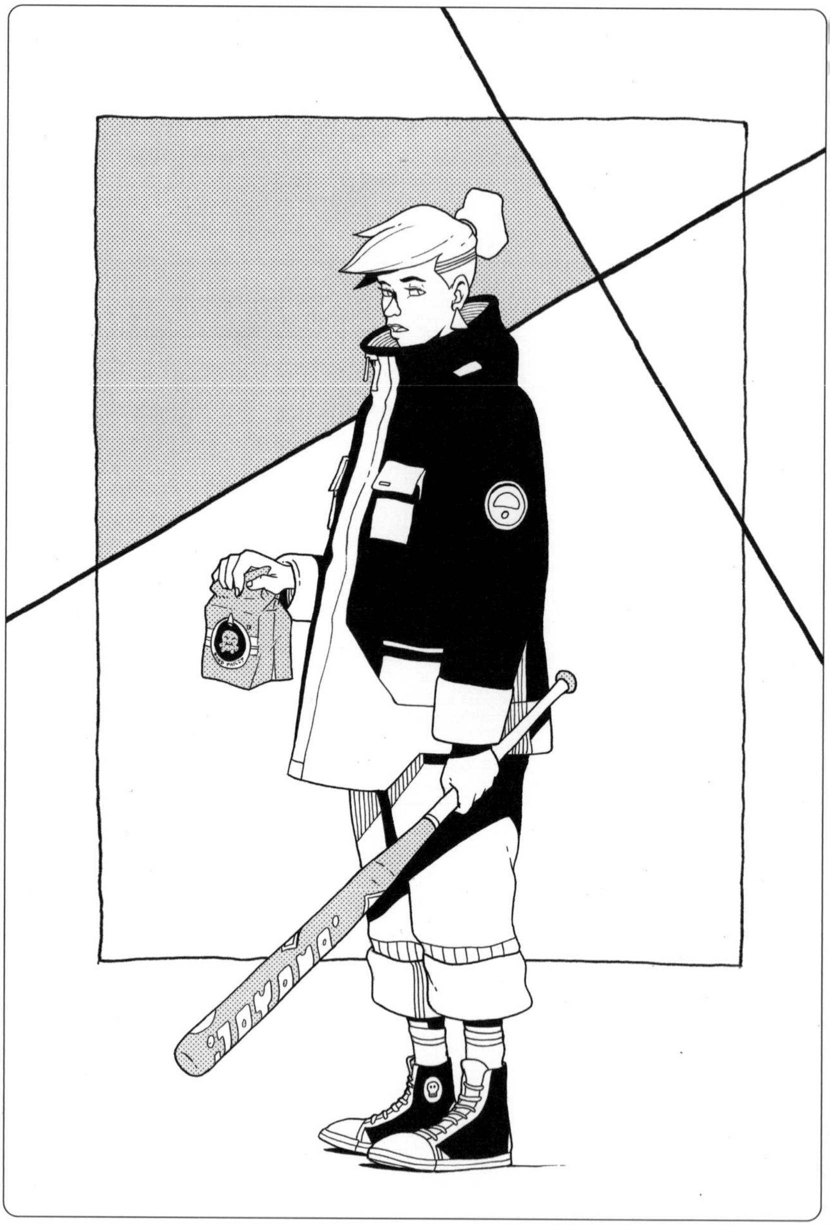

Character sketch of Juniper.

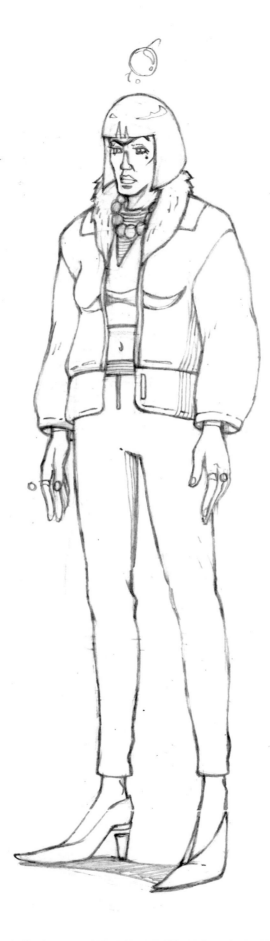

CREATOR BIOGRAPHY

Daniel Isles is an artist born in Birmingham, UK. He has been drawing since he was a child, and his work captures his unique perspective with a futuristic flair. He has created art for various clients throughout his career, including Apple Music, Yamaha Music Group, and Sega, as well as independently publishing his art book, *MONO*. He draws inspiration from a variety of sources—from family and friends, his hometown, and Eastern and Western cultures to fashion, animation, and retro video games. His work has been exhibited in galleries in the United States, Japan, and Australia. He currently resides in Hokkaido, Japan.

PRESIDENT AND PUBLISHER
MIKE RICHARDSON

EDITOR
JUDY KHUU

ASSISTANT EDITOR
ROSE WEITZ

DESIGNER
SARAH TERRY

DIGITAL ART TECHNICIAN
JOSIE CHRISTENSEN

JOYAMA VOLUME 1

Published by Dark Horse Books
A division of Dark Horse Comics LLC
10956 SE Main Street, Milwaukie, OR 97222

DarkHorse.com
To find a comics shop in your area, visit comicshoplocator.com

First edition: April 2022
Ebook ISBN 978-1-50672-393-8 | Trade Paperback ISBN 978-1-50672-390-7

1 3 5 7 9 10 8 6 4 2
Printed in China

Neil Hankerson Executive Vice President • Tom Weddle Chief Financial Officer • Dale LaFountain Chief Information Officer • Tim Wiesch Vice President of Licensing • Matt Parkinson Vice President of Marketing • Vanessa Todd-Holmes Vice President of Production and Scheduling • Mark Bernardi Vice President of Book Trade and Digital Sales • Randy Lahrman Vice President of Product Development • Ken Lizzi General Counsel • Dave Marshall Editor in Chief • Davey Estrada Editorial Director • Chris Warner Senior Books Editor • Cary Grazzini Director of Specialty Projects • Lia Ribacchi Art Director • Matt Dryer Director of Digital Art and Prepress • Michael Gombos Senior Director of Licensed Publications • Kari Yadro Director of Custom Programs • Kari Torson Director of International Licensing

Library of Congress Cataloging-in-Publication Data

Names: Isles, Daniel, writer, artist.
Title: Joyama / Daniel Isles.
Description: Milwaukie, OR : Dark Horse Books, 2022.
Identifiers: LCCN 2021044942 (print) | LCCN 2021044943 (ebook) | ISBN 9781506723907 (trade paperback) | ISBN 9781506723938 (ebook)
Subjects: LCGFT: Graphic novels.
Classification: LCC PN6727.I85 J69 2022 (print) | LCC PN6727.I85 (ebook) | DDC 741.5/973--dc23/eng/20211001
LC record available at https://lccn.loc.gov/2021044942
LC ebook record available at https://lccn.loc.gov/2021044943

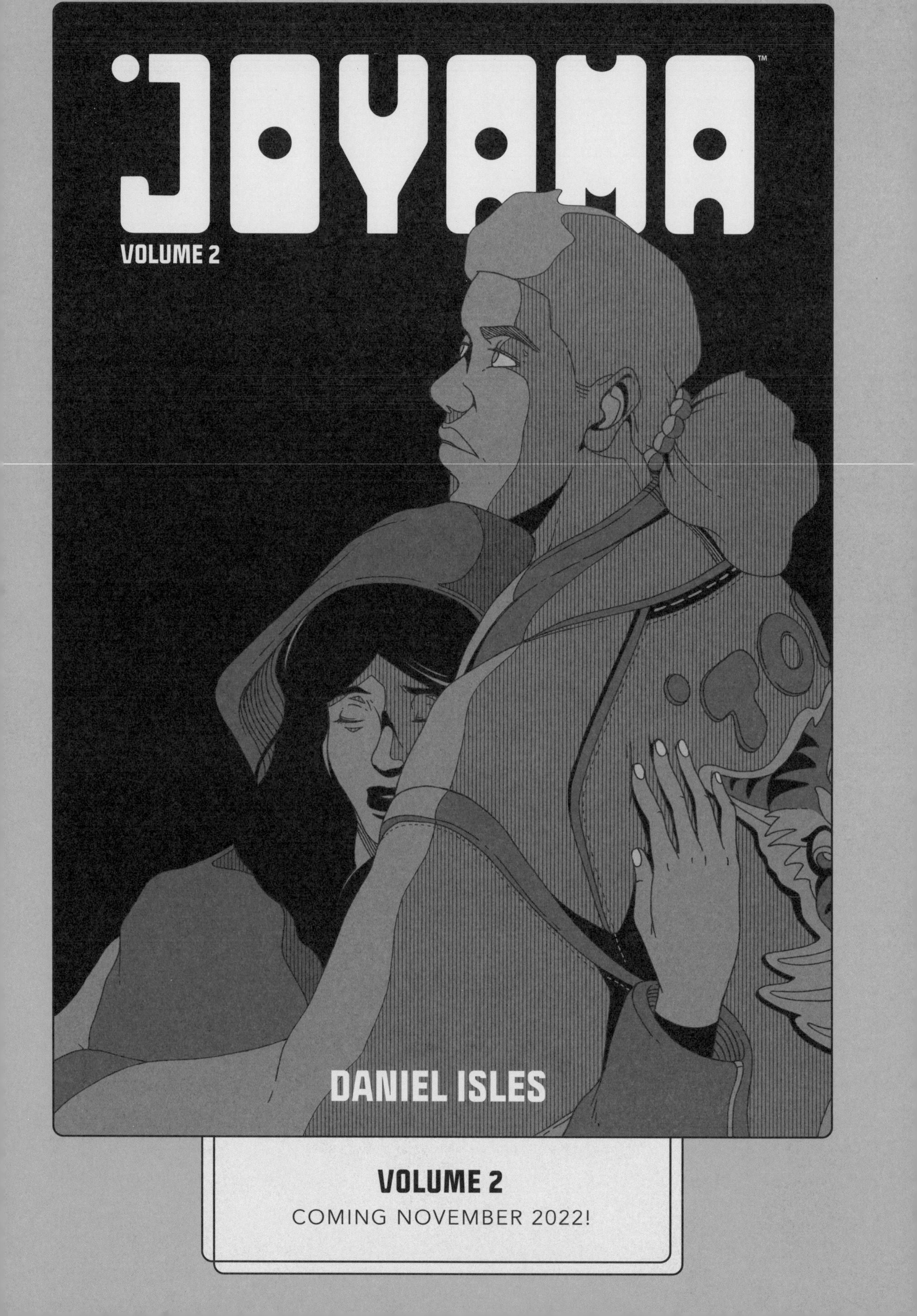
JOYAMA™
VOLUME 2
DANIEL ISLES

VOLUME 2

COMING NOVEMBER 2022!